Wheeler 7/10.
95

W9-AWL-748

Amber Beach

Elizabeth Lowell

Amber Beach

WHEELER
PUBLISHING, INC.
ROCKLAND, MA

★ AN AMERICAN COMPANY ★

Published in Large Print by arrangement with Avon Books, a division of The Hearst Corporation in the United States and Canada.

Wheeler Large Print Book Series.

Set in 16 pt Plantin.

Library of Congress Cataloging-in-Publication Data

Lowell, Elizabeth
    Amber Beach / Elizabeth Lowell.
        p. (large print) cm.(Wheeler large print book series)
    ISBN 1-56895-577-4 (hardcover)
    1. Businesswomen—Northwest, Pacific—Fiction. 2. Man-woman rela-
tionships—Northwest, Pacific—Fiction. 3. Northwest, Pacific—Fiction.
4. Amber—Fiction 5. Large type books.
I. Title. II. Series
[PS3562.O8847A8 1998]
813'.54—dc21   98-024020
                                                                    CIP

For Sunny and Al Runnells,
friends for all the seasons of life

1

Honor Donovan took one look and knew the man was trouble. On the other hand, she was already in the kind of trouble even her family's company, Donovan International, couldn't handle.

"If you're from the police, shut the door on your way out," she said. "If you're a reporter, go to hell."

"Been there. Done that."

"You have the T-shirt to prove it?"

He reached for the buttons on his stained denim jacket.

"Never mind," she said quickly. "Are you a reporter?"

"No. I'm a fishing guide."

"Piranha?"

"You *are* the Ms. Honor Donovan who advertised for 'a person with expertise in Pacific Northwest waters in general and Sea-Sport boats in particular'?"

She sighed and accepted the inevitable. The big man with the black beard stubble, light eyes, scarred left eyebrow, and clean fingernails hadn't wandered by accident into her missing brother's Puget Sound cottage. Despite this man's less-than-cozy looks, her instincts said he was a better candidate than the others who had come looking for the job.

One of the men had been a cop trying to pass for a fisherman. Another was a recent immigrant whose English defied understanding. A third man was convinced she really wanted the body he was so proud of. The fourth man's English was good, but his eyes had made her think of things that lived in swamps.

It had been three days since anyone else had applied for the job. She was going nuts counting minutes and waiting for Kyle to appear suddenly in the doorway with his crooked grin and a good explanation of why the cops thought he had stolen a million bucks in amber. She refused to consider any other reason for his disappearance, especially the one that kept her from sleeping, the one that made her throat close around tears she wouldn't cry.

Kyle had to be alive. He just had to be.

"Miss Donovan?"

Belatedly Honor realized that the most recent applicant was still waiting for her to say that she was indeed the one who had posted ads all over the small town of Anacortes.

"I'm the one," she said.

"You took the words right out of my mouth."

She looked at his mouth and knew how Little Red Riding Hood felt when she first saw "grandmother's" teeth.

"Excuse me?" she asked.

"Your ad could have been written with me in mind," he explained.

"Do you have references?"

"Driver's license? Fishing license? Boat handler's ticket? Tetanus shot?"

"How about rabies?"

The retort popped out before Honor could

think better of it. It came from a lifetime of dealing with big brothers.

"Sorry, Mr...."

"Mallory."

"Mr. Mallory."

"Try Jake. Saves time."

"Um, Jake. I meant references given by people you worked for in the past."

"You don't know much about fishing guides, do you?"

"If I did, I wouldn't have to hire one, would I?"

He smiled.

She thought of poor Little Red. "You should work on that smile. It really isn't reassuring."

Jake tried to look downcast. It wasn't any more convincing than his smile.

"If your hands are half as quick as your tongue," he said, "I'll make a fisherman out of you in no time."

"Fisherwoman."

"Ain't no such animal."

"Fishersan, then."

"Fishersan?"

"Man and woman both end in *an*. Do you want the job?"

"Fishersan," he said, rolling the word around on his tongue. "Yeah, I want the job. We'll be the only fishersen on the water."

This time Jake's smile was slow, warm, amused, and something more. It reminded Honor that she was a woman as well as the scared younger sister of a missing man. She looked down at her hands and cleared her throat.

"Fishersen?" she asked, distracted. "Oh, I get it. En. Plural. M*en* and wom*en*. You're pretty quick yourself. When can you start?"

"Do you have a fishing license?"

"No."

"Then we can't start yet. Too bad. The sun is out. The wind isn't. Slack tide in a few hours. It doesn't get any better than this in the San Juan Islands."

"What would we be fishing for?"

"Whatever we catch. Less disappointment that way."

"Is that your life philosophy?"

"Only after I grew up."

She lifted her head and looked at him intently.

"What's the matter?" Jake asked. "Are my ears on backwards?"

"I was just trying to imagine you as a child in need of growing up."

"Funny. I have no problem imagining you that way. Can you swim?"

"Like a fish."

"Considering my profession and all, you might want to rethink that description."

"You have a point."

"It's on the business end of the hook. First lesson of fishing."

Ambushed by Jake's slow, unexpected smile and deadpan humor, Honor laughed almost helplessly. Then she had to fight tears that were burning behind her eyes.

In the past few weeks she had been through too many sleepless nights. That was why after only two minutes with Jake Mallory she felt like she had been hit by a truck. His particular combination of rough edges, male warmth, and wry intelligence would have appealed to her under any circumstances. Right now, when her defenses were down and her emotions were all over the place, he was lethally attractive to her.

Bad choice of words, she thought. *Really bad.* If she started thinking about death she would cloud up and rain all over Kyle's messy desk.

Blinking hard, Honor stared through one of the cottage's many small windows. Beyond the panes of glass, fir trees swept down rocky slopes to the cold blue-green waters of Puget Sound. Amber Beach was a strip of tawny sand ringed by dark rocks and stranded logs bleached pale by the sea. Kyle's twenty-seven-foot powerboat gleamed whitely next to the floating dock he had built. He had named the boat *Tomorrow,* because he rarely had time to go fishing today.

Now Honor was afraid he might never have time.

She cleared her throat, rallied her thoughts, and said huskily, "The business end of a hook. Sharp. I'll keep it in mind."

"Better in your mind than in your thumb. How soon can you get the license?"

"Fishing?"

"Yeah."

"Any time, I guess. Where do I get it?"

"Anywhere they sell fishing gear."

"Fishing..." Slimy, slippery, smelly, disgusting fish. She sighed. "I can hardly wait."

Jake's eyes narrowed until little more than gleaming slits of gray showed between black eyelashes. He didn't know what he had expected of Kyle Donovan's sister. He only knew that it wasn't Honor.

"You should work on your enthusiasm," he said.

"I've had a rough month, as you probably know if you read the newspapers."

"Losing a husband—" Jake began, as though he didn't know who Honor was.

"Brother," she corrected.

"Brother, huh?"

"And he's not lost. Not really."

"A brother who isn't lost, not really. Is that why the police are expecting him to turn up here?"

"What do you mean?"

Jake shrugged and thought fast. It was something he was good at. Most survivors were. His first thought wasn't comforting: if the lady with the sad, sexy mouth, stubborn chin, and baggy black sweat suit hadn't noticed the plainclothes cop hanging around the turnoff to the cottage, she was either too stupid or too innocent for whatever game Kyle was playing.

Or had been playing. Missing could be another way of saying dead.

"The name on the mailbox is Kyle Donovan," Jake said. "He's the one who has gone missing, right?"

Honor nodded. The motion sent sunlight gliding through her short chestnut hair. Her unusual amber-green eyes gleamed with the same tears Jake had heard in her voice. He shook his head slightly. She looked much too vulnerable to be the sister of a liar, a thief, and a murderer.

But then, life had taught Jake that looks were a lousy index of character. Actions were what counted. Honor was a Donovan aiding and abetting another Donovan. She might look as sweet as a Girl Scout selling cookies, but when she advertised for a fishing guide, she had declared her entry into an international treasure hunt whose only rule was winner take all.

Jake intended to be the winner.

"You can tell me all about your problems while you show me the boat," he said.

"That's not necessary. I'm looking for a fishing guide, not a father confessor."

"All part of the service," he said, turning away. "Like bartending."

"Don't you want to discuss salary?"

"A hundred dollars a day."

"That's not a discussion."

He turned back toward her. "Two hundred."

"A hundred it is."

"Sold. Let's go look at the boat."

Wondering if she had made a mistake, Honor shoved back from her brother's desk. The sudden movement jarred one of the many small cardboard boxes scattered across the surface. One box skidded over papers and fell off the edge. A hunk of rich, transparent yellow leaped out of the cardboard, heading for a crash landing on the bare floor.

No sooner had she realized what was going to happen than Jake moved.

Nothing hit the floor.

"My God, you're quick," she said, startled. "Thank you. Kyle told me that amber can shatter like glass."

Jake didn't need Honor's words to know that he was holding amber. Nothing else on earth had quite the same warm, weightless, satiny feel. He shifted the piece into a shaft of sunlight coming through a window and let the light play through the golden resin. Unless he was mistaken—not likely—he was holding an exceptionally fine chunk of Baltic amber.

"That's part of a shipment my sister and I just received," Honor said. "I've never worked with amber before, but it's really fascinating. So old, so enduring, yet so exquisitely fragile."

Jake gave her a sideways look. "Are you a dealer?"

"No. A designer. The Donovan males wouldn't let mere females go out in the big, bad world and buy rough gems."

"Smart of them."

"That's a matter of opinion."

"Your brother didn't go missing in Disneyland."

Honor's mouth flattened.

The phone rang. She reached for it with a sense of relief. If another reporter was calling, she would enjoy slamming the receiver down in his ear.

"Donovan residence."

"Hi, Honor. How's it going?"

Her oldest brother's deep, impatient voice came through the receiver as though pushed through wet sand.

"You sound like you're on another planet," she said.

"Petropavlosk/Koryak Autonomous Region."

"Say again?"

"Eastern Russia to folks who don't live here. The Kamchatka Peninsula."

Honor's hand tightened as she tried to keep hope or dread from thickening her voice. "Have you found Kyle?" she asked starkly.

"No."

"Neither have the police."

"The police! Did you call them after I told you not—"

"I didn't have to call anyone," she interrupted. "For the last three days cops have been all over Kyle's cottage like a bad smell. What's going on?"

Static filled the line. She could almost hear Archer thinking fast and hard.

"What did they want?" he asked.

"Like you, they don't answer questions, just ask them."

"What questions?"

"Who am I, what am I doing here, when was the last time I saw Kyle, when was the last time I heard from him, have I received any packages"

Very carefully, Jake put the piece of amber

back in the box and set it on the desk.

"—do I know a man with two fingers missing on his left hand and Third World dental work—" Honor said as though reciting a lesson.

Jake wished he could swear aloud. Every word she said told him more than he wanted to know about Kyle and Honor and amber...and not nearly enough. Either she was a hell of an actress hiding knowledge of where Kyle had stashed the amber or she was an innocent sucked into a game only pros should play.

He hoped she was an actress. But whether innocent or as guilty as her brother, Honor still was Jake's only chance of finding the missing amber.

"—am I sure I haven't seen or heard from Kyle," she continued in a monotone, "when did he come back, why didn't he contact me when he landed in Seattle—"

"What?" Archer demanded. "When did Kyle—?"

"Ask the cops," she interrupted curtly. "It's their story, not mine. I haven't seen hide nor hair of Kyle. Reading between the lines, his passport came through SeaTac. Presumably with him."

Her brother let out his breath in a string of Afghani curses.

"I'm sure I would agree if I spoke the language," she said. "What's going on?"

"Have you checked Kyle's post office box?"

Her fingers clenched around the phone. "I repeat. What is going on?"

"What about his answering machine?"

Silence and static gathered.

As always, Archer outwaited his younger sister.

"Yes and yes," she said through her teeth.

"And?"

"No and no."

"Keep trying."

"It would help if I knew what I was looking for."

"Your brother. You remember him, don't you? Kyle of the charming smile and strange eyes."

"Don't forget the stolen amber," she retorted.

"What?"

"Stolen. Amber. Am I ringing any bells?"

"I'd ring your bell if I could get my hands on you. What kind of amber?"

"Ask the cops."

"That was all they said?" Archer asked. "Stolen amber?"

"Yes."

"Raw or worked?"

"They didn't say. What was in the shipment that disappeared along with Kyle?"

"Who said anything about a shipment of amber disappearing?"

"The cops."

Archer grunted. "Not good. Someone is telling tales out of school."

"Don't look at me. You haven't told me anything except to come here and wait. Is it true?"

"What?"

"Did Kyle disappear along with a fortune in stolen Baltic amber?"

"I don't know. Is that what the cops are saying?"

"Implying," she said distinctly. "There's a difference. The difference between being questioned and being charged. What about Lawe? Where is he?"

"Last I heard, he was still in Lithuania."

"What about Justin?"

"Kaliningrad," Archer said. "Is Faith with you?"

"No. She's on her way back to San Francisco from Tokyo. She's going to spend a few weeks in Hawaii along the way."

"For these small things, Lord, I am grateful."

"What does that mean?"

"It means that you and your dear twin get into more trouble together than apart."

"The same could be said of Lawe and Justin," she pointed out. "But look on the bright side."

"Show it to me."

"Mom could have had three girls. Faith, Honor, and Chastity. Can you imagine being saddled with a sister called Chastity?"

Her brother laughed, surprising both of them. "Thanks, I needed that."

"What?"

"A laugh."

Honor's smile was as sad as her eyes. "Archer?"

"Yeah?"

"You think he's still alive, don't you?"

The static had never sounded more unnerving. She held her breath, waiting.

"Until I see the body..." Archer's voice faded.

"Yes." She took a harsh breath. "Kyle isn't a thief or a murderer!"

Silence stretched. A chill went over Honor. "Archer?"

"Kyle was thinking with his hormones."

"What does that mean?"

"Some little prick tease had him tied up in knots."

"Are you saying that Kyle wanted this woman enough to steal for her?" Honor asked.

Eyes closed, breath held, she waited for Archer's answer. All that came was silence followed by static. After too long her brother swore wearily, drowning out the static. In her mind she saw him raking his fingers though his dark hair in a gesture of frustration that all of the Donovan men shared.

"We don't know what happened," he said. "The evidence against Kyle looks good. Too damned good. Almost like..."

Again, Archer's voice faded into static.

"Keep talking," she said. "Tell me you don't think what the cops think about Kyle."

"That he's guilty of theft?"

"And murder."

"Whatever happened, I think that the explanations I'm hearing are too tidy."

"What makes you say that?"

"Too long and involved. Just take my word for it."

"But—"

"Have you checked the boat?" Archer interrupted.

"For something smaller than my six-feet, two-inch brother?" she asked sweetly.

"Never mind. I'm sending you back home."

"What? I just got here."

"You're leaving."

"What about Kyle's boat?"

"Stay off it. Even tied at the dock, the *Tomorrow* is way out of your league. Pack up, Hornet. Go on back home and design gemmy little knickknacks for Faith."

Honor hated that particular nickname. She also hated being treated like she was addicted to all-day suckers.

"Archer, you—"

"If the cops bother you before you leave," he said, talking over her, "sic one of Donovan International's lawyers on them."

"What about reporters?" she asked tightly.

"No comment."

"No problem. I don't know anything."

"That's the whole idea. Start packing."

"But—"

She was talking into a dead phone. With a disgusted word she dropped the receiver back into the cradle. It would be a cold day in hell before she tamely packed her bags and left. She wasn't some schoolgirl to be ordered around.

"Trouble?" Jake asked.

Honor jumped. She had forgotten she wasn't alone. She spun around. Jake was standing a few feet away with a local newspaper in his hand. She wondered if he had read the mixture of half-truths and breathless speculation about Kyle Donovan, a mysterious corpse, and missing amber that passed for news in the morning edition of the Fidalgo Island *Patriot*.

"Family," she said tersely. "Can't live with them and they won't let you live without them."

Jake made a sound that could have been understanding, but it was hard to tell with a growl. She chose to believe the rumble offered sympathy.

She needed it. Her oldest brother could have taught tight lips to a clam, the cops thought her favorite brother was a murderous crook, said favorite brother had vanished ...and she had just signed up to learn how to fish.

A complete disaster all around.

"Ready to go look at the boat?" Jake asked.

"Why not? Everything else has gone wrong."

"Your enthusiasm bubbles over like a plugged toilet."

"Understandable. I'm sooo excited."

Black eyebrows climbed. "You did advertise for a fishing guide, correct?"

She took a deep breath. "Yes. Sorry. I'm a bit worn out."

"You look like you could use a cup of coffee," he agreed. "Does the galley work on your boat?"

"I think so."

"You think so." He shook his head. "Have you owned the boat long?"

"No. My brother...left it to me."

The explanation sounded lame even to Honor. She was terrified of small boats and hated fishing, both of which Jake would soon find out. Then he would wonder why she wanted to learn how to run a small boat and go fishing.

Maybe he would accept masochism as an excuse.

"I..." She swallowed and tried again. "It's still painful. I'd rather not talk about it."

Jake wasn't surprised. No matter how innocent Honor looked, she was hiding a lot.

But then, so was he.

"C'mon," he said. "Let's check out your boat."

2

Off to the southwest, a bank of clouds lay like a feather comforter on the mountains of the Olympic Peninsula. Overhead, the sun temporarily ruled the sky. The water was like fine blue satin, still and glistening. Only the secret, powerful flow of tidal currents disturbed the calm surface of the strait.

Honor hesitated at the head of the gravel path leading down the rocky bluff to the beach fifteen feet below. The air was cool, clean, scented with fir. The silence was a balm to her unsettled thoughts. She really didn't want to ruin the small peace she felt by going fishing. On the other hand, anything was better than sitting around and worrying about Kyle. She started toward the dock with a determined stride.

Jake didn't notice Honor's hesitation. He went down the path, onto the dock, and stepped into the open stern of the *Tomorrow*. Barely pausing in his stride, he popped open a small compartment on the stern gunwale and cranked the dial around to the on position for both batteries.

When he straightened, he realized that he was still alone on the boat. He turned to see what had happened to his reluctant fishersan.

Honor stood on the dock eyeing the *Tomorrow* the way a suspicious cat eyes a full bathtub.

"Something wrong?" he asked.

"It's moving."

He glanced quickly around. Both the bow and stern lines were securely tied to the fore and aft dock cleats.

"What do you mean?" he asked. "It's tied off at both ends."

"Then why is it bouncing around?"

Jake looked at the deck of the *Tomorrow*. The boat was swaying slightly as it adjusted to his weight and the gentle slapping of salt water disturbed by a breeze.

"Bouncing around," he said neutrally. "Honor, have you ever been on a boat before?"

"Of course."

"When?"

"The last time I took a ferry to Vancouver Island."

"Doesn't count. Those ferries are almost as big as aircraft carriers."

"That's why I like them. They don't bounce."

"You'd be surprised what they'll do in a good wind."

She ignored him.

"Have you ever been on a *small* boat before?" he asked.

"Once."

The look on her face said that she hadn't enjoyed the experience.

"What happened?" he asked.

"Lawe and Justin—two of my four brothers— took me fishing. A wind came up and the boat bucked like a rodeo bull. I had to lie in the bottom with the fish to keep from going overboard."

"How old were you?"

"Thirteen."

"Did you go out fishing again after that?"

"Do I look like a masochist?"

"For all I know you're wearing a hair shirt underneath that floppy sweat suit."

She whipped up her black sweatshirt, revealing a tourmaline-green sweater that fit very well.

"Regulation cotton," she said. "And my sweat suit isn't floppy. It's comfortable."

Hastily Jake looked away from the sleek torso Honor had so unexpectedly revealed. Beneath sweats that were big enough for a man his size, his employer was built just the way

18

he liked women. Not too skinny. Not too fat. Not too big. Not too small. Just right for his hands. Just right for his mouth. Just right everywhere.

Too bad she was a Donovan. Jake was long past the age of screwing a female he didn't trust.

Unfortunately, he couldn't remember the last time a female interested him as much as this one did. Besides, there were few better excuses to stay close to a woman than a new, red-hot affair. And he intended to stay close to Honor every step of the way to finding Kyle and the stolen shipment of amber.

Jake looked back at her and smiled.

"Comfortable, huh?" he said. "Well, if I get wet, I'll know where to find a dry sweat suit."

"Hold your breath. I'm more likely to get wet than you are."

"Standing on the dock?"

She sighed and looked at him. As soon as she went down into the boat, she would be looking up at him again. And bouncing around. With a silent prayer, she took the long step off the dock—and promptly caught the heel of her running shoe on some unexpected part of the gunwale.

Jake caught Honor as easily as he had stepped into the boat himself. He looked into her startled eyes, smiled slightly, and released her much more slowly than he had grabbed her.

"Thanks," she muttered.

"You're welcome. There's a place in town that sells deck shoes."

"Good for them."

"Better for you. When the deck gets wet, you'll think you're ice-skating unless you wear deck shoes."

"Wet! The deck isn't supposed to get wet. That's why I hired you."

"Water is wet. Boats float in water. Boats get wet."

"There goes your tip."

Jake snickered, then shook his head and laughed out loud. Whatever her bad taste in siblings, Honor Donovan was someone he could like.

The thought sobered him instantly. The last thing he needed was to like Kyle's kid sister. Just because she obviously had inherited a full dose of Donovan charm was no reason to like her, much less to slide downhill into trusting her. At the end of that slippery, treacherous slope was the kind of rage and disappointment he had felt when he discovered that Kyle was as crooked as he was good company. Jake's corporation would be years recovering from the damage Kyle had done, if recovery was even possible.

It had been a long time since Jake had misjudged a human being so badly. As far as he was concerned, hell would freeze solid before he made such a mistake again.

People died making mistakes like that.

"I'll survive without a tip," he said. "Get deck shoes when you get the fishing license."

Honor stared at him, surprise clear on her face.

He forced himself to smile and reminded himself that whatever else Kyle's sister might be, she wasn't stupid. She read him far too clearly for his comfort. And for hers, apparently. She didn't look happy with whatever she had seen in his eyes.

Nothing new in that. A lot of people got uncomfortable when he looked at them a certain way.

Jake held out his hand.

"I thought you didn't expect a tip," she said.

"Keys."

Without a word she dug into the pouch pocket of her sweatshirt and brought out a simple floating key chain. There were only two keys on it. One looked a bit like an oldfashioned skeleton key. The other looked like an overgrown luggage key.

"I don't know how to start the engine," she said.

"I do. That's why you hired me."

He took the old-fashioned key, inserted it into the door leading into the boat's cabin, and turned the handle. The door opened easily. Its big tinted glass panel flashed in the sunlight.

"Why don't you sit in the pilot seat for now," he said.

"Uh, sure. Where is it?"

"Up front on the port—left—side," Jake said, "directly across from the helm seat. The helm is the thing that looks like a steering wheel."

"There's one of those right behind you."

"That's the aft station. I want you inside."

Honor didn't move. "You're supposed to teach me how to run the boat. I won't learn anything sitting in there while you're busy out here."

"You're serious about that part of it?"

"Very."

Jake looked into her level, golden-green eyes and didn't doubt her words. Whatever lack of interest she had in fishing, she wanted to learn how to operate her brother's boat.

Both relief and disappointment coursed through him—disappointment because she was part of Kyle's scheme, whatever that was, and relief that she wasn't as clueless as she had sounded on the phone with Archer.

"Okay," Jake said. "Ready for lesson number one?"

Honor nodded.

"The first thing you do after coming on board is lift the engine cover and check the engine."

"That little compartment?" she asked, pointing to the stern.

"No. This big compartment."

He pointed to the squared-off hump that took up more than half of the standing room in the open stern of the boat.

"You opened the little compartment first," Honor said. "Then you opened the door to the cabin."

"I wanted to make sure you were out of the way before I checked the engine."

"Why?"

"The cover eats toes."

"Would it settle for a cheese sandwich?"

He tried not to smile, but couldn't help it. She was a very female, even more unsquelchable version of Kyle.

Kyle, who could charm rust off steel.

"Stand over here," Jake said, positioning Honor to his right, away from the dock. "Watch your toes."

He bent, hooked the fingers of his left hand in the engine cover, and lifted it back on its hinges. The compartment yawned open at the stern. With the lid tilted back vertically, there was barely enough room around the edge of the hole to stand without falling in. There was no room for a man to slide between the cabin door and the cover.

Honor whistled when she saw the gleaming black beauty that filled the compartment. "That's an engine!"

"Four hundred and fifty-four cubic inches," he agreed. "Goes like bloody blue blazes, if you don't mind buying gas."

"No free lunch?"

"Not even a snack."

He pulled out the dipstick, checked it, and held it out for her to inspect.

"Looks like oil to me," she said.

"Good news. Salt water in the oil is like sugar in the gas tank. Bad luck. So the first thing you do when you get on board is check to make sure nothing has seeped in since you docked."

He replaced the dipstick. Then he squatted easily on his heels and began a thorough inspection of various hoses, clamps, and fittings.

"What are you looking for?" she asked.

"Careless maintenance."

"Kyle is quick-tempered but he isn't careless."

Jake grunted and kept right on looking. In the short time he had known Kyle, he hadn't appeared to be careless. But then, he hadn't appeared to be a crook, either. When it came to Kyle Donovan, Jake wasn't counting on one damned thing he hadn't held in his hands and examined with a wary eye.

"Shipshape and looking good," he said, standing again. "Watch your toes. This cover is heavy enough to take them right off."

Honor crowded back against the side of the boat as Jake lowered the engine cover back down. There was no latch to keep it closed and no need of one. The weight of the cover alone was enough to hold it in place.

"What next?" she asked.

"Blower. Go in and sit to the left of the driver's seat."

"Driver? Aren't boat folks called captains or pilots or something important?"

"Depends. Personally, I drive boats and don't talk any more nautical than I have to."

Honor stepped down into the cabin, walked up the short, narrow aisle, and climbed up to a bench seat that looked forward over the bow. Unlike a car, the steering wheel of the boat was on the right-hand side. The "windshield" was three separate windows with a steep inward slant from top to bottom.

After a moment Jake came and stood beside her seat. He filled the narrow aisle. Every breath she drew in smelled of soap and heat and something indefinably male. His black beard was either new or very closely cropped. His skin was clean. His hair was a thick, gleaming black pelt that was combed away from his face. His mustache was slightly longer than the rest of his beard. It emphasized the crisp line of his mouth.

She was tempted to trace the sharp peaks of his upper lip and the promising curve of his lower lip. The thought startled her even as it intrigued her. She hadn't felt such an intense feminine curiosity about a man since puberty.

"This is the blower control," he said.

Reluctantly she looked at the console in front of the steering wheel. He was pointing to one in a row of black rocker switches.

"Blower control," she repeated.

"The blower sucks air out of the engine compartment. Never start this boat until the blower has run for several minutes."

"Why?"

"Gas fumes. If they've built up and you hit the ignition switch, the explosion could put you in near-earth orbit."

Her eyes widened. "Bad luck."

"The worst."

He hit the rocker switch. A fan kicked in somewhere at the stern of the boat, inside the engine compartment.

Jake lifted the bottom of the driver's seat and

tilted it toward the steering wheel. There was a small sink tucked away underneath the seat. He turned on the water pump, rummaged for a kettle and settled for a saucepan, and put some water on to boil on the small galley stove.

Then he turned back to the boat itself. He went over the controls, turning on electronics, checking dials, and listening to the marine weather report from Canada, twenty miles away. As he touched each piece of equipment, he gave Honor a short explanation of its function.

She watched, listened, and absorbed intently. Under normal circumstances she wouldn't have known a marine widget from a nautical whatsit and wouldn't have cared. But nothing had been normal since Kyle vanished.

The *Tomorrow* was her best chance of helping him. The logical part of her mind knew that the boat wasn't much of a chance. Her emotions didn't care. This was the only chance she had. She would make the most of it and ignore Archer's smug advice about going back home and catching up on her designing.

It was hard to design when she couldn't shake the feeling that the key to Kyle's disappearance—and reappearance—lay somewhere in the San Juan Islands, just waiting to be discovered by her. That was why she had plastered the town with "Wanted: Fishing Guide who knows SeaSports" notices.

She finally had the guide. Now all she had to do was keep her mind on cold electronics instead of on a stranger with clean hands and a wry, sexy curve to his mouth. Considering that she had given up dating precisely because she was tired of men who thought sex was as obligatory—and exciting—as breathing, keeping her mind on electronics shouldn't have been a problem.

But it was.

She wondered if Jake would mind not exhaling for a bit, just while he was so close to her. The coffee-and-cream scent of his breath was making her restless.

"Chart plotter," Honor said, trying to gather her thoughts.

"What about it?"

She frowned at the small computer screen to the left of the steering wheel. The screen, and assorted other electronic equipment, was mounted on a swinging arm that could be pushed out of the way into the V berth when the boat was at anchor. There were rows of buttons with cryptic labels bordering the screen. There was another number pad below, but it wasn't set up like any computer she had ever seen. None of the labels helped her to figure out what all the buttons did. In addition there was one of Kyle's crazy add-ons wired into the lot. She had no idea what modification her brother had made to the standard electronic setup.

But if he had an electronic "lock" on this computer, she knew the password he used to access his other computers. All she had to do was figure out how to use the basic electronic equipment while learning how to run the boat itself. Then she would access the special computer stuff—if any—with Kyle's password, find out the key to everything, fire up the SeaSport, and go rescue her brother.

Simple.

Honor ignored all the self-doubts and gaping holes in her plan. She had been over them all again and again in the past week and done nothing but wear paths on the cottage floor as she paced. The secret to success lay in doing one thing at a time. Right now, the thing was learning the *Tomorrow*'s electronics.

"How does the chart plotter work?" she asked.

"Well, I hope. If not, there's always the old-fashioned way to plot a course."

"What's that?"

"Compass, pencil, and ruler."

"Tell me about the electronic way."

Jake's eyebrows lifted slightly. The demand in her voice was polite but very real. Excitement whipped invisibly through his blood. She didn't like boats or water but she was dead set on learning about plotting a course. If the cops were right about Kyle sneaking back into the United States, the key to the stolen amber might very well be the *Tomorrow*.

The lady must have amber on her mind. That was the best news Jake had heard since the amber disappeared and the governments of Lithuania, Kaliningrad, and Russia had decided that J. Jacob Mallory's passport was no longer welcome in their countries. Nor was any representative of his company, Emerging Resources.

"I'm used to a different electronic setup," Jake said, which was true. "I'll have to study up on these before I can teach you much." Not true, but hell, she was a Donovan. Lies weren't new to the Donovan clan.

"We'll learn together," Honor said.

Jake would rather have pried the truth out of the computer without a Donovan witness. "If you're in a hurry, you can teach yourself."

"How?"

"Read the manuals that came with the equipment."

"I couldn't find any."

"Then we'll have to do it my way, won't we?"

"Hell."

He smiled despite himself. "Patience is a virtue."

"So is chastity. I don't hear many men standing foursquare behind it."

"Or women."

"Equality. Ain't it great?"

Jake looked at the bright, hard teeth filling Honor's smile and wondered if she enjoyed the sexual merry-go-round that passed for urban dating. Scorecards had never appealed to him. Neither had punchboards.

"Yeah, great," he said coolly. "The white button is the horn. These two levers over here are the gas feed and the shifter."

"Which is which?"

"Black knob is the shifter. Red is the gas.

You can turn off the blower now."

In order to reach the console, Honor had to lean across the aisle in front of Jake. Except for the horn, all the rocker switches looked alike. Black.

As she edged closer to read the fine white print beneath the dark switches, she discovered that Jake's body was a lot warmer than his voice. The living heat of him radiated through his stained denim jacket. Stained, but not dirty. The cloth was as clean as her own fingernails. She wondered if the rest of him was equally warm and well washed.

Think nautical, she told herself sharply. *Think fishing. Think root canal without anesthesia.*

Her clean, unvarnished fingernail pressed on the blower switch. The noise from the back of the boat stopped.

"I'm assuming this is like the other Volvo marine engines I've run," Jake said.

"Meaning?"

His big hand wrapped around the lever with the red knob. He pumped the gas feed up and down several times. "They catch fire faster if they're stroked a bit first."

"Is that some kind of salty saying that has double meanings?" she muttered beneath her breath, thinking Jake couldn't hear her.

"Like 'broad in the beam' or 'any port in a storm'?" he asked, deadpan.

Her head snapped around. He was looking at her from a distance of two inches. There were slivers of blue and green and black mixed in with the transparent silver of his eyes. His eye-

30

lashes were much too long for a man who wore a scruffy denim jacket and had calluses on his hands.

His eyes were beautiful.

"Don't tell me, let me guess," he said. "You like my eyes."

A hint of red stained Honor's cheekbones.

"Such manly modesty," she drawled. "Do all your female clients gush over you?"

"What do you think?"

"I think it's a good thing you aren't expecting a tip. You have the interpersonal finesse of a neutron bomb."

He gave a crack of laughter, inserted the small ignition key, and twisted. The engine growled to life. He tapped the lever, adjusting the gas feed. The engine settled into a contented, chuckling kind of rumble.

"We'll let it warm up for a few minutes," he said. "It—"

"Don't tell me, let me guess. Another salty homily about hot engines and smooth rides?"

"If the oil isn't circulating, friction is bad for the engine."

"No kidding. Would it interest you to know that Kyle and I used to build street racers together?"

"Then I won't waste any more time teaching you how to check fluid levels."

"Good."

"Yeah. Leaves more time for the interesting stuff."

"Electronics."

"Fishing."

Honor tried not to look like a plugged toilet running over with enthusiasm.

"Where did your brother keep his papers?" Jake asked.

"What kind of papers?"

"Boat registration, proof of ownership, insurance, manufacturer's instructions, that kind of thing."

"Behind you, in the second drawer."

He backed up and turned away. The tiny galley was just behind the driver's seat. In addition to the small propane stove, there was a cabinet and four drawers. He checked the coffee water, saw that it wasn't quite boiling, and settled for the papers. A quick jerk up and out released the catch on the second drawer.

Two large waterproof envelopes lay inside. The first envelope had the documents and certification he was looking for. The second envelope had warranties, instructions, and manuals for everything on the boat but the electronics.

"I'll make the coffee while you do whatever," Honor said.

He nodded absently and sat at the small galley table without looking up from the papers. For a time the only sounds were the small clatter of coffeepot and mugs and the mutter of the engine as it warmed up.

She handed him a mug of coffee.

"Thanks," he said, still reading papers. He took a sip and then glanced at her in surprise. "How did you know I liked cream, no sugar?"

"I smelled cream on your breath. Lucky for you, I like milk on my cereal."

She turned away and put the milk back in the small refrigerator under the dinette seat.

Jake watched her closely, wondering if she was flirting or just answering his question. He couldn't tell, because he couldn't see her eyes.

"As for the sugar..." She straightened, picked up her own coffee, and climbed into the pilot seat. "If you like sweet things, it hasn't made a dent in your personality."

Smiling slightly, Jake went back to scanning papers. When he was satisfied, he returned everything to its proper envelope and shut the drawer.

"Well?" she asked.

"All in order."

What he didn't say was that there were more warranties and instructions than there were items of equipment on the *Tomorrow*. Two auxiliary outboard engines were mentioned. One was permanently attached to the stern of the boat for use as a trolling motor while fishing. The other, smaller, engine was presumably for a Zodiac, which also had papers in the file.

Then there was the handheld Global Positioning System receiver unit whose warranty and receipt had been stuffed into the envelope as though Kyle had been in too much of a hurry to worry about keeping neat records. The date on the receipt was thirteen days ago.

Kyle had vanished four weeks ago in Kaliningrad and reappeared halfway around the world, in the Pacific Northwest, only to vanish again. The smaller engine and the Zodiac apparently had disappeared with him. Probably the GPS unit as well.

Jake made a mental note to pick up the portable GPS receiver from his own SeaSport tonight.

"Did your brother have any kind of tender?" Jake asked.

Honor looked at him blankly. "Excuse me?"

"A small boat."

"Another one?"

"No, just a little runabout. A skiff to take ashore when he anchored in a place without docks."

"I don't know. Is it important?"

"It's not required by the Coast Guard, if that's what you mean."

She didn't know what she meant, so she kept her mouth shut. Her tongue had already gotten her into trouble with this man. Her tongue or her hormones, or both working together without benefit of her brain.

"Where does he keep the PFDs?" Jake asked.

"The what?"

"Personal flotation devices."

"Oh. I don't know."

The look Jake gave her said he wasn't surprised. He bent low, quickly scanned the V berth in the bow, and found nothing that looked like it would pass a Coast Guard inspection.

And he suspected they would be having

34

one. It was the sort of thing he would have done if he couldn't think of a better way to get a look around the *Tomorrow*.

Honor tried to see past Jake into the V berth, but couldn't. He blocked the entrance and then some. A big man.

"Are the, uh, PFDs up there?" she asked.

"Nope. Nothing but clothes, fishing rods, a landing net, and two down-riggers."

"I take it that down-riggers aren't PFDs?"

"Not hardly. They float like anchors."

"Then what are they good for?"

"Fishing." He backed up slightly and turned toward her without straightening up. "Move your leg."

Her breath came in hard as one of his hands went between her calves. The instant of brushing contact was brief, but it was enough to rattle her. Quickly she shifted so that he could reach beneath the seat without touching her.

Though Jake said nothing, he had noticed the sudden, involuntary widening of her eyes when he touched her leg. If she had been riding the sexual merry-go-round, it hadn't been for a while. Instinctive body language didn't lie. The lady definitely wasn't used to being rubbed up against.

Too bad. It would have been a lot easier if she were the type who changed men every day and three times on Saturday night. Then he wouldn't feel like a ruthless son of a bitch if he followed up on the purely female interest he saw in her eyes.

Cursing silently at his inconvenient attraction to a thief's—and probably a murderer's—sister, Jake forced his attention back to the open area beneath the bench seat. That was where he stored his own PFDs when he was alone on the boat.

That was where he would have found them a minute before if he hadn't been thinking how nice it would be to reach beneath all that loose sweat suit cloth and find the warm, sleek leg beneath.

"Here we go," he said, reaching in. "Just what the Coast Guard ordered. One certified PFD."

She looked at the thick, bright orange jacket he was holding out.

"Looks more like Halloween to me," she said.

"Shows up real well against the sea, no matter how dark it is. If you're wearing this when you take a header into the drink, you'll be floating and easy to spot. Keeps the coroner happy."

"Coroner? I thought the point of floating was to stay alive."

"Then stay out of the water. Summer or winter, it's cold enough to kill you in thirty minutes or less."

Honor looked out the cabin windows at the blue-green water of the little cove. A fitful breeze had ruffled the satin surface into a shimmering kind of velvet. The ocean looked about as dangerous as cotton candy.

Yet she knew how quickly the wind could deepen and strengthen, piling up dangerous waves. It had happened to her when she was a girl. Justin and Lawe had managed to bring the skiff back to shore right side up, but it had been a terrifying experience for her. She hadn't been for a ride on a small boat since that day. If she had had her way, she never would. But finding Kyle was more important than leftover childhood terrors.

Jake put the float coat back under the seat. Then he looked at the two cheap PFDs that were stacked at the far end of the opening. Each thick, awkward vest had a Coast Guard stamp of approval on the bright orange fabric.

Silently he straightened and turned back to the woman who was either a fine actress or actually intrigued by him as a man. He kept hoping she was only an actress of the same high caliber as her brother. At the very least, she could have been as arrogant and high-handed as the rest of her family.

Somehow he didn't think he was going to be that lucky. Or unlucky. He couldn't decide which. And that bothered him even more than the fresh, vaguely peppermint scent of Honor Donovan.

Remember Kyle, Jake told himself savagely. *You liked him, too. And he screwed you but good.*

At least getting screwed by Honor would be a lot more fun.

"I assume your brother kept a log?" Jake asked impatiently.

"Yes. Could you hand me my purse? I've been looking through the log, hoping to find where he...uh, fished."

Jake looked over his shoulder, where she was

pointing. A dinette table stuck out between two more bench seats just across from the galley. The resulting booth could seat four, if they were friends. It made into a bed that would sleep two, if they were very, very good friends. Or planned on getting that way.

"This is a purse?" he asked, lifting the black leather backpack on the table.

"It works for me."

He held the backpack with one hand. "Find any?"

"What?"

"Good fishing holes."

"Er, no."

"So you decided to hire a fishing guide?"

"Er, yes."

Jake decided that Honor needed a lot more practice lying. Unless she really was a world-class actress pretending to be the innocent sister of a larcenous brother....

Impatiently Jake told himself that it didn't matter. Either way, the lady with the cat eyes and quick mind was definitely trouble in oversized sweats.

"Why are you looking so skeptical?" Honor asked. "Surely you've seen a woman's purse before."

"All sizes and shapes. I once saw a woman pull a live rooster and two chickens out of her purse. Of course, she was on the way to the market, so it wasn't all that surprising."

"Any fresh eggs?"

"Does scrambled count?"

"Nope."

"Then there weren't any eggs."

A smile changed the taut lines of Honor's face. The smile was brief and all the more beautiful for it.

"Ah, well," she said. "Maybe next time. Where was this market?"

Telling her that it was in Kaliningrad would raise the kind of questions Jake had no intention of answering.

"In the country," he said. "Is that the log?"

"Yes, but there's nothing interesting in it. Just rows of dates and gas consumption and maintenance records and that sort of thing."

Adrenaline pulsed through Jake. He had hoped that Kyle was the kind of captain who kept decent records. That, plus the chart plotter and computer, could tell a lot about where the boat had been recently.

Jake took the log from Honor. For a minute or two he flipped through it, frowning like a man working hard. Then he looked up at her.

"I can't say for sure that the boat is ready to go out until I look over this log more closely," he said. "Why don't I read it while you go into town and get boat shoes and a fishing license? If you hurry, we can still make the tide change."

She hesitated. "Okay, I guess."

"I'll meet you back here in ninety minutes," he said, sliding out from the helm seat.

"Wait! What do I do with the boat until then?"

He gave her an odd look. "What do you mean?"

"It's running," she pointed out.

Jake turned off the ignition key, pulled it out, and dropped it in Honor's lap.

"It's just an engine," he said with exaggerated patience. "It won't attack you. Treat it like a car."

All that kept Honor from saying *Bite me, big boy!* was the fact that he probably would.

3

Jake turned his battered four-wheel-drive truck into the muddy tracks that led to his cabin. Surrounded by dark, wind-sculpted fir trees, the small house crouched on a cliff above Puget Sound. This was his getaway from company headquarters in Seattle, the place where he caught up on work, his home away from home, the one place whose address and telephone number no one had.

That was why he swore when he saw a Ford utility vehicle sitting in what passed for his driveway. When a woman in a smart red blazer and black skirt climbed out and waved at him, he knew that the day had just gone from sugar to shoe polish.

Ellen Lazarus was old news from a time in his life when he believed in saving the world from itself. These days his goal was less grandiose: all he wanted was not to be at ground zero when that great outhouse in the sky unloaded.

He turned off the truck, climbed out, leaned against the door, and waited to find out how much crap was headed straight for his head.

"What, not even a smile or a wave of welcome?" Ellen said, walking up to him.

Jake watched her move with a cross between cynicism and male appreciation. She didn't have to work to add an extra swing and jiggle to her ass. She had been born with that special locomotion, the same way she had been born with wide blue eyes, black hair, and a brainy pragmatism that made Machiavelli look like a choirboy. Not surprisingly, once she got over wanting to play cloak and dagger games in the field, she became an exceptional intelligence analyst.

"I won't ask how you found me," Jake said. "The folks you hang with could find anything. *Why* did you find me?"

"My, we're in a bad mood, aren't we? And it's such a beautiful day, too." She waved an elegant hand at the sun-dappled forest. "I'd heard that it always rains in the Pacific Northwest."

He grunted.

"Does this mean you don't want to talk about the good old days?" she asked.

His scarred eyebrow lifted in a sardonic arc. "The good old days? That should take about three seconds. Bye, Ellen. Don't call me, I'll call you. Your three seconds are up."

Her cheerful smile vanished, leaving behind the restless, consuming personality that would never be satisfied with one of anything, including men.

"Hey, c'mon, Jake," she said softly. "It was good and you know it."

"Since when do you spend time looking over your shoulder at the ashes?"

"You're determined to do this the hard way, aren't you?"

"First thing a boy learns is it's gotta be hard to be good."

She made an impatient gesture. "Have it your way."

"I plan to. Good-bye. Don't give my regards to Uncle Sam."

Jake started to walk around Ellen to get to his cabin. She stepped out in front of him and looked up with eyes as blue and clear as a porcelain angel's.

"Would you be more cooperative if we sent someone else?" she asked.

"No."

"You don't even know what we want."

"I like it that way."

The wind gusted, rippling the black silk collar of Ellen's blouse. Absently she patted the collar back in place and examined her remaining options. It didn't take long. She wasn't a slow or timid thinker.

"I told them the old lover bit wouldn't work," she said calmly. "You haven't made any attempt to get in touch with me for years. In fact, you never did. When you say good-bye, you mean it."

Jake waited, knowing he wasn't going to get rid of her easily. What he was afraid of was that he wouldn't get rid of her at all. U.S. government intelligence types—no matter what part of the alphabet soup of agencies they might work for—didn't bother honest citizens unless the professionals were up to their lips in shit and the devil was coming by in a speedboat.

"I could appeal to your patriotism," Ellen said.

He smiled.

"Mother," she muttered. "Reformed idealists are the worst. Once the fairy dust gets out of their eyes, they don't want to play anymore."

"We've had this conversation before."

She tapped a manicured nail against her little leather purse and looked at the unfenced woods beyond Jake's truck. A bald eagle soared overhead, its pure white head turning as it looked for prey. Though the bird's shadow whipped over her face, Ellen didn't look up.

"All right," she said, deciding. "You want to find Kyle Donovan. So do we. We can help each other."

Jake's impassive expression didn't change. He had been expecting something like this since he had seen Ellen get out of her car.

"Why?" he asked.

"Why what?"

"Why are you after Kyle?"

"You know why. He stole a million bucks in amber."

Jake knew the amber was worth only half that. But if that's what the Donovan family was claiming on the insurance, no one would listen to him anyway. The Donovans had wealth and friends in high places—same thing, really.

"So Kyle stole some amber," Jake said. "So what? People steal ten times a million bucks and our dear Uncle doesn't break a sweat unless taxes aren't paid."

"Kyle stole this money from a foreign country."

"You're kidding, right?"

"Wrong."

"Get real. This is me you're talking to, not some freshman politician hoping to get in your pants. You'll have to come up with a better reason for chasing Kyle. A lot better."

Ellen considered her remaining options. Option, really. The truth. The only question was how little she could get by with—and how to shade it to the best advantage. But not too shady. Jake could be an abrupt bastard.

"Kyle was involved with Lithuanian separatists," she said. "We're afraid he took the amber to them to finance some grassroots terrorism."

Jake hoped she was wrong, but he doubted it. Even so, it still didn't explain why Uncle Sam cared.

"Still not good enough," he said. "When it comes to geopolitics, Lithuania is very small beer. So where's the damage to Uncle?"

She didn't want to answer but she knew she was going to. "I told them you would get to the bottom line."

Jake waited.

"Kyle's driver added something to the shipment before he was killed," Ellen said.

"What was it?"

"No answer."

"Don't know or won't tell?"

"Same difference. No answer."

Jake tried another direction. "I don't buy it. Kyle wasn't stupid enough to get involved with nukes."

"If it was nukes, we wouldn't be asking for anyone's help. We'd be demanding it."

He didn't disagree. "So it's more than raw amber and less than nukes, but still enough to bring Uncle running. Must be damned valuable. I don't think Kyle is that stupid."

"Idealism, fairy dust, and a piece of ass," Ellen said succinctly. "Makes 'em stupid every time."

"Are you talking about Marju?" Jake asked.

Ellen nodded. "She's the granddaughter of a hard case left over from World War Two. He fought the Germans. He fought the Russians. He fought the Soviets. He fought his own countrymen when they wanted peace."

Jake bit back some searing words of disgust. He knew full well how a woman could lower a man's IQ. "I told Kyle that Marju was more trouble than she was worth, but no, he was in love. He was going to be her bold knight in bright armor."

"I don't know about bright, but he's a bold son of a bitch. He killed the Lithuanian driver, got in the truck with the amber and headed off into the night."

"Tell me something I don't know."

"Tell me what you know and I won't bore you with repetition," Ellen shot back.

"Where did you lose Kyle?"

"We never had him to lose. He wasn't ours."

Jake wondered whether to believe her, then decided it didn't matter. "I managed to track him out of Kaliningrad and through Lithuania. I lost him when he crossed over into Russia."

"That's where we lost him," she agreed.

"And if I said I'd tracked him to Tallinn...?" Jake asked sarcastically.

"I'd be on the phone right now. We're being chewed up one side and down the other to get results. Did you?"

"Track him to Estonia? No. He went east, not north. I lost him about three hundred kilometers inside the Russian border. Before I could find him again, I started running into bureaucratic walls and some nonbureaucratic types with nasty guns. Officially, I was invited to leave the country and not come back."

"And unofficially?"

"I was offered permanent residence in a three-by-six-foot slice of Mother Russia."

She shook her head. "Whatever happened to Byzantine subtlety?"

"Same thing that happened to Byzantium. It lost."

"So about ten days ago you came back here to lick your wounds. And maybe to have a late-night look around Kyle's cottage?" Ellen asked.

Jake shrugged and said nothing. It was close enough to the truth to be uncomfortable.

"Then you noticed one of those cards tacked up all over Anacortes asking for a fishing guide and signed by H. Donovan," Ellen continued.

He waited, watching her.

"And then you turned on that Jake Mallory slow grin and got hired," she concluded.

"Half right. I got hired, which was more than your man did."

"How did you know about—hell," she said in disgust at falling into his trap.

"No harm done. Duping someone in as her guide was an obvious move."

"Did you tell Honor that you're looking for her brother?"

"The subject didn't come up."

"That's what we thought," Ellen said with cream-licking satisfaction. "The Donovans have stonewalled everyone overseas, including you. So you're going to backdoor them, using the younger sister in America."

There was no disapproval in Ellen's voice. If anything, there was a note of congratulations on finding an opening no one had before now. Jake would have preferred it if she had been shocked. But people with a low threshold for shock didn't last long in a world without fairy dust.

"We won't get in your way," she said quickly. "Just keep us informed."

"You're in my way right now."

"Get used to it, or I'll drop in on Little

Miss Muffet and tell her who her fishing guide really is."

For a few moments Jake simply looked at Ellen. Then he shook his head slightly. "I don't think so."

"What?"

"Right now I'm all you have inside the Donovan clan walls. You're not stupid enough to blow my cover until you're certain you can't use me at all."

Manicured nails tapped on black leather. A cool wind gusted and then gusted again, making a grove of slim, red-barked madrona trees shudder.

Jake knew without looking up that the clouds to the southwest were slowly reclaiming the sky. It would probably rain before sunset. The forests hadn't gotten green by accident.

"All right," she said. "What do we have that you want?"

"Did Kyle come through SeaTac about two weeks ago?"

"His passport came through. The Immigration guy we interviewed said he looked pretty much like his picture, given that he was coming off a two-week fishing trip on the Kamchatka Peninsula."

"What do you say?"

"We're betting if the man and the picture matched, neither was Kyle Donovan."

Jake's eyes narrowed. "Bad news."

"For Donovan, certainly. He probably got that chunk of Mother Russia they offered you. But bad for us? We don't know."

"Did—"

"My turn," she interrupted. "Have any of your Emerging Resources contacts heard rumors of prime Baltic Amber for sale from shady sources?"

"Raw or worked?"

"Both."

"Just the usual. Petty smuggling and theft in the mines are commonplace and not part of any larger conspiracy. The big-time smugglers are all connected to government. Hell, half the time they *are* the government."

"Welcome to the former Soviet Union," Ellen said sourly, "where a conflict of interest is your best hope of getting rich."

"When your currency is in freefall or you don't even have a currency to call your own, you have to expect a little creative bartering by the natives."

"Creative bartering." She smiled briefly. "That's good. Have any of your people turned up anything having to do with Russian amber specifically?"

"The usual small forgeries from Russian plastic factories. Some estate stuff that probably came from stolen World War Two household goods. A pretty decent replica of a corner table from the czar's legendary Amber Room."

Only someone who had once played the game would have recognized the subtle tightening of Ellen's features. Jake noticed the predatory sharpening of interest and felt a cold stone settle in his stomach.

More than raw amber and less than nukes.

The Amber Room.

Jake had heard rumors that the Amber Room had been found...but there were always rumors about World War II's most famous lost treasure. In 1941 the Nazis had dismantled one of the czar's extraordinary palace rooms, a room whose ceiling, doors, wall coverings, and furnishings—tables, chairs, lamps, knick-knacks, candlesticks, vases, knives, forks, spoons, snuff boxes, objets d'art, *everything*—were carved from solid amber or surfaced in mosaics of precious amber.

The only exceptions to the amber rule were the tall, gilded mirrors that doubled and redoubled the play of light throughout the magical room. When the room was intact, walking into it must have been like walking into a shimmering golden paradise suspended within the vast, icy gray of the Russian winter.

The Germans shipped their unique golden loot out of Saint Petersburg to Kaliningrad. From there, it vanished, thus beginning a treasure hunt that would endure as long as human imagination and greed or until the lost Amber Room was recovered, whichever came first.

"The table was fake?" Ellen asked.

"The mosaic inlay was real amber. The table itself was real and very well made, but it had never been part of the czar's Amber Room."

"How can you be certain?"

"It's my job."

"Convince me."

Jake thought it over for a split second and decided to be gracious. That way he had a fallback position.

"Quantities of Baltic amber are hard to come by," he said, "unless you're very well connected with a Baltic government or a local *mafiya* chieftain, take your pick. Mexican and Costa Rican amber are available to anyone with money. Whoever crafted the forged table was forced to use some clear amber from the New World."

"How can you tell the difference between New and Old World stuff?"

"Ask your experts."

"You're here. They're not."

Wistfully he looked at the sky. Clouds were thickening off toward the Olympics, but there was still plenty of time to try out the *Tomorrow* before the weather got nasty.

"Baltic amber is called succinite because of its high percentage of succinic acid," he said. "It's unique among ambers. In fact, some purists claim that succinite is the only real amber. All the rest is something else."

"All Baltic ambers are unique for the succinic acid content, no exceptions?" she asked.

"None that matter."

"Tell me about the ones that don't matter."

Jake looked at his watch. He would rather have been photocopying Kyle's log than telling Ellen what any amber dealer could have told her. He hoped that a little patience now would pay big dividends later on.

"About ten percent of Baltic ambers don't have succinic acid," he said, "but they didn't end up in the czar's palace."

"Why not?"

"That kind of Baltic amber is too soft, too brittle, or too ugly for decorative use. It was turned into varnish or medicine or burned as incense. The amber I saw in the forged table was as clear and radiant as liquid sunshine. First-class amber in the New World. The Old World still prefers bastard amber."

"Bastard?"

"Opaque or semi-opaque. Depending on its color and 'feel,' nontranslucent amber is called butter, bone, ivory, fatty, cloudy, semi-bastard—"

"I get the picture," she interrupted. "A lot of names."

"A lot of variations in color and transparency. Amber's link with human culture is long and richly textured, especially in the Baltic regions. They spent as much time describing and naming minute differences in amber as we did counting angels and pinheads."

Polished red fingernails tapped in slow counterpoint to the dying wind while Ellen ran what she had just heard through her first-class brain.

"Are color and clarity a reliable way to tell Baltic from other amber?" she asked.

"No. What I just gave you only skims the surface. There are literally hundreds of words in the Baltic languages describing varieties of amber. Each variation of clarity and/or color has its own passionate collectors and its own mythology."

"The czars traded all over the world," she said. "Could some high-quality non-Baltic amber have been used in making the original Amber Room?"

"Anything is possible."

"Is it probable?"

"Not really. The amber discoveries in Mexico and Puerto Rico are recent. The Amber Room dates from Prussian times, the early eighteenth century. Besides, why trade halfway around the world for goods you can get at home for a great price?"

"Meaning?"

"The Baltic amber mines were an imperial monopoly."

"Mother," she muttered. "What you're saying is, no matter what the color or clarity, every bit of amber in the Amber Room came from the Palmnicken mines."

"Or other mines along the shores of the Baltic Sea. Lithuania and Kaliningrad have the best mines, but not the only ones."

"Well, there goes that theory." She frowned. "What—"

"My turn," he interrupted. "Do you have proof that the Donovan family is part of Kyle's scheme?"

"Nothing to take to court. It's our working hypothesis. Do you have a better one?"

"No. Are you looking for the whole Amber Room?"

"Who says we're looking for it at all?"

"That's the problem with interrogation. You can't ask questions without giving away information. *Are you looking for the whole room?*"

Silence. Then Ellen shrugged. "They can't say I didn't warn them about you. At the moment, all we care about is the panel that Kyle stole."

"Does he have the whole room?"

"We don't know."

"Give me your best estimate."

"We think he may or may not be somebody's cat's-paw for the sale of the entire room. Either way, he ended up with a panel from the room as a calling card to excite the international market."

"Bloody hell. Who was the corpse that washed up in the San Juans, the one with Third World dental work?" Jake asked.

"Former KGB from the former Soviet Union."

"What was he doing lately?"

"People."

"Anyone in particular or was he an equal opportunity killer?"

"He worked for one of the Moscow *mafiya* chieftains for a while, then went freelance."

"Why was he after Kyle?"

"No answer."

"What do you have on Marju?"

"She was the usual loyal daughter of a

downtrodden, diluted, bastardized Baltic country. The losers keep track of feuds, wars, and bloodlettings going back centuries. They're good haters."

Jake already knew that. What he didn't know was whether Marju's brand of patriotism went beyond speaking an arcane language and taking up traditional Lithuanian crafts.

"How serious was she about freeing Lithuania?" he asked.

"From what we've discovered, good old Grandpa did a thorough job of infecting his granddaughter with a heavy dose of Father Country claptrap. She went to the usual 'secret' meetings, which were duly reported to the Russians by Lithuanian informers."

"There are meetings and then there are conspiracies. Which were these?"

"Babe, they haven't had a useful conspiracy in Lithuania since God wore knickers. There was lots of shouting over how our poor great-great-great-granddads were screwed, plus retellings of even more ancient rape and robbery."

"They would be better off shouting for a currency of their own, one not based on the Russian ruble," Jake said.

"Lacks sex appeal."

"What about—"

"Back to the missing amber," Ellen interrupted. "Have you heard any rumors about the Amber Room?"

"Sure."

Again Jake saw the shift in her, as though she had just come into hard focus.

"Tell me what you've heard," she said.

"You may have the rest of the day, but I don't."

"If I do, you do."

For a moment his impatience almost got the better of him. Then he reminded himself how much easier life would be if Ellen or someone like her wasn't sticking to him like lice.

"A few people say that the room never left Saint Petersburg, and therefore was lost when we bombed the place to a smoking ruin at the end of the war. Most people believe that the Nazis dismantled the Amber Room with hacksaws and pry bars in 1941, packed up the lot, and shipped it to Kaliningrad."

"And?"

"That's when the real fun begins. The crates the Amber Room was packed in vanished sometime in 1945. No one has seen them since. The bean counter types say the whole thing went up in smoke when we bombed the hell out of the city."

Ellen grimaced. "What do the rest of the people say?"

"You've heard of Erick Koch, a former Nazi from what was then East Prussia?"

"Have I?"

"He's the one who said the Amber Room is still buried in Königsberg, which the Russians renamed Kaliningrad. He ought to know. He's the one who buried it."

"Why didn't he dig it up?"

"He spent his life in jail after the Nazis fell. Various folks wooed him and whispered promises of freedom in his ear, but even on his deathbed he never told where the loot was hidden."

"Next theory," Ellen said coolly.

"Then there's Dr. Alfred Rohde, who said he locked up the amber in an underground cellar. Same city as Koch, different burial. Of course, that was before the Allies bombed the place to rubble and the Russians came, paved it over, and built a new city."

Ellen's expression didn't change.

Jake kept talking. His tone said that he thought it was all fairy dust and he was a man who no longer believed in the glittery stuff.

"One of the men looking for the Amber Room today thinks it's in a brewery in Kaliningrad," Jake said.

"What do you think?"

"I think that digging beneath the rubble of that old building is a good way to die. Live munitions left over from fifty years of war and revolution, flooded underground rooms, falling walls, that sort of thing. Dangerous."

Ellen made a sound that said she was listening.

"Then there's the shipped-to-America theory," he said. "Some wealthy, conveniently anonymous collector paid megabucks and hid the room in his modern American castle. A variation of that theory is the room went to South America—Uruguay or Argentina— with a departing Nazi as the Third Reich came crashing down around Hitler. Have I mentioned the Stasi?"

"No."

"Can't leave them out. The former East German Ministry of State Security, know as the Stasi to their friends, wasted years and millions looking for the imperial room. No luck, of course."

"Why do you say 'of course'? Do you believe the Amber Room won't ever be found?"

"I think it went up in smoke when the Allies leveled what was then Königsberg. Amber burns like what it is—pitch, the basic component of ancient torches. Great smell, a plume of soot, and a fast fire."

"But Boris Yeltsin told the Germans that the Amber Room was hidden somewhere in what used to be East Germany," Ellen objected.

"Yeltsin also said you could graft a free market economy onto a corrupt, self-destructing communist base, and do it in a year. I'm sure he would love to pull an amber rabbit out of his hat to please and excite the disgusted masses, but my money is on coming up empty-handed."

Again, nails tapped against leather. The wind gusted and set the fir trees to swaying. Streamers of cloud whipped by above the trees. Waves slapped against the cliff face with a stealthy sound.

Jake looked at his watch again. Only a few minutes had passed. It seemed like a lot more. Certain people had that effect on him. Ellen was one of them. It hadn't always been that way, but everybody grew up eventually—if they lived long enough.

"You're not after the Amber Room," Ellen said, looking closely at him.

"Like you said, I don't believe in fairy dust anymore."

"If you heard something useful, would you call me?"

"I don't have your number."

"We've got yours. I'll be nearby."

Jake didn't even try to look happy about the prospect. "Don't bother."

"No bother at all."

"Jesus," he said in disgust. "You really do believe Kyle is holding a piece of the Amber Room."

She hesitated, then said, "We have to proceed as though we believe that."

"Why?"

"The alternative is to be caught with our bare ass hanging over a buzz saw. You have seventy-two hours before I yank your ticket with Honor Donovan. My card is by your telephone. If you get lucky or smart, give us a call. You help us, we help you. Get smart, Jake."

"Good-bye," he said, walking around her.

"I mean it."

"So do I."

Before the door closed behind him, Ellen's car started up. By the time he picked up the telephone, she was disappearing down the winding dirt road. He didn't have to look up the number he was calling. As it started ringing, he opened Kyle's boat log and began scanning it.

"Emerging Resources, may I help you?" asked a pleasant voice.

"I sure hope so, Fred. Is my Number Two in?"

"Hi, Jake. She's talking to Kaliningrad."

"Hell of a time to do that."

"Apparently the contact was sampling local vodkas until well past normal business hours over there. He just returned her call. Oh, wait. Her line is open now. I'll put you through."

Eyes narrowed in concentration, Jake kept turning pages of the log. A few moments later Charlotte Fitzroy, vice president of Emerging Resources and one of Jake's oldest friends, came on the line.

"Hey, Pres. You making any headway?" Charlotte asked.

"Working on it. Has the government been all over you?"

"Like a rash. I tried to be helpful—"

Jake laughed and kept scanning the log.

"—but they wouldn't be specific about what they wanted," she said, "so I couldn't help them, could I?"

"They want the Amber Room."

"So does everyone who ever heard of it."

"Yeah. Other than that, how's it going?"

"Business in general or Kyle Donovan in particular?"

"Yes."

"Everything is lurching along without you,

but I'll be sending some contracts for your signature. As for Kyle, nothing new. No bodies with Western dental work. No *mafiya*-style hits related to the Baltic amber trade."

"You're sitting on something," Jake said.

"My delicate little butt."

"C'mon, Char. Remember who pays the bills."

"I want to wait until I have something solid."

"I don't."

"Oh, all right. One of our Kaliningrad contacts suggested we look on the other side of the former Soviet Union."

"Where?"

"Kamchatka."

Jake stopped turning pages of the log. The Kamchatka Peninsula was only a short hop from Alaska. "Why?"

"Kyle called a number there several times. A fishing resort, as near as we can tell. It's run by Russians. Vlad Kirov is the owner."

"Go on."

"Nowhere special to go. They know Kyle. He and other Donovans have fished with them several times. End of story."

Jake went back to turning pages. "Do we have anyone in Kamchatka?"

"Ed Burls, but he doesn't speak Russian."

"Get a picture of Kyle to Ed. He can work with a translator."

"He's a geologist, not a private investigator."

"If we don't prove that Emerging Resources

didn't have anything to do with the missing amber, Ed won't have a job."

"Good point. I'll tell him that when he starts screaming."

"Have Zack start asking around hospitals, urgent care clinics, that sort of thing."

"Where?"

"SeaTac to Anacortes."

"Is Kyle in the States?" Charlotte asked, startled.

"His passport is, according to Ellen Lazarus."

"Her! What's she doing in all this?"

"Looking for the Amber Room."

"Oh. My. God."

"Yeah. Life is just full of wonderment."

"I told you it wasn't destroyed! You owe me a thousand bucks!"

"I said she's looking for it, not that she found it."

"Details," Charlotte said.

"A thousand of them. Mine, not yours."

"Yet. Is Ellen still there?"

"No."

"What happened?"

"She offered an alliance."

"And?"

Jake looked at the business card by the telephone: "Ellen Lazarus, Consultant." The telephone number was of the 800 variety, no area code to give away location.

"I'm thinking about it," he said, "the way a pork chop thinks about teaming up with a starving wolf."

Charlotte laughed. "I hear you. Use her if

you can, but wear rubber gloves. Do you think they have Kyle?"

"They wouldn't be barking up my tree if they did."

"Do you think he made it to the States?"

"I don't know. But people are acting as though the amber might have come here, with or without him. It's not just Ellen. The government is guessing that Ms. Donovan wants to appear to go fishing while she retrieves the amber."

"What do you think?"

"Uncle is probably right. The cops are watching Kyle's cottage."

"Why?"

"Because they can," Jake said sardonically. "And because they want to question Kyle about the DOA with Third World dental work they found on the beach."

"Did you ever find the truck Kyle stole in Kaliningrad?" Char asked.

"Not yet, and it doesn't really matter. When we find it, it will be empty."

"You're full of cheer, aren't you?"

"Kyle isn't stupid. He would have had another truck stashed nearby, a truck no one would associate with stolen amber."

"Wouldn't he have needed help moving the amber to the second truck?"

"Amber is light," Jake said absently, scanning down a page of the log.

"You sound distracted."

"I am. I'm reading Kyle's boat log."

"Anything good?"

"The most interesting part is what isn't here."

"Such as?"

"The clock that automatically keeps track of engine time doesn't agree with the hours Kyle logged in."

"Translation?"

"Either he stopped keeping the log before he left for his last trip to Kaliningrad, or he came back and used the boat without writing in the log."

"Then he's alive?" Char asked quickly.

"Or was. Ellen said the corpse with the missing fingers was a Russian hit man. They usually hunt in pairs."

"Lovely."

"Yeah." Jake closed the log with a snap. "I've got to meet Kyle's sister soon. Anything else for me?"

"His sister? What's going on?"

"I'm teaching her how to fish on Kyle's boat."

There was a brief silence followed by a neutral "Convenient."

"That's one word for it. If you leave any messages on my answering machine, be careful. I probably won't be the only one listening."

"Gotcha. Do you think Ms. Donovan knows where the amber is?"

"If not her, then some other Donovan. She's the only Donovan within my reach."

"And you think the amber is in the San Juans?"

"I'm counting on it. Getting my hands on that shipment and clearing my name is the only way Emerging Resources will be allowed back in the Russian Federation."

"What's the sister like?"

Jake didn't say anything.

"Uh oh," Charlotte said. "A female version of Kyle?"

"Very female."

"Remember Ellen."

"Honor isn't Ellen."

"You're telling me? Ellen couldn't find honor with a dictionary."

He smiled wryly. "Honor Donovan is Kyle's sister."

Jake hung up before Charlotte could ask any other uncomfortable questions. He turned on the small photocopying machine and went to work.

It didn't take long to copy the log. Kyle had owned the boat for only fifteen months. He hadn't spent nearly the time on board that the boat deserved. The *Tomorrow* was too well named. Kyle hadn't had much time to play.

Don't feel sorry for the charming bastard, Jake told himself. *Nobody held a gun to his head and told him to work instead of going fishing.*

But all the same, Jake couldn't help thinking about the younger man's flashing grin and sudden laughter, the hours they had spent during the miserable Baltic rains drinking beer and talking about catching salmon when the sea was cold and the fishing was red-hot.

As soon as Jake finished copying the log, he went to work with a pencil in one hand and a chart book of the San Juans close by. By the time his wristwatch alarm started cheeping at him, he was sure of one thing.

Kyle's log didn't add up worth a damn.

Yet for all its tantalizing hints of secret hours spent on the *Tomorrow*, the logbook didn't say where Kyle was at the moment or if the amber was with him.

The more Jake thought about it, the more he was forced to accept the unhappy fact that Honor was his only route to the amber. To prove his own innocence, Jake would have to use her as ruthlessly as Kyle had used everyone else.

Even though Honor was a Donovan, Jake didn't like using her that way. But then, he hadn't liked much that had happened in the past month.

4

"Pretty as a postcard, isn't it?" Jake asked.

Honor jumped at the sound of his voice. Uneasily she stared out the side windows of the *Tomorrow*. The blue-green water of Rosario Strait did indeed look like a postcard. She wished it were. Ever since they had left the dock behind, she had been intensely aware of the lack of truly solid footing. She licked her dry lips.

"Postcards don't jig around beneath your feet," she said.

"Jig? It's dead calm."

She licked her lips again and said nothing.

Jake had noticed Honor's increasing restlessness. He was pretty certain of its source: she was afraid. He had been in enough tight places to recognize fear when he saw it. His employer was thin-lipped, pale, vibrating like a high-voltage line.

It took a strong motivation for someone to confront such a deeply rooted fear. He wished he knew whether love for her brother or greed for the fairy dust known as the Amber Room drove her out onto the water.

As Jake looked back at the smooth surface of the sea, he wondered what Honor would do when it got rough. He hoped she wouldn't come unglued. The thought of smacking sanity back into her didn't appeal to him. Instead of testing the *Tomorrow*'s seaworthiness the first time out as he had planned, maybe they should do something nice and calm and easy, like trolling for salmon. The local grapevine said fish were biting in Secret Harbor.

Normally the idea of salmon fishing would have made Jake eager, but at the moment things weren't exactly normal. He decided to head for more open water, where he could find out if Kyle's SeaSport performed the way it should.

Besides, if his employer was going to fall apart, they both should know it now, when everything else was calm.

Jake changed the course forty-five degrees and simultaneously kicked up the throttle

"What are you doing?" Honor asked.

She knew her voice was sharper than it should have been, but she couldn't do anything about it. She was feeling as edgy as broken glass. Going for a ride in a small boat was turning out to be much harder on her nerves than she had expected. She was thirty, but the overwhelming fear she had felt as a child was scraping her emotions raw.

"I was thinking about fishing," he said mildly, "but—"

"Good."

Surprised at what could have been mistaken for enthusiasm, Jake glanced across the narrow aisle to the pilot seat. "Good, huh?"

"Yeah. Thinking about fishing beats actually doing it."

He shook his head. "You've got to work on your attitude."

"Believe me, I have."

"Scary thought."

She didn't respond. Her hands gripped the bench seat as though she expected it to be yanked out from under her.

He said something under his breath. Using Honor was one thing; tormenting her was another. He was discovering that he simply didn't have the stomach for it. That was one of the reasons he had left Ellen to her spider games and never looked back. He hadn't enjoyed watching living things flutter in his sticky web.

With a muttered curse, Jake spun the wheel hard, turning the boat back toward the distant dock.

"What are you doing?" Honor asked quickly.

"Going back."

"Why? Is something wrong?" Her voice was as thin as the line of her mouth.

"Yeah."

"What?"

"You."

Her head snapped toward him.

"What are you talking about?" she asked through clenched teeth. "There's nothing wrong with me."

"And I'm the Easter Bunny."

"Wrong fairy tale. You appeared with the girl in the red coat."

Smiling slightly, he shook his head. Even scared white, she kept the keen edge to her mind. And tongue.

"Turn the boat around," she said. "We're going fishing."

He kept heading toward the dock, which was now about five minutes away. She gave him a sideways look.

"I mean it," Honor said. "Turn around."

"A little bit of fear is a healthy thing," Jake said matter-of-factly. "It keeps you alert. Too much fear is no good at all. It gets in the way of doing what has to be done."

"Such as fishing?" she retorted.

"Such as surviving."

Honor looked at his eyes. "What does a man like you know about fear and survival?"

"More than I ever wanted to." The flatness of his voice didn't invite questions.

She didn't even hesitate. "What happened?"

He gave her a sideways look. "The usual random violence."

"Oh. Six o'clock news stuff."

"Bar brawls don't make headlines."

"Bar, huh? Did you—"

"No," he interrupted.

"How do you know what I was going to ask?"

"I don't."

"Oh. None of my business, is that it?"

"That's it. Turn loose of the seat cushion before your hands go numb."

Very carefully she unlocked her fingers. Blood returned, changing the skin from white to pink. She sighed, swallowed, and licked her lips nervously.

"How did you know my fingers were aching?" she asked.

"Been there."

Afraid to take her attention off the water for long, Honor gave Jake a quick sideways look. He didn't look a bit scared. His left hand was curled over the top of the wheel. His right hand rested near the control levers and something baffling that he called trim tab switches. Every line of his body was relaxed, confident, utterly at home on the unpredictable surface of the sea.

"You, afraid?" she asked. "Pull my other leg."

"Don't tempt me."

"I wouldn't know how."

He gave her a disbelieving look. Without warning he moved the gas lever back to idle.

The boat stopped rushing through the water. Honor made a startled sound and braced herself on the bulkhead. After a few moments, swell from the wake surged beneath the boat, making it roll a bit. If Jake noticed what the boat was doing, it didn't bother him.

It bothered her.

"What are you doing?" she asked frantically.

"Laying out a few ground rules. Number one. You're damned attractive and you know it, so unless you're planning to follow up on all the lip-licking and sideways looks, save them for a boy who cares."

Her eyes widened. "What are you talking—"

"Rule number two," he continued without pause. "Refer back to rule number one. Got that, honey?"

"The problem exists in your mind," she shot back. "If I lick my lips it's because I'm nervous. Ditto for sideways looks. Got that, *honey?*"

Jake admired her brilliant, narrowed eyes. Anger had flushed her cheeks, taking away the pallor of fear. He smiled slowly.

"That's more like it," he said.

Her jaw dropped open. "Hello? Are we having the same argument?"

"Discussion."

Honor realized her mouth was still open. She closed it.

"Discussion?" she asked cautiously.

"Right. We were discussing how to get your mind off being afraid of the water. Simple. We give you something else to think about."

A dizzying combination of anger, laughter, and disappointment swept through Honor. The first two emotions she understood. The third she ignored.

"Ready?" he asked.

"To strangle you? Any time."

He laughed quietly. "You'll do, Honor Donovan."

"Promises, promises."

She let out a shaky breath, started to lick her lips, and forced herself not to.

"Okay?" he asked.

She nodded, surprised to realize that she meant it. "Your methods are crude but effective."

His smile turned down at the corners. "That's me. All the finesse of a neutron bomb and twice the fun."

"I didn't mean it as an insult."

"I'm used to it. Charm never was one of my virtues. I leave that for the con men of the world."

Like Kyle Donovan, Jake thought grimly. And his family. Don't forget them. They're the folks who gave orders that shut every door in your face that might have led to the truth.

And when all was said and done, Honor was a Donovan. He had to remember that.

He applied power, turned the boat, and accelerated. Very quickly he brought the Sea-Sport up on plane so that it skimmed over the water, balanced between speed and fuel efficiency. He adjusted the trims tabs the same way he did the throttle, unconsciously. The controls were as familiar to him as breathing.

That left him plenty of time to look around. He saw pretty much what he had expected to see but had hoped he wouldn't: as the *Tomorrow* raced back out into the strait, three other boats changed course and poured on the power to follow him.

Two of the boats had appeared shortly after the *Tomorrow* left its little dock. The third one was new, a big Coast Guard Zodiac in high-visibility orange. It was on an interception course with the *Tomorrow*. As the Zodiac got closer, one of the four men aboard began signaling for the SeaSport to stop.

"So much for fishing the tide change," Jake said.

"Did we miss it?"

"Not yet, but we will."

"Why?"

"See that orange Zodiac?"

There was only one orange craft on the water, so identifying it wasn't hard.

"It's more a raft than a real boat," Honor said.

"It can go ashore without a dock and catch anything on the water it's likely to chase."

Jake brought down the power to idle, but he did it slowly enough not to alarm Honor.

"Is something wrong with our boat?" she asked warily.

"I hope not. We're about to have a 'random'

Coast Guard inspection."

The brightly colored Zodiac was closing rapidly with them now that the *Tomorrow* was floating dead in the water.

"Do they inspect every boat?" she asked.

"Nope."

"Most boats?"

"Nope."

"A quarter of the boats?"

"Nope."

"One in ten?"

"I doubt if they stop one in a hundred."

"Then why are they bothering us?"

"Just lucky, I guess."

The cynical tone of his voice was echoed in her answering smile.

"Cops on land and cops at sea," Honor said. "Gosh, am I ever protected."

"Yeah. Makes you feel all warm and squishy, doesn't it?"

"So would a full diaper."

Jake was still laughing when he grabbed the *Tomorrow*'s papers from the drawer and went out to the stern to give the Coast Guard "permission" to board.

They didn't even go through the motions of asking about a previous Coast Guard inspection. Likely they knew exactly what Jake did; according to the papers in the galley drawer, Kyle had voluntarily taken the *Tomorrow* in for inspection less than six months ago. It had passed without a hitch. Normally, the boat wouldn't be up for inspection again for another six months.

The first of two Coast Guardsmen came over the *Tomorrow*'s stern by way of the swim step at the stern.

"Afternoon, gentlemen," Jake said. "What can I do for you?"

"Standard safety inspection, sir," the younger man said.

"Then we'll still have time to fish the tide change," Jake said. "This boat was inspected within the past six months. No violations. I have the ticket right here. If that's not good enough, call home base and check your own records."

The young man hesitated and looked over his shoulder toward the stern.

So did Jake. He stifled a curse and tried not to give the second official the kind of smile that made people nervous.

"Hello, Bill," Jake said. "Who did you piss off enough to be put on pleasure craft inspection?"

The second man winced. "Jake? What are you doing here? This boat is registered to Kyle Donovan."

"I'm teaching Honor Donovan how to use it."

"Oh. Well, uh, I'm sure she won't mind if we look around."

Jake turned and glanced back into the cabin. Honor was standing in the open doorway.

"How about it?" he asked. "Do you mind?"

"Should I?"

"You're within your rights to tell Captain Conroy to go spit in his mess kit."

"Is that your recommendation?"

Jake shrugged. "An inspection now should save us getting stopped at a more inconvenient time." He looked back at Conroy. "Right, Captain?"

"If I have anything to say about it, yes."

Jake's eyes narrowed slightly. "Message received. Hell of a job they handed you."

"There are worse." Conroy jerked his head at the other guardsman. "Check the usual."

"Yessir!" The young man turned briskly toward the cabin.

"Show him that the blower works," Jake drawled to Honor.

She went ahead of the young man into the cabin. The blower came on. Thirty seconds later it shut off.

"New recruit?" Jake asked, handing the registration papers over to Conroy.

"Somebody has to train them."

While the two men remaining in the Zodiac kept their craft close to the *Tomorrow,* Conroy thumbed through the registration papers. To no one's surprise everything was in order. He returned the papers to Jake.

"What is he looking for in here?" Honor asked from the cabin door.

"Compliance with regulations," Jake said.

"Such as?"

"Fire extinguishers, Coast Guard-approved PFDs for everyone aboard, the proper bureaucratic placards reminding you that it's illegal to put anything other than fishing gear into

Puget Sound waters, that sort of thing."

"So that's why Kyle had that tacky red garbage sign pasted over the stove."

"Don't forget the tacky black sign about the evils of motor oil that's pasted on the underside of the engine cover." He turned to Conroy. "Want to look?"

"I'll wait. Jimmy hasn't seen one of the big new Volvos yet. He'll get a kick out of it."

"I'm always glad to help in the education of our youth," Honor said, wide-eyed.

Jake snickered.

Conroy looked philosophical. As he had said, there were worse jobs out there.

When the time came to open the engine cover, it was Honor who conducted the magical mechanical tour with the detailed enthusiasm of a professor discussing the use of past participles in Shakespearean sonnets. She was especially careful to point out the dipstick, the leak-free fuel lines, and the flame arrester on the carburetor. She described intake, outgo, filters, ignition, water cooling, and the care and feeding of all four hundred and fifty-four cubic inches until even Jimmy's eyes began to glaze over.

Jake stepped in before she began dismantling the engine so they could inspect every moving part and some that didn't.

"Not today," he said easily. "You start field-stripping this puppy and we'll never get around to fishing."

For a moment he would have sworn Honor

looked disappointed.

"You sure?" she asked, looking at both Coast Guardsmen. "This is a really sweet hunk of machinery."

Reluctantly Conroy smiled. "I know a few engineers who would love to show you around below decks."

"Steam engines don't count. Neither do nukes. I'm the true-blue, all-American internal combustion type."

This time Conroy laughed out loud. Then he gestured for Jimmy to get back into the Zodiac. The young man scrambled to obey.

"Thank you for your hospitality, Ms. Donovan," Conroy said. "I'll never look at engines in quite the same way again."

"Off to make more inspections?" Jake asked.

"You never know."

"If you get bored," he said, pointing over the stern, "there are two civilian boats back there. Or are they yours?"

"Not so far as I know."

"Going to inspect them?"

"Not today."

"Tomorrow?"

Conroy's mouth flattened. It was obvious that he wasn't happy with this particular assignment. "When did you get back in town?" he asked.

"Not long ago. You off tonight?"

"Yeah."

"I'll buy you a beer."

Conroy relaxed. "Sure. How about the Salty Log? Eighteen hundred hours."

Jake glanced at his watch. It was nearly five, or seventeen hundred to military types. He wouldn't have time to do much with the SeaSport before he had to head back for the dock. But he wasn't complaining. Finding out whether the guy putting pressure on the Coast Guard was local, state, national, or international was more important than anything Jake could do on the water.

"I'll be there," he said. "Bring Janet if you like."

"Not this time," Conroy said in a low voice. "I don't want her anywhere near this mess."

That wasn't good news, but Jake smiled anyway. "Right. See you at eighteen hundred."

Enviously Honor watched while Conroy stepped up on the engine cover, down to the swim step, and into the Zodiac with a dancer's grace.

"How does he do that in rough water?" she asked Jake.

"Carefully."

He turned and headed back into the cabin. She stayed in the stern for a moment longer, watching the open Zodiac with a combination of horror and fascination. The four men had no cabin to retreat to when the wind drove spray into the boat, no shelter when black clouds turned to icy rain.

She wondered if the bottom of the Zodiac smelled like fish. Shuddering, she turned and hurried back inside the cabin, closing the door behind her. After the little Coast Guard craft, her brother's SeaSport seemed like a haven of comfort and security.

Jake was already sitting in the chair behind the helm, watching the water and the boats around them. She stepped up into the pilot seat across the aisle from him. The bench seat was wide enough to seat two comfortably, three if they were kids.

"Since when does the Coast Guard wear orange uniforms?" she asked.

"Survival gear."

"They expect to sink?"

"Regulations. Open boats and cold water equals survival gear."

"Day-Glo orange for the coroner. Lovely."

"They're wearing dry suits. They could float for days and stay alive."

"Talk about diapers..."

Laughing, Jake hit the throttle. The engine growled happily as more fuel rushed through its lines and caught fire deep in the engine. The controlled explosion known as internal combustion slammed through machinery, turning the prop and driving the SeaSport across the cold blue water.

Smiling, Honor closed her eyes and listened to the bass music of a muscular, well-tuned engine. Though they were whipping along through the water at good speed, the sound of the engine told her there was power to spare. Right now only two of the four barrels of the carburetor were working. The other two were in reserve, waiting for the demand that would bring them to life.

"I'll bet it sounds wonderful when the other jets kick in," she said.

Jake glanced aside, saw her savoring kind of smile, and told himself not to think about how satisfying it would be to make her respond like that in bed. He told himself he was stupid to even think about her like that. This was business, impure and simple.

But no matter how hard he tried to control his thoughts, images kept sliding into his mind, the kind of images that made his pants fit tighter with every heartbeat.

"Listen up," Jake said, increasing the gas feed. "Here goes three and four."

The boat surged forward. The sound of the engine changed, becoming both deeper and higher. It ran through Honor's blood like hard liquor. Her smile widened until she laughed out loud.

"Gorgeous," she said. "Eat your heart out, Beethoven."

Jake smiled, too, especially when he glanced over his shoulder. The three boats following him were having to scramble to keep pace. He looked forward again, scanning the water ahead for floating logs, rafts of seaweed, or other navigation hazards. There was nothing in sight but clean, flat water.

"Might as well see what this puppy will do," he said.

Better now than later, when lives might depend on it. But he didn't say that aloud. He liked the smile on Honor's face too much to remind her that she had a lot more to fear than cold blue water and the smell of fish.

Then it occurred to him that maybe, just maybe, she was too innocent to realize her danger.

Instantly he told himself that was ridiculous, of course she did. But he kept remembering that she hadn't even noticed when Kyle's cottage was under surveillance. Yet she was hardly stupid or unobservant.

That left innocent.

She certainly had sounded like it when she was talking to Archer. Her older brother had slammed the same kind of doors in her face that he had slammed in Jake's.

Savagely Jake told himself he was a fool for even thinking that Honor might be as honest as her clear, amber-green eyes. Not that it mattered—honest or crooked, Honor was his ticket into the closed world of Donovan International. He didn't have to love, respect, or even dislike the means to an end. He just had to grit his teeth and use it.

The *Tomorrow* fled across the flat, cold waters of Puget Sound. The widening white V of the wake spread out from the stern like a fan-shaped contrail. One of the pursuing boats fell back rather quickly. The other hung on. So did the Zodiac.

Jake eased the power up more. With a throaty roar of delight, the SeaSport hit thirty-four knots.

"I knew there was a reason Kyle is my favorite brother," Honor said over the sound of the engine.

Jake glanced at her. She was smiling dreamily, eyes closed. Whatever fear she had of small boats and big water wasn't as great as her pleasure in a powerful, well-tuned engine doing what it had been made to do. He couldn't help smiling back at her.

While he held the revs at four thousand, he divided his attention between the water ahead and the dials on the console. Nothing changed but the speed of the boat as it skimmed over currents and eddies caused by the slackening tide.

He nudged the throttle lever higher. The Sea-Sport had more speed to give. And then more. The motion of the boat became less predictable as a smaller and smaller fraction of the hull actually met the water. He held the boat with a light, relentless touch, finding out what it was made of, what it had in reserve, and where it would fail.

The gauges remained well within normal range. The *Tomorrow* sliced cleanly through the water. There were no sheets of spray fountaining on either side of the bow. Jake was too experienced a driver and the hull was too well designed for that kind of inefficiency in calm water.

Twenty minutes later, satisfied that the engine didn't have any hidden weakness, he finished a wide loop around an island. As he brought the revs down to thirty-four hundred, he looked over his shoulder to see who was still with him.

The Coast Guard was hanging back, little

more than an orange spot. Jake knew it was Conroy's choice rather than mechanical necessity; the big engine pushing the light Zodiac could have kept pace with the SeaSport. One of the private boats that had been following was no longer in sight. The other was well behind and making hard work of it, bouncing and smacking down on the water, jolting sheets of spray into the air.

Jake wondered if the driver was wearing a kidney belt. He certainly needed one.

"Well?" Honor asked.

"Nice boat."

"Mmm. I begin to understand the lure of fishing."

"Fishing? In your dreams. At the speed we were going, you'd have to be trolling for flying fish."

"Better and better."

"Do you like to eat fish?"

"Yum!"

"Fresh fish?" he asked.

"There's no other kind worth eating."

"I'll make a fisherman—er, fishersan—out of you yet."

"No need. I've already buttered up my local fishmonger. He makes sure my fish are fresh."

"Nothing is as fresh as when you catch it yourself."

Honor gave Jake a sideways look that said she didn't believe a word of it. "I'd rather learn how to drive the boat."

His smile would have made Little Red turn

and run. "Okay. First thing you need to know is that the owner always buys the gas."

"Is that supposed to worry me?"

He eyed the half-empty gas gauges. "It will. Until then, listen up. Under good to fair water conditions, the most efficient ratio of speed to gas consumption for this boat is about thirty-four hundred rpm. At that speed, the boat is very responsive to the helm. There's a direct ratio between speed, trim, and…"

Jake headed back for the dock at a sedate speed, talking the whole time. He kept at it long after Honor's eyes glazed over, burying her in facts and figures and nautical terms, demonstrating with every relentless word how much he knew about the SeaSport and how little she did.

It was a lousy way of teaching her how to run the boat. But it was a great way of teaching even a stubborn Donovan female how much she needed one J. Jacob Mallory to help her do what she really wanted to do—find a fortune in stolen amber.

5

The Salty Log was an old hangout for the loggers, fishermen, and crabbers of Anacortes. The fortunes of the place had declined along with the local fish stocks, the discovery of the spotted owl, and the rise of Native American fishermen who worked according to tribal rules rather than federal or state regulations. Never an upscale place to begin with, the Salty Log could most kindly be described as "atmospheric."

When Jake walked in the atmosphere was stale smoke and old complaints about know-nothing Fisheries bureaucrats, city-born tree huggers, and greedy Natives. The rants were as old as the reality of declining resources and much easier to understand. Jake had heard each of the arguments before, believed in some of them at one time or another, and now took a sour view of all of them.

Conroy was waiting at a small table in the far corner, away from toilet traffic. Off-duty, he wore gray work pants and a flannel shirt with colors as muted as the bar itself. He looked tired and irritated. The beer in front of him hadn't been touched.

Jake picked up a beer at the bar and went over to the table. No one took note of him beyond the uninterested glances regular patrons gave folks who looked local but weren't part of the Salty Log's hard drinking fraternity.

"I told you I was buying," Jake said, sitting down.

Neither man had his back to the room. The bar might be long in the tooth but the teeth were still sharp. Fights were common, brutal, and ignored by the local law unless guns or fishing knives were involved.

Conroy lifted his beer in ironic salute.

"Evening, buddy. I'll buy my own, thanks. From what I can see, you're way out from shore in a leaky skiff and small craft warnings are flying all over the place."

"It could be worse."

"How?"

"So far it's just warnings."

"What the hell have you done?" Conroy asked bluntly.

"Nothing."

"Bullshit. I've been told to keep the *Tomorrow* in sight."

"I don't own the boat, remember?"

"Then stay off it."

"Is that official?" Jake asked.

"No. It's a hangover from the days we used to fish and tear up bars together."

"This whole talk is unofficial?"

"You have my word."

Jake nodded, settled more comfortably, and took a sip of his beer. In the background he heard cigarette-roughened voices arguing over which was worse, tree huggers in penthouses or morons who thought a man could survive fishing seasons that were only open for four hours once every three months.

"Did your superiors mention Kyle Donovan?" Jake asked in a voice too soft to be overheard.

"Just as the owner of the *Tomorrow*."

"Did they say what you're supposed to be looking for when you board us?"

"Nothing specific, so I assume Donovan is

smuggling cigarettes north to Canada or Chinese south to the U.S., or dope both ways, or a combination of all three. Or worse. There are a lot of unsolved murders in Anacortes, particularly for a town this size."

"Murder? Is that what the local newspaper is saying now?"

"Dead man floating facedown with his throat crushed by an elbow or a karate chop, missing Kyle Donovan nowhere to be found, an expensive pile of Russian amber lost somewhere, government of Russia asking for help from its new ally the U.S. of A. to find the amber. The rest is typical infotainment crap to sell ads—insinuations about local boy Kyle Donovan, who might be murder victim or a murderer or both, hard breathing about fabulous wealth up for grabs, short stroking about murder in paradise and oh-ain't-it-awful."

Jake smiled at Conroy's obvious disgust. "You're more cynical than you used to be."

"I've been in charge of search-and-rescue operations that I couldn't recognize when I read about them the next day. Makes you wonder about the rest of the so-called *facts* behind the headlines."

"I always knew you were bright. You get tired of the Coast Guard, you can work for me." Jake's smile faded. "If I still have a business."

"Stay off the *Tomorrow*. Whatever Kyle Donovan did isn't going to go away. He's the biggest local interest story since the plywood factory shut down."

"I'd love to stay clear of the whole mess. I can't."

"Try harder."

Jake took a sip of his beer, decided that the risk of telling Conroy the truth was outweighed by the potential of gaining an ally, and started talking.

"The amber Kyle stole came from a government mine in the former Soviet Union. Emerging Resources brokered the deal. The amber was being transferred from Emerging Resources's care to the purchaser, Donovan International. The U.S.—and apparently the Russian government—believes that a piece of stolen art might have been part of the shipment. The Russians want it back."

"Why are they breathing on you?"

"Either Kyle took it or I did," Jake said flatly. "Donovan International is pointing the finger at me. All I know is that I signed over the shipment to Kyle Donovan. It was the last time I saw him. Donovan International says the transfer never was made."

Conroy's eyes narrowed.

"The Donovans have a lot more leverage with governments than I do," Jake said. "My company is being set up to take the blame for the theft of the raw amber and whatever else might have been along for the ride. If I don't prove my innocence, Emerging Resources goes under and I go with it."

Conroy whistled softly through his teeth.

"The Donovans are slamming doors in my

face all around the world," Jake said roughly. "I've already been kicked out of the Baltics and Russia for asking too many questions. I want Kyle Donovan's ass."

"You think he's still alive?"

"I was pretty sure he wasn't. Now I'd bet on either side of the question. Frankly, I'm hoping he's alive. I'd really like to have a talk with that boy."

"You aren't the only one."

"Don't tell me that he violated Coast Guard regulations," Jake said dryly.

Conroy hesitated, then reached his own decision. "I wish it was that easy. This whole thing stinks of politics, the international kind where nobody wins and everybody loses."

Jake grimaced and drank more of his beer. "I hear you."

"Are you sure you can't walk away?"

"I don't have anywhere to walk."

"Shit."

Conroy took a drink, pulled out a cigarette, and set fire to it with an ancient Zippo lighter.

"I thought you quit," Jake said.

"Four times and counting."

"Try getting off the light cigarettes. From what I hear, they have more nicotine than the regular ones. The better to keep you health-conscious sorts hooked, no doubt."

Conroy looked at the cigarette with distaste but no surprise. "Figures." He took another drag and blew out smoke. "If my superiors find out about this talk tonight, I'll need that job you mentioned."

"Since when is having a beer with an old friend a crime?"

"Since I ran the registration numbers on the boats that were playing tag with you."

In the bar's dim light, Jake's eyes glittered like crystal. "You don't have to say another word."

"Just trying to even the odds. Any time nameless men in suits start giving direct orders to men in uniform, I get real nervous."

"Politics."

With a grunt, Conroy flicked ash into the smudged ashtray next to his beer. "Some Washington type—and I mean D.C., not state of—has been camped by a radio, waiting for me to call in every time you change heading."

Without looking away from the other man, Jake took a drink. The expression of distaste he wore could have been due to the luke-warm beer, but it wasn't. He was thinking about fairy dust and the fabled Amber Room.

"You don't look surprised," Conroy said.

"I don't look like anything but what I am—pissed off and interested in equal parts. Did the suit say which branch of the government he works for?"

"No. He didn't give me name, rank, serial number, or anything but a code name for this operation you don't need to know. He could be military. The twenty-two-foot Bayliner hanging on to your wake—the one with the blue canvas—is owned by a navy captain based at Whidbey."

"Was he driving it?"

"Couldn't tell. The kid at the helm looked too young to be a captain."

"Maybe we're just getting old."

Conroy blew out smoke. "Hell of a thought."

"Or the boat could be on loan to the suit brigade," Jake said, "complete with an enlisted navy driver."

Abruptly Conroy stubbed out his cigarette, as though impatient with himself for being addicted. "The second boat, the beat-up little Bayliner driven by an amateur, is a local rental. I didn't get the name of the renter, but I can."

"Don't stick your neck out. Tomorrow I'll make sure I get close enough to look over the competition. I may recognize him."

"A local boy, huh?"

"I hope so, but I wouldn't bet a ruble on it."

Conroy said something under his breath and looked at the dead cigarette with a combination of irritation and regret.

"If you have to board the non-navy Bayliner," Jake added softly, "don't take anything for granted. The corpse with the Third World dental work was a Russian killer. Where there's one, there's usually at least two."

"Nice folks you run around with."

"It's a brave new world over there. You work with the survivors. The other people aren't buying and selling anything anymore."

Conroy shook his head. "I can't wait to find out who was driving the third boat."

Jake sat up straighter. "What third boat?"

"The Olympic with the big black dip net hanging next to the radar and the name *Tidal Wave* on the side. It could have been just a fisherman curious about who else was chasing salmon, but he looked you over with the binoculars real good. He looked over both Bayliners, too."

"Who was the boat registered to?"

"I don't think you're going to like this."

"Try me."

"One of the Russian immigrants who settled around here two years ago. Vasily Baskov. I've checked Vasi's seiner before. I know what he looks like. He wasn't driving the Olympic."

"You're right. I don't like it."

Conroy picked up the half-smoked cigarette, lit it, and made a face at the taste. Even so, he kept on smoking.

"What did the driver of the Olympic look like?" Jake asked.

"Male, about my height and weight, more blond than I am. He had a line in the water but never checked it."

"Then he wasn't a fisherman. Anything else?"

"There was at least one other person inside the cabin. He was too coy for me to get a good look at and I had orders to keep you in sight."

"Anything else?"

"The guy's an okay boat driver, but nothing special. He hasn't figured out how to handle Puget Sound's short chop yet."

"I'll keep it in mind."

"You're going to shake his fillings loose, aren't you?" Conroy asked, smiling thinly.

Jake's smile wasn't the one that comforted people. "Did you see anyone else who might have been too interested in me for my own good?"

"Just the pretty lady. Is she really Kyle Donovan's sister?"

"She really is."

"Does she know why you're interested in her brother?"

"No."

Conroy shook his head. "Well, shit happens, I guess. She looked like a decent person."

"Stubborn, too."

"She likes you."

Jake looked at his beer. It was as flat and sour as he felt. "She'll get over it as soon as she finds out why I signed on to help her."

"Yeah, I'll just bet she will. Does she have a temper?"

"Amen."

"Should be interesting."

"Not for me."

Smiling faintly, Conroy picked up his glass, drank until a swallow or two remained, then set the glass down with a thud. His cigarette hissed when it hit the flat beer.

"If I hear anything that might help," he said, standing up, "I'll give you a call."

"Don't say anything over my phone that you don't want your superiors to know."

For the first time Conroy looked shocked. "Is it that bad?"

"If it isn't already, it will be."

"Seems like a lot of trouble to go to for a million bucks worth of amber."

"Half a million, plus change, is what I turned over to Donovan International's rep— Kyle Donovan."

"Would that much amber fit in the *Tomorrow?*"

"Not comfortably. Why?"

"My orders are to board you once a day, or whenever the goddamn suit grabs his phone and says the word. It sounds to me like they're expecting you to pick up something."

"Fairy dust."

"What?"

Jake just shook his head. "Someone upstairs has been bitten by the lost treasure bug."

"What does that mean?"

"You know what the Amber Room is?"

"No."

"With luck, it will stay that way. Goodbye, Bill. And thanks. From now on stay as far away from this foul-up as you can."

"Hey, what are friends for?"

"To keep," Jake said softly. "When the suits question you about our little chat, tell them what they already know."

"What's that?"

"We're old friends, and you're the kind of stiff-necked, honorable man who doesn't like screwing friends on orders from men in suits.

95

So you met me, we had a beer, and I told you I thought Kyle might be hiding out in the San Juan Islands but I hadn't found any trace of him or the amber. Then Honor Donovan showed up and I signed on with her, figuring she had a better line on Kyle—dead or alive—and the missing amber than I did. You listened to me and decided that whatever I was doing was nothing you wanted any part of. You left. End of story."

"What happens when I tell them that you're every bit as stiff-necked and honest as I am?"

"Save us both a lot of trouble. Don't tell them. And don't shake my hand when you leave."

Conroy looked at his glass. The remains of the cigarette floated facedown among ashes. As he watched, the butt began sinking. He looked up. "I'd like to help you."

"You have," Jake said. "Now help yourself. Stay away from me until the fairy dust settles."

For a moment Conroy hesitated. Then he turned and walked out of the bar. He didn't look back.

Jake forced himself to sit and drink a few more swallows of beer before he stood up and left. Once he was outside, he walked swiftly around the corner. Then he stopped, turned just enough so that he could see behind him, and bent down to tie his shoe.

Though he fiddled with the laces for more than a minute, no one came around the corner to follow him.

Alone in Kyle's cottage, Honor rubbed her

eyes, sighed, and wished she had a second brain to hold all the new information. She hadn't worked so hard since she had slogged her way through genetics on her way to a liberal arts degree. Muttering to herself, she went back to poring over a chapter in the oversize book her fishing guide had insisted she read before they went out the next day at dawn.

Summer fog wrapped around the cottage like a hungry cat hoping to be fed. She barely noticed. *Chapman Piloting, Seamanship & Small Boat Handling* had her full attention. The page she was reading, and rereading, described the "danger quarter"—how to find it, how to tell whether you and another vessel were on a collision course, and who had to give way under the law of the sea.

"Only for you, Kyle, would I do this," she said into the silence. "Only for the brother who talked me through endless variations of the old algebra problem about the train leaving at noon and averaging twenty-two miles per hour, and how long will it take me to catch up with the blasted thing at thirty-nine miles per hour."

She sighed and rubbed her forehead wearily. She hadn't been sleeping well since she came to the cottage. In truth, she hadn't been sleeping particularly well since she turned thirty and realized that the men she dated always turned out to be too...quiet. She came from an outgoing, rough-and-tumble, shouting and hugging and laughing sort of family.

When she was growing up, the Donovan men

often drove her nuts. Bigger, quicker, stronger, arrogant in the way of healthy animals, they were true believers in "might makes right." After losing too many contests of strength to her brothers, she had vowed she would never go out with anyone who reminded her of the large, confident, forceful males of her childhood.

She had kept her vow. Now she wondered if she had done the right thing.

Twice she had made the mistake of taking one of her clean-shaven, quiet, reserved gentlemen home. The first time her brothers got her date so drunk he couldn't find the floor with anything but his face. The second time Kyle had handled the intrusion alone. He quietly, relentlessly baited her date until the nice man fled in confusion.

Honor hadn't fled. She had stayed behind and ripped a strip off Kyle from heels to forehead. He had laughed and laughed until she was tempted to hit him with a skillet. Then he told her what she really didn't want to know.

You would have destroyed that jellyfish the first time you lost your temper. Try dating something from the vertebrate branch of the animal kingdom. You'll both enjoy it more.

Nice doesn't mean spineless!

Hell, sis, I know that. When are you going to figure it out?

With that Kyle had picked her up, hugged her hard, and told her what a great sister she was—and would she help him adjust the valves on his old Thunderbird?

Anger, laughter, tears, love. So many memories of Kyle. Honor hadn't known how deeply she was tied to her brother until she lost him.

Instantly she corrected herself. She hadn't lost Kyle. She was going to find him no matter what.

Frowning, she forced her attention back to the "danger quarter" and the rules of the sea. Thinking about childhood and Kyle and men who were too nice for her own good wouldn't help anyone. Finding her brother would.

The Donovan males had the rest of the world covered. She had the entire group of San Juan Islands to search, and maybe Canada's Gulf Islands as well. To do that, she had to be able to get herself around the islands. To do that, she had to learn how to drive a boat, because the local ferries stopped at only a handful of the major islands.

It would have been easier to hire a boat, but she had decided it wouldn't work. If Kyle was hiding—for whatever reason—approaching him on his own boat was the only way to get close. He might be too proud to ask his family for help in a private mess, but he wouldn't run from them once they showed up.

Yet in order to get close to Kyle in his own boat, she had to learn how to drive the boat. To do that, she had to spend hours reading about danger quarters and other arcane things that made her head ache.

Sometimes she was afraid that what she was doing was more complicated but just as futile as flinging a symbolic lei of flowers on the sea where a ship had sunk, killing all aboard. On a map the islands looked so small, so accessible, so *easy*.

But they weren't.

They were rank upon rank of fir-covered rock thrusting up from a cold sea. Wrapped in rain and wind, sun and night, the islands were isolated and starkly beautiful; many of them were also inaccessible to the point of mystery.

Don't think about it all at once, Honor told herself for the thousandth time. *Just think about the next step. Then the next. Then the next. If you can't do that, then just go buy flowers and stand on the shore and snivel about Kyle while you throw petals into the sea. What you're doing might not seem like much, but—*

The phone rang, scattering her unhappy thoughts. She picked up the receiver and spoke eagerly. "Archer?"

"Jake."

"Oh. Hi."

"Like I keep saying, you should work on your enthusiasm."

She smiled and straightened in the chair. Matching wits with her unexpected fishing guide had proved to be a great antidote to fear. Energy sparked through her.

"Give me something to be enthusiastic about," she challenged.

"Have you had dinner?"

She looked at her watch. It was after seven. No wonder her stomach was growling. "I haven't eaten since lunch, if you call half a cheese sandwich lunch."

"Do you like crab?"

"No. I adore it. I worship at its crabby little altar. I would kill for—"

"Not necessary," Jake interrupted. "I already did. After dinner I'll show you the basics of the fishing gear we'll be using."

"I just lost my appetite."

"You'll get it back."

"Do you really have fresh crab?" she asked suspiciously.

"I really do. Two Dungeness crabs, eight inches across, pulled out of the water by yours truly this morning, cooked, and put on ice for dinner."

"You're right. I'm hungry."

"My cabin or your cottage?"

"Where's your cabin?"

"Close to Deception Pass," he said.

"Oh. I assumed you lived in Anacortes."

"Not anymore. The San Juans are my getaway place, not my home."

She hesitated and thought about the call from Kyle she kept hoping to get. "I'd better stick close to my phone."

"Okay. I'll be there in half an hour. How are you fixed for bread and salad?"

"I can manage that."

"Wine?"

"That too."

"Have you figured out how to avoid a collision at sea yet?"

"Stay on land."

"Wrong answer. Look under 'danger quarter.' "

"Why look for trouble?"

"Beats having it sneak up on you. See you in thirty."

Smiling, Honor hung up the phone and leaped to her feet. She thought about a fast shower and a change of clothes, then decided against it. The black sweat suit and new white boat shoes were all the occasion called for. Jake was her teacher, not her date. She hadn't expected that learning to handle a boat would involve bookwork on land, but it did. The more she learned at night, the faster she could begin searching for Kyle by day.

All things considered, a hundred bucks a day was cheap wages for Jake. He was willing to put in long days.

And long nights?

The unexpected thought shivered from Honor's breastbone to her knees. She started to chew on herself for being so frivolous as to be interested in a man while her brother was in trouble, but the lecture had no real force behind it. The cold truth was that she needed something to keep her mind off the depressing things that could have happened to Kyle. For all Jake's rough edges—probably because of them—he was a world-class distraction.

"Still, this is a really stupid time to rediscover your hormones," Honor muttered. "You need an affair right now like you need to go fishing."

Put that way, fishing sounded almost appealing.

Smiling wryly, she went to the kitchen, stuck a bottle of white wine in the freezer, and went back to learning more than she wanted to know about small powerboats and big water.

The phone rang.

"Damn," she muttered. "I almost understood that last bit."

The phone rang again.

She ignored it and tried to visualize the changing swath of ocean that was a boat's danger quarter when under way.

The phone rang twice more. She grabbed it.

"Hello," she said curtly.

Silence.

"Hello?"

There was a soft click as someone hung up.

She stared at the phone and told herself she was foolish for being uneasy. Wrong numbers happened all the time. Especially here, "at the end of the grid," as Kyle put it. No big deal.

But recently it had been every night. Even twice a night.

Though she tried not to, Honor kept remembering one particular candidate for the job of fishing guide. He had showed up at the cottage without warning. His eyes were greedy, shiny. Reptilian. The kind of man you never want to meet in fog-draped twilight.

Telling herself she was being silly every step of the way, she got up to check the front and back doors of the cottage. Both were locked. She hesitated, then closed the curtains.

"Kyle would laugh himself sick if he could see you. Frightened of the dark! Maybe you should check under the bed, too. And don't forget the closet."

Her sarcastic words echoed in the small room. Her breath caught. It was so quiet she could hear the fog dripping from fir branches onto the cottage roof.

"Kyle, where is your twenty-two pistol when I need it?" she whispered.

Nothing answered her but random drops of water.

She knew her brother had the gun because she had found the permit. Yet no matter how carefully or how often she searched the cottage, the gun hadn't turned up. Nor had she found it on the boat, despite all the nifty little compartments she had discovered while searching for any clue to Kyle's disappearance.

"Where could he have hidden it?" Honor asked the cabin.

The only answer was Archer's curt advice as he saw his two younger sisters off to college: *Anything can be a weapon if you need it. But your best weapon is your brain. Use it.*

In addition Archer had taught Honor and Faith some brutal little tricks to use if a date wouldn't take no for an answer, but he had always emphasized that it was better never to get into trouble in the first place.

Honor wondered if he had given Kyle that same advice. And if so, had he followed it?

"A million dollars in amber gone," she said to the cabin. "A dead man. A missing brother. If that's what comes of following Archer's advice, I'll stick to Miss Manners."

Restlessly Honor checked the windows again. For the first time she noticed that the window locks were shiny, unscratched, obviously new. Curious, she looked at the doors more closely. New dead bolts reinforced the tarnished old locks.

"This is industrial-strength stuff," she said, surprised. "Those dead bolts should keep out anything short of a battering ram. Why doesn't that make me feel better?"

Probably because she kept thinking about why her brother—who was hardly weak and had a handgun to use if pushed to it—felt he needed to install city dead bolts on a rural cottage.

A fortune in stolen amber.

A dead man.

A missing brother.

"Where are you, Kyle?" she whispered. "Why haven't you called us? You know we'd help you no matter what. We may all drive each other nuts from time to time, but so what? We're family. We're supposed to drive each other nuts!"

The dripping of fog onto the roof was the only answer Honor got. Rubbing her arms against a cold that existed more in her mind than in the cottage itself, she paced through the small rooms—bedroom, kitchen-dining

room, living room, kitchen-dining room, bedroom, and back again.

When the sound of her own footsteps began
to get to her, she did what she should have done
in the first place. She picked up her sketch pad,
a pencil, and the piece of amber Jake had
rescued from a hard landing on the floor that
morning.

Soon she forgot her fears, her worries, and
the empty sound of dripping water. Since
Kyle introduced her to amber a few months
ago, she had become fascinated by its unique
physical characteristics—an organic gemstone created by once-living trees rather than
the more usual gemstone created by geolog-
ical processes. Amber was the only gemstone
that was also a fossil.

It was also beautiful in a mysterious, satiny,
sensuous way. The piece she was holding
now had been rounded by time, a distant sea,
and the very nature of fossilized resin itself;
the fist-sized lump of amber was both a window on the past and a tantalizing glimpse of
the future sculpture that lay concealed within
the translucent golden mass.

Honor had been studying the amber in her
apartment in Laguna Beach, California, when
Archer called and asked her—ordered her, actually—to Kyle's cottage. The idea of her fiercely
self-contained older brother's actually needing something from her had been so startling
that she simply had swept the recent shipment
of amber into a suitcase along with some
clothes and grabbed the first plane out of

John Wayne International Airport to SeaTac.

The days that followed were so hectic and unsettling that there had been little time for work. Yet she and Faith had a show to prepare for in Los Angeles in less than six weeks. All of the jewelry and decorative art for the show already was designed, created, polished, and ready to display. All of it was in the traditional, inorganic gemstone material she was accustomed to working with.

But ever since Honor saw the recent shipment of Baltic amber from Kyle, she had been haunted by its possibilities. There was something within this one piece of amber. Something remarkable. She was certain of it. She just hadn't been able to discover it.

Amber in her left hand, pencil in her right, Honor stared at the shifting lines of light and shadow within the ancient resin. Shadow and light twisted, turned, twined, slid achingly close to becoming...something.

A knock at the door made her jump. A vision of new, strong dead bolts replaced the elusive image in the amber. Her heartbeat doubled. She swallowed in a throat suddenly gone dry and licked equally dry lips.

"Who is it?" she asked in a raw voice.

6

"It's Jake Mallory."

With a long sigh Honor set aside the amber

and closed her sketch pad. She shouldn't feel relieved that Jake was here, but she did. His solid, if sometimes overpowering, masculine presence reassured her in a way she couldn't put into words. Instinct, hunch, she didn't care. She simply knew that he wasn't the type to make scary, one-sided telephone calls to women.

She walked quickly to the door, opened the locks, and gestured Jake inside with a smile that was too bright, too brittle.

"A fishmonger who delivers," she said. "I'm in heaven."

"Wait until you taste these beauties."

He reached into a paper shopping bag and pulled out one of the "beauties" for her to admire. She stared at the huge, rust-red crab dangling from his hand. Half a crab, actually. A ragged half.

"What happened to it?" she asked.

"What do you mean?"

"Crabs in the shell come whole, with their legs tucked so that they can crouch neatly on your plate. What you're holding looks like the loser in a crustacean demolition derby."

"That's because I cleaned it before I steamed it."

"That makes a difference?"

"A big one. No belly flavor."

"Belly?"

"Guts. I clean the crabs after I kill them, rather than boiling them alive, guts and all, the way most people do. You clean everything else before you cook it, why not crabs?"

"Ugh. I'm sorry I asked."

"Supermarket predator, huh?"

"Devoutly."

He smiled. "Have any plates?"

"I'll get them."

"Where do you want me to put the Chapman?" he asked.

Honor glanced at the big, open book that covered half of the table. "It would make a heck of a tablecloth."

"It makes a better reference. It's saved my butt more than once. Besides, this table doesn't need protecting. Look at those scars. It's been through wars you've never even heard of."

She glanced from Jake's scarred eyebrow to the scar on his lip that was almost hidden beneath his mustache. "Like you?"

He gave her a sideways look and wondered if Archer had called his sister again and started comparing notes on her "fishing guide." Kyle had always called him Jay rather than Jake, but that was no guarantee that Archer wouldn't put the two names together and come up with one J. Jacob Mallory.

Ellen's deadline was bad enough, but he might be able to talk her into an extension, especially if he was getting closer to the truth about Kyle. The instant Honor knew what Jake was after, the game was over. He had to make sure Honor didn't find out the truth too soon. Despite the female interest in her eyes when she watched him, he had no doubt that she would slam the door in his face as soon as she found out what he really wanted.

Without seeming to, Jake watched Honor pick up the big reference book and put it on the kitchen counter. He liked the way she moved, no hurry, no fuss, no fluttering. He liked the way she looked when she stripped off the man-sized sweatshirt. The blue-green knit top fit over her like a hungry man's hands. The curve of her black jeans told him what he had already guessed: with Honor, a man would have a soft landing and a snug, hot fit.

Damn it, Jake thought angrily, looking away as his body leaped with hunger. Honor turned him on like he was a teenager again, but her last name was *Donovan.* He had to remember that. The Donovans stuck together and let everyone else go hang.

"Here," she said, handing Jake plates and silverware. "Put these on the table while I do the bread."

Watching her from the corner of his eyes, he started setting the table. She surprised him by wetting her hands and running them over a loaf of French bread.

"Do you have some kind of clean fetish," he asked, "or are you part raccoon?"

She gave him a blank look.

"Not many people wash their bread before they eat it," he pointed out.

"French bread crust is more crunchy that way."

"Washed, huh? Well, that's a new one."

Honor had a feeling that not many things

were new to Jake. There was a seasoned look about him that went deeper than the scars and the lines at the corners of his eyes and mouth. It should have warned her away. Instead, it lured her.

"You'll need something to crack the crab shell," he said, looking at the silverware he had put out.

"Two crab crackers, coming up." She began sorting through a drawer of kitchen tools. "I hope."

"I can get by without one. Dungeness shells aren't that hard. Red rock crabs are different. You have to take a hammer to them to get the meat."

"I'm sure Kyle has something in this rat's nest. He loves crab as much as I do."

Jake's mouth flattened at being reminded of her brother, but all he said was, "I'll open the wine."

"It's in the freezer."

"Of course. Wash the bread and freeze the wine. Why didn't I think of that?"

"You're too conventional?" she retorted.

"Yeah, that's it. I'm too conventional."

He pulled the wine bottle out of the freezer, peeled off the foil, upended the bottle, and whacked the bottom with the palm of his hand until the cork came halfway out. He pulled it the rest of the way with a quick twist of his fingers.

Honor stared. "I suppose you catch bullets in your teeth, too."

"I don't catch any bullets I can avoid."

111

"Could you teach me to?"

"Avoid bullets?" He looked at her, startled.

"Open a bottle of wine without benefit of corkscrew," she said with exaggerated patience.

"Why? It's easier with a corkscrew. I just didn't know where one was."

"I'd like to see Kyle's jaw drop. Archer's, too. Maybe even the Donovan himself."

"Who?"

"Dad," she said, handing Jake an empty wineglass.

"Sounds like you come from quite a family."

"Quite a family." She laughed without humor. "That's one way of putting it. Five large, overbearing males. Faith and I had to leave home to keep from strangling them one and all in their sleep."

Jake just shook his head. He knew what it was like not to get along with your family, to barely tolerate your parents and siblings, much less love or even like them. For all of Honor's supposed trials with the men in her family, her voice softened with affection when she spoke of the Donovan males.

It didn't surprise Jake. He had learned the hard way that Donovans stuck together like wolves in a pack; and J. Jacob Mallory had been the dumb lamb nominated for the slaughter.

"No mother?" he asked, pouring wine, fishing as always for information about the Donovan wolf pack. Know thy enemy was one of the oldest rules of survival.

Honor took the glass of pale gold wine he held out to her and waited for him to pour his own.

"Mom is incredible," she said. "The woman barely comes up to my shoulder, but she manages to do exactly what she wants, when she wants, and not ruffle masculine egos in the process."

"Sounds like a good plan."

"I've tried it. Doesn't work for me. Mom has this kind of cast-iron nonchalance. No matter what roadblocks the men throw up, she just kisses them on the cheek, gives their hairy chests a pat, and goes on her merry way." Honor shrugged. "Maybe it comes of being an artist."

"Artist?" he asked, picking up his own wine.

"Painter."

"What kind?"

"Good."

Laughing quietly, Jake clicked his wineglass against Honor's, and said, "To learning how to fish."

She grimaced. "To learning, period."

He raised his glass in silent salute, drank, and made a sound of surprise. "I didn't know Australia had a good white wine."

"Kyle told me about it. Avoid the pure Chardonnays and head straight for the blends."

No new information for Jake in that. Kyle had been able to find decent wine in some of the most desolate rat holes in Kaliningrad. Then the two men would go back to what passed for a hotel, open tins of fine caviar and stale

113

crackers, and discuss sex, politics, religion, loneliness, and how to negotiate long-term deals in a country that was even younger than the wine they were drinking.

Kyle Donovan was as close to a friend as Jake had had in a long time. Too bad Kyle had turned out to be a con man, a thief, and a murderer. It would have been better if he were simply a fool whose brain was being run by his dick. Jake could understand that. He had been a fool from time to time himself. But Kyle had never struck Jake as the foolish sort.

That left the crooked sort.

"When will the bread be dry?" he asked.

"Dry? Oh, hot. A few more minutes. What do you want on the crab?"

"My mouth."

"The man is hungry."

"The man is ready to eat shell and all."

"You want it with lemon or seafood sauce?"

"Both. I'll make the sauce."

By the time Honor had salad on the table, the sauce was ready. They sat down and began eating. There was an intimacy about the informal meal that surprised her. It was hard to be standoffish with someone while sucking tidbits of crab from your fingertips.

"You're right about the bread," Jake said, crunching into a piece.

She had her mouth too full of crab to answer.

"Isn't that the sweetest crab you've ever eaten?" he continued.

She nodded vigorously.

"Next time I'll show you how to kill and clean

114

it before you cook it," he said.

Her hair whipped from side to side with the force of her silent, negative response.

Laughing silently, he cracked crab legs between his fingers and picked out the meat using one of the smaller claws. With surprising speed a mound of succulent white meat grew on his plate.

"I thought you were hungry," she said.

"I am."

"Then why are you ignoring all that luscious crabmeat?"

Jake's slow smile brought every one of Honor's female senses to red alert.

"I'm not ignoring it," he said. "I'm anticipating it. Different thing entirely. Then I'll savor it. Three times the pleasure that way."

"And only a third the calories. All the same..."

He saw the look in her eyes as she measured the pile of crab on his plate.

"Don't even think about it," he said.

"What?"

"Stealing some crab."

"It wouldn't be stealing if you gave it to me."

Smiling, he slid his fork into the crab to give her some. Then he realized what he was doing and stopped. That old Donovan magic. People turned themselves inside out for it.

"That wide-eyed charm may work with your other men, but it won't get the job done with me," Jake said, forking the crab into his own mouth.

She stared at him in disbelief. "Wide-eyed charm?"

He grunted and chewed crab.

The idea of being thought charming silenced Honor more effectively than a hand over her mouth. None of the men in her life had accused her of being charming. Stubborn, impulsive, too smart for her own good; yes. Charming?

Never.

"Thank you," she said.

His head came up swiftly. Before he could ask her why she responded to his insult with thanks, the phone rang.

Honor jumped as though she had been stung. She stood up so quickly that Jake had to catch her chair before it toppled over. The phone barely finished its second summons before she grabbed the receiver.

"Archer?" she asked breathlessly.

No one answered.

"Hello?"

Silence.

She slammed the receiver back into the cradle.

Jake's eyes narrowed. He was beginning to understand that Honor was strung a lot tighter than she looked with her teasing amber-green eyes, quick smile, and casual, silky brown hair. At the moment she was rather pale, her mouth was drawn in anger or fear, and she held her hands clenched together as though to keep them from shaking.

Fear, not anger. Something had frightened the charming Ms. Donovan.

He had an unexpected urge to put his arms

around her, to soothe and protect her. Ruthlessly he swept the impulse aside and concentrated on what had dragged him to Amber Beach in the first place. Murder, robbery, treachery, and Kyle Donovan.

"Problems?" Jake asked.

"Are cops into this kind of harassment?" Honor asked tightly.

"What kind?"

"One-sided phone calls."

Adrenaline stirred beneath Jake's calm surface. He had wondered if he was the only one outside the law who had an interest in Ms. Donovan.

"Heavy breathing?" he asked.

"No. Just the kind of silence that makes your hair stand on end."

He pushed out her chair with his foot. She took the hint and sat down. Even though her appetite had vanished, the wine looked really good. She reached for it, took a drink, and then another.

"Maybe the caller is a woman," Jake said.

"What makes you say that?"

"This is your brother's cottage, right?"

"Yes."

"Your missing brother, right?" Jake asked, careful to sound like someone who had only read the newspaper accounts of one Kyle Donovan.

Honor nodded.

"Then the explanation is simple," Jake said. "Someone who looks like Kyle would be scraping women off all the time. Hearing your voice on the phone would be an unhappy shock for a girl whose motor was humming and ready to go."

"I'm a girl and I don't think Kyle is sexy."

"Siblings don't count. They don't see things the same way normal people do."

Kyle sure hadn't, Jake thought sourly. He had mentioned his great-sense-of-humor, dead-bright twin sisters, but he hadn't said that Honor had a sweet little body and a way of looking at a man that made him feel ten feet tall and solid as a stone cliff.

"Besides, how do you know what Kyle looks like?" she asked.

Jake hesitated just long enough to call himself a fool for not thinking that far down the road. Then he remembered the picture in the local paper. A passport photo, likely.

"Newspaper," he said. "They ran a photo."

"Not a good one."

She was right, but admitting it wouldn't help his cause any. "Siblings," he retorted. "Can't see worth a damn."

Honor's smile was wan. He could tell that she wasn't buying the lovelorn explanation for the phone caller.

"Have you been getting a lot of calls?" he asked after a moment.

"For a while there were reporters who wouldn't take no for an answer, but that dropped off in the past few days."

"How many times have you picked up the phone and no one answered?"

"Oh, five or six times."

"A day?" he asked, startled.

"No. In the last week."

"The phone system is going to hell."

"Maybe." But she didn't sound convinced.

The fear lying beneath Honor's careful smile made Jake wish that he had no more on his mind than helping her. That damned Donovan charm.

"What are you thinking?" he asked without meaning to.

"About the man who just called. That's his second time tonight."

"If he didn't say anything, how can you be sure it was a man, much less the same one?"

While Honor picked at her crab, she thought of ways to sidestep the question. None came to mind. Nor did any explanation that wouldn't make her sound like a New Age wacko.

"Honor?"

Sighing, she quit fiddling with the crab leg and looked across the table at Jake.

"Are you the macho kind who feels all superior when a woman talks about pretty reliable, really nonlinear ways of getting information?" she asked.

It took Jake a moment to sort out what she was trying to say. Even then he wasn't sure, until he remembered Kyle's famous hunches, a kind of gambler's luck that he laughingly said came to him from the Druid side of the Donovan blanket. His mother's side.

"Nonlinear information," Jake said neutrally. "Is that a fancy way of saying your woman's intuition is at work?"

"I prefer to call it a hunch. Men don't make sarcastic jokes about hunches."

"Okay. You have a hunch that the same man has called you twice tonight and had nothing to say. What else?"

"You're going to think this is weird."

"So are crabs. Did that stop me?"

She smiled crookedly.

If he hadn't already known she was Kyle's sister, Jake would have been certain now. That off-center smile was a big part of the Donovan charm.

"One of the men who answered my ad in the paper made my skin crawl," Honor admitted.

"Did he touch you?"

Though Jake's voice hadn't changed, her breath caught. She sensed that he was angry as certainly as she had sensed the mysterious caller's malevolence.

"No," she whispered. "I didn't even let him in the front door."

"Why?"

"His eyes." A shudder worked through her. "They made a snake look friendly."

"Most of them are."

"You and Faith. She says the only kind of snakes she worries about have two legs."

"Drink some more wine," he said, filling her glass. "You look tighter strung than a steel guitar."

She took a few quick sips, then a healthy swallow. With a whispery sigh she settled into her chair and began looking at the crab with interest again.

"Other than eyes," Jake said, "was there anything memorable about the guy?"

She hesitated, fork halfway to her mouth, and thought about the short time the man had been at her front door.

"He was Caucasian," she said, "over thirty, medium height, medium weight, medium brown hair, medium everything except his voice. He had an odd accent."

"European?"

"Maybe, but it wasn't French, Italian, or German."

"Are you sure?"

"Pretty sure. Faith and I have worked with a lot of Europeans in our business."

"There's a group of recently arrived Russians in Anacortes," Jake said slowly. "They're day workers, mostly. Then there are the Finns and the Croatians, but those families have been here so long that only the grandparents talk with an accent."

"For someone who lives in Seattle, you sure know a lot about Anacortes."

"I was raised here."

"Oh. Is that where you met Captain what shisname, he of the bright orange Zodiac?"

"Conroy. What kind of clothes was Snake Eyes wearing?"

"Generic stuff. Dark wind shirt and pants, like a warm-up suit. Leather jacket, cheap from the look of it. Some kind of athletic shoes, not new. A baseball cap that looked like it had hitchhiked from hell."

A picture of a snake-eyed man half a world away flashed through Jake's mind. Even as he told himself it was extremely unlikely, he couldn't shake the memory of Dimitri Pavlov's little black eyes and standard E-Bloc thug couture, the kind of clothes that would be thought fashionable only in a country where Western consumer goods were rare.

The problem with Pavlov as Snake Eyes was simple: no money for a ticket to the United States. Half the time Pavlov couldn't even afford vodka. On the other hand, rumors that the Amber Room had been found would bring quite a gathering of international carnivores. Compared to the dead czar's priceless amber art, the cost of a plane ticket was nothing. Some crooked entrepreneur could have financed Pavlov's travel expenses in the hope of making an astronomical profit when the Amber Room was found.

"Did the man have all his fingers and thumbs?" Jake asked.

Honor grimaced, remembering the cops' questions about the dead man who had washed up on a rocky island beach.

"I didn't count," she said slowly, "but I didn't notice anything missing."

"When was the first time you saw him?"

"About four days ago."

"When was the last?"

"Ten seconds after the first time. I told

him the job had been filled and closed the door in his face."

"Was he angry about it?"

"I didn't ask. He didn't say anything or make rude gestures."

"And you didn't see him after that?" Jake asked.

"No, thank God."

He frowned. "Not much to go on, but I'll ask around the rougher bars."

"You don't have to do that," she said quickly.

"Afraid I'll stub my toe on a bar stool?"

Honor laughed despite her tension. "I don't like to think of anyone getting into trouble because of me, that's all."

"I'll be okay."

"Does that mean you're at home in tough bars?" she asked, curious about Jake. He rarely answered questions about himself, but that didn't keep her from trying.

"I stopped going to tough bars a long time ago," he said. "But it's like riding a bike—you don't forget which moves work and which ones will leave you flat on your butt wondering what hit you."

"I didn't know that being a fishing guide was such rough work."

"It isn't. Growing up is, at least in downhill sliding towns like this one."

Honor looked up from her crab, which she was eating again with pleasure. "What did your father do?"

"A bit of everything." Jake picked up his wine-glass and took a drink. "Is that a sketch pad I saw next to the Chapman's?"

She sighed. The subject of Jake Mallory was closed. But when it came to a non sequitur, she could give as good as she got.

"I can only take so much talk of vectors and angles of intersection before I overload," she said.

He followed her train of thought without dropping a beat. "Then you start drawing?"

"It's part of my work. I design things using semiprecious stones."

"Jewelry?"

"Jewelry, decorative art, things to please the eye and touch and spirit. Or 'gemmy little knick-knacks,' as my patronizing brothers would say."

Jake smiled faintly. "Could you draw a sketch of Snake Eyes?"

"Sure."

She leaned back in her chair and snagged the sketch pad off the counter. The pencil was a longer stretch. She pushed back on the chair, balancing it on two legs. It rocked, seemed to steady, then teetered on the edge of falling over.

With startling speed Jake shot to his feet, righted her chair, and handed her the pencil.

"Didn't your mother ever tell you not to tip back on your chair legs?" he asked.

"Regularly."

"Did you ever listen?"

"Does any kid?" she retorted. "No peeking. It makes me nervous when someone watches."

After a brief hesitation Jake sat down and went back to eating crab.

Honor bent over the pad, eyes narrowed in concentration, hand relaxed yet firm on the pencil. Recalling the man's appearance wasn't difficult. Although she hadn't spent much time looking at Snake Eyes, her instincts had been sending out wave after wave of chemical warnings. Adrenaline had burned his appearance into her memory very well.

Too well. After the first crank phone call she had seen the man in her dreams, the kind of dreams that left her wide awake, straining to hear every tiny sound of wind and forest and wave.

Very quickly a likeness of the would-be fishing guide appeared on the sketch paper. First Honor drew the shape of the face, then the stance of the body, then the details of clothing and expression. Not once did she pause. She drew slowly only when she was creating something that hadn't ever existed before. What she was drawing right now was a direct translation from reality. Unfortunately.

After a minute she held the pad at arm's length, tilted her head, and studied it.

"Done?" Jake asked, reaching for the pad.

"Not quite."

She touched up the eyebrows and the line of the mouth, added shadows, and held the result out to Jake. His whistle of surprise and approval of her talent rippled up and down the scale. It reminded her of Kyle's expertise with flutes and penny whistles.

"You're one hell of an artist," Jake said, recognizing Dimitri Pavlov instantly. As Honor had said: Snake Eyes.

"That's illustration, not art."

"Says who?"

"Folks who are paid to know the difference."

He grunted, unimpressed by her reasoning. Then he looked at the sketch with unfocused eyes and thought of all the good, legitimate reasons that one of his best Lithuanian amber connections might be in the United States trying to pass himself off as a fishing guide.

Jake couldn't think of a single good reason. Bad ones were easy. He had always suspected that the son of a bitch was working for more than one master. Now the only question was, which two or three or four? Politics in the Baltic states was a blood sport based on thousands of years of grudges. Everyone could play. No entry fee necessary. No way out of the game.

"Was he alone?" Jake asked, flicking a finger at the sketch.

"I didn't see anyone else."

"What about a car or a truck?"

"I didn't look for one. Once I opened that door, all I could think of was getting it closed again. Fast."

"I don't blame you. This guy looks like a nasty bit of business."

And he was. Pavlov might not be real long on brains, but he had the kind of contacts that were invaluable in a society where the good guys and the bad guys were a matter of opinion and nobody agreed on anything, even the color of the sky. Both Donovan International and Emerging Resources had purchased Pavlov's expertise in the past.

Jake wondered who was buying it now.

Carefully he folded the sketch and tucked it into his jacket pocket, even though he no longer needed to ask around to find out the man's identity. He didn't want Honor asking how he knew Pavlov.

"Did you lock up the boat good and tight?" Jake asked.

"Somehow I don't think theft will be a problem."

"Because this is such a small, backward town?" he asked dryly.

"No. Because after you left I took the rotor cap out of the distributor. The *Tomorrow*'s engine won't start."

His eyebrows lifted. So much for his idea of offering to keep an eye on the boat by sleeping on it—and using the time to go through the electronics without having Honor looking over his shoulder.

There were several ways to hide something the size of the amber shipment. The quickest, cheapest way was to bury it under the sea and mark its location electronically. Salt water didn't leave trails and didn't hurt amber. Kyle's Zodiac, diving suit, and handheld GPS receiver were missing, along with an anchor heavy enough to sink a fortune in amber. All Jake needed to do was ferret out the electronic treasure map from the *Tomorrow*'s computer.

"So you disabled the engine, huh?" he asked. "Did you bring the electronics up to the house?"

"I didn't even think of it. Isn't everything bolted down?"

"Not quite."

She frowned. "Are you saying that the electronics are easy to remove and reinstall?"

"Not the way your brother has them rigged."

"Leave it to Kyle to do things the hard way. Now what?"

"No problem. I'll just move aboard the *Tomorrow* for a while. That way nobody can break in and make off with thousands of dollars in electronics."

"You think somebody is after Kyle's computer?"

Honor was awfully damned quick, Jake thought uncomfortably. Not that it should surprise him. The other Donovans he had met weren't stupid.

"Computers are expensive, portable, and pawnable," he said. "That makes them a target."

"I locked the boat."

He hesitated, then mentally shrugged and went for the gold ring. After all the instructions he had heaped on her head today, plus reading Chapman's, she should have figured out that she wouldn't turn into a boat driver overnight. If she was after the amber, she needed a trusty native guide.

Or at least a knowledgeable one.

"After reading the newspaper," Jake said, "it wouldn't surprise me if every amateur hard-ass with dreams of finding a fortune in amber is after your brother. A locked cabin door with a glass panel isn't much of a barrier against that kind of ambition."

Without meaning to, Honor looked around the small cottage. The newly installed locks taunted her with all that she didn't know about Kyle, stolen amber, and questions Archer wouldn't answer.

"I guess I can sleep on the boat," she said.

Clearly the idea didn't appeal to her.

"Why bother?" he asked. "I like being on the water. You don't."

She grimaced but didn't argue the point. "Are you sure you don't mind sleeping on the boat?"

"Positive. Put the engine back together while I get some stuff from home. I'll move aboard tonight."

"But what if a burglar does try to break in?"

"I'll scream."

"That will be a big help."

"Don't knock it until you've tried it. Or are you the type who carries a can of pepper spray and a purse pistol?"

"No to the gun," she said. "I've thought about buying some pepper spray but it never got farther than that. Thinking."

"How are you at screaming?"

"I used to be about nine on the Richter scale. Faith has more volume, but Archer swore that I could pierce eardrums at fifty yards."

Jake smiled. "How worried are you about those one-way calls you've been getting?"

"Worried enough to be glad that someone will be within screaming distance," she admitted.

"Does that mean you don't think I'll give you reason to scream?"

"If I thought that, I wouldn't have hired you."

"I'm no Snake Eyes, is that it?"

Honor toasted him with her glass of wine. "I've never met a gray-eyed snake. Lucky for you, huh?"

Luckier than she could imagine, Jake thought. She was as wary as any intelligent urban female, but she lacked the bone-deep spookiness of a wild animal—or someone who had been burned to the bone by trusting the wrong person.

Jake raised his wineglass. "To luck." He would need a lot more of it to get out of this mess intact.

And whether Honor knew it or not, so would she.

7

It was still dark when Honor's alarm clock went off. The alarm began as a gentle chiming, graduated to a reasonably polite buzzer, then moved on to an alley-cat-ecstasy imitation, the kind of screeching that gets mating felines in trouble with the neighbors. The whole cycle took fifteen minutes. She had been asleep for the first fourteen minutes and fifty-five seconds. She still wanted to be asleep.

Groaning, she pulled the pillow over her ears and burrowed beneath the covers. The alarm clock's shriek followed her. The sound was electronically created, electronically amplified, and absolutely impossible to ignore. Not for the first time she cursed Kyle's inventiveness with bits and pieces of technology. Somehow he had spliced the horrific scream into an otherwise normal battery-driven clock.

"All right, *All right! I'm awake!*"

The alarm was neither bright enough to accept her surrender nor stupid enough to believe it. The wailing, gnashing sounds went on until she shot out of bed, stalked across the room, and silenced the infernal machine.

"At least I'm sure Kyle isn't a drunk," Honor said, rubbing her eyes. "No man who suffered regular hangovers would invent an alarm clock like that."

A pounding sound came from the direction of the front door.

"Honor! Are you all right?"

She hadn't known Jake long, but she had plenty of older brothers; she recognized the voice of a man who was one inch from doing something physical. She raced to the front door,

131

shot the bolt open, and jerked on the handle.

The porch light showed Jake with his fist raised above the door frame out of her sight. She had no doubt that he was lining up for another blow to the innocent cottage.

"The sun isn't even a prayer on the eastern horizon," she snarled. "Why in God's name are you hammering on my door?"

"Are you all right?"

"I'll let you know as soon as I wake up. Now was there anything in particular you wanted or are you just a born-again pain in the ass?"

Jake leaned his weight against the fist that was out of sight above the door. He put his other fist on his hip.

"What in hell is going on?" he asked.

His tone sliced through the lovely fog of sleep Honor had been trying to hang on to. Her eyes widened as she really looked at Jake for the first time. He had shaving cream smeared across one bearded cheek. An oddly carved amber medallion on a black silk cord gleamed against a pelt of rumpled male chest fur. Dark blue skivvies rode low on his hips, cupping the remains of an early-morning erection.

"Good grief!" she said, staring. "Do you always run around in your underwear?"

"Only when I'm racing to the rescue of screaming idiots."

"Screaming...ohmygod. Could you hear it clear down on the boat?"

"The boat, hell. I'm expecting them to scramble a squadron from Whidbey Island Naval Air Station."

She groaned and covered her eyes. "It's all Kyle's fault."

"What? Is he here?" Jake asked sharply, looking past her.

"No. Just his alarm."

"Alarm? As in clock?"

She nodded. "Kyle and I have one thing in common. We are *not* morning people."

"So?"

"So he built an alarm clock guaranteed to get me up. It was a birthday present."

Jake closed his eyes and tried to calm the storm of adrenaline that had exploded through him when he heard the awful screaming.

"Birthday present," he said. Breath hissed through his teeth. "It's a wonder Kyle survived your gratitude."

"Yeah. Sorry about waking you up."

"I was already awake and thinking about shaving for the first time in a month. Are you finished staring or were you planning to stuff money in my jockstrap?"

Honor's mouth dropped open. Her eyes narrowed. The door slammed in his face.

Jake let out another hissing breath, turned away, and lowered the hand that he had kept out of her sight. The gun he held was dark and every bit as efficient as it looked. He figured it was a little soon in his relationship with the sexy Ms. Donovan to explain why a fishing guide needed a handful of matte-black death.

Thank God for the Donovan temper. Making her mad enough to slam the door had been pure inspiration. It had been brought on

133

by the knowledge that if he had to stash the gun out of sight in the cottage's rain gutter, he was in for an hour of penance with the cleaning kit as soon as he retrieved the weapon.

Not to mention the fact that a few more seconds of being admired by those wide, amber-green eyes of hers and he would have popped right out of his Jockey shorts.

"Down, boy," he muttered, walking quickly toward the little dock.

Boy wasn't having any of it. That was the problem. Boy had seen what he wanted—it had tangled chestnut hair, a sleep-softened mouth, and a hip-length green T-shirt that fit just enough to make him want to get inside it.

"I don't need this."

But he sure wanted it.

"Of all the butt-dumb, ass-stupid...ouch!"

Even as he cursed the cold, uneven rocks he hadn't noticed when he sprinted barefoot up to the cottage, he welcomed the discomfort each step brought. It helped to get his mind off his crotch.

On the way to the boat, he decided to hell with shaving. After four weeks the stubble had become beard-soft and didn't itch anymore. Besides, winter was coming eventually and he had it on good authority that women hated face fur. They liked the clean-shaven pretty boys or the way-cool types who had to plan their dates two days in advance so they would have just the right amount of fuck-you bristle on their city cheeks.

Muttering every step of the way, Jake tried to find the silver lining in his particular cloud. The best he could come up with was the fact that by now everyone watching the cabin would know the prey was up and about.

The thought of Ellen getting a predawn wake-up call made him smile.

Honor pulled herself together, dressed, and hurried down to the dock. It was still dark. The *Tomorrow*'s lights were on, the engine was chuckling to itself like a tree full of ravens, and fishing gear was laid out. She looked at the rods standing upright in the rod holders next to the cabin door. Then she measured the big black dip net waiting in what Jake called a "rocket launcher" mounted on the roof. Exotic bits of fishing gear dangled from the rim of a white plastic bucket. Inside the bucket a package of frozen bait fish was slowly thawing.

"For this I got up way before sunrise," she said under her breath. "For this I should have my brain scanned."

With a feeling of doom, she stepped onto the dew-laden boat and opened the cabin door. The aroma of hot coffee curled around her like a caress. Jake was seated at the helm, holding a mug in his big hand.

"I forgive you," Honor said instantly, reaching for the mug.

"For what?" he asked, startled.

"Anything. Just hand over your coffee."

"Actually, it's yours. Both sugar and cream."

"Heaven in a chipped mug. Gimme."

He gave her the coffee. She drank cautiously, persistently, then shuddered with the first, ecstatic wave of hot coffee lighting up her throat all the way to her belly.

"Other than the alarm, how did you sleep?" he asked.

"How do I look like I slept?"

"Badly."

"Ouch. I thought all fishermen lied."

"Only about things that matter."

"Like fish?"

"Yeah. Any more calls?"

She shook her head, sipped again, then drank greedily despite the heat. "God, you make good coffee. How come some smart woman hasn't married you, taken off your shoes and socks, and chained you to the kitchen stove?"

"Because I can't get pregnant."

"Ah, well, nothing is perfect. Except this coffee." She finished the last drop in the mug and smiled winningly at him. "Do we really have to go fishing?"

"We really do. But nice try. I especially liked the bit about taking off my shoes and socks before you chained me up."

Honor laughed and let the last of her grouchiness slide away. Dawn with Jake wasn't all that bad.

"Truce?" he asked dryly.

She shrugged. "Yeah. I'm awake, now."

"So am I," he said, turning back to the chart plotter he had been working over when Honor appeared. "Sorry for that crack about staring."

"Sorry for staring," she muttered. "I'm not used to mostly naked men in the morning."

"Whatever happened to women's liberation?"

"AIDS, among other things," she said, reaching for the coffeepot on the stove. "Celibacy is back."

"Sounds boring."

"So is sex." She yawned. "You want some?"

Jake's head snapped up. He saw her pouring coffee into her mug and told himself he was relieved rather than disappointed that she was offering him coffee, not sex.

"Yeah, thanks."

She creamed the coffee and handed it to him.

"You do that like you're used to fixing coffee for...someone," Jake said.

"Faith. She likes loads of cream and sugar. Actually, cinnamon lattes are her favorite." Honor shuddered delicately. "What a breakfast."

"That reminds me. Did you eat something before you left the cottage?"

"My alarm clock."

Jake's head snapped around toward her.

She burst out laughing. "You should see the look on your face."

"I'd like to. I'm trying to imagine how you'll sound at dawn tomorrow morning."

"We aren't going to be up then."

"Of course we are. Would you like an omelet to go with your alarm clock?"

Honor gave him a look of wide-eyed awe. "Can you actually cook?"

"Do I look like I'm starving?"

"There are restaurants."

"Local restaurants are the number one reason I learned how to cook."

She wanted to ask if he had ever been married but couldn't think of a subtle way to do it. "Have you ever been married?"

"Yeah. Have you?"

"Nope. I never found a man brave enough to take on the Donovan clan. How long were you married?"

"What makes you think I'm not married now?"

It was Honor's turn to be caught with her jaw hanging open.

"It was twelve years ago and it lasted less than a year," he said, smiling slowly. "I was in the navy and she was a party girl who didn't like being alone. No kids and no regrets. Any other questions?"

Honor winced. "Sorry. I was just curious and it's too early in the morning to be clever about asking."

He tugged lightly on a flyaway piece of her hair. "I'm the direct sort myself. No kids for you either?"

"I told you I wasn't married."

"Honey, if you think it takes marriage to get a woman pregnant, you should watch daytime television." Shaking his head, he turned away from her. "Can you cook?"

"Sure. Do you want me to peel the eggs for the omelet?"

His head turned swiftly toward her before

he realized that he had been suckered again. Smiling, he turned toward the stove. Kyle had been like that—quick-minded, quick to tease, quick to laugh at himself. Good company.

"What would you do if I said yes to peeling the eggs?" Jake asked.

"Make a mess."

"That's what I figured."

He started cracking eggs into a bowl. While he made an omelet, Honor looked at the computer screens.

"What's on the screen?" she asked.

"I found a batch of stored routes."

"Where do they lead?"

"Out in the islands."

"Fishing holes?"

"Seem to be."

She made an impatient gesture. "The fishing can wait. I want to learn how to run the boat."

"You can do both at once."

Honor grimaced. "Whatever. Let's get to it."

"Eat breakfast first. You learn better when your stomach isn't empty."

What Jake didn't say was that he wanted to be certain that the elusive fourth boat, the Olympic, had time to get into the predawn parade. He would really like to get a look at whoever was aboard. It made him edgy not to know the names of all the players.

He poured the egg mixture into a hot pan. As the eggs set, he started adding ingredients.

"Did Kyle ever say anything to you about diving?" Jake asked casually, watching the eggs.

"Here?"

"Yes."

"Not really. He dove off of Australia some years back, when Archer was investigating Broome's potential as a pearl supplier."

"But Kyle never talked about diving here?"

"Only in the negative. As diving goes, I gather the San Juan Islands aren't much."

"Compared to the tropics, they aren't. Diving here is hard, cold work. The currents are always tricky and often dangerous."

"Do you dive?"

He shrugged. "Some. Is Kyle's diving gear stored up at the cottage?"

"No."

"You're sure?"

"I turned that place upside down looking for his twenty-two pistol. I didn't find any diving gear."

"What about the pistol?"

"It's missing, too." Then she added quickly, "But the guy who washed up on the beach wasn't shot, if that's what you're thinking."

"All I'm thinking of is not burning the eggs." He swirled the mixture around and tested the edges. Not ready to fold yet. "Did you see anything like this when you were searching?" he asked, turning toward the galley table.

Honor looked at the small electronic gizmo he picked up off the table.

"What is it?" she asked.

"GPS receiver."

"Hello?"

"Global Positioning System. A receiver

140

tells you where you are within a few yards or a few hundred feet, depending on how the government has dicked with the signal."

Eyebrows raised, she glanced at the modest-looking bit of electronics again. "I didn't see anything like it."

He wasn't surprised. He suspected that Kyle had the GPS unit with him. For whatever reason, Kyle had chosen to leave the SeaSport behind and use the Zodiac instead. Locating things at sea was dicey. A GPS made it almost easy. Almost, but not quite.

"Where else might Kyle keep dive gear?" Jake asked.

"Not in his car. I checked it first thing."

Jake focused on the omelet. He didn't want to be too obvious about finding out where Honor's brother might store things he didn't keep on the premises, but subtlety wasn't getting the job done.

"Does Kyle have one of those U-rent storage lockers in that place on the edge of town?" Jake asked finally, folding the omelet with a flip of the spatula.

"If he does, I didn't see anything about it in his checkbook. That omelet smells heavenly. What's in it?"

"Cilantro, sweet onions, jack cheese," he said absently. He was digesting the information that Honor had been through Kyle's check register in search of anything that might lead to her brother. For all her talk of nonlinear information sources, she didn't overlook the linear kind. "Any unusual deposits or withdrawals?"

"No big ones, if that's what you mean."

"That's what I mean."

"The only sort of unusual check was to a wine seller in California. And for Kyle, that's not really unusual. He likes decent wines, but not the kind it's high drama to drink."

"High drama?" Jake asked, looking at her.

"You know. The kind you have to open with a sterling silver corkscrew, pour into Baccarat crystal, and roll around on your tongue while someone whispers in your ear about all the fine points of the vintage that you, slobby peasant that you are, would overlook in quest of good old alcohol."

Smiling, Jake lifted a corner of the omelet and decided it could wait for a few more moments. "What about his post office box?"

"Junk mail. Household bills. More junk mail."

"Telephone bill?"

The last traces of humor left Honor's expression. "That too."

He waited, hoping he wouldn't have to drag information out of her like a cop on cross-examination. He was walking a very fine line between making her suspicious by asking too many questions about Kyle and wasting time by not asking questions.

"There haven't been any long-distance calls charged on this number since Kyle went to Kaliningrad," Honor said finally. "At least, none that have been billed yet."

Jake didn't point out that dead men don't make phone calls. Neither did men who were

142

on the run with a fortune in stolen amber and didn't want to be traced.

He slid the omelet onto a plate and put it in front of her. "Eat while I cast off. The tide isn't patient."

"What about you?"

"Under the right circumstances I can be very patient."

She watched his slow smile and wondered if it had been registered as a lethal weapon. "Um, I meant the omelet. Aren't you going to eat breakfast?"

"I already did."

Jake shut the cabin door behind him as he left, keeping out the chilly wind that was rising with the distant dawn. The *Tomorrow*'s navigation lights burned colorfully against the slowly fading night. He cast off the bow and stern lines, stepped aboard, and took the aft controls. As soon as the boat was headed in the right direction, he ducked back into the cabin and took the helm seat.

"Any company?" Honor asked.

"Not yet."

"Do you suppose Captain Conroy is going to show up and board us again?"

"It wouldn't surprise me."

"I don't think much would."

Jake gave her a swift glance, wondering what she meant. She was licking the tines of her plastic fork. Not a scrap of omelet remained after her tongue passed over. He looked away, but not quickly enough. His pants were getting tight. He concentrated on the water and cursed his body's quick response to Honor's agile little tongue.

"Wonderful," she said.

He grunted.

"No, I mean it," she said. "That was a great omelet."

"It's the cilantro. Gives it just enough edge to be interesting."

"You're sure you're not married?"

"Positive. It's not the kind of thing a man would forget."

"Good grief. Talk about people who should spend a week watching daytime television..."

She licked the fork again and sighed.

"It's a fork, not a sucker," Jake muttered.

"What?"

"Did you bring binoculars?" he asked clearly.

"Yes." She stuck her hand into the leather backpack she had brought aboard and pulled out a small pair of glasses. "Right here."

He glanced at the dainty glasses. "Use mine. They'll do a better job in low light. Check out the boat coming up on our right."

"Port," she said promptly. "See? I learned something nautical yesterday."

"You learned it wrong. Port means left. Same number of letters in each word."

"What about right and starboard?" she asked, smiling slyly.

"What about it?"

"Never mind. You aren't up to my speed yet."

For an instant Jake thought of telling her to put a hand in his pants and check out just how

144

up he was. Then he saw lights approaching from another quarter.

"Use the binoculars on those boats," he said, pointing.

"What am I looking for?"

"Names, registration numbers, model of boat, anything you can see."

"Let me drive while you look," she said. "You know what you're looking for."

Jake noticed that Honor didn't say it as an accusation or even ask him why a fishing guide was curious about the other boats. Probably because she wanted to know who was in those boats for the same reason he did—Kyle and missing amber.

"Right now I'm looking for logs," he said.

Honor's eyes widened. She stared at the darkly shimmering water. "Is that why we're creeping along at eight knots?"

"Only a fool or someone with a life at stake races around the San Juans in the dark in a small boat."

"Right. You look at logs. I'll look at boats." She took Jake's binoculars from the rack just above the table and fiddled with the focus until she found the first boat. "I can't be positive, but it looks like the name is *Bay Timer*."

"Bayliner. It's a name brand, like Ford or Honda. How many people aboard?"

"Can't tell."

"Try the starboard boat."

"That's the one on our right, right?"

"Yeah, yeah."

She smiled. "It looks a little smaller than the first boat. That's about all I can tell right now."

"Probably the other Bayliner."

"What?"

"There were two of them yesterday. Any other boats?"

"I'm looking."

Slowly Jake brought up the speed, pushing the limits of visibility. Dawn was coming on hard now, a silent explosion of color and light sweeping across the arch of the sky.

"A bright spot of orange just popped up," Honor said. "Must be Conroy."

"Probably. Anyone else?"

"I can't be sure, but I think there's a fourth boat way off to the left—port."

He looked in that direction. "I don't see any lights."

"Neither do I. But there's something out there against the dawn and it's shaped like a boat."

"Keep an eye on it."

Jake killed the *Tomorrow*'s spotlight and navigation lights. Then he shifted course and headed for the mysterious boat.

"Let me know when we're close enough to make out the features of the folks on board," he said.

"Won't they see us first?"

"Look behind us."

She did. It looked a lot darker in that direction. "Clever."

"Thank you."

"Are we looking for anyone in particular?"

"Snake Eyes."

Honor lifted the binoculars and began looking. After a few minutes she made a soft sound, leaned forward, and stared through the binoculars.

"What is it?" Jake asked.

"It's gone. The boat. I can't find it anywhere."

"Get up here in the pilot seat."

Without a word she jumped to her feet and shifted seats. Only then did she look at Jake in reluctant admiration. "What a tone. Were you a drill sergeant in the navy?"

"They don't have them. Hang on. This won't be a smooth ride."

"What are you going to do?"

"Get close enough for a look."

8

The sound of the SeaSport's engine deepened and expanded like the dawn as Jake brought up the throttle. The boat rose up on plane, speeding across the indigo sea. A combination of wind and tide chopped up the surface of the water. Every few seconds, sheets of spray lifted on either side of the bow.

"You see him yet?" Jake asked.

"No."

"You see any wakes?"

"We're splashing so much ourselves, I can't be sure."

He nudged up the throttle some more.

"What about those logs you mentioned?" Honor asked through clenched teeth.

"It's a big ocean."

As the *Tomorrow* shot over the top of a small wind wave, he chopped back on the throttle just enough to soften the landing. Honor made a startled sound and braced herself against the dashboard when he brought the speed up again. Spray burst over the bow. He flicked on the three wipers long enough to clear the windows and trimmed the bow down. The ride became less rough.

When they came out of the lee of an island, the water turned more choppy. The ride went from occasionally bouncy to rough. He kept the revs high and readjusted the trim so that the chine met the waves at a better angle.

"The rest of the parade is falling behind," Honor said.

"Their problem, not mine. Can you see the fourth boat yet?"

"No."

"Use the glasses."

She picked up the binoculars with one hand and braced herself on the dashboard with the other. The rough water made focusing on anything through the glasses nearly impossible. After a few minutes she put them down and hung on to the dashboard with both hands.

"See anything?" Jake asked.

"Not really."

"Keep trying."

"Forget it. If I look through those glasses

again at this speed, your wonderful omelet might reappear."

"Uh-oh. I didn't know you were the seasick type."

"I wasn't until I tried to focus through the binoculars on something that was jumping all over the—" She swallowed hard. "Can we talk about something else?"

Jake looked at the radar screen. Nothing showing ahead. *The bastard has legs,* he thought sourly, *and the balls to go between them.*

"Are we still pulling away from the crowd?"

"Yes. All I can see is the Day-Glo Zodiac."

"Hell." Jake eased back on the throttle, breaking off the futile chase. "I don't especially want to put Bill through a wringer."

"He's a big boy. He can take it." Honor's tone said that she had no sympathy to spare for the official types who kept dogging her. "If he can't keep up, he can always drop off."

"He has his orders."

"So does every good soldier."

"He's not that bad, honey."

She started to tell him that her name was Honor, not Honey. Then she realized that he sounded friendly rather than patronizing. All the same...

"Are you sure, darlin'?" she asked mildly.

He gave her a fast, surprised look, followed by a slow, slow grin that made her wonder if she hadn't bitten off more than she could chew.

"Darlin', huh?" he asked.

"It was that or buttercup."

He gave a crack of laughter. "Buttercup. My God. You must have driven your brothers around the bend."

"I did my best. When I wore down, Faith took over."

The rueful affection in Honor's voice when she spoke of her family took the smile right off Jake's face. It reminded him of how close Honor was to them—and how far away from him.

"Giving up on the other boat?" she asked.

"Yeah."

She waited but he didn't say anything more.

"So now what?" she asked.

"Gas."

He didn't say anything more to her until he cut back to a snail's pace at the mouth of a public marina.

"Go to the bow and get ready to toss a line to the gas jockey," he said.

Even if Honor had felt like arguing, she wouldn't have. The look on Jake's face wasn't the warm and friendly kind. She stepped up onto the port gunwale and edged carefully to the bow. The landing line was hardly necessary. The *Tomorrow* came up alongside the fuel dock like a well-trained dog.

The attendant was a curvy girl with big hair who didn't look old enough to drive. She tied off the bow quickly, then leaned out and grabbed the stern cleat so the boat couldn't drift out from the dock.

Hastily Honor retreated from the bow, handed over the stern line, and watched enviously as the attendant secured the *Tomorrow* with a few fast turns around the dock cleat. As the girl started dragging the heavy gas hose toward the boat, Jake opened the cabin door.

"Hey, Kyle," the girl said brightly, "long time no— Oops, you aren't Kyle." She checked the name of the boat again. Definitely the *Tomorrow*.

"No problem," Jake said, smiling at her. "Sounds like Kyle is a regular."

"Between gas and compressed air, he's in here twice a week. Or was," she added wistfully. "I haven't seen him in a while. Guess he's on vacation."

"Guess so," Jake said easily.

The look he gave Honor told her not to say otherwise. If the gas jockey didn't read newspapers, who were they to trouble her with reality?

"Cool boat," the girl said, looking at the *Tomorrow*.

"Yeah." Jake put the key in the gas cap and began unscrewing the bright chrome disk. "I'm keeping it in shape for Kyle. I figured I'd better fill up the tanks before I went anywhere. He didn't give me any fuel-consumption figures."

The attendant laughed, tossed her breast-length mane of kinky ringlets, and gave Jake a smile that said she would be happy to go over any figure with him, especially hers.

Sourly Honor thought that not reading the newspaper had its points—the girl obviously didn't know her hair was years out of date. Not that it mattered. A figure like hers would always be in fashion with men.

The girl handed Jake the gas nozzle and watched while he deftly slid it into the mouth of the tank. Vapor curled up as he began pumping fuel.

"This baby uses a lot of gas if you run it at top speed," she said. "Kyle sure must have. He'd go through a hundred gallons or more every few days. He must be rich."

"He gets by," Jake said. "When was he in last?"

"Oh, about two weeks ago."

Honor barely smothered a startled sound. Jake didn't even look up from the gas tank.

"He didn't top off, though," the girl continued. "Just stayed long enough to fill his dive tanks and the tank for his Zodiac."

"A tank for his Zodiac?" Honor said, confused.

"Gas for the outboard engine that drives his tender," Jake explained.

She still wasn't sure she knew what was going on, but at least Jake seemed to.

"What was he diving for?" Honor asked the girl curiously. "There aren't any sunny coral reefs out there."

"Some of the guys go after the local version of king crab. Some of them go after cod with a speargun. Some get sea urchins for the Japanese roe trade." The attendant tossed her head again. "Some just dive to get away from the old lady. Is he married?"

"Who? Kyle?" Honor asked.

"Yeah."

"No."

The attendant brightened and hurried off to help another boat dock.

"Do you really think she saw Kyle two weeks ago?" Honor asked in a low voice.

"She doesn't have any reason to lie."

"But..."

Jake waited. He wanted Honor to sort through all the unhappy implications herself. Then she wouldn't shoot the messenger who brought the bad news, namely J. Jacob Mallory.

"Why wouldn't he call us?" she asked.

"You know him better than I do. Why wouldn't he call you?"

Her only answer was silence.

Jake glanced at the dial on the gas pump, listened to the sound of fuel going into the tank, and began easing up on the feed.

"Something is wrong," she said.

He gave Honor a look that said she had the brains of a pet rock. "You're just figuring that out?"

"No, I mean really *wrong*," she said tightly. "It's one thing for me to have a strong hunch that Kyle is in the San Juans. It's another for him to actually have been here and not called any of us. Why would he cause us so much worry? He knows we love him, no matter what."

The hurt and confusion in her voice made Jake wince, yet she still hadn't arrived at the obvious and most painful conclusion: Kyle had avoided his family because he had something to hide.

Like murder and a fortune in hot amber.

Without a word Jake screwed the cap back onto the port gas tank, unscrewed the cap to the starboard tank, and resumed pumping gas. A cool, salty breeze ruffled his short hair, bringing with it the promise of open water and a day without limits. Beneath a layer of high cloud, the air was "severe clear." Visibility unlimited. The sea was gentle. A great day to go looking for amber treasure sunk beneath the sea with a missing anchor.

Jake pumped gas and wondered if Kyle had done the standard pirate thing and sent a corpse to the bottom to guard the treasure. Maybe that was how the man with the missing fingers had died.

And maybe it was Kyle who had died, Kyle who was sunk on the bottom of the sea with all his secrets locked behind dead lips.

"What are you thinking?" Honor asked.

"You don't want to know."

"What does wanting have to do with this mess?" she asked in a rising voice. "Did anyone ask me if I wanted any of this to happen?"

Jake held out his hand. The look of surprise on her face told him that it was about the last thing she had expected him to do. Yet she didn't hesitate. She took his hand and allowed him to draw her close.

"We'll talk about it later," he said against her cheek, "when the wind isn't blowing every word we say right back to the chatty Miss Ringlets."

Honor drew a ragged breath and leaned her forehead against his shoulder.

"Jake?" she whispered.

"Yeah?"

"I'm scared."

"It's about time."

"For Kyle, not me."

"Be scared for you."

"I can't believe he...stole anything. But I'd rather believe that than believe he's dead."

Jake let out a long breath. Honor had gotten to the bottom line without his help, which meant that she wouldn't waste time being angry with him for telling her what she really didn't want to hear. Now if he were very, very careful, he might win enough of her trust to get past the solid wall of Donovan family silence to the truth about Kyle, amber, murder, and treachery.

Unless Honor found out who her fishing guide was first.

That wasn't a happy thought. Jake hoped that Ellen would keep her perfectly painted mouth shut for two more days, as promised, but he wasn't counting on it. When her boss put on pressure, she immediately would go to Plan B, whatever that was. Jake would just as soon not be around to find out.

He finished filling the tanks and turned on the blower while Honor went to pay the bill. When she came back, she was suffering from a kind of sticker shock. She looked at the

Tomorrow's gleaming length as though expecting to see fuel pouring into the marina.

"This puppy sucks gas," she said.

"The price of getting there fast. I can keep it to sailboat speed, if you like. It wouldn't take much more than a few hours to get home, if the tide and currents are right."

"Hours?" She stared at him. "How fast do sailboats go?"

"Depends on wind, weight, sail, and hull design. If they're burning fuel instead of wind, most of them go six to eight knots."

"What were we doing on the way here?"

"Normal cruising speed, most of the time."

"What is that in miles per hour?"

"Oh, maybe thirty-five, depending on tide and currents. We went faster when all four jets of the carburetor kicked in, but it's hard on the fuel consumption."

"I'm glad my credit card is good."

"So am I," Jake said, thinking of the plot charter and the stored routes he had found. "We've got a lot of places to go. Unless Kyle told you about any places he particularly liked...?"

"Every time he talked fishing, I changed the subject."

Jake wasn't talking about fishing, but he wouldn't get anywhere pointing that out. Nor was he getting any help from Honor in narrowing down the search. If she knew where her brother or the amber might be, she sure wasn't giving out any hints.

It looked like the bright lady hadn't figured out the simple truth: there was no way

156

she was going to learn enough to set out alone into the San Juans anytime soon. Yet she acted as though she had all the time in creation.

If Ellen kept her mouth shut, Jake had until day after tomorrow. A big *if*.

He bit back on his impatience and set about casting off from the fuel dock. None of the boats had been brave enough to follow him to the dock, especially the Olympic, but it wasn't long before three small craft appeared from different quarters and began pacing the *Tomorrow* as it headed out into the San Juan Islands.

Jake looked, but didn't see the Olympic. Nor did the Bayliners come close enough for him to identify passengers.

"Can we outrun them?" Honor asked.

"Probably, but why waste gas? The bite won't be on for a while."

"The bite?"

"The time when fish bite. We're supposed to be going fishing, remember?"

"To hell with fishing," she said tightly. "Teach me how to use the electronics and drive the boat."

Jake clamped down on his temper. As he had feared, she still thought a few quick lessons were all that stood between her and the freedom of the open sea. Ms. Donovan needed a dose of reality therapy. For starters, they would work on knots.

"Boating, huh?" he said. "Okay. There's some spare line in the back cupboard. Bring me two pieces."

After a minute Honor reappeared with a piece

157

of red line and a thinner piece of blue. She looked at them doubtfully. "What good will two little pieces of rope do?"

"On a boat it's line, not rope. It's for tying in knots. We'll start with a bowline."

"A what?"

"A basic knot every boat driver should know. You do it like this."

Jake let go of the helm and took the blue line. Like the well-designed little craft that it was, the SeaSport continued to streak happily over the water, holding true. Reassured, Honor watched closely as he took one end of the blue line in each hand, did something fast and mysterious, and the rope—*line*—flipped into a tricky-looking knot. Unlike most knots, it was asymmetrical and unattractive.

In fact, the bowline had more than a passing resemblance to a hangman's noose.

"Now you do it," he said.

"Sure. Right after I walk on water."

"Use the blue line as a guide."

"But I—"

"But nothing," he interrupted, turning back to the helm. "You wanted to learn. I'm teaching you. Knots are the easiest part of running a boat. While you do that, I'll explain some of the most basic aspects of boat handling, so you'll know what to expect when you take the helm for something more demanding than trolling."

Honor set her mouth in a straight line, looked at the blue knot, and tried to make one just like it. The first knot fell apart. So did the second. And the third.

Meanwhile Jake kept up a steady lecture that included the location of the pivot point on a powerboat versus a sailboat. Then he went on to the responsiveness of the helm under varying conditions of speed, trim, thrust, wave, wind, current, and the most common combinations of those elements.

The knot Honor was trying to tie kept falling apart. Her lips became thinner and thinner. Spots of color burned on her cheeks. She knew she had a good visual imagination, but she couldn't visualize where the little loop came from, the one that held the whole big loop of the knot together.

"Here," Jake said finally. "Try a different knot. This is a double sheet bend. You use it to tie two lines together. It doesn't slip, even with synthetic line."

His hands moved swiftly. First the knot in the blue line—the one she had been trying to copy—came undone. Then another one appeared with astonishing speed. He handed the blue line to her and took the helm again.

She eyed the new knot in disbelief. It looked like the blue mother of all night crawlers had doubled back and looped around itself. If it had been a design, she would have chucked it into the trash.

"I thought knots were beautiful, like macramé," Honor said.

"Two lines that stay tied together when you need them are beautiful. The rest is aesthetics, and aesthetics won't save your butt when a pretty knot comes undone."

Honor turned the knot over and over in her hands, trying to trace which end of the line was which where the knot came together. Just when she thought she saw the pattern underneath the chaos, Jake started talking again.

"Remember when you're coming up to a dock, you always check wind direction, currents, and the general 'feel' of the boat before you commit to docking. There aren't any brakes on a boat, so if you're going too fast you have to put it in neutral and then wait a second and put it in reverse. Of course, unless your helm is dead center, going in reverse will pull you off course. Remember that, because that's how you suck the stern over next to the dock when—"

"Stop," Honor said loudly. "It's much too much, muchtoofast!"

"Are you kidding? I haven't even scratched the surface."

"All right. So I'm slow."

Jake knew it was his method rather than Honor's mind that was at fault. But the time Ellen had given him was slipping away like the tide.

"You're not slow," he said curtly. "You're stubborn. So am I. Guess who's more stubborn?"

"*Merde.*"

"Try the knot again. Keep trying it until you get it right. While you try, I'll tell you more about how to trim the bow for various speeds and water conditions."

Honor bent over the knot while Jake talked quickly and relentlessly. The result was confusion rather than understanding. There was fear, too, fear that she simply didn't have what it took to help Kyle. She hadn't felt this inadequate since she had tried to play football with her brothers.

The knot she was working on fell apart. Again. If Jake noticed, he didn't even pause in the mind-numbing flow of facts.

"What was that about chine?" she asked desperately. "Is that even a word?"

"Chine is the line of intersection between the side and bottom of a boat. If you present the chine correctly to the water, you get a smoother ride."

"Oh."

And that was just the beginning. The longer Honor listened, the more she realized how silly she had been to think that running the *Tomorrow* was something she could pick up like skiing—a few hours, a few pratfalls, and watch her fly.

Jake measured the dismay growing on Honor's face, but didn't let up on the ruthless flow of information and instruction. The lady had hired him to teach her how to fish and how to run the boat; not one word had been mentioned about finding a missing brother or stolen amber. By God, he would bury her in teaching until she figured out that she wasn't going to turn into a boat handler overnight. Then she would have no choice but to ask his help in her real hunt.

He didn't think it would take long. Every instant they were on the boat made it more obvious to him that she was fighting herself—and him—on the subject of fishing and small boats. Under other circumstances he might have found her stubbornness amusing. But knowing that some hard, crafty people were after the same amber treasure that could prove Jake's innocence took all the humor out of the situation.

Time was wasting, and Honor was the one wasting it.

"Let's try something really simple," he said. "Go out on the stern."

"And jump overboard?" she asked sarcastically.

"That comes later, when we do the 'man overboard' practice."

"Like bloody hell."

But she turned and went out the door to the stern. Jake joined her a moment later and continued driving the boat from the aft station.

"Go to the stern cleat," he said, gesturing to one of the bright chrome fixtures that was fastened to the gunwale.

He cut speed, looked around, and let go of the wheel.

"Tie your line on the cleat like this," he said.

With startling speed, the blue line formed into two figure eights lying neatly around the cleat.

"Nifty," Honor said approvingly. "That's the first knot you've made that doesn't look like half a can of worms."

Despite himself, Jake smiled as he took hold of the wheel again, throttled up, and looked over his shoulder. The knot was an easy one, but not as easy as it looked. The trick was in making the loops lie flat and parallel.

Honor soon found that out for herself. Making the figure eights was easy. Making them pretty wasn't. Especially when Jake was pouring a river of facts and instructions into her ear.

"Twist the other way," he said for the third time. "The second figure eight is supposed to lie flat around the first one."

"I followed the blue line exactly."

"Really? Then why did the knot fall apart?"

"Don't ask me. You're the expert."

"Keep it in mind," he shot back. "Now twist the line the *other* way."

She looked at the length of line in her hands. "Why don't you teach me something useful?"

"Such as?"

"How to drive the boat."

"This knot is as useful as it gets," Jake said. "It's how you make sure your boat stays at the dock so that it's there when you come back."

"Why didn't Kyle buy a rowboat?" Honor asked under her breath. "Even twelve-year-olds run them."

"Big or small, if it floats you still have to tie it to the dock." Jake looked over the stern at the other boats. Still following. Still too far back to see anything useful. "Try the second figure eight again."

She flipped a loop and yanked on the loose end of the knot. To her surprise the result lay in clean, obedient curves, just like the blue line.

"I did it!"

At first he didn't answer. Then he said absently, "Sure you did, honey. Anybody who can draw the way you do can tie a simple knot."

Honey.

Her head came up sharply. She opened her mouth to tell him what she thought of men who used condescending nicknames for women.

The words never got past her lips. He was staring over the stern. She turned to see what he was watching.

A bright orange Zodiac was flying over the water, closing the distance between them.

"Don't tell me," she said.

"Okay."

"Don't they have anything better to do?"

"Guess not."

"What if I don't let them aboard?"

"Let's keep on being good citizens. We might be glad to see them later."

"I doubt it."

Jake's glance shifted from the approaching boat to Honor. The combination of anger and impatience in his eyes startled her.

"You're a bright lady," he said. "Use that brain for something more than being stubborn."

"You sound like Archer, all-knowing and oh-so-superior."

"Screw your brother. Screw the whole damn family. You're so busy looking over your shoulder to see if any Donovans are watching that you're going to trip and break your stiff neck."

"You're fired!"

He let go of the wheel and stepped back. Unguided, the *Tomorrow* raced through the calm water, holding steady.

"What do you think you're doing?" she demanded.

"I'm tired of playing games." He gestured toward the aft helm station. "It's all yours, Ms. Donovan."

She looked from him to the helm. Whatever you called it, the helm looked like a steering wheel to her. The rest of the boat might be a mystery, but she knew about steering wheels and go-fast engines.

Besides, she recognized a dare when it was flung in her face.

She stepped into place behind the heavily chromed helm wheel. The first thing she learned was that boats and cars didn't respond in the same way. The second thing she learned was the same as the first, underlined. She simply couldn't predict what the boat would do next.

The *Tomorrow*'s wake went from a straight, even line to a wildly uneven Z.

"Throttle back," Jake said. "The boys in the Zodiac are getting impatient."

With a muttered word, she grabbed the throttle lever and pulled back hard. The boat slowed so suddenly that she was thrown against the helm.

Jake staggered once and caught himself. Knowing what was coming next, he spread his legs and flexed his knees. The *Tomorrow*'s own wake boiled up under the stern and bucked beneath the boat in a powerful wave.

Honor gave a startled cry and hung on to the helm for balance.

"Lucky for us this is a SeaSport," he said curtly. "You can swamp most boats in their own wake stopping that quick. Take it out of gear."

Shaken, she reached for the black-knobbed lever and pulled gently. Nothing happened. She pulled harder. The lever moved a bit, but she could tell by the sound of the engine that it was still in gear. She gave the lever a good jerk. It slid past neutral and hung up halfway to reverse.

The boat kept going forward.

"You missed the gate," he said. "Try again. No, not that way. Take the gearshift all the way up to the top, then back to neutral in the middle."

This time she found neutral. Instantly the boat stopped responding to the wheel. She turned the wheel frantically. Nothing.

"What happened?" she asked anxiously. "I can't make it go where I want!"

"You're in neutral."

"I know that! Why doesn't the boat respond to the steering wheel?"

"Unless the boat is under power the helm is useless, remember?"

The look Honor gave Jake said she didn't

believe a word he was saying.

The look she got back said he didn't care.

"Right now you're on a very expensive piece of drifting junk," he said bluntly.

"But—"

"The faster you go," he interrupted, "the more responsive the boat is to the controls. The reverse is true, too. Remember?"

Now she did. Before, it had been simply one of a thousand unrelated facts racing around her head.

"No velocity means no steering," she said shakily. "Got it."

The next thing Honor learned was that wallowing around on the choppy water like a pig on ice made her very nervous. Her stomach kicked.

"I don't like this," she said abruptly.

She snapped the gear lever forward and shoved up on the throttle. Obediently the SeaSport leaped forward, but it veered off at an unexpected angle because the wheel was still cocked from her previous efforts to get a response.

"Watch it!" Jake yelled.

He leaped forward, grabbed the wheel with one hand and Honor with the other, and spun the bow away from the Coast Guard Zodiac. Startled cries and angry shouts came from the smaller boat.

Swiftly Jake shut down the throttle, put the boat into neutral, and looked toward the Zodiac.

"Everything okay?" he called.

What came back wasn't Coast Guard-approved language.

"Sorry," Jake said loudly. "Honor was trying out the controls. We're ready for you to come aboard now."

This time Conroy was the first one over the stern. He came aboard alone and fast.

"Another stunt like that and I'll impound the boat," he said furiously to Jake.

Honor stepped around Jake and faced Conroy. She was still shaken by the near accident. Like most Donovans, she responded to that kind of adrenaline surge with pure, flaming anger.

"No one is born knowing how to run a boat," she said icily. "We were inspected yesterday and we acted like good little citizens. If you want to inspect us from now on, you'll have to take my inexperience into account. I didn't know that would happen. Hell, I still don't know what happened."

"What happened was that you damn near rammed us!"

"Yes, but I don't know why!"

Conroy looked from Honor's pale, tight-lipped face to Jake, who nodded.

"She's as rank an amateur as ever took the helm," Jake said simply. "She didn't like the feeling of being adrift, so she shoved it in gear and hit the throttle."

"Without checking the wheel position first?" Conroy asked, his voice rising.

"Yeah."

"Shit." But there was understanding rather

than anger in his voice. He turned back to Honor. "Ma'am, I've got a small thing to check on your registration papers. Do us all a favor. Let Jake handle the controls until I'm done and we're at least a hundred yards apart."

"What 'small thing' are you checking?" she demanded.

Conroy hesitated.

She threw up her hands. "Oh, never mind. Just do it. I want salmon for dinner."

Jake waited until Conroy was inside the cabin before he turned to Honor. "Salmon? I thought I was fired."

"I get a little impatient when I'm stressed. I didn't mean it."

"I did. I'm calling your bluff."

"What bluff?"

"You no more want to learn how to fish or run this boat than I want to paddle a canoe to the moon. So what are you really after, Ms. Donovan?"

Honor looked at Jake's hard face and laser-clear eyes and knew he wasn't going to budge. Even worse, her instincts were screaming at her that if finding Kyle depended on her ability to drive herself around the San Juans in the *Tomorrow*, her brother was well and truly lost.

She had a choice. She could do as Archer wanted and design "gemmy little knickknacks" while waiting for the Donovan males to straighten things out or she could openly enlist a not-quite-stranger to help her. A man her instincts trusted.

A man she wanted.

"I—" she began, only to stop when Conroy emerged from the cabin.

"Everything in order?" Jake asked him without interest.

"Fine. Sorry to bother you," Conroy said, not meaning it.

"See you tomorrow," Jake said dryly.

Conroy shrugged. "Likely."

"Does that mean you'll be around if I send up a flare?"

The captain's expression changed from irritation to interest. "Send it. I'll come running."

"But whose side will you be on?" Honor asked sardonically.

"The good guys, who else?" Conroy retorted.

Jake waited until Conroy was in the Zodiac and speeding off before he turned to Honor.

"Well?" he demanded. "What are you after? The amber?"

"Kyle. Just Kyle. Beginning, middle, and end."

With an effort, Jake didn't show his anger. *So close and yet so far.*

She still didn't trust him enough to let him all the way inside the Donovan family walls.

"All right," he said evenly. "I'll lose our escort at twilight and pick your brother up. Which island is he on?"

Honor stared at Jake as if he was crazy. "How would I know? He didn't exactly leave a trail of bread crumbs!"

"Shit. You're not going to do this the easy way, are you? *Where is your brother?*"

"Jake. Listen to me," she said with exaggerated patience. "I. Don't. Know."

He barely managed to swallow a torrent of Russian curses. It was such a satisfying language to swear in. And if ever a situation deserved cursing, this one did.

Jake believed her.

Neither one of them knew where Kyle or the amber was.

"Okay," he said, reassessing quickly. "What do you know that will help us find Kyle?"

Honor let out her breath in a long, hidden sigh of relief. *Us.* Ever since she had admitted to herself that she could spend weeks learning the boat and not get any closer to Kyle, a chill had spread in her soul.

She knew her brother needed help. She was certain of it. She just didn't know how to give it to him. With Jake along, she felt a lot better about her chances of finding Kyle.

"Then you'll help me look for him?" she asked.

"I insist on it," he said ironically.

"I'll pay you, of course. Just like you really were teaching me how to fish and run the boat."

"I really will be."

"What?"

"Teaching you how to fish and handle the *Tomorrow.*"

"But I don't want to know!"

"Okay. I'll give on the fishing, but not on the boat handling."

"Why?"

"If something happens to me, you'll have to run the boat. Deal?"

Honor took a shaky breath and held out her right hand. "Deal."

The hand that took hers was slow, male, and very warm. So was Jake's smile.

"Congratulations, honey. You just hired yourself a fishing guide and boating instructor. Again."

9

This time Jake took the helm. Honor didn't argue. But that didn't stop her from asking questions.

"Where are we going?"

"A place called Secret Harbor."

"Why?" she asked, intrigued by the name. "Do you think Kyle might be there?"

"Doubtful."

"Then why are we going?"

"To fish."

"What!"

He almost smiled. "I thought you wanted a salmon dinner."

"I can buy it at the grocery store."

"This is better. Trust me."

"I don't have much choice, do I?" she asked evenly.

Jake's hands held the wheel too hard. He didn't like to think about that part of what he was doing. Honor was damned if she trusted him and damned if she didn't.

And so was he.

He wished he had a soothing, charming, amusing response, but he didn't. All he had was the cold comfort of knowing that, like Honor, he didn't have much choice.

"We're going to Secret Harbor because the trolling line there is a long ellipse that will give us a chance to look over the competition," he said. "Since Secret Harbor is also one of the places Kyle mentions in his log, we'll scan the shore for anything that might have...washed up."

"Like what?"

"The missing Zodiac, dive tanks, an anchor, anything that shouldn't be there."

"What if we don't find anything?"

"Then we go on to the next place Kyle mentioned in the log. And the next. And the next. Unless you have a better idea?"

"No. It's what I was going to do once I learned how to drive the boat."

Jake grunted. "The good news is that no one else has a better idea."

"How do you know?"

"If they did, they wouldn't be following us."

Honor blinked. "So if we look around and no one is following, we know we're on the wrong trail."

Jake wondered if he should tell her about his near certainty that Kyle had altered the chart plotter enough to hide or add routes. There was also a good chance that Kyle had decided to hide the route in plain sight and had wired some useless stuff into the computer to confuse anyone who came looking. It was the sort of double reverse that would have appealed to Kyle's sense of humor.

After a moment Jake decided to spend the day going over the stored routes and another night trying to hack into Kyle's plotter by himself. He should have more than twenty-four hours before Ellen started whispering in Honor's ear. If Ellen kept her word....He smiled cynically. Ellen's word wasn't exactly cast-iron.

"We'll do the close-in spots first," he said. "That way we'll waste as little time as possible just getting from here to wherever."

The *Tomorrow* sped across the blue-green sound. A white, surprisingly flat wake unfurled behind the SeaSport. The other boats followed. Honor kept turning around to check on them. Jake didn't. He was watching the radar screen for a fourth boat. One way or another, he really wanted to get a good look at the driver.

"Rest your neck," he said to her after a few minutes. "The radar will keep track of our escort."

"Good for it. I'd rather do it the old-fashioned way. Then I know what I'm looking at."

"I've set the radar screen at a quarter mile. That means each of those three rings on the screen covers about eleven hundred feet." He began pointing to the radar screen mounted above the dashboard. "That ragged chunk of green to the port—left—is an island. That bright spot over there is a channel marker. That big ellipse is a freighter headed for the docks to pick up logs for Japan. Those three specks behind us are our admirers. The ferry off to the starboard—right—doesn't show yet, but it will as soon as it gets closer."

Honor glanced from the screen to the water and back again. It took a little practice, but soon she began to associate the electric green blobs on the screen with the reality outside.

"What's that?" she asked, pointing to the screen, where it appeared as though the freighter was separating into two uneven pieces.

"Looks like another boat was in the radar shadow of the freighter but is pulling away now." He glanced outside. "A purse seiner. See it?"

She stared out the side window and saw a ratty-looking commercial fishing boat pulling away on the far side of the freighter. The seiner's paint sat on rusting metal like gangrene on flesh. The freighter itself was no prize in the glamour department—streamers of rust spilled down its sides. The name on it was Japanese. The name on the fishing boat was Russian.

"Don't we have any American boats around here?" she asked.

"You're riding in one."

"I mean commercial boats."

"There are a few, but most of the nonpetroleum haulers that go out of Anacortes these days are foreign."

Honor looked at the freighter and tried to forget she was in a small boat heading out into the San Juans in search of answers that she might not want to know.

It didn't work. She couldn't forget. Kyle was a knot in her stomach and an ache across her shoulders that didn't go away. She forced herself to concentrate on the *Tomorrow*, which might do Kyle some good. Worrying sure hadn't.

As the boat arrowed through the shipping channel, she compared shapes on the water with the shimmering green blips on the radar screen. Once they were out of the main channel, the number of big ships went down. The number of small pleasure craft soared. She felt like part of an unannounced parade.

"I didn't think there were that many crazy people, even in the Pacific Northwest," she said, waving a hand at little boats zipping around on the cold water like speedy white bugs.

"Crazy? Oh, you mean boaters. The San Juans are a mecca for small boats, especially in the summertime."

"Then Kyle wouldn't exactly have stood out...."

"No. Don't be alarmed. I'm going to slow down and get the fishing gear in the water."

"Oh joy. I can't wait. Be still my beating heart." She gave him a sideways glance. "How's my enthusiasm index?"

"Right off the bottom of the scale."

Carefully, slowly, Jake brought the boat down to idling speed and put the shifter in neutral. The wake swelled up beneath them very gently. He didn't want to make Honor nervous. Just because he had to use her to save himself didn't mean that he had to torture her in the process. It wasn't much of a sop to his conscience, but it was all he had.

Silently Honor watched while he set out the fishing rods. He kept up a running commentary about down-riggers, rod holders, cannonballs, flashers, spoons, and other words she let pass right out of her mind. Then he started in on the difference between fishing with cut plug herring versus whole herring versus artificial lures. Then he went on about trolling versus mooching versus buzz bombing.

His enthusiasm should have been catching. It wasn't. She tried not to yawn in his face, but she didn't try hard enough. When he got to the part about how many "pulls" behind the boat the lure should be positioned to catch silver versus coho, and what the trolling speed should be in order to avoid getting dogfish, she held up her hands in surrender.

"Enough," she begged. "You've made your point."

He looked surprised. "I have?"

"Yes! Fishing is a lot more complicated than squeezing eight inches of worm onto a one-inch hook and dunking the mess over the side."

"I just kept talking because I didn't want you to be nervous."

"Nervous? I'm comatose. Why would I be nervous?"

"No reason."

Jake hid his smile by bending over to fire up the small trolling motor. If Honor hadn't noticed that they were adrift and the wind was starting to chop up the surface of the water, he wasn't going to point it out. Not that there was any danger—the SeaSport could ride out a gale, much less the refreshing breeze that had come up—but Honor wasn't at home on the water yet.

As soon as he was satisfied with the trolling speed, he checked the two rods in their separate holders and went back into the cabin. He picked up the remote throttle control for the kicker, climbed into the helm seat, switched the computer display from the chart to the depth sounder/fish finder, and took his place in the long, elliptical line of boats trolling for salmon.

The two Bayliners that had followed the *Tomorrow* swung into place much farther back. Jake had brought the SeaSport into line just behind the only Olympic he could see. He doubted it was the elusive fourth boat; the fish landing net was a faded blue and the driver was old enough to be Honor's grandfather. Not the sort of person who would be playing tag in the dark with a speeding boat and then racing off to start fishing at Secret Harbor while the Coast Guard practiced climbing on and off the *Tomorrow*.

"Take the helm and keep us in line with the boat ahead," Jake said.

"What are you going to do?"

"Use the binoculars."

"I can do that."

"I know what the shoreline should look like. You don't."

Warily Honor took over the controls. She soon discovered that the boat responded very slowly when it was on the trolling engine. In fact, it was a pig to hold in line.

While she learned the rhythm of steer, correct, overcorrect, oversteer, repeat as necessary, Jake picked up the binoculars and scanned the shoreline. He didn't see anything unexpected. There was a small settlement tucked way back at the mouth of the harbor, plus some salmon pens farther out along the edge of the bay. None of the small craft he saw matched the specifications in Kyle's registration papers for the Zodiac. No dive equipment was lying carelessly about on the shore. No anchor was stranded on the rocks. No unusual debris decorated the beach.

When Honor managed to bring the SeaSport about and begin the return leg of the troll, Jake switched to watching the other boats as they passed by thirty or forty yards away. They couldn't escape from his scrutiny, because the SeaSport was between them and the open sea.

Jake smiled. It was the nervous-making kind of smile.

"Well?" Honor asked.

"Well what?"

"What do they look like?" she asked impatiently.

"Idiots. They don't have any fishing gear in the water."

"I'd say that speaks highly of their intelligence," she retorted.

He didn't answer. He had just spotted a double-dealing Lithuanian trying to look like a salmon fisherman. As though realizing too late that he was on center stage with a spotlight in his face, Dimitri Pavlov turned away from the passing boat.

"Snake Eyes," Jake said distinctly.

"What? Let me see."

"Keep steering. He's not going anywhere. I want a look at the other boat that was following."

Honor stared over the distance separating the two boats. She couldn't make out the features of the man who was driving the boat. To her eye, he seemed to be bouncing around a lot.

"Why is his boat wallowing around on the water more than we are?" she asked.

"Bad hull design, bad trim, bad driver, or any combination thereof."

"What difference does...never mind. I passed my limit on useless facts for the day somewhere between dogfish and buzz bombing."

"You sure?" he asked.

She looked at the smile spreading on Jake's mouth beneath the binoculars. Her pulse kicked. That slow grin of his was deadly.

"Positive," she said. Her voice sounded husky. She cleared her throat. "Recognize anyone in the second boat?"

"Two men. One woman. Two fishing rods."

"Why just two?"

"Only two fishing licenses on board would be my guess."

"His and hers?"

"His and his. Most fishermen are—"

"Men?" Honor interrupted dryly.

"Yeah."

He didn't say that the woman in question was Ellen Lazarus, who had a mind like a bear trap and thighs to match. He didn't recognize the men with her, other than that the guy driving the boat was a clean-shaven, close-cut, squared-away generic military type. And Conroy was right—the driver looked too young to be a captain in anyone's navy.

Jake wondered which of the Whidbey Island NAS boys had been pressed into service as a fishing guide for Uncle Sam's entry into the amber treasure hunt. Whoever it was, he knew how to fish. The rods made a clean arc against the gray-blue water. Each rod tip moved in slow rhythms that told of a flasher turning beneath the surface of the sea, luring fish to come up, have a look, and stay for dinner.

The man with Ellen might have been a sport fisherman in his spare time, but he was working now. He didn't even glance at the rods arching off to port and starboard of the stern. The man had a pair of binoculars against his eyes and he was memorizing everything about the *Tomorrow*.

Jake gave him a casual, one-finger salute and lowered the glasses. Honor snatched them up, adjusted them for her own eyes, and looked at the first of the two boats.

"You sure that's Snake Eyes?" she asked. "I can't see much beneath that miserable cap he's wearing."

"I'm sure."

She started to object that she wasn't that good an artist—her sketch and a glance through binoculars at forty yards weren't enough for certain identification. Then she looked again. What she could see of the man was unappetizing enough to go with her memory of Snake Eyes. Clothes that were as cheap as they were ill fitting. A hat that should have been burned as a health hazard. Hands that were allergic to soap.

Not that she was a fashion queen herself in her black jeans, blue-green sweater, blue-green wind jacket, white deck shoes, and hair combed by the playful wind. But at least she was clean. Snake Eyes wasn't.

"Yuck," Honor summed up, and focused on the next boat.

"He's a regular Prince Alarming," Jake agreed. "Recognize anyone in the second boat?"

"Nope. The woman looks a bit overdressed for fishing. Nice jacket, though. Red that clear is hard to find."

Jake preferred Honor's sleek, sea-colored wind shell and sweater to Ellen's expensive red jacket, but he didn't say anything. He couldn't help wondering if the rest of Ellen's clothes would catch up with her before she ruined the ones she had. Obviously she had been yanked

out of whatever office job she had been working on and shot into Anacortes to seduce one
J. Jacob Mallory. No time to pack. No time
to say good-bye. Just grab a cab and blast
off to the next brushfire.

He had enjoyed that kind of life once. Now
he didn't miss it at all.

A glance over his shoulder told Jake that nothing was happening with the fishing rods. He
wasn't surprised. None of the other circling
boats had dropped out of line to fight a fish.
He glanced at the fish finder. Nothing was
returning a sonar echo except the flat bottom
of the bay.

"Nobody's catching anything," Honor said.

"Tide won't change for half an hour."

"So?"

"There's a saying around here that ninety-
five percent of fish are caught during the ten-
minute bites at tide change."

"Then what are all these people doing here
now?"

"Praying for the other five percent."

"I was right the first time. They're crazy."

"Relax. The best-kept secret about fishing is
that it's a grand excuse to do nothing."

Honor didn't look convinced. Or relaxed.

He switched the screen to the chart plotter
and called up the Secret Harbor route Kyle
had stored. For the moment he was assuming
that the dashed route on the chart was simply a preferred trolling route and the cross marks
along that route were places where Kyle had
caught fish.

"What's that?" she asked.

"A chart showing Secret Harbor. That's Cypress Island. Across the channel is Guemes Island."

She leaned into the narrow aisle to get a better look at the screen. "What's the dotted line that loops around?"

"I'm assuming it's the trolling route Kyle preferred. It's real close to the contours of a little rise that shows on the charts."

"What are these marks?"

"Probably places where he caught fish."

"But you're not sure?"

"No. That's why I'm retracing this route."

"How will doing this help us find Kyle?"

Jake hesitated. Even his quick mind didn't see a useful way of ducking the question. Besides, the sooner Honor accepted that her brother was a thief, the less she would feel betrayed by Jake when she found out that he was no more a fishing guide than she was a woman who was yearning to learn how to fish.

Jake didn't want to be classed in the same lying category as Honor's ruthless, treacherous, charming brother.

"I think you'll agree that your brother and a fortune in amber disappeared at the same time?" Jake asked mildly.

Honor closed her eyes, then opened them and met his level glance. "Yes, but that doesn't necessarily mean he's a thief."

Even more than a month's growth of beard couldn't hide the impatience and anger that drew Jake's mouth into a hard line. He switched the lower screen from chart to depth sounder and stared at the colorful red and blue screen. Flat bottom. Ninety feet down. No fish showing. Nothing had changed.

Including Honor's stubborn belief in her brother.

"You're a loyal sister but a lousy thinker," Jake said. "You'll get a lot closer to where your brother is if you take the most likely explanation for the facts as we know them and work from there."

"You think Kyle stole the amber."

Jake glanced up from the screen. "Can you think of a better explanation?"

She opened her mouth. Nothing came out. She swallowed. "I've spent a lot of time thinking about it."

He raised one dark eyebrow and waited.

"I...I just..." Her voice died into a painful silence.

"Never mind," he said roughly. "Believe whatever you have to, but don't expect the rest of the world to worship at the altar of Kyle Donovan."

"The man driving the amber shipment was killed when it was stolen," Honor said in a strained voice. "Could you believe that your brother was a thief and a murderer?"

"I'm not close enough to my stepbrothers or half brothers for it to get in the way of my judgment."

Jake looked back at the fishing rods. Nothing new there, either. He turned back to Honor.

"Whatever the circumstances," he said in a neutral tone, "I'm assuming that Kyle and the amber are together. Some other people in official positions seem to be assuming it, too. Can we agree on that much, at least?"

She nodded.

He let out a hidden breath and sorted quickly through the information he had gotten from the newspapers rather than first-hand in Kaliningrad or from Ellen and Conroy.

"Okay," Jake said. "Do you know how much bulk we're talking about?"

"Six feet, two inches, about one-ninety," Honor said in a clipped voice.

"I meant the amber. How big a shipment are we talking about?"

"I don't know. Depends on the quality, I guess. The newspaper mentioned a million dollars. From the cost of the one shipment Kyle just sent me, a million dollars would buy a lot of ordinary amber."

"Is that what Donovan International is claiming from its insurer—a million bucks?"

"We don't have a claim. We never received the amber, so it wasn't ours to lose."

Bullshit, Jake thought savagely, but he didn't say anything aloud. Obviously the Donovan males were hiding a few things from their beloved little sister.

"How about the amber itself?" he asked. "Was it raw or worked?"

She frowned. "I'm not sure, but I think both."

Excitement threaded through Jake. Honor

was the first person who had mentioned worked amber as opposed to material fresh from the mine. Unless he took Ellen's talk about the Amber Room seriously. He really didn't want to do that. He was still praying that Ellen was chasing a ghost.

The last thing he needed was the kind of trouble a stolen Amber Room would bring down on his head. Financing a handful of wannabe rebels was one thing. A dumb thing. Stealing a piece of a country's cultural history was quite another.

Wars had been started for less.

"What kind of worked amber?" Jake asked casually.

"What do you mean?"

"Old or new stuff? Cups, sculptures, boxes, rosaries, tables, candlesticks, mosaics, jewelry? What was the worked amber like?"

"Really old. Neolithic. Kyle started collecting Stone Age pieces when he was handling the jade trade for Donovan International. Then he discovered the small Neolithic figurines or pendants carved of opaque amber. Bastard amber is what he called it."

Jake knew the type of amber object Honor was describing. It was another of the things he and Kyle had found in common: Jake had a long-standing fascination with fossil resin shaped into art by people who had been dead thousands of years. The Amber Room's history was a lot more recent. The eighteenth century rather than thousands of years B.C.

He let out another hidden breath. Let Ellen

grab hold of the fairy dust. He had something more real to chase: a shipment of top-quality raw amber from Kaliningrad. He knew just what the shipment looked like to the last gram—he had packed it himself—but he didn't know how much the Donovan family knew.

"Kyle used to send jade he had collected back with the other stuff Donovan International bought," she said. "When he started collecting Neolithic amber carvings, I assumed he would transport them home the same way, with a commercial shipment."

"So, any worked amber in the missing shipment was just old stuff for his own collection," Jake said.

"As far as I know. But he was working with another collector, too."

Jake tensed. "Who?"

"Kyle just called him Jay. He really liked him. Said he was the kind of man I should be dating instead of—" She broke off sharply.

Jake raised his eyebrows in silent question.

"My brothers think I should date men like them. Stubborn. Arrogant. Too big for my comfort. Hardheaded." Then Honor sighed and admitted, "Intelligent. Enough integrity and backbone for a regiment. Loyal. Occasionally quite wonderful."

"But only occasionally," Jake said dryly.

"Hey, I'm a sister. That's as good as it gets."

"So you've been dating spineless, hesitant, stupid, weak men."

"They weren't stupid!"

"Okay. Smart, spineless, and weak."

"They weren't weak. Not really."

"Spineless and hesitant."

"Polite."

"Spineless."

"Sold." Then she laughed sadly. "But I'll never admit it to my brothers."

"Something tells me they already figured it out."

"Yeah, well, Jay whatshisname can stay in Kaliningrad and collect Neolithic amber. I don't want another big, overbearing man in my life."

"I doubt if he's all that bad," Jake said blandly.

"I don't. Anyone who can fight Kyle and win is no fragile little flower of chivalry."

"They fought?" Jake asked, surprised. He didn't think Kyle would have passed along the tale of the beer barrel, the barmaid, and the boy who bit off more than he could chew.

"Sure did. Kyle ended up on his butt in a puddle of beer. Jay put him there. But Kyle really respects him. Talks about him like he was a stepbrother to God or another Donovan. Same difference, I suppose."

Jake didn't know what to say. Apparently Kyle had conned his family as thoroughly as he had conned Jake; they believed Kyle liked and respected the very man he had betrayed.

It should have made Jake feel better that he wasn't the only one who had been fooled by Kyle. It didn't. He found himself hoping that Honor would never have to know how different

Kyle was from what he seemed. The discovery had been painful enough for him; he could imagine how terrible it would be for Honor.

"Okay," Jake said. "What else do you know about amber and your brother?"

"Not much. He called about six weeks ago and told me to start designing some fantastic stuff, the kind museums and very rich collectors buy. He had just heard about some big pieces of clear raw amber, chunks of a size for tabletop sculptures rather than earrings or inlay."

Jake hoped his surprise didn't show. Kyle hadn't said a word to him about that kind of treasure trove. But then, Kyle hadn't said anything about a lot of things that were on his mind, as Jake had found out too late.

"Sounds expensive," he said carefully.

"It would be. Big pieces like that are really rare. When Kyle first started working in Kaliningrad, I asked him to bring me a cantaloupe-sized chunk of clear red amber. He laughed so hard he nearly dropped the phone. How was I to know I might as well have asked for a ten-carat diamond?"

"Um," was all Jake could think of to say.

He was trying hard not to laugh himself. He looked at the bright blue screen of the fish finder and hoped his face was as blank as the screen.

Not a fish showing. Not a bump on the bottom worth investigating. He cleared his throat and turned back to Honor. "Then we'll assume we're looking for something that is bigger than a man and smaller than, say, a room in Kyle's cottage."

"Why?"

Jake thought fast. "Logic. Would he bring it here if he couldn't hide it?"

"How did he get it here, then?"

"Good question. I'll be sure to ask him."

"First we have to find him."

"I'm working on that."

"From here, it looks like you're fishing. And not very well, I must say. Good thing I got some chicken for dinner."

"I'll bring the wine."

Honor smiled and wished she knew Jake well enough to kiss his hard cheekbone just above his beard. She had been hoping not to spend the evening alone, waiting for the phone to ring, wondering if it would be bad news, worse news, or Snake Eyes on the other end of the line.

"What are you looking for?" she asked, leaning close to the blue screen, needing to think about anything except the unnerving silence that came when she said hello and no one answered.

Jake tried not to take an extra-deep breath, savoring the sweet smell of woman so close to him. Then he tried not to think how nice her chin-length hair would feel tickling his bare skin. Then he tried not to think about her lips doing the same thing, tickling so fine.

"Jake? What are you hoping to find?"

"I'm..." He stared at the screen for a few seconds while he tried to think of a nice way to say that he was looking for her brother's dead body or a cache of stolen amber sunk to the bottom by the missing anchor.

There was no nice way.

"I'm looking for fish," he said. "That's all. Just fish."

"The screen looks blank to me."

"It is."

Jake hit one of the buttons on the bottom number pad. The view changed back to the chart. Trying to see more clearly, Honor shifted position until she was half standing in the aisle. He hit a few more buttons and the picture changed again. A new route was laid out.

"Steer while I reel in," he said, sliding out from behind the helm seat.

There was no way he could avoid touching her quite thoroughly as he passed her in the narrow aisle. There was no way he could avoid noticing the way her breath broke and her lips parted at the contact. And there definitely was no way he could help his elemental male response.

At least one thing was working well today, Jake thought ironically as he brought the fishing lines in. Rock hard and ready to go.

"What now?" Honor asked when he came back into the cabin.

"Now we find out if their gas tanks are as full as ours."

10

Ten hours and fifteen fishing spots later, Jake still had what he had started out the day with: unanswered questions and an ache in his crotch.

It did nothing to improve his temper. He had pushed the speed hard getting to the sixteenth fishing hole, if only to watch the navy Bayliner scramble. Snake Eyes hadn't made the cut. He had turned off to refuel at Fisherman's Bay several hours before and hadn't caught up again. The other Bayliner had dropped out for a time, but hadn't had any trouble finding them again. A direct line to the Coast Guard no doubt helped.

The only good news was that Honor had gotten so restless he had talked her into learning a few basics of fishing. He started by teaching her the fine art of casting a lure and buzz bombing on the retrieve. The buzz bombing part of it didn't particularly interest her. What did was casting. She had a natural sense of timing and leverage that made her casts long and accurate.

When Jake cut the speed back to an idle, Honor looked around. There were no other boats in sight. He had really burned up the water getting there.

"Now what?" she asked.

"Kyle entered a 'hit' in the log here. If the date is accurate—and I have no way of checking it—then this is one of the places he came to but didn't record in his written log after he got back from Kaliningrad."

"Date? What do you mean? I didn't know the *Tomorrow*'s electronics recorded dates."

There was a lot about the electronics that Honor didn't know. Jake would just as soon it stayed that way. He didn't want her to get any ideas about going off on her own if Ellen spilled the beans the next day. The way Honor had taken the helm and shot off over the water still haunted him. She had more guts than sense.

"Some programs record all kinds of things," he said. "In any case, Kyle tinkered with this computer the same way he fiddled with your alarm clock. All I know for sure is that this isn't like any other chart plotter I've ever used. I'm still trying to figure out half the stuff I find."

That wasn't quite true, but it wasn't entirely false, either. Jake supposed there was some kind of poetic justice in using a mixture of truths and half-truths, omissions and distractions on Honor Donovan. That was what a Donovan had done to him. There was no single thing that he could have pinned on Kyle, yet the proof surely was in the result: J. Jacob Mallory accused of theft and Kyle Donovan making off with the amber.

Jake went out on the stern and looked around, ignoring the rods waiting to be used. He didn't feel like setting up the trolling gear again.

Honor slipped past him and grabbed a rod out of the holder. The rod tip bowed over with the weight of the lure. Once she had discovered that lures came in weights from a quarter of an ounce to sixteen ounces and up, she had gone right to the heavy stuff. Smiling like a kid with a new toy, she started casting.

"What are you aiming for?" he asked.

"Straight ahead of me, where that chunk of wood is floating."

She gripped the long rod with two hands, lifted the tip up and behind her right shoulder, then snapped the rod forward smartly. At the same time she released all restraint on the fishing line. The lure shot out straight in front of her, peeling off translucent line in a blur of speed.

As though it had been on rails rather than monofilament line, the lure dropped into the water near the floating wood. The distance was at least fifty feet.

Jake shook his head at the waste of talent—to cast like that and not care if you ever got a bite. In fact, he had the distinct feeling that Honor would welcome a fish like ants at a picnic.

"Why are you shaking your head?" she asked. "I came pretty close."

"Pretty close? Hell, you're better at casting right now than ninety percent of the people who ever picked up a fishing rod."

She reeled in as though there were a prize for highest speed through the water by a lure. "Really?"

"Yeah. But your retrieval technique needs work. A lot of it."

She ignored him.

He thought about setting up the trolling gear again and decided again that it wasn't worth the trouble. They wouldn't be there long; Kyle had marked only one "hit" on the chart plotter for this area.

"I'm not going to bother with the trolling gear," Jake said.

"Fine with me."

"Reel in. I'm going to take a few slow passes over Kyle's route."

"It won't interfere with my casting."

"It would interfere with catching a fish."

"Like I said..."

Jake gave up and went back into the cabin. He drove over the marked spot twice at idling speed. He saw nothing on the fish finder. Not fish, not bubbles, not even an interesting lump rising from the flat bottom.

"Wrap it up," he called over his shoulder. "We're heading out."

Honor didn't argue this time. She reeled in, put the rod in the holder by the door, and went into the cabin.

"Do you think we lost our escort for good?" she asked, looking at the empty little cove.

"No. Conroy never really lost me. He should be rounding the head any second now."

"Then why did we race here?"

"If we're predictable, we're a lot easier prey."

"I don't like the sound of that word."

"Little supermarket predator," he said, smiling despite his edgy mood. "You're one of a kind."

"Wait until you meet Faith."

Jake's smile faded. All things considered, he didn't think he would be meeting any more Donovans. Certainly not under friendly circumstances.

He picked up the binoculars and studied the shoreline. It didn't take long. The islet was not only small and uninhabited, it was pretty much sheer rock except for a ragged crown of fir trees.

"Anything?" Honor asked.

"The usual."

Switching his attention to the computer, he started punching instructions into the chart plotter. The picture on the screen changed and then changed again.

Honor knew just enough to tell that Jake was looking at some kind of map—*chart*, she corrected herself silently. But she couldn't figure out what kind of chart. It could have been the route back to Anacortes or it could have been the bottom of the South Pacific colored blue with little black dash marks going crazily in every direction.

When the screen changed she peered over Jake's shoulder. As usual, nothing made sense. She bent over to see more clearly. Being so close to him reminded her of the time before dawn, when he had looked at the hem of her night-shirt and risen like a phoenix from the ashes of a morning erection.

Are you finished staring or were you planning to stuff money in my jock strap?

Anger, embarrassment, and something hotter licked over Honor. She stepped back quickly and glanced around, trying to think of anything but Jake Mallory's very male body.

He called up the last route to be checked— or at least the last route he could find stored in the modified computer. The route was well off the normal run of fishing or sailing places. It led to a waterless, uninhabited cluster of small islets, reefs, and rocks whose presence was known but not marked by warning lights or beacons.

It wasn't the kind of place he wanted to tiptoe through in the late afternoon on a falling tide. In any case, there wasn't enough daylight left to get to the next route, check it over, and still make it back to the cottage's little dock before full darkness.

Jake reset the radar to reach farther out. A tiny blip was boring in from the east. The Zodiac, no doubt. He glanced sideways at Honor. She was doing everything but putting her head in the bait bucket to avoid looking at him with her speculative, hungry eyes.

He knew just how she felt. The more he looked at her, the better he liked what he saw. If something didn't happen to lower the level of sexual heat in the boat real soon, he would do something really stupid.

He could hardly wait.

Jake hissed a disgusted word, furious with himself for not being able to get his mind off his crotch. He looked at the fish finder. Nothing was showing. He switched to the chart and gauged distances. He looked at his watch and then the sky. Still not enough time to do anything useful.

Still plenty of time to do something really stupid.

On the other hand, he could go fishing. Real fishing instead of just dragging lures through the water no matter what the time or tide.

"I wonder if the kings are still running at Falcon Cliff," he said aloud.

"Kings?" Honor asked. "As in royalty?"

"As in twelve to sixty-five pounds of pure dynamite waiting to bite on our freshly sharpened hooks."

"Kings are fish?"

"Around here they are."

"Are you saying that we're really going fishing?"

"Right."

"*Merde.*"

"Wrong answer," Jake said, revving up the SeaSport, turning it about. "Enthusiasm, remember?"

"Oh, I just can't wait. Can we go there right now, please pretty please with sugar on it, et cetera."

"Your enthusiasm still needs work. But don't worry, I'll give you lots of chance to practice."

The Zodiac closed in quickly as the *Tomorrow* retraced part of its previous course. Jake waved as they passed. Conroy didn't wave back. He didn't try to board them, either. Apparently he was getting as fed up with the game as Jake was.

Honor sighed and watched dark water whip beneath the *Tomorrow*'s bow. She tried not to worry about Kyle and the cold sea, missing amber, and a murdered man.

"Do you want to talk about it?" Jake asked.

"What?"

"Whatever is making you look so grim."

"No thanks. I'd rather talk about anything else."

"Okay. Do you live alone?"

She looked over at him, startled.

"Well, you did say you'd rather talk about—" he began.

"—anything else," Honor finished dryly. "Faith and I share a condo in Southern California, but one or the other of us is gone a lot of the time."

"What does your sister do?"

"Turns my designs into breathtaking bits of art. While she does that, I'm usually on the road looking for new materials at gem and mineral shows across the country. When I'm home designing, she'll take her turn rounding up raw materials."

"Is that where you got the amber I saw on your desk?"

"No. Kyle sent it to us."

Jake's hands tightened on the helm. He didn't say a word.

"All our brothers keep an eye out for interesting stuff for us to use," Honor continued. "Even the Donovan collects for us."

"Are your father and brothers in business with you?"

"With mere females?" she retorted. "Bite your tongue. Donovan International is the last of the Old Boy Clubs."

Though her voice was sardonic, there was no real anger in her words. She and Faith had learned to be grateful they were women. In some ways it made getting out from under Donald Donovan's benevolent tyranny much easier. Archer had fought for his freedom with a ferocity that was still legend in the family. Lawe and Justin had double-teamed the old man and worn him down that way. Kyle was still struggling. He had the added burden of being the youngest male, which meant that sometimes he had to fight his older brothers, too.

"Donovan International," Jake said slowly, looking at the radar. Three boats showing now. Apparently Snake Eyes had managed to find the bright orange of the Coast Guard again. "I've heard the name somewhere..."

As he had hoped, Honor took the bait.

"On Wall Street, likely," she said. "Dad's company discovers, recovers, buys, and/or sells metals and rare minerals."

"Nice setup. Your brothers will never lack for a job."

"Lousy setup. They want to be boss."

"Every Eden has a snake."

"Well, my brothers bypassed the old serpent and started their own company, Donovan Gemstones and Minerals."

Jake smiled despite the raw male hunger prowling through his blood every time he thought about Honor's soft mouth and softer body. "The sons went into competition with the old man, is that it?"

Honor winced, remembering. "That's it. The salsa really hit the fan when Dad discovered that he had been outmaneuvered by his own sons."

"Did he disinherit them?"

She looked shocked. "Of course not. Dad is bullheaded and stiff-necked, but he's not vicious. The Donovan males went head-to-head for a year on various mineral surveys and such. When Dad was convinced the boys would make it without him, he offered a palace alliance."

"Did they take it?"

"Sort of. They do work for him on a contract basis, but never enough that Donovan International is their only customer, or even their best one."

"Smart." But then, Jake had already known that. The Donovan males he had met were as intelligent as they were hardheaded.

"I suppose. Sure makes for some interesting Thanksgivings and Christmases, with Dad praying at every meal for stray lambs to return to the fold and said lambs running as hard as they can to stay out of reach of the old wolf."

The idea of the Donovan brothers as "lambs" made Jake laugh out loud.

"Are your holidays like that?" Honor asked.

"Like what?"

"Fighting off family."

"Nope. We can't get far enough away from each other."

"Sounds...lonely."

"You know what they say about freedom."

"No, what?"

"Another way of saying nothing left to lose."

Jake changed course, ducked around a little island, shot across a narrow strait, and shut down to an idle at the base of a rugged stone cliff. He punched a button. The fish finder glowed in blue and red on the lower screen.

Honor didn't bother to ask where they were. Even with a chart, she had a hard time sorting out which San Juan island was which. There were a lot of islands, many so small they were barely rocks. She had tried orienting herself with the chart while they raced from place to place, but all she got for her efforts was a headache and a sour stomach.

"Hot damn!" he said. "They're here."

She leaned in for a better view. The screen looked like somebody had been drawing yellow dashes on it between forty and ninety feet. Before she could ask if the random clumps of color were fish, Jake was gone. She followed him out into the stern well and watched while he started the kicker engine and set up the fishing rods. The gear didn't particularly interest her. Watching Jake's easy, economical way of moving did.

He mistook her presence for a desire to learn more about fishing.

"We've dragged all the dead herring through the water that I'm going to for today," he said. He bent over the white plastic bucket and picked up a lure that had been dangling from the rim. "Know what this is?"

"Looks like two little hooks from here. Incredible. I don't know if I can stand the excitement."

But there was no real sarcasm in her voice. She was having too much fun watching Jake enjoy himself. And she knew he was enjoying. It was there in his voice, in the brilliance of his eyes, in the springy way he moved. The man loved fishing.

Well, she reminded herself, nobody is perfect. I've got some industrial-strength flaws myself.

"The hooks," he said, "are attached to a nifty, semi-flexible lure called the Tormentor. I'm going to bend it just enough so that it imitates the action of a cut-plug herring. Now I'm going to attach the Tormentor's leader to the dodger and—"

"Foul!" she interrupted.

"What?"

"You aren't going to teach me fishing. I signed on for boat handling, period."

"I didn't think you really meant it."

"Wrong."

"Okay."

Just like that, Jake went back to setting up the fishing gear. After a few minutes he started whistling. The sweet clarity of the sound reminded Honor of a nightingale at moonrise. It was startling to hear something so beautiful coming from the lips of such a hard-looking man.

Then Honor realized there was something else about Jake that was surprising. If he had been one of her brothers, she would have been in for a battle of wills over the issue of learning or not learning to fish. But Jake not only accepted her decision without a fight, he didn't sulk.

Very quickly there were two fishing lines in the water, Jake was in position at the aft station, and they were creeping past the cliff at a pace only slightly faster than that of grass growing.

Jake looked up, eyes narrowed against the glare of the descending sun. The Zodiac had taken up a position a hundred feet out to sea, paralleling the *Tomorrow*. The Bayliner with Ellen aboard was even farther out. No other boat was within sight. Either Snake Eyes had gone home or he was off the scope somewhere.

Ignoring the escort, Jake looked back at the arch of the fishing rods and the subtle, hypnotic dip and sway of the rod tips as each responded to its dodger.

"Now what?" Honor asked.

"We fish."

"Goody. Like watching paint dry, only less exciting."

"You'll change your mind as soon as you feel a salmon on the other end of the line."

"Be still my beating heart."

Shaking his head, Jake looked at the shoreline. There were no houses or cabins to interrupt the wildness of the place; there were only stone cliffs, wind-twisted fir trees, and a clean, cloud-layered sky. Between the clouds, random, slanting shafts of sun spotlighted rocks and water. A bald eagle soared overhead and the boat swayed gently beneath his feet. For the first time in weeks, a sense of peace curled through Jake.

Honor looked at the softened line of his mouth and knew she was getting in over her head. Just seeing his pleasure made her want to smile and hold out her arms.

Stop looking at him, she warned herself. *Do something useful. Anything. Just stop thinking about Jake Mallory.*

But as soon as she did, thoughts of Kyle and amber and death haunted her. Now she just wanted to crawl into Jake's arms and be comforted.

Merde, she said silently, disgusted with herself.

She went back into the cabin, pulled a sketch pad and pencil out of her backpack, and flipped to the design that was still eluding her. After a few minutes she took a box out of the backpack, opened it carefully, and stared at the amber inside.

No inspiration came.

Gently she picked up the amber, cradling it in her hand, turning it slowly. But no matter how hard she stared at the tantalizing lines, creative lightning didn't strike. Maybe direct sunlight would help.

She tucked the amber into the pocket of her wind shell, grabbed pad and pencil, and went outside. She discovered that the engine cover made a surprisingly comfortable seat. She settled in with her back against the stern. Without taking out the amber, she began trying variations on her design's basic theme, working from memory alone.

Jake stood in the doorway, driving the boat from the aft station while watching the fish finder in the front of the cabin.

Soon a rill of nightingalelike notes rose into the quiet afternoon. Though there was no obvious melody in his whistling, Honor found it both relaxing and mentally stimulating, rather like listening to Gregorian chants. Her pencil flew over one page, then another, then another, trying out various ways of balancing line and shape, evocation and representation, creating the blend of flow and meaning that made her creations unique.

Belatedly she realized that the whistling had stopped and Jake was watching her. She looked up.

"Sorry," he said. "I didn't mean to distract you."

"You didn't. The whistling actually helped me to concentrate. I only noticed when you stopped."

It must be something in the Donovan genes, Jake thought wryly. Kyle had enjoyed "dueling whistles"—Kyle with his pennywhistle and Jake with only his lips.

"What are you working on?" he asked. "Or is asking like peeking over your shoulder?"

She smiled. "It's not peeking if I show you." She turned the pad so that it was right side up for Jake.

"That's the piece of amber you had at the cottage, isn't it?" he said, recognizing the shape and combination of smooth and rough surfaces. "The one I caught before it hit the floor."

"You have a good eye."

"You're a good artist."

"Illustrator."

"Buttercup."

She shot him a sideways glance out of eyes that were nearly as golden as amber touched by slanting, late-afternoon sun.

"Most people can't tell one chunk of amber from another at a glance," she said.

"I suppose so."

"But you can."

Jake shrugged, hating to spoil the peace of the moment with evasions and half-truths. "Amber is an interest of mine. Has been since I was a kid."

"Really? Is that why you asked so many questions about the amber Kyle is supposed to have stolen?"

Jake nodded, but he was cursing silently. Honor was too quick. The less he said right now, the better off he would be when she found out. On the other hand, it was getting tiresome to always teeter along the sharp edges of half-truths and lies, wondering when he was going to be pushed off and cut himself to the bone. If he had liked living that way, he and Ellen would still have the same boss.

"What attracted you to amber when you were a kid?" Honor asked curiously.

"I felt sorry for the flies stuck in the past. What are you drawing?"

She could tell by looking at Jake that she wasn't going to get anywhere if she pursued the subject of why a child would identify with insects trapped in amber. So she answered his question instead of asking another one of her own.

"I'm drawing what Faith will sculpt. Kind of."

"Kind of?"

Honor looked back at the sketch. "I mean, the piece won't be a real sculpture, finished in three dimensions. More of a bas-relief." She frowned at the paper and admitted, "Actually, I'm beginning to think it's a mistake. I'm not getting there from here."

"What do you mean?"

Without answering, she reached inside the loose pocket of her wind shell. When her hand came back out, a hunk of amber gleamed on her palm like every hope of sunlight and warmth ever dreamed by a cold, shivering man.

Jake whistled softly. In the pure light, the amber showed its true worth. It was transparent but for a swirl of tiny bubbles and intriguing flecks of ebony. Polished on one side and delicately crazed on the other, the amber had a satin radiance that redefined the word *golden*.

It burned.

"Ardent stone," he said softly.

"What?"

"That's what amber means. Stone that

burns. May I? I didn't really get a chance to look at this piece before."

"Sure, but there aren't any flies in it."

He didn't say a word. He just held the amber between himself and the descending sun.

Honor caught her breath at the sudden, incandescent beauty of the gem. It was as though she had never really seen it before. The random swirls suggested a man's closely cropped hair and beard, and the ebony flecks evoked half-opened eyes as deep as the human soul...a man caught forever in amber, free only because he had no more to lose.

"Don't move!" she said urgently.

Jake froze in the instant before he realized that there was nothing wrong. She flipped to a new page and began drawing with a speed as dazzling as the amber bathed in sunlight. He watched and held the stone so that its golden shadow fell onto the paper.

A rod tip jerked, catching his eye.

"Uh, Honor..."

"Not yet. I've been trying to see that face ever since I was born."

From the corner of his eye Jake looked at the rod tip closest to him. It was moving up and down much faster and harder than the dodger could account for.

"Honor..."

She made a go-away noise and kept on drawing.

The line did what it was designed to do. It popped out of the down-rigger clip and headed off at an angle.

"Well, hell," he muttered in disgust. "We can always have pizza tonight."

"There. Got it! Or most of it." She looked up. "Pizza? I'd rather have salmon, if it's all the same to you."

"So would I!"

He bent, stuffed the amber back into her pocket, and yanked the rod out of the holder in one continuous motion. A quick upward jerk assured him that the fish was still on the line. The motion of the rod told him the fish was a salmon and it was well and truly hooked.

"Here you go," he said, handing the rod over to Honor and taking the sketch pad. "Reel in our dinner. I'll handle the boat."

"But I can't—I've never—" The rod leaped and quivered in her hands. "My God! Jake, there's really a fish on the other end of this line!"

"Sure is. Reel, buttercup."

11

It was full dark by the time Jake buttoned up the *Tomorrow* for the night and drove to his own cabin to check the answering machine. There was no news from Emerging Resources, but there was a surly message from Ellen on the subject of racing boats and their testosterone-freak drivers.

"Tough kibble, lady," he said. "If you can't run with the wolves, stay in your kennel."

Smiling with a wolfish kind of satisfaction, he grabbed some wine and headed back to Honor. There was another message, of sorts, at the turnoff to her driveway—an unmarked car parked in a little turnout just off the county road. In case anyone wondered what the car was doing there, a radar unit poked out the open window.

Jake wasn't the only one who had noticed the cop's presence. Local traffic, which normally went at least ten miles over the twenty-five-miles-per-hour speed limit on the little road, was going precisely what the law allowed. In Washington State, speed traps were considered a valuable, ecologically sound, endlessly renewable resource that was nourished by ridiculously low speed limits.

Honor opened the front door as soon as the truck coasted to a stop. It shouldn't have pleased Jake that she was watching for him, but it did. What pleased him even more was that, like him, she had showered and changed her clothes. Her hair looked slightly damp and she was wearing casual slacks and a loose blouse that were the same color as her green-and-golden eyes. Talk about looking good enough to eat...

Jake wrenched his mind out of its single track and got out of the car. "Is everything all right?" he asked.

"No. The charcoal is ready and so am I."

He blinked. "For what?"

"Salmon, what else? I'm starved."

So was he, but salmon was distant second to what he really wanted—Honor Donovan, naked, in bed. He grabbed the bottle of cold Chardonnay he had brought from his cabin and followed her into the cottage.

While he made a marinade for the salmon and put it on the barbecue, Honor was right on his heels, proud as a duck with fourteen ducklings.

"Well, the day wasn't entirely wasted," she said, gloating over the fish. "But it's too bad you didn't catch one."

Jake smiled, remembering her dancing excitement when she finally managed to reel in her fish. She had lit up like a Christmas tree. Just watching her had been more fun than he could remember having in a long, long time.

"It doesn't matter," he said, putting the cover on the barbecue. "There will be other salmon for me."

Honor looked uncertain as she followed Jake back into the house. None of the Donovan males had been worried about being outdone by a woman, but some of her dates hadn't taken it very well.

"You're sure?" she asked, shutting the back door.

"Uh huh," Jake said, tugging lightly on a strand of her hair. "I don't mind, honey. Even if I caught a salmon, I would have turned it loose."

"Why?"

"Even after I cleaned it, yours weighed fourteen pounds. By the time you finish eating it in sandwiches, pastas, omelets, and salads, you'll be thinking salmon is another name for too much of a good thing."

"Ha! I've never gotten my fill of fresh salmon. Or good smoked salmon, either."

"In that case, we'll have to get you a big salmon."

"A big one? What do you call that?" She gestured toward the barbecue.

"Good eating. But if you're going to get the best smoking fish, you go for ones over twenty-five pounds. Thirty and up, way up, is best. Unfortunately, there aren't many that big left in the San Juans."

"Thirty pounds?" Her eyes widened. "Good grief. I better start lifting weights. I had a heck of a time bringing this little shrimp to the boat."

"You did fine."

"Really? Then why were you always yelling at me to keep my rod tip up?"

"I wasn't yelling."

"Ha! I thought Captain Conroy was going to fall out of his Zodiac laughing."

"That's because he'd never seen anyone trying to hold a net full of struggling salmon in one hand and an armful of over-the-moon woman in the other."

"Don't forget the fishing rod."

"It's hard to forget holding that in my teeth," Jake said dryly.

It was the only thing that had prevented him from returning Honor's excited kiss. That was just as well. He had a feeling the kiss would have gone from congratulations to raw hunger in a heartbeat. That would have been dumb.

At least, that's what he kept telling himself. But himself wasn't listening. In his mind, Jake kept seeing that crotch-length T-shirt Honor slept in. He couldn't help wondering if she wore underpants beneath. Thinking about that led to other things, like what she looked like when she opened herself to a lover.

"Hello," she said, waving a hand in front of his eyes.

"What?"

"Where are you?"

For an instant he considered telling her that he had been mentally pushing her nightshirt up her hips and searching through her spicy thicket with his tongue until he found the soft woman flesh beneath.

Dumb. Really dumb.

"I was just thinking," he said.

"About dinner?"

"Um...yeah. Dinner."

"How does pesto sound? Or would you rather stick to hot sourdough bread and salad?"

"It all sounds good."

"You must be hungry."

"Yes," he said curtly, stepping away from her. He was also dumber than a row of stumps for even thinking about how good it would feel to slide into her.

"Why don't we have some crackers and cheese right now?" Honor suggested warily. "As grouchy as you are, we'll be at each other's throats before the salmon is done."

Jake knew he was in a rough mood, just as he knew that cheese and crackers wouldn't satisfy the hunger riding him. But food was better than what he had now.

Nothing.

He munched on cheese and crackers, drank a beer, and watched while Honor tossed pesto and pasta together.

"Do you mind if I draw while the salmon cooks?" she asked, setting the pasta aside. "I keep thinking about that face in the amber."

"I don't expect to be entertained."

She gave him a slanting, rather wary glance and headed for her sketch pad.

The telephone rang. Jake expected Honor to hurry across the room and grab it eagerly. Instead, she walked slowly and extended her hand to the receiver as though she expected to be bitten.

"Hello," she said.

"Disassociate yourself from Mr. Mallory or your brother will suffer."

"What? Who is this? Where is—"

The phone went dead. She looked at it in disgust and slammed the receiver back into the cradle. "Damn him!"

"Who was it?"

"I don't know. Not Snake Eyes. This jerk started talking as soon as I said hello."

Jake shut the front door and walked to her. She was pale except for bright spots of anger and adrenaline burning on her cheeks.

"How can you be sure it wasn't Snake Eyes?" he asked.

"Linear logic sure or hunch sure?"

"Either one."

"Actually, it's both. I knew it before he started talking. The silence was different. Anyway, his accent isn't as broad as the one Snake Eyes had when he mumbled around at my front door."

"What kind of accent did this caller have?"

"Not French," Honor said, replaying the words in her mind. "Not quite German. Not Spanish. Not British."

"What do you mean, 'not quite German'?"

"I don't know. It just wasn't."

He didn't push. There was no reason. The odds were nearly one hundred percent that the caller was from Russia itself or one of its satellite states on the Baltic Sea. Nothing new there.

"What did he say?" Jake asked.

Honor took a deep breath. It broke into pieces. Carefully she took another one. Then she looked at Jake with shadowed eyes.

"He told me to get rid of you or Kyle would suffer," she said simply.

Jake's eyes narrowed. "Divide and conquer."

"What?"

"The oldest tactic in the book. And the best. Someone wants you isolated."

She looked out the window. The wild gold of the sun and restless blue of the sea were long gone, leaving only the kind of deep black she didn't want to face alone.

"Kyle..." Honor whispered. "My God, what am I going to do?"

The anguish in her soft voice was like a knife in Jake's conscience. He wanted to comfort her, to reassure her; and if he did, she would only feel all the more deeply betrayed when the truth came out.

He told himself he would be doing everyone a favor if he pointed out all the logical, rational reasons why she shouldn't send him away. He was still listing those reasons in his mind when he found himself holding out his hand.

"Come here," he said softly.

Honor walked into his arms as though she had always known she belonged there. He held her the same way, cursing Kyle with every heartbeat.

"What should I do?" she asked finally.

"Whatever you can live with."

"What about Kyle?"

"He's a big boy. Worry about yourself."

"You keep telling me that."

"I keep hoping you'll listen."

She laughed raggedly. "Talk to me, Jake. I need...to talk."

His arms tightened around her. "I'll go or I'll stay. Your choice, Honor."

"I don't want to choose." She burrowed against him as though the chill she felt was physical rather than mental. "Do you think whoever called has Kyle?"

"No."

"Why?"

"If he already has Kyle, there's no point in hamstringing your search, is there?"

She let out a shaky breath. "That was my second thought. A bluff rather than a real threat."

Jake brushed his lips against her hair too gently for her to feel. Each breath he took was sweet with the scent of warm woman.

"What was your first thought?" he asked.

"I was glad I wasn't here alone. I'm beginning to hate the telephone."

"I'll get you an answering machine."

"I have one. I just can't bear to turn it on when I'm here. I keep thinking that Kyle might be on the other end."

There was nothing Jake could say to that. Certainly there was nothing that Honor would want to hear. So he simply stroked her chin-length, shiny hair and held her until she finally let go of him and moved away.

"Thanks," she said self-consciously. "I didn't mean to, well, you know."

"Er, no."

"Cry on your shoulder."

He touched the dark blue flannel shirt where she had laid her head. "What are you talking about? It's dry as a Baptist revival."

She laughed almost helplessly. Then she took a shaky breath and turned toward the kitchen. "About that wine..."

"I'll get it as soon as I check on the salmon."

The telephone rang again.

Honor flinched. Jake headed toward the

phone. She stopped him by grabbing his wrist.

"No," she said quickly. "I can handle it." She picked up the phone. "Hello?"

Jake tensed and watched her expression.

"I'm sorry," she said automatically. "He isn't here right now. May I take a message?" She frowned. "Really? Can you hang on to it for a while? It's paid for? Good. I'll be in to get it when I can. Thank you."

"Who was it?" he asked as soon as Honor hung up.

"A woman from Watermark Book Store. They have something that Kyle ordered."

"When?"

"They didn't say. Odd, though."

"What?"

"I didn't know my brother was interested in Russian history."

Neither did Jake, but saying it would raise more questions than he wanted to answer.

"Modern stuff?" he asked casually.

"No. She said the book is a catalog of the contents of Russian palaces before the Revolution. He had wanted one specifically on the palace known as Tsarskoye Selo, but there weren't any available."

Jake went still. Before the Nazis invaded Russia, the Tsarskoye Selo had been the home of the Amber Room. His lips thinned and he wondered if alcohol would cut through the bitter taste of fairy dust in his mouth.

"I'll open the wine," he said.

Honor watched Jake stalk to the kitchen. She

knew that he had just lost his temper, but she didn't know why.

"And men say that women are moody," she muttered.

If Jake heard her, he ignored the bait. He opened the wine, poured her a glass, and went out to brood over the barbecue.

Honor didn't make the mistake of tagging along. Her own temper was too uncertain. She picked up her sketch pad, took the amber out of its box, and lost herself in drawing. The Amber Man was still elusive, but she was certain of ultimately drawing him out of his golden prison.

She didn't know when she realized that what she was drawing looked like an echo of Jake's strong features, but after she accepted it the drawing went much faster. It was both Jake and not-Jake, man and shadow, darkness and light, a smile from one direction and a cynically curving mouth from the other.

After a while she became aware that Jake was standing nearby, watching her. She wondered if he recognized himself in the drawing. Probably not. Most people accepted the reversed image of themselves they saw in the mirror as reality.

"Make yourself useful," she said, handing him the piece of amber. "Hold this between me and a strong light source. I need to make certain that the flecks are deep enough to survive if the surface is smoothed and polished."

Jake took the shade off a table lamp and held

up the amber. She bent her head and went back to work.

He tried not to notice that there were shades of gold buried deep in Honor's hair, that her mouth was just full enough to tempt a saint, that the slim fingers holding the pencil would have felt good inside his pants, and her mouth would have felt even better. But nothing would feel as good as watching her come apart when he was buried to the hilt in her.

The direction of his thoughts was echoed in the hard length of his erection. He was grateful that she was too busy drawing to notice.

"You're making me nervous," Honor said after a time.

"Afraid I'll drop the amber?"

"Nope. I'm feeling like Little Red again. Dinner-ish. Think the salmon is done, Granny?"

"Do I look like your grandmother?"

"Well," she said without looking up, "you both have a nice mustache...."

Shaking his head, smiling despite the hungry ache in his crotch, Jake handed Honor the amber and went to check on the salmon.

As soon as he was out of sight, she let out her breath and looked at the place where he had stood. She wouldn't have been surprised to see smoke curling up from the floor. Or from her own chair. The way he had watched her was hot enough to cook both of them.

She told herself that she didn't need the kind of complication that an affair with Jake would bring. She didn't have the emotional energy for it. And her emotions would definitely be involved. Without that, sex was more trouble than it was worth.

Face it, she reminded herself briskly. *Even with emotion, sex is more trouble than it's worth.* At least for a woman it was. Men did just fine on autopilot. *Wham, bam, I'm outta here. No fuss, no muss, stuff it back in your pants and see if there's a good game on TV.*

With an impatient movement Honor set aside her sketch pad and closed it. Yet the face locked within amber haunted her, calling silently to her. No matter how she felt about its living model, she couldn't leave the face caught forever within time.

Unfortunately she didn't know how to free it. She only knew that her normal approach to designing sculpture wouldn't work for amber in general and this piece of amber in particular. She simply hadn't worked with amber enough to understand it the way she did harder stones.

When Jake came back into the room carrying a platter of salmon, Honor was sitting and frowning fiercely at the amber. Her glass of wine hadn't been touched.

"I'm not the only one in a bad mood, am I?" he asked neutrally, setting the salmon down on the table. "Did you get another call while I was watching the fish?"

She jumped, wondering how much time had passed. It was often like that when she started thinking about a design. The world simply went away.

"No calls. I was just thinking about that face. If I try to design my usual bas-relief..." She shook her head and stood up abruptly. "It just won't work. I'm sure of it."

"What about intaglio?"

Honor stopped in the act of reaching for her wineglass. What she knew about intaglio could about be summarized very briefly: the opposite of cameo.

"I've never tried designing something to be viewed through the gem rather than on its surface," she said.

"Why? Don't like the result?"

"It's not that." She put her wineglass on the table and went to the refrigerator. "I'm usually designing for quite small pieces or stones that aren't translucent enough for intaglio to show through. Sometimes the gem is simply too hard for Faith to carve that way. Plus I never designed with amber until a month ago."

Honor set out the pasta and salad. Her eyes had a distant look in them that told Jake she was thinking about amber and intaglio.

"Intaglio was popular in the seventeenth and eighteenth centuries," he said, "especially for amber. In some cases the internal carving would be backed with gold foil. When viewed from above, through the amber itself, the result is very striking, almost alive."

"How do you polish the carved area before you add the foil?"

"Same way you carved it—carefully, with itty bitty tools."

When he leaned past her to pour wine for

himself, his arm brushed hers. She jumped.

"Sorry," Jake said. What he didn't say was that even when she was thinking about her work, she was strung so tight she damn near vibrated. "Didn't mean to startle you."

"It's not your fault. No matter what I'm doing, underneath it all I'm still worried about Kyle," she admitted.

"Understandable. Sit down and eat. Or are you too jumpy?"

"No worse than breakfast or lunch." She smiled wryly and sat. "I'm afraid I'm not one of those women who become artfully thin from worrying. Just the opposite."

"So what's the problem? You could use a few more pounds."

"Bite your tongue."

"I'd rather bite your salmon."

Honor assured herself she had imagined a slight hesitation before Jake said "salmon." Then she reached for the delectable pink fish and told herself to quit hoping. It was pretty clear after the long day on the boat that he wasn't going to do anything about the prowling sexual tension that had grown between them. Though he obviously was a healthy male fully capable of getting an erection, he just as obviously wasn't going to pursue it. Or her.

Maybe he felt the same way she did about sex. About as exciting as cleaning the toilet.

Depressing thought.

Jake noticed that Honor hadn't started eating. "No appetite after all?"

Rather than answer, she forked in a bite of

salmon. A moment later she made a throaty sound of surprise and delight.

"Like it?" he asked.

"Orgasmic."

His eyebrows climbed. "That good, huh?"

"Better."

"Nothing's better."

Since *orgasm* was just a word to her, Honor decided not to argue the point. She tucked another bite into her mouth and savored the salmon. She didn't say another thing until she had eaten two servings of the fish and cleaned up her share of the salad and pesto. Then she settled back in her chair with a sigh of pleasure.

"You should open a restaurant," she said, covering a yawn.

"You did the salad and pesto. Is your pesto recipe a Donovan family secret? I've been buying mine and it's not half as good."

"Nope. My pesto recipe is the result of years of selfless sacrifice in the hope of a better future for all mankind."

"They don't hand out a Nobel for pesto."

"Next thing you'll tell me there isn't a Santa Claus."

"Now that you mention—"

"I'm crushed," she interrupted, "just crushed. Anyway, the pesto was nothing compared to the fish," she added with a wave of her hand that ended up covering another yawn.

Jake stood up and began clearing the table.

"I'll take care of it," she said, yawning again.

"You'll fall asleep first."

"Your point?" she muttered.

"Go to bed. Tomorrow is already racing across Europe toward you."

"What an awful thought."

He laughed and ruffled her hair casually as he passed by her chair. "Don't forget to brush your teeth."

For an instant Honor considered biting him. Hard.

Instead, she decided to get even by taking him up on his offer. "Okay. Thanks."

Breath held, Jake watched Honor walk to the tiny bathroom that was just off the bedroom. For a second there, he had been sure she was going to sink her neat little teeth into his hand. He didn't know what he would have done next, but he had no doubt about the ultimate outcome—the two of them locked in the kind of sweaty, hand-to-hand combat that had no losers.

Cursing silently, he finished the dishes, scrubbing them hard enough to leave ruts in the shiny surface.

The door to the bathroom opened. From the corner of his eye he saw the flash of color that was Honor as she went from the bathroom to the bedroom. The door didn't quite shut behind her.

When Jake finished cleaning up, he let himself out of the cottage. The door locked automatically behind him. The metal sound was cool and final. He walked down the gravel path to the dock. Every step of the way he congratulated himself on what a fine, honorable, noble, dumb son of a bitch he was, going off alone to a cold bed.

12

It was still dark when Honor was startled awake. Her alarm clock wasn't screaming at her, but her instincts were.

She could hear the scratching sounds from the living room with terrible clarity. It sounded like someone was fumbling a key into the front door lock. Her heartbeat speeded. *Kyle?*

But if it wasn't...

She realized suddenly that she hadn't shot the bolt before she fell asleep.

The vague scratching sounds continued. A chill prickled over her skin. She had a sickening feeling that it wasn't her brother out there trying to get in.

Part of her wanted to pull the covers over her head and pretend she wasn't there at all. Part of her wanted to scream down the house.

In the end she didn't do either one. Making as little noise as possible, she eased from beneath the blankets and went barefoot to the bedroom door. It was open a few inches, just enough for air to circulate.

A gust of cold swirled through the living room to the bedroom. The front door was wide open. A silhouette moved through the moonlight pouring inside. A human figure.

A pencil of light came from a small flash-light. The beam played over Kyle's desk. When the figure bent over and started opening drawers, reflected light showed only the black of a ski mask, dark jacket, and leather gloves.

Fear and rage burst through Honor. The combination left her light-headed with adrenaline. *The burglar was already inside.*

Silently she retreated from the doorway and went to the window. The new lock didn't squeak when she opened it, but the old wooden frame did. It was much louder than the scratching noises had been.

Fear of being trapped in the bedroom by the intruder slammed through Honor. She shoved upward with all her strength and then kicked through the bottom half of the opening, taking out the screen as she went through. She stumbled when she hit the ground, recovered, and ran toward the dock.

Honor didn't know she was screaming Jake's name until he ran toward her from the direction of the dock. He was naked as a hook.

"Honor, what's wrong!"

"A m-man. In the cottage. He—"

"Is he armed?" Jake interrupted.

"All I s-saw was a flashlight."

"Lock yourself in the boat. Don't open up until you see me."

"But—"

It was too late. Jake was already headed for the house at a run. Unlike her, he didn't use the moonlit path. He stuck to the shadows. When he reached the house, the front door was wide open. Papers were scattered across the porch. No sounds came from inside.

He went in low and hard through the open door. Crouching, listening, he turned swiftly in an arc that covered the whole room. The gun in his fist was a darker shade of night.

Even in the faint moonlight, the interior of the cottage looked like it had been through a storm. The only question was whether the prowler was still hanging around or if he had run out the door when Honor started screaming. If he was smart, he was gone. But Jake knew that fairy dust had a bad effect on brain cells. It shrank them.

Quietly he eased along the edges of the room until he was within reach of the bedroom door. It was ajar. He kicked it hard enough to make the door slam open against the wall or anyone who might be hiding there. The instant his bare heel connected with the door he spun aside and waited, listening. He heard nothing but his own careful breathing.

Then, from somewhere well beyond the driveway, came the sound of an engine starting up. The prowler, presumably. But not certainly.

With a silent curse, Jake grabbed a heavy book from the mess at his feet and heaved it into the bedroom. Before the book finished making a racket on the floor, he was in the bedroom, crouched as he had been in the living room, his gun a swift arc taking in every corner.

He was alone.

Just to be certain, he went through every space

in the cottage that was big enough to hide a man. Then he started circling the exterior. He was almost finished when he heard faint footsteps behind him.

Jake sank down into a deep patch of shadow and waited, breathing lightly. He was ninety-seven percent certain who was out there, but that last three percent could be fatal. After a few more breaths a shape went by. He attacked as silently as he had waited.

Honor would have screamed but his hand was clamped over her mouth. She would have bitten him but his fingers were cupped so that she couldn't reach them. She would have kicked but he was holding her so that she couldn't reach anything vital. She would have run but her feet were dangling six inches off the ground.

"The next time I tell you to stay put, you damn well better stay put," Jake said roughly against her ear.

"Mmmph!"

"Is that an apology?" he asked, lifting his hand.

"Listen, you arro—"

His hand descended again. "No, *you* listen. I wasn't expecting anyone out here but a prowler who might or might not be armed. You should be damned grateful that I'm not the kind who empties a gun into the night just because a shadow moves. I could have killed you. Do you understand?"

Honor went completely still. She understood all too well.

"Good," Jake muttered.

He lifted his hand from her mouth and put her back on her feet. He could tell the exact moment she spotted his gun. Her breath broke and she looked up at him sharply.

"Don't worry, it's on safety," he said. It had been since he felt her breasts flattened beneath his forearm and her nice ass rubbing on his thigh. But he didn't mention any of that. He had a feeling she wouldn't want to hear it.

"I'm—I'm sorry," Honor said. "I didn't hear anything and I was worried that you were hurt."

"Just my feet."

"What?" She knelt swiftly. "Where? I don't see any blood."

Jake's breath came in hard and fast. Her hair was drifting across his skin. If she moved her head just an inch or two, she would be touching something a hell of a lot more sensitive than a bare thigh.

His heart slammed. At this rate, she wouldn't have to move at all. He was rising to her like a blind moth to a particularly hot flame.

"Jake?" she asked, looking up. "Where does it—oh!"

"Don't let it worry you."

"Why? Is it on safety, too?"

He gave a crack of laughter and stepped back. "Go see if anything is missing."

"Doesn't look like it from here," she said under her breath.

"Unless you want to be flat on your back in the dirt, go into the cottage."

She shot to her feet, embarrassed that he had

overheard her. "Sorry. I'm a little rattled."

"So am I."

"You? Rattled?"

He grunted. "If this keeps up, I'm going to start sleeping in shoes."

Honor winced in silent sympathy as he stalked down the path to the boat. Her own feet ached and stung from her barefoot run to the dock.

Even knowing the cottage was empty, she hesitated before going inside. Adrenaline still coursed through her blood, making her shake. Or it could have been the temperature of the night air. She hadn't noticed it until now, but the shirt she had pulled on at the boat—Jake's shirt, in fact—let in a lot of breeze around the bottom. Beneath her usual night-time T-shirt, her rear was frankly cold.

Her hands were even colder. She could hardly feel the switch inside the door. When she finally managed to flip it on, she wished she hadn't. The cozy little room looked like it had been turned on end and shaken.

For the first time Honor really understood that the small sounds she had heard were those of an intruder ransacking the room, not the noise made by someone fumbling to get past the front door's old lock. The knowledge that she had been asleep while a man systematically trashed the place not fifteen feet from her head made her feel sick. She crossed her arms over her stomach and swallowed hard. Then she swallowed again.

"I thought that was my shirt," Jake said.

She made a sound as though she had been struck. Her knees began shaking.

"Honor? Honey?"

She tried to talk, couldn't, and simply held on to herself as wave after wave of adrenaline and nausea swept through her.

"Easy, sweetheart," he said. "Did he hurt you?"

She shook her head.

"Aftershocks," he said quietly, relieved. "Don't worry. They don't last long. It just seems like it." He shot the dead bolt home and turned back to her. "Breathe in through your nose and out through your clenched teeth. It will help the nausea."

After a few attempts Honor got it right. By the time Jake had gone from room to room, making certain that the cottage was buttoned up, she no longer felt like throwing up. She was still shaking, though. When she stopped clenching her teeth, they chattered.

Keeping a wary eye on her, Jake knelt and made a fire in the small fireplace. "Come over here," he said when the flames started to dance. "It will help you get warm."

"C-can't."

He wasn't surprised. The way Honor's legs were trembling it was a wonder she was still standing. He dragged the old couch close to the fire, grabbed a blanket from the bedroom, and went back to her.

"Don't be startled," he said in a soothing voice. "I'm going to pick you up."

Even with the warning, she jerked when he lifted her.

"It's all right," he said. "I won't hurt you, honey. I'm just bringing you closer to the fire."

Her breath came out in too many pieces to be called a sigh, but she relaxed against him. Her cheek was almost cold against the bare skin of his shoulder. When he started to put her on the couch, she wrapped her arms around his neck and hung on hard. After a moment of hesitation, he sat down on the couch, still holding her.

He couldn't fold the blanket around her unless she let go of him, and she showed no signs of doing that. Her skin was as white as salt. Her eyes were dry and wild. She was still shaking. He dragged the blanket over both of them as best he could and held her while she trembled.

"Adrenaline is a funny drug," he said. "Especially if you aren't used to it. Knocks you over like a tidal wave."

She made a sound that he took as agreement.

"When adrenaline hits some people," he said, "they freeze and stay frozen. They couldn't scream or run if their life depended on it. Other people holler loud enough to put your alarm clock to shame."

Honor's lips tried to smile. As smiles went, it wasn't much, but Jake felt like he had been given a gift. She was shivering less now and leaning into him more. Slowly her skin was warming against his.

"Either way," he said, "freeze or scream, hide or flee, the choice usually isn't a conscious one. Your body decides and you go along for the ride. When the crisis passes, there you are, still loaded with adrenaline and no place to go. So you stand there and shake or you pace everywhere and shake or you throw up your toenails and then you shake."

"How—" Honor's voice cracked. Her dry tongue tried to moisten equally dry lips. "How do you know?"

"The usual way. Been there. Done that. And yes, I have the shirt to prove it."

"Where is it?" she said, rubbing her cheek against his bare chest.

"You're wearing it."

Honor started laughing and kept on. She knew what Jake had said wasn't that funny, but she couldn't stop laughing. She tried to explain or to apologize or just to say his name. Her voice kept breaking over the laughter she couldn't control.

"It's okay," he said. "Don't fight it. Let it out. It's a harmless way for your body to let off steam."

He gathered her closer and held on to her until the laughing jag ran down to a ragged kind of breathing. Finally her breaths evened out and the waves of trembling passed. She drew air in deeply and sighed so hard that it stirred the hair on his chest.

Jake's body pulsed to full alert. So did his conscience. For some people, danger could act as a world-class aphrodisiac. Honor might well be one of them. He would be a selfish, insensitive, exploitive bastard if he took advantage of her.

And he wanted to. That was the problem. He had gotten used to the effects of adrenaline, but he wasn't making any headway getting used to his inconvenient lust for Honor Donovan.

Subtly he changed position, trying to get more distance between their bodies. She followed him like water following gravity. Utterly natural. Completely unstoppable.

Jake told his conscience to get stuffed. Honor was old enough to decide if and when and where and how to take a lover. If the time was here and now, he was ready, willing, and able to the point of outright pain.

He shifted his hold on her, curving her more deeply into his body. "Better?" he asked, his voice husky.

"Yes, but..." Honor sighed again. "Is it always this bad? I feel like an idiot."

"You get used to it after a time."

"Feeling like an idiot?"

"That too."

She laughed softly. This time it was amusement rather than the crumbling edge of hysteria.

"More lessons learned in rough bars?" she asked.

"Among other places. The first few times you run slam into danger are the worst."

"After that it's no big deal?"

"After that it isn't new anymore. You react,

237

but not as much. Want some wine or brandy to settle your nerves?"

"Only if neither one of us has to move. I'm just getting warmed up."

Jake was already warm and then some. He liked the feel of Honor's cheek on his bare chest and her breath like a hot silk brush against his skin. He liked even better the feel of her hips snuggled into his lap. He would have liked it best of all if he were still naked, but he was smarter than that. Half smart, anyway; he had pulled jeans on before coming back to the cottage. If he asked nicely, maybe Honor would give him the shirt off her back. And the T-shirt, too.

"Jake?"

"Yeah?"

"That—that creature. He was here while I was asleep. He could have—"

"Try not to think about it," Jake interrupted.

"Try not breathing," she retorted.

"Okay."

With that he lowered his mouth to hers. He meant to be gentle and polite and patient and all those things a man is supposed to be the first time he kisses a woman he wants to seduce, but adrenaline was still lighting up his blood. Even if it hadn't been, he would have been in over his head with a single taste of her. His body had been on a sexual red alert since the first time he saw Honor.

The kiss went from simple contact to raw passion with the speed of a burning fuse.

Honor didn't fight it or the man who was holding her. She was discovering that she had never needed anything as much as she needed the heat of Jake's body against hers, the hunger of his tongue thrusting into her mouth, the friction of his big hands rubbing over her from shoulders to hips and back, rocking her against him.

She responded without hesitation or thought, matching him hunger for hunger, thrust for thrust, her hands kneading his body with a liberty that would have shocked her if she were thinking at all. But she wasn't. She was just feeling, and what she was feeling made her melt and run in his hands like liquid silk.

When he finally tore his mouth free of hers, she was on her back, her thighs were wrapped around the rough fabric of his jeans, and she was making husky noises in her throat. Hot, sexy, reckless, she rubbed against him until the satin fire of her heat sank through his jeans and into him.

Even as Jake raked his fingers through his pocket, seeking a condom, he knew he should slow down, give Honor a chance to change her mind. But he didn't want to. He didn't even know if he could. He needed her too much.

Just when he was on the point of finding out how much self-control he had left, she arched, dragging herself over his erection. He stopped thinking at all. He barely managed to slow down long enough to put on the condom before he sank into the heat between her thighs. She fit him better than the high-tech condom, hotter, sleeker. He groaned and pushed into her until she could take no more of him.

But he wanted to go even deeper. She was tight and wet and he would go crazy if he couldn't bury himself completely in her.

Honor made a low sound and tried to ease the stretching feeling of having Jake inside her body. Sex had never been particularly comfortable for her. It was one of the reasons she had tried it only a few times.

"Jake?"

"Easy, honey. Take a deep breath and let it out."

"I can't. You haven't left me any room!"

"Sure there is." He bit her lower lip tenderly. Her breath jerked in, then unraveled in a broken sigh when he ran his tongue over her lip like a cat licking cream. "See?" he asked.

She wasn't sure what she was supposed to see. She knew only that he filled her in a way that made her restless. But it wasn't really uncomfortable. Not anymore. Nothing like her memories, where discomfort and disappointment in sex finally became boredom and impatience to get the whole thing over with.

"Go ahead," she said. "It's okay now."

"Okay isn't nearly good enough."

Jake shifted just enough to get his hand between their bodies. He circled around the tight, sensitive lips holding him until she shivered and sultry heat licked over his fingers. He captured the sleek love knot and rubbed until her breath broke again and passion welled up slick and hot between them.

"Lock your legs around me again," he said, his voice almost rough.

"But—"

Honor's voice broke as his fingers plucked, sending the most incredible sensations splintering through her. Her hips jerked and jerked again, seeking him hungrily, sliding over him, taking all of him and wanting every bit of it.

He fought against losing control as he sank deeply into her. He told himself to slow down, to take her with him over the edge, but it was already too late. His whole body corded as he came with a violence that made him shout through his clenched teeth.

Arms tight around Jake's back, Honor held him close, his body locked to hers. The shudders that racked him set off silvery shivers deep inside her, like light stirring before dawn. The feeling was as new as her pleasure in holding a man buried deep inside her. She found that she liked Jake's weight, his powerful body completely relaxed against hers, his broken breathing gradually evening out, his skin sleek and sweaty beneath her hands.

Without understanding why, she turned her head, tasted his salty shoulder, and bit him not quite gently. She felt the ripple of response that went through him. Relaxation changed into tension. He burrowed against her neck and returned the love bite with slow deliberation.

The odd, glittery feelings swirled through Honor again. She shifted restlessly. He bit her again, harder. Heat splintered through her. With a soft cry she arched, giving herself to the startling pleasure of his mouth against her neck. He sucked on her hot skin and rocked slowly between her legs. With every motion he made, the quicksilver sensations increased in her until she couldn't breathe.

"Jake?" she whispered, not even realizing that she spoke.

"I know. I'll take care of it."

Before she could ask what he meant, he lifted himself off her and reached for his jeans again.

"No," she said, grabbing hold of his arm, afraid that he thought she wanted him to stop.

"You want to put it on me this time, is that it?"

Honor didn't know what she wanted. It took her a few moments even to understand what Jake was talking about. Then she grabbed the small packet, tore it open, and looked from the condom to him. Curious in a way she never had been before about a man, she ran her fingertip from the blunt base of his erection all the way to the broad tip. Smooth but not soft, not cool to the touch

"Amber man," she said. "Stone that burns."

His breath hissed in at her words and delicate, questing touch. "A side benefit of going off like a teenager seems to be the speed of recovery."

"What do you mean?" Honor asked without looking up. She was finding that she liked all the textures of his masculinity. She more than liked them. She was fascinated by her amber lover.

"I know I didn't please you," he said.

That got her attention. "What are you talking about? You gave me more pleasure than I've ever had from sex."

Jake stared at her for a moment, trying to subdue the sudden, wild hammering of his blood. He might as well have saved his energy for what was coming. He wanted her as much as he had the first time. Then with a sense of shock he realized that he wanted her even more.

"You know," he said as he reached for Honor, "I was thinking that the second time was going to be easy for me, lots of patience for technique and no worrying about too soon or too late or not at all. Wrong again."

Honor blinked. "I'm missing something."

"You sure are."

His smile was slow and thorough. It set every one of her nerves alight.

"So tell me," she said.

"Put that on me, honey. There are times when words just don't get the job done."

With a sideways look, she began smoothing the condom into place. She wasn't experienced enough to be quick about it, but Jake didn't complain. He just watched with eyes that burned. When she was finished, she faced him.

"Now what?" she asked.

"Now I do what I've been wanting to do ever since that alarm clock of yours interrupted my one attempt at shaving in the past month."

He slid his hands up Honor's calves and kept on going until her thighs separated beneath his caressing palms. She made a startled sound when he bent and tasted her as though she were an exotic dessert. Then her breathing shattered into a word that was his name.

"Don't worry about a thing," he said, circling the hot love knot with his tongue. "This one is on me."

She didn't know what he meant until the quicksilver feelings of pleasure changed into sharp, burning claws raking her into full arousal for the first time in her life. When she thought she could bear no more of the twisting, relentless, fiery tension, she told him to stop the sweet torment. He laughed and slid long fingers into her, stretching her even as he sucked on the sweet knot of her desire. Suddenly she had no voice, no words, nothing but an ecstasy so unexpected and astonishing that she would have screamed if she had the breath.

Jake entered her at the peak of her climax, driving her even higher, teaching her with every stroke of his body that she had reservoirs of sensuality and strength that she had never suspected. He was teaching himself, too. The soul-deep honesty of her response took his own arousal to new heights, new intensity, new possibilities.

Her broken words of passion and love pushed him over the edge. His last coherent thought was that he was a fool to give and take so much from a woman whose love would turn to hate as soon as she found out who he really was.

A few hours later Jake came close to throwing Honor's alarm clock through the wall. Swearing in a bastard combination of Russian and English, he fumbled for the shrieking monster, silenced it with a blow from his fist, and pulled the covers back into place.

Mumbling something sleepy, Honor burrowed into his warmth. He wrapped his arms around her and looked out the window. Not even the barest hint of predawn light showed.

"Wake up, honey," he said, biting her ear gently. "It's time to be up and about and fishing."

A warm hand drifted down from his chest to his belly and just below. He felt as much as heard her laughter when she discovered him.

"Fishing, huh?" she said. "Dibs on this rod. Wonder what I'll catch?"

He sucked in his breath. Hard. "Uh, Honor..."

She made a low sound that was part laughter and mostly pure female pleasure at what she held in her hand.

"Honey," he said, "you keep that up and you're going to spend the day the same way you spent the night."

"Promises, promises."

Jake grabbed the last of his self-control, pulled her hand to his lips, and kissed it rather fiercely.

"That wouldn't be a good idea," he said.

"Why not?"

He slid his fingers down to the spicy, wonderfully female center of her. "Because I'm betting you're sore, that's why." He probed lightly. "Right?"

Her breath hissed in as her body stretched and awakened, remembering ecstasy and hungering for more of it in the same instant.

"Yes and no," she said. "I'm a little sore, but it would be a great idea."

Regretfully, Jake withdrew from the warmth he ached to bury himself in. "We'll give you time to heal."

"How much time?"

"A few days."

The look of dismay on Honor's face made him want to ravish and cherish her at the same time.

"Way too long," she said.

"I don't want to hurt you," he said simply. "I can wait."

"I've spent my life waiting and didn't even know it. To hell with more waiting."

He laughed and tugged lightly on her tangled hair. "Does that mean I didn't bore you?"

"Bore me? What are you talking—ohmygod," she said, remembering. "I actually said that sex was boring, didn't I?"

"Yeah."

"You're the exception that proves the rule." She gave him an off-center smile. "Come here and be exceptional."

As Jake bent down to her mouth, he told himself that he could kiss her and pet her a little—

hell, a lot—and please her wildly without riding her.

Honor was well on her way to ecstasy when the phone rang. She made a muffled sound of denial and rejection, but the phone kept ringing. Jake took one more deep, drugging taste of her and forced himself to lift his head.

"Did you remember to turn on the answering machine?" he asked.

"When would I have done that? You haven't let me out of bed. And vice versa."

Jake laughed, then kissed her so delicately that she hovered on the brink of shattering climax.

The sound of the phone was shattering, period.

"Go ahead and answer it," he said. "I'll remember where we left off."

The phone rang again. She grabbed the receiver because it was the only way she could think of to shut up the phone.

"Do you know what time it is?" Honor snarled.

"I thought so!" Archer said, sounding as angry as she did. "What the hell do you think you're doing at Kyle's house after I told you to leave?"

Amusement flickered over Honor's features as she looked at Jake lying so hard and ready between her legs. "You don't want to know what I'm doing, Archer."

Jake's body stilled.

"You're right," her brother snapped. "All I want to know is that you've hauled your stubborn butt out of town."

"No can do. I'm staying."

"Honor, listen to me. Leave right now."

"Allow me to point out that there isn't a thing you can do about your commands. I'm here and you're there and life's tough all over."

"Listen to reason—"

"Beats listening to your orders," she interrupted, yawning. "Say something reasonable. I'm listening."

There was a seething silence followed by a heartfelt *"Shit."*

"Now that's really reasonable, big brother. Any other little pearl of wisdom you want me to listen to? *Crap,* maybe? How about *caca?* And let's not forget the all-purpose *merde.*"

"Honor, this isn't funny."

"I'm sorry your sense of humor stinks. See how reasonable I'm being? Polite, too."

Jake muffled his laughter against her thigh, but that put him very close to real temptation. He remembered all too well where he had left off.

Honor sucked in her breath. He was teasing her in the most delightful way, drawing hot designs on her skin with his tongue and then nibbling along the cooling lines.

"All right," Archer said harshly. "I didn't want to scare you, but you don't leave me any choice. I'm hearing rumors that some really ugly folks are after Kyle or the stolen amber or both."

"Do you think they found Kyle?" she asked,

afraid all over again for her missing brother.

Jake paused in his sensual play. The fear in Honor's voice was echoed in the sudden tension of her body, a tightness that had nothing to do with rising desire.

"I don't know," Archer said, his voice rough with frustration. "I only know they're looking."

"But why go to all this trouble for some amber that could be replaced with a few trips to the mines?"

"It's not that simple."

"I'm listening."

"I don't have time to educate you in the bleak, bloody stupidity of clan warfare carried on in the ruins of empire. Take my word for it. You're in danger as long as you stay there. Get out."

"I believe you, but—"

"No buts," he interrupted. "I'm coming down the instant the weather lifts enough for a plane to get out."

"What's the rush? Do you think Kyle is here?"

"I think someone should be there."

"No problem, I'm here."

"Damn it, haven't you been listening? You could be right in the line of fire! The men looking for Kyle aren't the churchgoing, baby-kissing, kind-to-mother type."

"I figured that out for myself after the one-way phone calls and the boats following me, and the—"

"Boats?" Archer interrupted swiftly. "Have

you been out in the *Tomorrow*?"

"Yes. I think Kyle—"

"Are you crazy?" he interrupted

"I'm your sister, does that count?"

Archer exploded. "You don't have the faintest idea how to handle a boat! You have no business playing around with—"

"I hired someone," she interrupted loudly.

"To do what?"

"To teach me to run the boat."

Jake tried not to tense. He wasn't successful. Not that Honor would have noticed. She was already strung as tightly as a recurved bow.

"Did you ask for references?" Archer asked.

"Yes." It was the truth as far as it went. She *had* asked. She just hadn't gotten any. "Jake is a very good boat driver. He knows Sea-Sports and he's learning how to deal with Kyle's chart plotter. We went through a lot of stored courses yesterday."

"Are you doing what I think you're doing?"

"Looking for Kyle? Of course. I may be your sister, but I'm not completely crazy."

"Honor. Listen. Please. It's too dangerous."

"Jake can handle himself." He also could handle her exceptionally well, but she didn't think Archer would appreciate that discovery nearly as much as she did.

"Does Jake have a last name?"

"So you can have Donovan International detectives vet him?" she asked sweetly.

"Jake who?" was Archer's only response.

"Mallory."

There was a charged silence.

Honor didn't like it. She knew all about the quiet that preceded a major Donovan storm.

"Is he about six feet two, moves like a fighter, light eyes and dark hair, scar on one eyebrow and a small one on his lip?" Archer asked softly.

Honor felt the room falling away. She didn't know what a fighter moved like, but the rest fit. "Yes," she whispered.

"You little fool. He's the one who framed Kyle. He could even be Kyle's killer. Get out of that house and stay out."

13

Honor's horrified expression told Jake everything he didn't want to know. She was looking at him the way a kid would look at the man who shot and mounted Santa's reindeer on the den wall.

He took the phone from her hand before she could stop him. "Hello, Archer. Telling lies again, I see."

Silence came, then a swiftly drawn breath. "Mallory!"

"Yeah."

"*You son of a bitch.* If you so much as touch Honor I'll—"

"Shove it," Jake said through his teeth. "You're the one who sent her to the firing line, not me."

"I didn't know—"

"Shove that, too," Jake interrupted. "There's a lot you don't know but it hasn't stopped you from shooting off your goddamn mouth, has it?"

"Listen, you assh—"

"You listen," Jake said, talking right over Archer. "I've had it with you Donovans riding roughshod over all the rest of us. Kyle took that amber and ran, and all your Donovan lies won't pin that stinking rose on me. Got that?"

"Put Honor back on."

"When I'm finished."

"Oh, you're finished all right," Archer said softly. "You hurt Honor and I'll bury you alive."

"Better make sure she isn't buried with me."

"Are you threatening to—"

"I'm telling you," Jake snarled. "I'm not the only one here. Dimitri Pavlov showed up on Honor's doorstep a week ago."

"What?"

"He answered her ad for a fishing guide."

"Jesus."

"Then there's the guy who tossed Kyle's cottage last night. He was a pro, too. He left a mess as a warning, but he was so quiet about it Honor almost didn't wake up and get out the window to me before he got around to questioning her."

Honor stiffened as though she had been slapped. It was one thing to fear a burglar who maybe had more on his mind than theft. It was another to hear violence talked about as though it were so many ounces of amber, jade, or pearls.

Jake flicked a glance at Honor, then concentrated on Archer again. The silence on the other end of the line would have bothered most people. It didn't bother Jake. He knew Archer well enough to know that he had put his emotions on hold; right now Archer was sorting through the mess in search of solutions with a speed and clarity that had overwhelmed more than one competitor.

Besides, Jake had plenty to keep him occupied without Archer snarling in his ear. Honor was edging away from him, easing closer to the point where she could lunge out of bed and beyond his reach. He didn't know what was going on behind her wide, green-gold eyes, but he had no doubt that if he let her go he wouldn't see her again.

"Anything else?" Archer asked after a moment.

"Does the Forest Brotherhood have a line on the Amber Room?" Jake asked.

Archer started swearing.

"I'll take that as a hearty yes," Jake interrupted, watching Honor without seeming to. "Which means that Kyle knew about it through Marju, right?"

"You'll have to ask Marju," Archer said.

"Ask her for me."

"We'd have to find her first."

"Shouldn't be tough. Try your home office."

"What makes you think she's there?"

"Before I was kicked out, I got a frantic phone call from her saying that Donovan International had sent their hounds after her and had I heard from Kyle."

253

"Good question. Have you?"

"Not since I handed over the amber shipment to Donovan International's representative—Kyle Donovan."

"So you say."

Jake went still. "Yes. That's what I say. My word is good, *Donovan*. Ask anyone, anywhere."

"Everyone has a price. The Amber Room was yours."

"Not mine. Kyle's."

"This isn't getting us anywhere. Put Honor on."

"Give me your number."

"Put her on," Archer said. "Now."

"Give me your number."

Honor gathered herself for a lunge off the bed.

Jake's hand flashed out and grabbed her thigh, pinning her in place. He met the silent rage in her eyes head-on. Despite his facade of cool control, he was as furious as both Donovans put together.

"She'll call you after we've sorted out some things," Jake said softly.

The quality of the silence that came over the line was somehow different this time. He guessed why. Archer was probably trying to squeeze the receiver into a thin paste. That was the problem with telephones—you couldn't get your hands on the guy who was pissing you off.

"I'll call in five minutes," Archer said. "If Honor doesn't answer, my next call will be to the cops."

"Fifteen minutes."

"Five."

Jake was holding a dead phone. He hung up without looking away from Honor.

"Go ahead," he said. "Say it."

"Let go of me."

"No. You'll run, I'll catch you, and we'll be a lot less comfortable on the floor than we are right here."

There had been many times in Honor's life when she wished for the size and power of her brothers, but never had she wanted that stature so savagely as she did now. It would have given her a great deal of satisfaction to hammer Jake Mallory between the cracks of the hardwood floor.

He knew it. He was watching her with a wariness that would have pleased her if she weren't so furious.

"Well, at least you aren't physically afraid of me," he said after a moment. "You trust me that much."

"A moron's trust. How gratifying for you."

The cool acid in Honor's voice told Jake that five minutes wouldn't be nearly enough to make her understand.

"If I had come to you," he said roughly, "and told you that the Donovan clan was trying to frame me for what your beloved brother Kyle did and I needed you to prove that I was innocent, you would have slammed the door in my face."

"Delightful thought."

"Not for me. My company has been booted

out of the Baltics and shit-listed in Russia. Unlike the Donovan brothers, I don't have a vast family fortune to cushion my fall. I fight or I go under and stay there. I'm not going under."

Honor looked at the grim lines of Jake's face and didn't doubt a word he said.

"I'd like to meet the man who gave you those scars," she said. "I'd hire him on the spot."

"They don't post want ads in hell."

There was nothing warm and reassuring about Jake's eyes at the moment. They were winter cold and as unforgiving as the hell he had just mentioned. She swallowed and wondered for the first time if she shouldn't be afraid of him.

She wanted to be. It would make everything so much easier. But she wasn't.

Rather distantly she wondered what the IQ of a moron really was. Probably close to absolute zero, if her own so-called brain was any guide—she was the one who had been babbling about love to a man who hated her brother. Her only, bitter, comfort was that Jake had been too busy screwing her to listen.

"What would you have done in my place?" he demanded.

"My options would have been limited. I'm not as strong as you are. And I'm not a world-class liar."

His hand tightened on Honor's thigh. "I haven't lied to you. Not in the way you mean."

"Really? What way *do* I mean?"

"I didn't make love to you in order to get to your brother," Jake said bluntly.

256

"I believe you."

He let out a long breath. "Thank God."

"You didn't make love to me, period," she continued with a thin smile.

"What would you call it?"

"Sex."

"Whatever. As long as you know it didn't have anything to do with the Kyle mess."

Honor stared at Jake and wondered which one of them was crazy. One of them had to be.

"Let me get this straight," she said. "You came to me under false pretenses—"

"You hired me under false—"

"—and then you—"

"—pretenses," he said, talking over her. "You didn't want to learn how to—"

"—take advantage of my fear to crawl in bed and—" she continued relentlessly.

"—fish and you're afraid of—"

"—then you have the balls to suggest that the sex and the Kyle mess have nothing—"

"—small boats and—"

"Stop yelling!"

"*I'm not yelling.*" Jake's breath came out in a rush that was also a disgusted curse. "This isn't getting us anywhere."

"On that we agree. Let go of me."

"You'd rather finish this conversation on the floor?"

"There's nothing to finish. It was finished when Archer told me who you were."

"Just what did your brother tell you?"

"That I was a little fool and you could be Kyle's killer."

A stillness came over Jake.

For the first time, fear breathed a chill over Honor's skin.

"Is that what you believe?" he asked softly.

She made a trapped, frustrated gesture. "I don't believe Kyle is dead, so I could hardly believe you killed him, could I?"

"Talk about damned by faint praise."

"It's more than you deserve and less than a smart woman would give you," Honor said, her voice flat. "But then, you've already proved just how stupid I am, haven't you?"

"No. I proved how passionate you were. That's a different thing entirely."

Honor closed her eyes and wished with all her soul to be somewhere else. Anywhere else. And with no memory of the past few days.

The pain and humiliation beneath her anger made Jake wince. His hand on her thigh became less confining, more caressing. "Honor, sweetheart, I'm sorry you had to find out this way, but I'm not sorry about last night."

"Don't. Touch. Me."

The softness of her voice made the hair on Jake's neck stir in primal reflex. If he pushed her any harder, she would go for his throat like the cornered animal she was. Very gently he lifted his hand. She let out a shuddering breath and opened her eyes. He didn't like what he saw in them any better than he had liked the tone of her voice.

"Right now you don't ever want to see me again—" Jake began.

"Bingo."

"—but we don't always get what we want."

"More salty philosophy?"

Jake took a grip on his own uncertain temper. "Too bad Archer couldn't have waited for a few more days."

"Is that how long you figured it would take to finish screwing my brains out?"

"Last night has nothing to do with the rest of this mess!"

The smile Honor gave him could have cured sharkskin, but she didn't say a word. She simply waited and watched him with the wide, cold eyes of a cat. He looked at the clock on the bedside table. There wasn't much time left.

"You want to find Kyle, right?" Jake asked.

She nodded her head slightly.

"I want to find your brother, right?" he continued.

She shrugged.

"Believe it," he shot back. "There's nothing I'd like better than to have a chat with my good buddy Kyle Donovan."

Honor nodded. If she believed nothing else about Jake, she believed he wanted to get his hands on her brother.

"You," he said, "need me to run the boat and keep the rest of the players off your back."

"I'll hire someone else."

"Too dangerous. Snake Eyes has friends. Besides," Jake said smoothly, "you want to stay close to me. Real close."

"Like hell I do."

"Think. How else will you be sure Kyle doesn't get hurt when I get my lying, cheating, murderous hands on him?"

The phone rang.

Honor didn't even flinch. Nor did she make a move to answer it.

"You know who it is," Jake said. "You can do what Archer says and go home like a good little girl, or you can be a big bad girl and keep on looking for Kyle with me."

She didn't so much as glance toward the phone.

"Answer it," he said tightly. "Or do you want to spend the rest of the day talking to cops? If you think you're embarrassed now, wait until you tell them why we spent the night in the sack instead of calling in a burglary."

She snatched up the phone. "Hello."

"Are you all right?" Archer demanded.

"Fine," she said distantly.

"You don't sound like it. Does he have a gun on you?"

For the first time Honor remembered Jake's gun. If he had it, it wasn't on him. There wasn't one inch of him she couldn't see.

"Honor?" Archer asked urgently.

"No. He's not holding a gun on me. Why would he? I trusted him. As you pointed out, I'm a little fool."

Jake's eyes narrowed with barely leashed rage. Honor's voice was so very calm, so completely reasonable. It was like dripping acid onto his raw conscience.

He never should have touched her.

But he had.

There was no going back. He didn't even want to. He wanted more of what he had found with her last night. A lot more.

"You're not a fool," Jake said softly. "You're a passionate woman with good instincts about when and who to trust."

Honor ignored him as though he were a stain on the sheets. She was ignoring Archer the same way, although her brother didn't know it. She needed every shred of control she had just to think through the unholy tangle that passed for her emotions. If she could get past the humiliation and rage, then she might be able to use her brain for something besides silently screaming names at herself.

Abruptly she realized that the line was open and silent. Archer was waiting for an answer. Unfortunately she couldn't remember what the question had been.

"Sorry," she said in a clipped voice. "One way or another, it's already been a hell of a day. What were you saying?"

"Are you sure you're all right?"

"Archer, I could be standing crotch-deep in crocodiles and there isn't a damn thing you could do about it right now except yell at me for being so stupid as to wander into a swamp!" She took a jagged breath. "Other than that, I'm fine. Peachy wonderful fabulous. Now, what haven't you told me about Kyle and stolen amber and any other little thing that might seriously inconvenience or kill me between now and tomorrow?"

"When I told you to go to Kyle's cottage, I didn't have any idea that he had returned to the States or that other people were after the amber or that the police had been alerted. If I'd known, I'd never have sent you there."

"Okay. It was April Fool all the way around. What else haven't you told me?"

There was silence, a few muttered words in a language Honor didn't recognize, and then a pungent curse in English.

"I know that one," she snapped. "Tell me something I don't know."

"Have you ever heard of the Amber Room?" Archer asked finally, reluctantly.

"Sort of. It belonged to a czar, the walls of the room were covered in amber mosaics, and it's supposed to be some of the most beautiful decorative art ever made."

"The Nazis stole it. No one has seen it since the end of World War Two. Or if they have, they're not talking."

"So?"

"A panel from the room was stashed with the shipment of amber Kyle supposedly took from Jay."

"Jay? Who is— Oh, you mean Jake."

"A son of a bitch by any other name is still a—"

"Son of a bitch," Honor finished, looking right at the naked stranger in her bed and trying to forget that she was equally naked herself. "So Jay/Jake got his hands on a chunk of the Amber Room, slipped it into a legitimate shipment of raw amber, and set up Kyle to look like the thief?"

Jake's eyes could have been borrowed from hell, but he didn't say a word.

"That's the simplest explanation," Archer said. "Unless you prefer to think that Kyle did it."

"Who is this Mar-you person?"

"Marry-you? Oh, Marju. She's the one Kyle lost his head over."

"The one he might have stolen for, except that Jake beat him to it?" Honor asked coolly, watching the thief in question.

"That's about it," her brother said.

"What does Marju say about this mess?"

There was a pause.

"Archer," Honor said, biting off her brother's name, "don't hold out on me again."

"Hell, sis. All we have is second- or third-hand gossip."

"I'm all ears."

"Marju says that Kyle pretended to be in love with her in order to get his hands on the Amber Room."

Honor's eyelids flinched. "What about Jake?"

"She thinks he was in partnership with Kyle. Informally, if you get my meaning."

"A collaboration of crooks."

Silence.

"What do you think, Archer?" she asked.

"I think there's more to this mess than we've been able to uncover."

"That's not what I meant and you know it."

"I'm given a choice of trusting Mallory, who I've known for less than a year, or I can trust Kyle."

"How well do you know him?"

"Kyle?" Archer asked in disbelief.

"No."

"Oh, Mallory."

"A son of a bitch by any other name," she agreed bitterly.

"Until the Amber Room came on the scene, I would have trusted Jay with my secrets, my business, and my life if it came to a fight in a dark alley. But every man has a price. The Amber Room was Mallory's."

"But not Kyle's."

"Kyle doesn't need money and he's not a serious collector of amber. His first love is jade. Jay doesn't need money, but he loves amber the way some men love God. Love isn't a particularly reasonable emotion."

Honor's throat closed. She had a growing suspicion about just how irrational, unreasonable, and unruly an emotion love could be. She was, after all, the fool who had declared her love to a man who was merely an exquisite lover.

"Do you think he killed Kyle?" she asked baldly.

"I don't think Kyle is dead."

"That's not an answer."

"It's the best answer I have. Hell, anyone can kill in the right circumstances, even you."

"No argument there," she said, looking right at Jake.

"What is this about Dimitri Pavlov?" Archer asked.

"Dimitri who?"

"Snake Eyes," Jake said clearly, guessing the

course of the conversation.

"Oh, him," she said. "I didn't hire him."

"Stay away from him," Archer said. "He's the kind of person you hate to do business with but don't have any choice if you want to work in the modern Russian Federation."

"What do you mean?"

"Russian *mafiya*," he said succinctly. "The new interface between capitalism and chaos in the old Soviet Union. They have the morals of a mink and the scruples of a shark."

"That's how Snake Eyes struck me," she agreed. "He's following me whenever we go out fishing. So is the Coast Guard and at least one other private boat. Maybe two."

"Bloody wonderful," Archer said under his breath. "Well, at least you're safe on the water. Who ransacked Kyle's place last night?"

"I don't know." She looked at Jake. "Do you know who was here last night?"

"No."

"He doesn't—" she began.

"I heard," Archer said. "Ask him if he has any guesses."

"You ask him. I've had it with being caught in the middle."

She threw the receiver at Jake. He caught it without taking his eyes off her. He watched while she got out of bed and stalked toward the bathroom. When the shower came on he let out a silent sigh of relief and lifted the receiver to his ear.

"What?" he asked curtly.

"Who was the guy last night?"

"He wasn't from this side of the ocean."

"How do you know?"

"The U.S. government thinks it has an in with me, so they have no reason to do a dicey black bag job on a very private residence."

Archer absorbed that. "The government has already approached you?"

"Yeah. Seems the Russians asked for help recovering the Amber Room."

"Have you seen it?"

"No. I don't expect to, either. I think it's a wide load of fairy dust."

Archer grunted. "Is Honor in danger?"

"From Uncle Sam's players? Probably not. After that, all bets are off."

"Put her back on."

"She's in the shower."

"Shower! Just how close are you and Honor?"

"About ten feet."

"What?"

"The phone is about ten feet from the shower."

"Mallory, you're pissing me off."

"Do unto others and all that. Are you still in Kamchatka?"

"Why do you care?"

"If I get taken out, I'd like to think that help was on the way for Honor. The body that washed up here was former KGB. After the wall came down, he hired out his talents. He had a traveling partner. The partner hasn't washed up yet. The good news is, neither has your brother."

"Christ, what a mess. Get Honor out of

there! I'll pay you more than the Amber Room is worth."

"I don't want the Amber Room. I want the truth."

"That's all the Donovans want."

"Like hell. What you want is to clear Kyle by hanging me."

"If you get Honor out of there, I'll spread the word that you're innocent."

"Then who's guilty? Kyle?"

Archer didn't answer.

"Nice try," Jake said sardonically, "but I'm not buying any more Donovan bullshit. If you find out anything that might help keep your sister alive, don't forget to call."

He hung up on Archer, listened to the shower, and tried to think of how he could keep Honor safe. He was still sorting through possibilities when the shower shut off. A few minutes later Honor walked into the room wearing her baggy black sweat suit. Above the collar she looked fresh and sleek.

Then Jake saw her eyes. He had been wrong when he told Archer that she was only ten feet away. The kind of distance he saw in her now couldn't be measured.

"Who was the guy last night?" she asked calmly.

"I don't know."

She ran her fingers through her chin-length hair in an automatic fluffing gesture and didn't say a word.

"I really don't know," Jake said angrily. "He didn't exactly leave a business card."

"Anything else?"

Her voice was like her expression, cold enough to leave frost.

"You said you have a sister in Hawaii?" he asked.

Honor spun toward him. "Why? Is something wrong with Faith?"

"Archer wants you to visit her. It's one of the few things we agreed on."

"Too bad. I don't agree."

"Snake Eyes is a professional killer."

Her eyelids flinched. "All the more reason to keep Faith out of this."

"All right. Take a vacation on Tahiti or Easter Island until this is over. Donovan International can hire some bodyguards to haul your luggage. If they don't know anyone up to the job, I do."

"No."

"Why not?"

"As you so cleverly pointed out, I should be around when you find Kyle."

"I won't hurt him. You have my word."

"That's nice. I'm staying."

Jake played his last card—the famous Donovan temper. "Just can't get enough of me, huh?"

"Yeah, how'd you guess?" she said without interest. "Let's go fishing."

For a few electric seconds Jake measured Honor. Everything he saw convinced him that fishing not only was the best offer he would get from her right now, it was the only one. She was fully capable of walking out and casting off in the boat herself, leaving him standing around with his fine intentions hanging out.

He grabbed his clothes and started pulling them on.

14

The weather was better than Jake's mood, which wasn't saying much. Low clouds, lower clouds, fog, drizzle, rain, and choppy water could be seen along various parts of the strait. At one point there was a pool of sunlight glittering way out on the water, but it didn't last long. Wind closed the hole in the clouds and a hundred shades of gray settled seamlessly over land and sea.

The *Tomorrow*'s blower was already on when Jake reached the dock. Before he had taken two steps the engine roared to life and settled into a muscular muttering. He went aboard fast.

"Going somewhere?" he asked, closing the cabin door behind him. Hard.

"It's time I learned how to drive the boat."

He grunted. "There's no way you can learn enough to search the San Juans alone."

Honor sat behind the helm and didn't say another word until the SeaSport's engine had warmed up to operating temperature.

"Cast off," she said without looking at Jake.

"Not this time."

Without a word she got out of the helm seat and went to the dock. She undid the bow line and the stern line, stepped on board, and headed for the cabin. Jake was already in the helm seat.

"I meant it," she said through the open door. "I'm driving."

"Use the aft controls."

A moment later she put the gear lever in reverse and eased up on the throttle. The boat began backing away from the dock, out into the shallow cove. She started to turn the boat away from the dock the same way she had seen Jake do it, waiting until the bow was just clear of the end of the dock.

Wind gusted, catching the *Tomorrow* full on the side. More quickly than Honor would have believed possible, the boat whacked broadside into the end of the dock.

Jake came out of the cabin carrying a boat pole. He pushed the *Tomorrow* off the dock. "Try again."

She did. This time the bow banged against the dock.

"Reverse," he said.

She missed the gate for the shift. Before she could find it, wind had blown the stern back onto the dock. Jake shoved off. She went into reverse, but somehow the wheel position was wrong. Instead of backing away, the stern was sucked against the dock again.

Honor set her teeth to hold back the kind of language her daddy said only men used. She tried again. The bow scraped against the dock. Even as she jammed the gear lever into neutral to kill speed, she jerked the wheel as though to turn the bow away. It didn't do any good, of course. In neutral, the steering wheel was useless.

"Better," Jake said, pushing the boat off the dock again. "It would have worked if the wind hadn't stopped blowing the stern."

She reached for the shifter again.

"No," he said curtly. "Check your helm position first or we'll ram the dock but good this time."

After a few more tries, Honor got the *Tomorrow* away from the dock despite the unpredictable wind. Bleakly she admitted to herself that it was more due to Jake's instructions than to any of her own skill. She wouldn't have believed how much a little wind could push around something as big as the *Tomorrow*. The thought of landing in a real wind made cool sweat break out on her spine.

"Now take the forward helm," Jake said. "Head for that point of land."

Honor looked where he was pointing and went into the cabin. He stood by the aft controls until he felt them respond to her hands. When he climbed into the pilot seat across from her, she didn't so much as glance in his direction.

"Where are we going?" she asked.

"To the marina to top off the tanks."

The thought of docking the *Tomorrow* made

Honor cringe. She knew that coming up along-side a dock was a lot more tricky than simply pulling away from it—and she had made a real hash of that.

She worried all the way to the marina.

"I'll take the aft station," Jake said. "If I tell you to let go of the controls, do it."

She nodded and hoped her relief didn't show. He went out on the stern and began calling directions to her. She didn't argue or hesitate. She simply did what he said as best she could, even when she thought she should be doing the opposite.

The dock approached with unnerving speed. She missed the gate on a shift into reverse.

"Let go!"

Even before Honor lifted her hands, the control levers took on a life of their own. While she wiped damp palms on her sweatshirt, Jake killed the forward momentum and tucked the boat alongside the dock with a few swift maneuvers.

Honor let out a shaky breath. The whole time the gas tanks filled, she thought about what she had done wrong on the landing. Besides missing the shift gate, she had been coming in too fast and at too steep an angle. Easy enough to figure out now, but at the time everything had happened all at once and yet had taken forever, like fast-forward on a video machine and slow-motion terror at the same time.

When she came back from paying for the gas, the blower was on and Jake was in the cabin.

He killed the blower and started the engine.

"Take the aft station," he said, pulling the fenders aboard. "I'll cast off."

She set her jaw and went to the controls. The wind was doing the same thing it had in the little cove, holding the *Tomorrow* against the dock like an invisible, relentless hand. She couldn't back away and there was a boat blocking the front exit.

Jake told her where to set the wheel before she engaged reverse. He gave the stern a shove, grabbed the bow, pushed hard, and swung himself up and over the bow railing. It took him only a few seconds to walk the gunwale and drop lightly into the stern well. The *Tomorrow* was well away from the dock.

"Okay," he said. "Take her out of the marina. Remember, no wake."

They got out of the marina without incident. Once they were in more open water, Honor began to relax—until she noticed the clouds. In places they covered the water like draperies of dove gray muslin. Where islands appeared, they were low dark lines capped by mist.

"The weather report hasn't changed," Jake said, turning down the marine radio. "Drizzle and patchy fog in the early morning. Winds out of the southeast at ten to twenty knots. Squall lines possible this afternoon. Haro Strait might be a problem, though. There are small craft warnings at the mouth."

"Are we going there?"

"It's the shortest way to the last route Kyle stored. At least, it's the last route I can make the machine show me. He might have something hidden. If he does, I don't have the code."

Honor thought she did, but she wasn't going to share that information with someone who had a grudge against Kyle.

"Put the route up," she said.

Jake's mouth thinned. "The place is ninety minutes out in good weather. It will be a lot longer if the wind gets strong enough to make us sneak along in the lee of the islands."

Honor looked at the water. It wasn't exactly smooth, but there weren't any whitecaps. "Looks good to me."

"The chop isn't bad," he agreed, "but adjusting to it will add time, unless you want to hammer your spine."

"How much time?"

"It depends."

"On what?"

"Wind, tide, and visibility."

"We have radar."

"You want to drive blind?"

Honor's fingers clenched around the wheel. "Not particularly."

"That makes two of us. In case you hadn't noticed, some mighty big ships share those narrow passes between islands with us. On a boat this size, you bet your life on radar only when fog catches you short of land. You don't just blithely fire up and head out into the soup for the hell of it."

"I'm not doing any of this for the hell of it."

She leaned over and pushed a button on the

lower electronic unit. She had been watching him closely yesterday; she got the screen to switch from the depth sounder to the chart plotter on the first try. She hit the menu button, scrolled down to the stored routes, and punched the last number on the list.

A chart popped onto the screen.

"This the route?" Honor asked.

Jake said something savage under his breath.

"Right," she said. "This is the one."

She swung the boat around until she was headed for the first way point on the stored course.

"Do you remember the most efficient rpm for speed versus fuel efficiency?" he asked.

"Yes."

"Bring us up on plane."

After several tries—and a few hair-raising zigzags caused by badly deployed trim tabs—Honor got the SeaSport up on plane. She could tell when she had done it right; if she lifted her hands from the wheel, the boat held a true line. She soon realized that, unlike a car, the boat did better when she left it alone.

"That's better," he said. "You're learning not to oversteer."

Honor looked over her shoulder at the water they had covered. Even through the gloom she could see that the wake wasn't as straight as when Jake drove. But it wasn't all that bad, either. She was getting the hang of driving on a road that had no markings and didn't stand still.

The computer cheeped. Honor flinched.

"It was just telling you that we've passed the first way point on our route," Jake said. "Watch the radar screen. With the next sweep it will show what your new heading should be. So will the lower screen, but it's not as easy to read."

Saying nothing, she waited and watched the screen. A few seconds later she turned the wheel, adjusting course. Immediately the boat became harder to handle. It didn't like taking the chop at this angle. Though the rpms hadn't changed, the speed dropped.

"Bring the bow down two clicks on the left trim tab and one on the right," he said.

The ride evened out. Adjusting the trim got back some of the lost speed, but not all.

Jake looked out the stern. The usual boats were pacing the SeaSport. He didn't envy Conroy in the open Zodiac. Today the Coast Guard would be grateful for their bright orange dry suits. He looked at the sky and thought about their destination.

His thoughts were as unhappy as the set of his jaw. Kyle's last fishing hole was almost on the invisible border between Canada's Gulf Islands and the San Juan Islands of the United States. Right now the SeaSport was more or less paralleling the weather front, but the front would overrun them before too long.

He turned up the marine radio. Even though it was after the hour, the forecast hadn't changed. No small craft warnings had been posted yet, though advisories were out along the strait.

That didn't make Jake feel much better. Forecasting weather was an art, not a science, especially in the San Juans. The islands were notorious for sudden winds and unexpected squall lines.

Silence settled into the cabin like carbon monoxide. Jake wondered how long it would be before Honor looked him in the eye again, or at the very least stopped treating him like something that had stuck to her shoe. The tilt of her jaw didn't predict a turn for the better anytime soon.

Half an hour dragged by. Jake had never thought of himself as a particularly chatty person, but the roaring silence was getting to him. Honor didn't seem to notice it—or him. She hadn't actually looked at him the whole time they had been on the boat. The way she acted he could have been a voice speaking out of the air.

More than once he caught himself checking in one of the boat's windows to see if he still had a reflection. He opened his mouth to tell her what he thought about sulky women. Then he remembered the way she had looked that morning when he had held her in bed with his hand on her thigh.

Direct confrontation hadn't worked very well.

The radio crackled to life. The weather bureau had changed its report. Winds from thirty to fifty knots were expected in Haro Strait before noon. Twenty to thirty in the islands.

"Turn around," Jake said.

Honor started to look at him, caught herself, and stared ahead. "It's only nine-thirty. We've got time."

"No. Turn around."

"But—"

"Get out of the helm seat."

With a hissed word, Honor turned the Sea-Sport around. If it came to a contest of strength, she would lose. Big time.

Jake reversed the chart plotter so that it would give them way points back to the dock.

Silence settled in once more with the weight and color of lead.

Honor glanced from the rumpled water in front of the bow to the "heads up" radar display. She was off course. Carefully she corrected, then waited for a few seconds before deciding whether she needed to correct again. She had learned that boats and cars didn't drive at all alike. Most of the time boats were a lot less sudden. Sometimes they were a lot more.

The solid line on the radar merged with the dotted line of the course she was supposed to follow. She took visual sightings on the islands ahead, kept alert for floating logs, checked the angles and speed of approaching craft, and spared a few seconds to glance at the gauges for anything unexpected.

After fifteen minutes of watching Honor watch the water, Jake's jaw ached from the tension of biting back all that he wanted to say about stubborn Donovans. He set his jaw even tighter and decided to try a more subtle approach. Somewhere beneath all that icy female fury was an intelligent, reasonable woman. More to the point, she loved him.

He had it from her own sweet lips.

"I met Kyle about two months ago," Jake said, "when Archer sent him to the Baltics to be the liaison between my own company, Emerging Resources, and Donovan International. Usually I work out of Seattle. The only reason I went to Kaliningrad at all was that my rep there had a bad appendix."

He waited for some sign that Honor was listening. If she was, she didn't respond to the lure. He made a disgusted sound, reined in his temper, and asked in a voice dripping with reason, "How can we settle anything if you won't talk to me?"

"What's to settle? I need you to teach me about the boat and you need me to get to Kyle."

"What about last night?"

"Was it good for you, too?" she asked with a total lack of interest.

"It was the best I've ever had."

"That's nice. Why isn't the outdrive gauge showing dead center?"

"It's not supposed to be. Honor, I'm not going to let you turn your back on last night."

"Should I be worried about those clouds? It's getting really black along our course line."

Jake didn't even bother to look at the

weather hanging low over the San Juans. "Talk to me."

"I am, but you aren't listening. Those clouds go all the way to the water."

"We're like a frog's ass. Waterproof. How long are you going to make me pay for not cutting my own throat and telling you everything the first time we met?"

"A watertight frog butt. Now there's a thought."

"You were a Donovan and the Donovans got me kicked out of the Russian Federation."

Honor held on to the wheel and her own temper. She had always thought that Kyle could talk anyone into anything. Now here was Jake with his earnest whiskey-and-velvet voice, his razor-edged mind, and a body that had taught her things about herself and overwhelming pleasure that she would spend the rest of her life trying to forget. Or duplicate.

Even worse, she kept going over and over it in her mind. Not just the sex, the whole mess. She hadn't been honest with him. He hadn't been honest with her. But she damn well hadn't slept with him as a means to finding her brother.

Jake couldn't say the same.

Why else would he have been so careful to give her the kind of incredible pleasure he had? She had made it pretty plain that he attracted her; he had followed up in a way that was guaranteed to keep her happy about having him around.

She was a fool. She had been a fool since Jake walked into her life, a life that was already thrown off balance by her brother's disappearance.

Silence expanded until it was a living, smothering presence in the cabin.

Jake watched Honor for any sign of response to his words. All he saw was increasing tension and a disgust she couldn't quite hide beneath her careful lack of expression.

"Is it so impossible," he asked through his teeth, "that Kyle might, just might, have gotten in over his head with Marju and done something really stupid?"

"You know her better than I do."

"She's about the sexiest thing since Eve."

"Kyle is hardly a kid. He's been chased by experts."

"Marju is different."

"This will come as news to you, but we're *all* different."

"You know what I mean."

"No, I don't," she said, staring out through the increasing rain. "I do know that asking me to choose between my brother who has never betrayed me and a man who has just betrayed me isn't very bright."

"I didn't betray you!"

Rain poured down, drenching the *Tomorrow* in transparent sheets of water.

"You didn't betray me," she said indifferently.

"Right. Where are the wipers on this thing?"

"Here." Jake's hand shot out and slammed on all three wipers at once. Then he let out a seething breath and tried sweet reason again. It wasn't very successful. His voice

281

was more angry than sweet. "I didn't betray you and you damn well know it."

"That's what I said."

"*Shit.*"

"Another point of agreement. See how easy it is?"

Jake took several slow breaths and another, hopefully better, grip on his temper. Honor's newfound habit of agreeing with him and not meaning a word of it was sawing away at his self-control. It was impossible to argue with someone who was so damned agreeable.

The computer cheeped, signaling a way point successfully passed. Honor watched the radar screen until it completed a sweep of the circle and put the new course in place. She corrected the wheel, looked where her new course would take them, and instantly changed her mind about staying on it.

One of the massive Washington State ferries was barreling toward them out of the rain. In addition to the *Tomorrow* and its three watery shadows, there were three more small craft to keep an eye on, plus a huge tanker with accompanying tugs, and a shrimper criss-crossing the water while dragging its strange-looking net in search of even stranger looking prey.

"A boat with nets out has the right of way," Jake said.

"What does he think he's doing in the center of the shipping channel?" Honor muttered, adjusting course.

"Fishing. And he's not in the center. He's

at the crotch of the Y where two shipping channels merge."

"What about the freighter and the ferry?"

"They'll miss each other. And unless the shrimper is nuts, he won't push the right-of-way issue. Just like we won't. We're in the ferry's danger quarter, but we'll give way to him instead of vice versa. Man-made rules are one thing. The natural laws of mass and momentum are another thing entirely. There's something known as being dead right."

Cold rain made the windows start to steam up. Jake reached past Honor and turned the defrosters on low. She flinched and jerked back when his arm brushed against her. He ignored it, adjusted the radar to reach out into the rain for miles in all directions, and studied the new display. No new boats showed up along the *Tomorrow*'s course.

"All right," he said. "Imagine an old-fashioned clock. We're at the center. Straight ahead of us is twelve o'clock, straight back is six o'clock—"

"Three o'clock is ninety degrees to the right," she interrupted impatiently, "and nine o'clock is ninety degrees to the left. Now what?"

"Head halfway between one and two o'clock," Jake said.

Honor glanced uneasily at the closing gap between the freighter and the ferry. That was where Jake's directions would take the Sea-Sport.

"Do it," he said flatly. "The longer you

hesitate, the worse it will be."

While she changed course, he brought the radar back in to sweeping only the nearby water. The rain was letting up, but not the clouds. They were coming right down to sit on the ocean. Though the resulting condition wasn't the same as fog, it had a bad effect on visibility.

"Jake, I can't see the—"

"Look at the radar," he interrupted, pointing to the screen. "That's the ferry. That's the freighter. That's the shrimper. That's the sailboat. That's the Grand Banks cruiser. That's the idiot in the skiff. You're going here. Bring your speed up."

"What about the boats behind us? One of them is veering toward shore."

"Conroy. His Zodiac has a really shallow draft. The tide is low, but he'll be able to scoot along the shoreline out of traffic. The rest of them can drop back or take their chances."

"What about us?"

"At high tide we could get away with what Conroy is doing. But there are rocks that come within two feet of the surface at low tide. We need more water than that. The freighter and the ferry need a hell of a lot more. They'll stay well inside the channel markers. We'll stay just outside them. Watch for logs. Two currents come together right around here, which means debris collects. Remember what I told you about a log if you can't avoid it?"

"Steer into it, not away from it. Jake, that freighter—"

"I see it," he interrupted.

What he saw was that the freighter wasn't holding the expected course. It was staying in the *Tomorrow*'s danger quarter, which meant there would be a collision unless one of them changed speed or course.

Quickly Jake checked the radar. Instinct ran cold fingernails over his spine. Normally he would have cut back on the throttle and waited for the traffic to clear. It was the sensible thing for a small craft to do when playing with seagoing elephants.

But if the *Tomorrow* slowed down now, they would be swamped by the oncoming ferry. The ferry's captain would get a reprimand and an early retirement for not suspending natural laws by giving way to the SeaSport in the ferry's danger quarter. Jake and Honor would get an early grave.

"I'll take over," he said.

If she had any objections, she didn't get a chance to voice them. He pulled her out of the helm seat and dumped her in the pilot seat before she could open her mouth.

"Hang on," he said as he reached for the throttle.

The second set of carburetor jets kicked in with a throaty growl of delight. Jake's fingers danced over the controls as he set a new course, adjusted the trim, turned the defrosters onto high, and settled in for a short, rugged run through the narrowing window of safety.

The *Tomorrow* raced across the water. There were moments when it was more like riding a skipping stone than a boat, but it worked. The freighter began shifting out of dead center in their danger quarter.

Even so, it was going to be close. Very close.

The freighter gave three short blasts of its horn.

"Stiff-necked bastard," Jake muttered. "He's got better radar coverage than we do. He could change course without endangering or even inconveniencing himself."

Obviously the freighter wasn't going to do that. In fact, if it had changed course at all, the result was to bring the huge ship closer to rather than farther away from a collision with the SeaSport.

Honor gripped the dashboard with one hand and the fixed armrest with the other. Even so, the force of the boat hurtling through the choppy water lifted her off the seat and slammed her back down with spine-rattling force. In tight silence she watched the freighter loom closer and closer on the radar.

She could tell by the position of the throttle that the *Tomorrow* had more speed available, yet Jake didn't use it. Before she could ask why, he spun the helm, sending the boat hard to the left. Something slammed against the hull. From the corner of her eye she caught a glimpse of a dark shape sliding away in a boil of foam. A log.

Jake spun the wheel back onto the old heading and gave the radar a flicking glance. Where there should have been one image, he saw two. The second one was much smaller, but still many times bigger than the *Tomorrow*.

And it was heading straight at them.

"Hang on," he said grimly.

"I am!"

He slammed the throttle forward. The SeaSport's bow exploded wave tops into wild sheets of spray.

The radio crackled. Most of the words were drowned out by the noise of going too fast over choppy water.

"...Conroy. Do you read me, Jake? There's a ship in the radar shadow of the freighter. Change course to..." The noise of the *Tomorrow* slamming into a bigger wave drowned out whatever Conroy was saying.

Though Jake appreciated the warning, he didn't have a spare hand for the radio right now. It was taking all of his skill to keep the *Tomorrow* right side up. Even the most seaworthy boat had its limits, especially at speed. He knew he was crowding the SeaSport's.

Sheets of spray drenched the windshield. Salt water overpowered the wipers for seconds at a time. It didn't matter to Jake. He was running on radar, skill, nerve, and necessity.

Honor didn't bother screaming or pointing out the new blip on the radar screen. Obviously Jake had already seen it. There was no other reason he would have the SeaSport going flat out over choppy water. With unnatural calm she watched the radar screen. The gap they were racing toward closed in little jerks with each new sweep of the radar.

The freighter leaned on its horn again. She looked out the window and saw an immense shape looming. Her breath locked in her chest. She couldn't have screamed if she had wanted to.

The *Tomorrow* flew over the chop and across the freighter's bow with seconds to spare.

No sooner had they cleared the freighter than a new threat leaped out. Jake had an instant to recognize the outline of a big Alaska seiner before he brought the bow around hard. The SeaSport skidded, jerked, and bit into the water again.

They shot past the second boat. They were so close Honor could count the rust streaks streaming from the anchor chain. She knew she would be counting them in her nightmares.

The seiner's wake hit them like a fist, but Jake was prepared. He had already chopped back speed and angled the bow to minimize the impact. Even so, the boat lifted and dropped sickeningly, slamming into the surface of the sea as though it were concrete rather than salt water.

Honor stared at the radar like a bird at a snake, waiting for the next piece of bad news.

The screen was clear of everything but a small boat racing toward them from the solid mass of the island ahead. Even as she spotted the Coast Guard Zodiac, it must have spotted them. The radio crackled to life.

Jake switched channels and picked up the microphone to answer Conroy's query.

"*Tomorrow* here. No damage."

"Nice bit of driving," Conroy responded. "Vasi's seiner couldn't see you."

"Didn't the freighter warn him?"

"From what I gathered while you were out-running them, the freighter's radar has been 'spotty' and no one on board the seiner spoke enough English in any case. Or was it Russian they didn't speak and the seiner's radar that was spotty?"

Conroy's sarcastic tone said plainly that he wasn't impressed by the explanations he had heard.

"No harm, no foul," Jake said.

"That was too close."

"No argument here."

"Maybe you should stay off the water for a while."

"Officially?"

"Since when has common sense been official?" Conroy shot back.

Jake laughed and signed off the air. Before he could hang up the microphone, another call came in on the hailing frequency. He listened to the request, switched channels, and looked at Honor before he turned on the micro-phone.

"Are you okay?" he asked.

She nodded.

"You're sure?"

"A few bruises on my rear end. No big deal."

He smiled slowly, relief and something more, something hotter.

"Anything that happens to your rear end is a big deal as far as I'm concerned," he said. "You fit like you were made just for me."

"Stop talking about—"

A burst from the radio cut across her words. "Jake, it is Petyr. Profound apologies, my friend. Are you me listening? Ah, excuse please. Excitement too much. Are you hearing me?"

Jake looked at the microphone as though it had just bitten him. Of all the bad news he had heard since Kyle disappeared, Petyr Resnikov could easily be the worst.

"I'm hearing you," Jake said into the microphone. "Which boat are you aboard?"

"The freighter. The captain is quite angry, but you know how silly seafaring peasants are. He insists it was your fault even though his radar is, shall I say, inconsistent?"

"So I was told. What are you doing in this half of the world?" Jake asked bluntly.

Laughter came out of the speaker. "Ah, Jacob. You have not changed."

"Have you?"

"Cheerfully, not a whittle. If you will come on board as soon as we dock, you and I may toast one another with some of Russia's best vodka."

Jake had no intention of getting aboard anything with Petyr Resnikov until he knew who was paying the Russian.

"Not this time," Jake said easily. "I'm doing

something else this afternoon."

"But of course. Bring the beautiful, artistic Miss Donovan with you. If she is as charming as the brother Kyle, she will be a glowing companion."

Jake glanced toward Honor. At the moment she looked more rattled than charming.

"Some other time," he said into the radio.

Like never. He had no intention of letting Honor within a hundred yards of the elegant, rapierlike Russian.

"Ah, Jacob, you sadden me," Resnikov said calmly. "May I insist? For—how do you say it?—reason of older times?"

The gentle tones didn't mislead Jake. He had just been given an invitation he shouldn't refuse.

"Meet me at the Chowder Keg in two hours," Jake said.

15

Silently Jake turned off the ignition of his truck. He looked at Honor. She had changed into fitted black jeans, a bronze turtleneck sweater, and a black linen jacket. She wore a hand-wrought gold necklace. Its pendant was a stylized, rock crystal and jet spiral in the ancient yin and yang design. He knew without asking that she had designed it.

He looked across the sidewalk at the weathered, windowless front door that belonged to the Chowder Keg and wished he had chosen one of the town's more upscale diners. It had been years since he had braved the smoke and sour smell of grease in order to eat what was arguably the best clam chowder in the Pacific Northwest. He had forgotten just how disreputable the place looked. And was.

Honor reached for the door handle on her side. Jake's long arm shot across her and held the door closed. She yanked her hand out from under his as though she had been burned.

"Look," he said. "This isn't your kind of place. Too many guys from the fish boats."

"You don't know me well enough to know what kind of place is or isn't my kind."

His hand tightened over hers. He gave her a look that said he was remembering everything about last night.

"Honey, I know you from your forehead to the soles of your feet and all the sweet places in between. The Chowder Keg is hard, dirty, ratty, and rough. You aren't."

Honor knew she was probably blushing. She hoped the color would be written off as anger.

"You're wasting time," she said, refusing to look at Jake. "I'm going inside with you."

"Why?"

"Guess," she said through her teeth.

"You don't trust me."

"Aren't you a clever boy. But we already knew that, didn't we?"

For a few moments there were no sounds but those Jake made controlling his breathing.

"You're going to push me until I lose my temper, aren't you?" he asked evenly. "Then you're going to tell me what a nasty, overbearing, untrustworthy son of a bitch I am."

"Why would I tell you something you already know?"

"Do you want to find your brother or do you want to keep baiting me?"

Honor looked at the powerful arm barred across her body. Jake wasn't touching her—but if she took a deep breath she would be touching him.

"Don't bother to loom over me," she said. "You need me too much to threaten me physically."

"You need me just as much. Remember that and bridle your tongue."

For an instant Honor saw nothing except the hot rush of her own blood darkening the world.

"Look who's talking about pushing," she said when she could trust her voice. "If you're trying to make me lose my temper and rush off in a snit, forget it. Kyle means too much to me."

"You love him."

"Of course I do."

"What about me?"

"What about you?" she retorted.

"You sure do fall out of love easily," he said in a soft, cold voice.

Honor flinched. Until that moment she had actually hoped Jake hadn't heard her foolish, whispered declaration of love.

"Easy come, easy go," she said with a tight shrug. "Move your arm."

"Look at me."

She didn't turn her head one bit.

"Stop acting like a spoiled child," he said. "Petyr Resnikov is a shrewd, handsome womanizer who supposedly no longer works for the KGB. I don't believe it. You shouldn't. At best we might be able to use Pete to find the amber. At worst he'll use us. If you don't stop acting like I'm a bad smell, I can guarantee that we'll be the ones who get used."

"What do you want from me?" she asked tightly.

Jake looked at Honor's stiff posture and was tempted to shock her by telling her exactly what he wanted, when he wanted it, and how he wanted it. But that wouldn't improve the situation one bit.

"An act," he said.

"What do you mean?"

"I want you to act like I'm an all-day sucker and you can't wait to lick me. I'll do the same with you."

"I'm not that good an actress."

"You were before Archer called the second time."

She started to retort that it hadn't been an act then. Just in time she saw the trap and bit off the protest. "I'll do what I can."

"You can start by looking at me."

Honor clenched her hands. Then she deliberately relaxed her fingers and turned to look at Jake. Not his eyes, though. She really didn't want to see the male contempt in them for a silly, easy female conquest.

"Anything else?" she asked through pale lips.

"Pete will want to know what our relationship is."

"I hired you to handle my brother's boat."

"And?"

"That's what you're doing."

"Then why are we sleeping together?"

"We aren't."

"Wrong answer. If you think I'm going to lie awake in the boat wondering when some other *mafiya* hopeful will prowl through the cottage, you're nuts."

"No. I'm not sleeping with you."

"Whether you sleep or not is your problem. Mine is making sure I'm the only one in your bed."

"No."

"All right. We'll do it your way."

At first Honor didn't think she had heard correctly. Before she could ask Jake to repeat it, he was talking again.

"I'll arrange your ticket to Tahiti and some husky types to handle your luggage."

"I'm not going anywhere."

"Wrong again. You have two choices—me as your roommate while we look for Kyle, or Tahiti and bodyguards. Take your pick, Ms. Donovan."

"You can't force me to—"

"I can damn well make sure that you're taken out of the game," he interrupted savagely. "If you don't believe me, keep pushing. The only way you'll find out about Kyle will be in the newspapers."

This time Honor looked at Jake, really looked at him. There was nothing smug or superior about him. He was as coldly furious as she was. If she hadn't known better, she would have thought he was the one who had been betrayed rather than her.

"Where do you get off being angry?" she demanded. "I'm the one who got screwed!"

"So that's it," he said. "Forget all the huffing and puffing about truth. My crime was teaching you how good sex can be." His voice softened. "Don't be mad, honey. I learned the same thing. Or is it just that I didn't say I love you right on cue?"

"At least you don't tell lies in bed," she said thinly.

"Keep it in mind. Now take your pick—put on a good act or get out of the game."

"It isn't a game. It's Kyle's life."

"It's mine, too, a fact that you didn't bother to tell me when I hired on as your 'fishing guide.' "

"I didn't know!"

"You didn't want to know. You live in a fantasy world where money means nothing. In the real world people will kill you for a handful of shit, much less for a million dollars."

"You knew that before I hired you as a fishing guide. I didn't have to tell you."

"I didn't know it was going to turn into an international mud-wrestling match over the Amber Room."

"Then you shouldn't have hidden a piece of it in with ordinary amber!"

Jake's eyes narrowed. "Is that what Archer said I did?"

"It's what he said happened. Either you did it or Kyle did it."

"And Kyle, being a Donovan, couldn't have done it," Jake said icily. "That leaves me, the world-class chump who thought Kyle was his friend."

"He was. He likes you!"

Jake looked at Honor's face and saw all the outrage, hurt, and confusion she felt. And love. She would go to her grave believing that Kyle had done no wrong.

"Kyle likes me, huh? Thank God he didn't love me. I wouldn't have survived." Suddenly Jake removed his arm. "In or out, Honor. Your choice. It's more choice than I was given."

The weary edge of bitterness in his voice slid past Honor's defenses. He was no happier than she was. It shouldn't have made a difference, but it did. She didn't know what the difference was; she only knew that something had changed.

"In," she whispered.

Jake got out, pulled a battered overnighter suitcase from behind the seat, and shut the door of the truck. Without looking to see if she was coming, he headed for the Chowder Keg.

Honor barely caught up with him before he reached the front door. He opened it and ushered her into the smoky room. One glance told her it was more bar than café and hadn't been cleaned since she was in diapers. Several men who were drinking lunch glanced up from their beers. They looked Honor up and down. Twice.

Jake's hand pressed lightly low on her back. She stiffened at his touch. In the next breath she realized there was no need for her to worry. No matter how intimate his touch might look to an outsider, she knew in her gut that it was impersonal.

I want you to act like I'm an all-day sucker you can't wait to lick. I'll do the same with you.

A tall, athletic-looking blond man with wide cheekbones and an equally wide mouth stood and walked toward them. He skirted the few locals without appearing to notice their sullen dislike of having an outsider in their territory. His clothes were informal, expensive, and neither Russian nor American. Smiling, he held out his hand to Jake as though greeting him at a private home for a cup of tea.

"So good of you to come," Resnikov said, shaking Jake's hand firmly. "This is the charming Honor Donovan, yes?"

Honor shaped her mouth into a social smile, nodded, and allowed her hand to be gently taken between both of the Russian's. His accent teased her. It was similar to Snake Eyes's, but less coarse. She felt she had heard it before-...but as Jake said, there were a lot of Russian immigrants around.

"Those marvelous eyes," Resnikov said. "Does every Donovan have them?"

"Two each," she said. "Standard issue."

He laughed as though she had said something amusing. "You have wit as well as beauty. Surely you are the smaller sister of Kyle."

Jake removed Honor's fingers from the lingering trap of Resnikov's hands. "Quit drooling, Pete. She's spoken for."

Resnikov looked from Honor to Jake and sighed. "I am devastate."

"Desolate," Jake corrected dryly, "or devastated. Your choice."

Behind them the Keg's door opened. Jake turned just enough to see who was coming in. A man and woman walked through the door with a confidence that visibly irritated the locals.

Jake turned his back on the couple. At this point in the game, Ellen and her pinstriped escort weren't going to stick a knife in him.

"Let's get out of the doorway," he said.

Honor spotted the woman and frowned. No red jacket, but the rest looked real familiar, even without binoculars. "Isn't that the wom—" she began.

Jake shut her up with a hard kiss. "Move, darlin'. We're blocking progress."

"Of course, *buttercup*. Whatever you say."

He gave her a warning look. She gave him a wide-eyed, innocent, empty smile and turned to follow the Russian to his table.

Ellen took a table nearby. Her partner went to the bar and ordered two mugs of chowder and two beers. Jake watched the couple without appearing to. He held out Honor's chair, then sat down beside her so close that their thighs rubbed. She flinched subtly but didn't move away.

The bar door opened again. Resnikov's pale blue eyes narrowed. Jake glanced sideways toward the front of the bar.

"Old home week," he murmured.

"What?" Honor asked.

"Snake Eyes. Don't look. Trust me."

She bit back the obvious retort. "Who's his date?"

"He's solo."

"No surprise there. Even a mirror wouldn't want to be seen with him."

Jake smiled faintly. He looked toward Resnikov. "Friend or competitor?"

"Pavlov?" He shrugged. "I don't know."

Jake didn't believe him.

The door opened again. Conroy walked in with a young, burly man who was probably a recruit. Jake saluted silently. Conroy responded with a nod and headed toward the bar.

"Who is that?" Resnikov said sharply.

"An old friend."

"Will he want to join us?"

"I don't know. Will he?"

Resnikov appeared to think about it, then shook his head in the negative. "On the whole, for you it would be better to renew old friendships elsewhere."

Jake wasn't surprised. "Right. What's on your mind?"

Before Resnikov answered, he looked around

the smoky room. The tables close to them were full. Then came a swath of empty chairs. Then came a knot of regulars who looked frankly surly at the invasion of their turf.

"I was told this was a quiet place," the Russian said. "Perhaps we should return to my ship. It would not be wise to show you the amber here."

Honor took a swift breath. Before she could speak, Jake's hand clamped down on her thigh beneath the table.

"What amber?" he asked. Though the words were clear, they didn't carry any farther than Resnikov.

"A, er, sampling? Is that correct word?"

"Close enough. Samples of what?"

"Amber, but of course. My employers would like your opinion of the worth of these pieces."

"Why didn't they ask you?"

"They wanted the best. I am merely quite good."

Honor looked from Resnikov's handsome, surprisingly elegant features to Jake's rough-edged face. Beneath his offhanded expression, she sensed an intensity in him that compelled her. It reminded her of the single-minded lover who had turned her world inside out in the space of a night.

But sex wasn't the center of Jake's attention right now. Amber was.

He loves amber like some men love God.

"There's a back room here," Jake said. "I'll see if it's available."

Two minutes and forty dollars later, he led

Resnikov and Honor into a dingy private room. The Russian set down his beer and a small suitcase not unlike Jake's. Resnikov pulled out a cigarette, lit it, and settled into a chair. In front of him was a circular table whose ruined cover might once have been green but now was the color of dirty hands. So was the deck of cards stacked near the overflowing ashtray.

Jake chose a chair that had a view of the door they had just come through. There was another door that led out to the alley. He could see that one, too. He pulled a chair very close beside him, patted it, and smiled at Honor.

"Come to papa," he said.

"You're old, buttercup, but not *that* old," she said, deadpan.

Resnikov snickered. "She is like her brother, yes?"

"Not in the ways that really matter," Jake said, giving Honor an up-and-down look and a slow grin.

She blew a kiss to him through lips that wanted to snarl. When she noticed the Russian giving her an odd look, she took Jake's hand and nipped at the pad of his thumb. "You promised this wouldn't take long, remember?"

Jake's eyes narrowed. He made no attempt to hide the leap of hunger caused by Honor's playful bite.

"You heard the lady," he said in a husky voice. "Let's see the amber."

Resnikov opened his briefcase, pulled out a piece, and set it on the table. Jake picked up the stone. It was half the size of his hand. In bright light it would have been a rather thin yellow. The amber was unpolished, still in its oxidized, opaque "shell."

He set the piece down, put his own briefcase on the table, and opened it. Honor got a quick glimpse of a heavy needle, a lighter, various bottles and implements whose uses she couldn't guess, and a black gun whose purpose she understood all too well. The top half of the case held what looked like samples of amber in see-through compartments.

Jake pulled out a tightly stoppered bottle, put a drop of fluid on the pale surface of the stone, and pushed the stopper in firmly again. The penetrating smell of ether curled up. He waited a few moments, then touched the surface.

"New Zealand copal," he said dismissingly. "You're wasting my time."

He tossed the piece to Resnikov, who caught it with an easy, quick movement of his hand.

"It isn't amber?" Honor asked, surprised.

"Not for a million years," Jake said. "Amber is fossil resin. That piece is way too young to qualify."

"How can you tell?"

"Ether makes copal sticky. It doesn't do a thing to true amber." He looked toward Resnikov. "If your employers can't do better than that, they don't need me. They need a decent source."

Resnikov smiled gently. "Patience, my very American friend. These people do not know you as I do. They insisted that I, er, show your gaits."

"Do you mean they want me put through my paces?" Jake asked dryly.

"Is that the idiom? Put through paces...very nice. They hope to hire you for the smallest possible price, you understand."

"American dollars, British pounds, German marks, Japanese yen, Russian rubles?"

"A more fitting coin. Amber."

"They'll pay me in amber?"

Resnikov nodded, making light run like pale water over his blond hair. "The amber will be from items such as I have with me now."

Jake's black eyebrows rose. "Interesting. If I settle for a fraud, I'll get paid in kind."

"But of course. Is it not always so?"

"What happens if I prove to be very, very expensive?" he asked.

"They will wail. They will scream. They will pay."

Jake grunted. "I hope you have something a hell of a lot better than copal."

With a thin smile, Resnikov brought out something wrapped in dark, soft cloth, set it on the table, and gestured for Jake to go to work.

Jake unwrapped the cloth quickly but carefully. A piece of jewelry lay inside. The oval cameo was several inches long, opaque, somewhere between butter and cream in color, and had a nice satin shine. A woman's face was carved in relief. A delicately wrought Victorian silver setting displayed the brooch very nicely.

"I don't have an ultraviolet lamp with me," Jake said, balancing the brooch on his palm, "but I suspect this will fluoresce white."

"Truly?" Resnikov asked.

Jake weighed the brooch and said only, "Do you object to a hot needle?"

"No. You will be careful, of course."

Setting the piece aside, Jake took a lighter and a sturdy steel needle from his briefcase. Flame leaped. He held the tip of the needle in the fire. When he was satisfied that the metal was hot enough, he turned the brooch over and touched the needle to an inconspicuous edge of the stone, where the tiny mark wouldn't show. Immediately the bitter scent of burned milk bit into his nostrils.

"As I thought," he said. "Casein."

"What?" Honor asked.

"Imitation amber made of milk protein and formaldehyde. It's a third again as heavy as the real thing." He ran the ball of his thumb lightly over the carving, appreciating its fragile lines. "Very nicely crafted. Probably a hundred years old. Is it for sale?"

"Why?" she asked, before Resnikov could answer. "You just said it's a fake."

"Half the items in museums are fakes. This," Jake said, rubbing his thumb over the brooch again, "is an artfully carved bit of history from the time before plastic made counterfeiting amber easy and cheap. It would fit right into my collection."

"Of fakes?" Honor asked in disbelief.

Resnikov laughed out loud.

Jake's smile showed as a flash of white against his short, dense beard. "Not all of my collection is fake."

"You are too modest," Resnikov said. "Your collection of antique carved amber is one of the finest in private hands."

"What else do you have in the case?" Jake asked.

Shaking his head, the Russian replaced the samples Jake had already seen and took out a box. He opened it and presented the contents with a subdued flourish.

"You may handle it with your customary care," the Russian said.

Honor leaned forward. "What is it?"

"A pendant, probably," Jake said, looking closely at the item without lifting it out of the box. "Etruscan style with oversized eyes and the kind of nose we call Roman today. Broken and mended where the boy's leg lies between the woman's."

"Boy? It looks like a girl to me," Honor said, peering at the carving. "It's a smaller figure than the other one, with bigger eyes and more delicate features."

"Cultural bias," he said succinctly. "Etruscan goddesses, and probably the wealthy Etruscan women as well, had much younger lovers. A mature woman's face is more fully formed than a boy's. In any case"—he handed Honor the loupe—"look where the figures are almost joined."

After a short silence, Honor handed back

306

the loupe. "Right. Definitely not female. Not real delicate, either."

Jake laughed quietly. "From the position of the figures, this probably was a fertility fetish."

"Then it is a genuine piece," Resnikov said with the air of a man stating the obvious.

"I wouldn't buy it."

Surprise and something less pleasant flashed across the Russian's aristocratic face. It made Honor wonder if, like Jake, Resnikov had a gun stashed in his suitcase along with all the other odds and ends.

Jake must have wondered, too. As the uneasy silence expanded, he watched Resnikov's hands.

16

Resnikov spread his fine-boned hands on the table as though he would have preferred to wrap them around Jake's neck.

"What are you saying?" the Russian demanded.

Jake shrugged, but there was nothing casual about the way he was gathering himself for a fight, if it came to that. "There's something about this carving I don't like."

"Explain. But do not question or test the amber substance itself. It is real beyond a doubt. I will guarantee it."

"It's not the amber that bothers me."

"Excellent. Continue."

"I'm not an art historian," Jake said calmly, "but there's something wrong about the drapery or wings or whatever they are on the woman's figure. It's hard to tell which on such a small piece."

"Examine it more closely." Then, as though hearing the cold anger in his own voice for the first time, Resnikov forced himself to smile. "If you please."

Jake picked up the amber, set it on the lens of his flashlight, and turned on the beam. Light glowed through the tiny sculpture, setting it afire.

"The crazing isn't thick," he said, looking at the network of hair-fine cracks all across the surface that gave a textured appearance to the amber.

"If the piece came from a grave, locked away from oxygen and light for all the long centuries, then crazing would not develop greatly," Resnikov pointed out.

Though Jake nodded, he obviously wasn't convinced. He bent over and examined the small carving for a long minute through the loupe.

"Look at this edge," he said, straightening. "It's ragged and the others are smooth, as though a piece was broken off after the carving was finished. Yet the crazing is the same on the ragged edge as the smooth."

"It could have broken during the burial ceremony."

"It could have."

"You do not think so," Resnikov said.

"No. I think this is a copy of a real piece,

a copy that was made without benefit of magnification and baked in an oven or hot sand to simulate the natural aging of time."

Resnikov took the flashlight and carving. Without waiting for a request, Jake handed over the loupe. Silence condensed in the room while the Russian bent over the amber. He began speaking softly in his native language. The look on his face said that he wasn't composing love sonnets to the carving.

Unhappily he stuffed the amber back into its box. His lack of care said more than words about how his opinion of the artifact had changed.

"As I said," he muttered, "I am merely quite good. You are best."

As he opened his small suitcase wider and reached in for another item, the door leading back to the main café swung inward. Jake didn't have to move his head to see Ellen look around the room. Though her glance was fast, it missed nothing.

"Oh," she said, as though surprised. "Excuse me. I was looking for the rest room and thought this was the door." She smiled prettily and withdrew.

The door didn't quite close behind her.

Resnikov got up, grabbed an extra chair, and wedged the back of it under the doorknob. He secured the alley door in the same way. Only then did he open another box and hand it to Jake.

Displayed against burgundy velvet, a piece of jewelry gleamed in shades of ivory. In fact,

Honor assumed it was ivory, until Jake picked it up with a care he showed only when handling amber—or a lover. He had touched her like that, as though she were distilled of moonlight and time.

"Rosary," Jake said. "Decade type. Probably sixteenth century. Possibly earlier. Faceted white amber beads with a few 'pine needle' inclusions. Quite rare. Excellent metalwork. Gold filigree beads separating the decades. Very fine silver filigree cross. May I have my loupe back?"

Resnikov dropped the magnifying device into Jake's outstretched hand. He put the glass to his eye and studied the beads.

"First quality," he said simply after a time. "I could set a needle to the beads, but there's no real point."

"Why?" Honor asked.

"The edges of the facets and the drill holes in the beads all show the subtle wearing down expected in jewelry of this age. Imitation amber doesn't wear like that simply by moving against the silk strands holding the beads together. True amber does."

Jake returned the rosary to its box with gentle care and an odd smile.

"What?" Honor asked.

"Just thinking about amber and the human mind," he said. "In all its hundreds of colors, amber's earliest use was as a talisman, a means of warding off evil and luring good. Paternosters like this were so proudly displayed by their owners that some orders banned the use of amber in rosaries during the thirteenth and fourteenth centuries, saying that simple knotted cords were all the pious needed to count their prayers."

Honor looked from Jake's long index finger to his half-closed eyes, gleaming like quicksilver in the dim light. Yet it was his voice that held her, deep and husky, rich with memory and emotion, resonant with a shared human hunger for that which is rare and beautiful.

"I'll bet the ban didn't stay in place for long," she said. "People have always used beauty to celebrate their gods and their own lives."

"No, it didn't last," he agreed. "The amber trade has flourished from the time women who gathered firewood on the shores of the Baltic Sea discovered that the 'sea stones' washed up on shore burned more readily than wood."

"They burned amber?" Honor asked, horrified.

"I can't prove it, but I'm sure they did. The Baltic climate is cold, wet, and miserable. Anyone who has ever tried to set fire to wet wood couldn't help but value something that burned as quickly and sweetly as amber. The peasants and soldiers in the amber mines certainly knew it. During the wars, they burned raw amber just to stay alive."

"My God. Imagine the gems they must have destroyed."

"No thanks," Jake said dryly. "I'd rather think of the women who collected firewood and carved up the carcasses brought home by the men. I'm betting those women were the first artists who worked in wood and amber. If they carved in driftwood, it rotted and vanished in a century or two. If they carved in amber, it never rotted. So the same women who burned amber in hearth fires also made rare, extraordinary pieces of Stone Age art, pieces that outlasted their creators, their children's children, and their culture itself."

Honor remembered what Kyle had said about the man he called Jay—a collector of Stone Age amber carvings. What Kyle hadn't said was that Jake's passion for the amber remains of past cultures was intellectual and sensual rather than simply greedy and possessive.

Resnikov set out another box. This time the piece inside was set off by cream-colored satin. The amber itself was a deep shade of cinnamon and radiantly clear along most of its four-inch length. A portion of one end had been left untouched. The rest of the object was carved into the shape of a vaguely tapering, irregular cylinder, with the thicker end embedded in the rough amber.

Honor frowned as she looked at the piece. The shape itself was teasingly familiar. Where it was polished, there was a surge of fluid lines and intriguing, shadowed ripples that made her want to run her fingertips over each curve and hollow. She was reaching out to do just that when she realized why the shape seemed so familiar. Instantly she snatched back her fingers.

"Go ahead," Jake said, amused. "It won't bite."

"Another fertility fetish?" she asked dryly.

"Probably not. Amber has always been thought of as supernatural. In Baltic lore, an amber necklace was believed to choke anyone who spoke lies. Talismans were carved in various shapes to ward off sickness or accidents or ill wishes. An amber phallus like this one was believed to be the most powerful of all talismans, guarding its wearer against any evil sorcery."

"Must have been a patriarchal culture that dreamed that one up," Honor said.

"No doubt. Most cultures were."

"Only after women taught them how."

Jake smiled. "Hold this while I get something."

Before she could object, she was holding the palm-sized amber phallus. Once she got past the subject matter, she saw that the workmanship on the carving was both exquisite and accurate. The amber itself was warm to her fingertips. It wasn't the first time she had noticed amber's unique property of feeling warm to the touch, but it was the first time she had blushed over it.

Yet even as she did, she couldn't help thinking of ways to turn the ancient talisman into decorative art. A brooch, possibly. Or a pendant. Yes, a pendant on a handmade golden chain, with long, elegant vines curling around the phallus, cupping it in the rich warmth of beaten gold...

"Rub it with this," Jake said without looking up from his briefcase. "See if it will pick up a bit of tissue."

Still thinking of design possibilities, Honor took the cloth he held out to her and rubbed it briskly over the smooth part of the phallus.

"That should do it," he said. "Now the tissue."

She passed the blunt, smoothly rounded tip over a small piece of tissue. The paper lifted and clung to the amber like a hungry lover.

"Lots of electricity," she said, her tone carefully neutral.

"Some plastics have that property," he said as he fiddled with his lighter and a pressurized canister of butane. "May I use the needle?" he asked Resnikov.

"If you must," the Russian said dryly. "I admit that I find the prospect troubling."

"I'll do it," Honor said, looking at Jake with wide-eyed malice. "I'll be really careful, just like it was still attached."

Jake shot her a sideways look as he heated the needle with the recharged lighter. When the steel was good and hot, he touched the rough end of the carving very delicately. After a few moments the scent of ancient resin and million-year-old sunshine curled sweetly into his nostrils.

"Not plastic," he said.

He got out the jeweler's loupe, turned on

a flashlight, and examined the phallus in strong light.

"Ambroid," he said after a time. "You can just make out the flow lines and bubbles flattened by the pressure of the mold."

"Another fake?" Honor asked.

"To some. To others, merely an 'enhanced' form of amber. In any case, the piece isn't ancient. The technique for creating a big piece of amber out of little chips was discovered in the late nineteenth century."

Jake gave the piece back to Resnikov, who put it away. Honor watched rather wistfully as the carving disappeared.

"It would make a dynamite necklace," she said. "Just think how safe I'd be."

"You already have an amber phallus," Jake said. "Remember? You're safe from the inside out."

She willed herself not to blush. "I haven't put it to the hot needle test. It might be fake."

"Trust me. It's real."

"That's what they all say."

Snickering, Resnikov set out a shallow box on the table and took off the lid.

Jake turned to the new item. Inside the box, pieces of amber interlocked to form an intricate, exquisite mosaic in the shape of a royal crest. Several pieces were missing.

"Amber?" Honor asked.

"Ask me in a few minutes," Jake said. "Amuse her, Pete. Tell her about *ginteras*."

"It is an old Lithuanian word," Resnikov said to Honor. "In general it means 'defender' or 'protector,' but it particularly refers to an amber talisman worn around the neck. Jake wears one in the shape of twined dragons. It is of Chinese making. The ancient Chinese believed amber to be the soul of a dead tiger."

Honor had a flash of memory—a translucent cinnamon-gold pendant lying against the black pelt on Jake's chest. She had noticed the amber when her alarm clock screamed and he showed up nearly naked at her door. She hadn't noticed the pendant last night.

"Are you wearing it now?" she asked Jake.

"Yes."

"Why weren't you wearing it last night?"

"Later," he said without looking away from the amber in front of him.

While Jake worked, Resnikov told Honor about the amber woven like sunlight through the darkness of ancient Baltic cultures. Amber to cure illness, amber to protect the body in war, amber to speed the soul on its final journey. Amber as the sign of the Celtic male sun god. Amber as sacred to the ancient mother. Amber as the precious residue of tears cried by the goddess Juarate, who fell in love with a mortal man and thereby ensured his death and her eternal grief....

Amber, always amber, the only stone that was warm to the touch, the only stone that could be carved with a simple knife, the only stone that crackled with life when rubbed by fur, the only stone that floated on the mysterious breast of the ocean. Amber, the divine made tangible. Amber, the burning stone of man's desires.

"Very nice," Jake said, looking up finally. "An excellent sampling of eighteenth-century carving techniques. And someone resisted the temptation to fill in the missing pieces with Dominican amber."

Resnikov laughed softly. "You have not forgiven me for that table, have you? But it was an honorable mistake."

Jake grunted.

"I would like to have seen the whole of the Amber Room," the Russian said, watching him more closely, "*or even just a single panel. To enter the room was said to be like being reborn into a world made wholly of sunlight.*"

Instinct and intelligence combined into a coolness sliding down Jake's spine. "I'm betting on the side of those who said that room burned to ash." He pushed his chair back as though to leave.

"Not so quickly, my friend," Resnikov said. "There are other pieces that require your fine touch."

Jake looked at Honor.

"You couldn't drag me out of here with amber horses," she said instantly. "This amber is fantastic. Designs are going through my mind like chain lightning."

The smile he gave her was as warm as the touch of amber. She found herself responding before she could think of all the reasons she shouldn't.

Resnikov lifted out a long, shallow box that had been constructed with a care that bordered on obsessive. The box itself was wrapped in intricately tooled leather that had designs embossed on it in gold. The clasp and hinges were hammered from solid gold. The lining inside the box was a dark, very fine suede. Eight uneven compartments held amber carvings that seemed simple, almost crude, next to the elegance of the box itself.

Jake whistled. "How many people did you kill for this lot?"

"Ah, Jacob. Always the jokester, yes?"

"Not this time."

"Then you will be pleased to know that no blood was spilled," the Russian said smoothly.

"I would be pleased if I believed you."

"It is the truth."

"Then some folks must have died of natural causes," Jake said, unconvinced. "You would have to pry these pieces out of a collector's dead hands. Or a curator's. No one would willingly part with these artifacts...if they're real."

"That is what you are here for, is it not? To determine if these are genuine."

Without another word Jake bent over the box. The difference in him was obvious to Honor. When he handled the other pieces of amber, he had been intent, interested, and appreciative. Now he was utterly focused. He radiated a kind of intensity she had seen in him only once before—last night, when he had taught her so much about the nature of sensuality and passion.

The first piece of amber appeared to be a small, worn head of an ax carved out of pale butter. When Jake gave it a delicate, questing

318

touch with his fingertip, a flush of memory and new hunger coursed through Honor. Holding her breath without knowing it, she watched while he ran his sensitive fingertips over the miniature ax head as though he were blind and reading Braille.

"Unbelievably smooth," he said after a time. "The drill holes that decorate it feel like they were polished after the piece was made."

"Is it a fetish?" Honor asked.

"Of a kind," Jake said. "Amber was believed to give immortality to its owner. Neolithic hunting societies sometimes buried their members with amber grave goods. Amber axes were probably a highly valued gift to the dead."

Resnikov nodded, but said nothing. He was watching Jake rather than the amber.

Shifting his grip on the artifact, Jake ran his thumbnail over the surface with measured force. As he had expected, his nail didn't leave a mark.

"I won't put the hot needle to this," he said.

"Is it real, then?" Honor asked.

"I don't know. But if it is, it would be a crime to mark it in any way at all."

"Stalemate?" she asked.

"No."

Gently Jake replaced the ax head in the box. Then he turned to his own case and began pulling things out. When he was finished, he had several tightly sealed jars in front of him. Each was about the size of a big coffee mug and partly filled with a clear liquid. He unscrewed the top of one jar, took the small ax head, and dropped it in. The amber dipped and settled to the bottom of the container.

"What's the liquid?" Honor asked.

"Distilled water."

Jake fished out the artifact, dried it carefully, and unscrewed the top of the second jar. Though the liquid looked the same, the ax head floated on it like thin, opaque ice.

"What's in that one?" Honor asked.

"Salt water with a specific gravity of one point zero five," Jake said without looking away from the ax head. "If this were transparent amber instead of opaque, I would have used the third jar. That water has more salt in it, which means a higher specific gravity." He lifted the ax head out and dried it carefully. "Clear amber is more dense than the cloudy kind, because the 'clouds' are caused by very tiny air bubbles."

Jake returned the ax head to its compartment in the elaborate box and selected another piece. Honor sensed his increasing excitement in the clarity of his eyes and the slight tension in his mouth. The change in him was so small she wouldn't have noticed it if she hadn't spent the night learning the depth of emotion he concealed behind his beard and impassive expression.

She looked at Resnikov, wondering if he had noticed anything different. If he did, it didn't show in his face. The Russian was watching Jake the way a fisherman watched a baited hook disappearing beneath the surface of the sea—uncertainty and hope combined.

Jake picked up another artifact from the box. The figure's shape suggested a horse. It was perhaps four inches wide by three inches tall.

Though crudely made by modern standards, the artifact was nonetheless oddly powerful. A series of tiny drill holes, like tattoos, ran down the horse's thick neck and over its short back to its stocky haunches. Its feet were close together. The piece had a shape that was both bowed and supremely centered in its own life.

"It looks like one of those ancient horses," Honor said. "The kind they just discovered running wild in Nepal or Tibet."

"It probably was modeled after an animal just like that," Jake said. "They weren't as scarce seven thousand years ago as they are now."

"Seven thousand years?" she asked, startled.

"At least."

She leaned closer, staring at the small object more closely. It looked like it had been carved from fossil ivory or bone. Yet the way Jake handled the horse told Honor that he believed it was amber. Gently he put it into a jar of liquid. The figurine floated just as the other had.

"Amber," she said.

Neither man answered. The gentle motion of the horse floating on salt water said it all.

In silence Jake lifted piece after piece out of the box. Each one that was small enough to fit in the container floated. None of them tickled his instincts, telling him that there was less to an artifact than it appeared.

The eighth piece he examined was a primitive statuette of a person. It was perhaps five inches tall, two inches wide, and obviously had been broken off below the knees so long ago that the scar had blended with the whole. The facial features were minimally carved—brooding, sunken eyes and a straight-lined, strongly defined nose. The mouth was either worn away or hadn't been considered important enough by the carver to command attention. There were two small holes drilled where the armpits would have been.

"Perhaps a pendant, perhaps a badge of office, perhaps a fetish hung by a cave door to protect the family within," Jake said. Then he added softly, "A very, very fine piece."

"Some of the others are more carefully carved," Resnikov pointed out.

"And less powerful for it." Jake cradled the object in his hand. "It's as though the artist didn't want to make the mannequin too real, for fear of what it had been or might become. Stone Age people didn't view life as we do, a straight line to death. I suspect they knew many kinds of life, many levels of death."

Jake replaced the statuette without performing any tests on it other than simply weighing it in his hand and running his fingernail over its surface.

"Is it real?" Honor asked.

"It looks right, feels right, and didn't scratch beneath my nail. In any case, it's too big for the containers I brought."

"No hot needle?" she asked.

"Bite your tongue." Then he looked up from the statuette and smiled slowly at her. "Never mind. I'll do it for you later."

"I'm breathless."

The words didn't carry quite the sting Honor wished. There was something about Jake's smile that could disarm a tank. Unfortunately for her peace of mind, she was made of much softer stuff than armor plate.

"Superb," Jake said, touching the figurine delicately as it lay in the box. "Art, artifact, and gemstone in one. Literally priceless."

"Everything has a price," Resnikov said. Though he said nothing more, his attitude made it obvious that he included Jake in the things that were for sale.

Honor held her breath, expecting him to go for Resnikov's throat. Instead, Jake smiled. It wasn't the kind of grin that made a woman feel all warm and tingly.

"I'm listening," Jake said, packing up his small suitcase as he spoke.

"If you agree to work for me, Emerging Resources will once again be welcome in all of the Russian Federation."

Jake's hands stilled for an instant, but no more. It was his only reaction to being offered exactly what he had been looking for—a means of removing his company from the Russian least-wanted list.

"When you successfully complete your task," Resnikov continued, "you will become the sole representative to the world of all Baltic amber, whether raw or worked. If you wish, every single piece of Russian Federation amber will pass through your own hands before it is sold."

Honor drew in a swift breath at what Resnikov was offering to the man who loved amber more than he loved anything else. Yet when she looked at Jake, he was closing up his suitcase as though nothing important had been said.

"Whether or not you are wholly successful in your task," the Russian added, "you will receive one hundred amber artifacts that equal or exceed the quality of those which you have deemed genuine tonight. You will be allowed to choose them yourself from a selection of four hundred museum-quality goods."

Jake's eyes widened fractionally, then narrowed. "Then you're still working for the Russian government."

"Does it matter? No matter who is my employer, the quality of your payment is assured by your own expertise."

Silence. Then Jake asked, "What do you want me to do?"

"Find the panel from the Amber Room that Kyle Donovan stole in order to—"

"My brother didn't steal anything!"

Resnikov gave Honor a hooded glance and a smile that was no deeper than the enamel on his teeth. "Of course. Forgive me. I will modify my request." He looked back at Jake, who was closing his suitcase. "Find the panel of the Amber Room that was hidden in the shipment that Kyle Donovan drove from Kaliningrad to Russia. The panel is intended to be a bona fide for the sale of the entire room. I believe sixty million U.S. dollars was mentioned as a beginning price in the auction."

Honor made a startled sound.

"What makes you think I didn't steal the amber panel and set Kyle up to take the blame?" Jake asked blandly.

"You?" The Russian laughed. "You are too—how is it said?—honorable as a long day?"

"As honest as a day is long."

"Yes." Resnikov nodded quickly. "That is it precisely. Even if you were less honest, betraying a friend is not your style."

The Russian's certainty irritated Honor. "Just how long have you known Jake?"

"Many years, both as ally and, shall we say, competitor. I have intimate experience with his lack of desire to betray friends." He looked back at Jake. "What do you say?"

"Whose interests do you represent?" Jake asked.

"The amber you will receive has no blood on it. Each piece was dredged from lagoons behind Samland Peninsula."

"Recently?"

"No. Many museums donated pieces to the owner who had this box made."

" 'Donated,' huh? Nice of them."

"The Soviet Empire was once quite large and wealthy." Resnikov shrugged. "Now it is smaller and much poorer."

"It happens."

For a moment longer Jake looked at the incredible pieces of art that had been carved in reverence and awe by human hands so long, long ago. Slowly he reached out, closed the lid of the box, and fastened its gold catch.

"No thanks, Pete. I only work for one friend at a time."

Resnikov went very still. "I cannot believe that you are part of Kyle Donovan's scheme."

"I'm not."

"Then why do you refuse to work with me? Our countries are no longer enemies."

"It has nothing to do with politics." Jake's big hand closed around Honor's. He lifted her cool fingers to his lips. "I'm working with Miss Donovan. We're...very good friends."

She couldn't hide the shiver of response that went through her as his breath warmed her skin. Nor could she hide her relief.

Until that instant, Honor hadn't known just how alone she would feel if Jake left her to search for Kyle by herself.

"You do not have to answer me tonight," Resnikov said through tight lips. "Think about it for one day. Do not let your stiff neck rule your mind, Jacob. You are not strong enough to own the Amber Room."

"I don't want to."

The Russian looked at Jake for the space of four long breaths, then nodded, believing him.

"In that event, I have an alternative suggestion," Resnikov said smoothly. "Take your lovely *friend* to Paris or Rome or London at my expense. Stay for at least a month." Deliberately he opened the box of amber once more. "No matter your decision after that month, keep these as a small token of our friendship."

Tucked among shadows, ancient amber gleamed with time and mystery and the yearnings of people long dead.

Jake stood up, pulling Honor with him. "It won't be any different tomorrow. No sale and no time-outs. Do you understand?"

Slowly Resnikov nodded. "And you, J. Jacob Mallory, do you understand?"

"You can bet your life on it. Say good-bye, Honor."

Jake handed her the suitcase, grabbed her arm in his left hand, and headed for the back door.

"When you change your mind," Resnikov said clearly, "I can be reached at the Ana Curtis Hotel."

"I won't."

"I believe you will. My employers can be very persuasive."

Jake kicked the chair from beneath the door handle and pulled Honor out into the alley. She didn't realize he was holding a gun down along his right leg until he let go of her, pulled the truck keys out of his pocket with his left hand, and tossed them in her direction.

"Drive."

For once she didn't argue.

17

"Turn here," Jake said. "We're going to my cabin."

"You may be," Honor said, ignoring his instructions, "but I'm going back to Kyle's cottage."

He turned his head to look at her. Her stubborn chin was tilted up, as though to meet the darkness head-on.

"Allow me to explain what happened back there," he said softly.

"I was there, remember?"

"Your body was. Your brain wasn't, or you would know how silly you sound talking about going alone to Kyle's cottage."

Honor's instincts told her that Jake was right, but she had no intention of sharing that gut feeling with him. She felt too off balance to trust herself to keep her distance if he reached for her in the darkness of a shared cottage.

Or if he didn't.

"Resnikov believes you won't betray me," Honor said. "But then, he doesn't know what happened, does he?"

"What happened is that I spent the past hour examining some world-class amber artifacts, artifacts that—"

"I was there, remem—"

"—could only have come from Russian state museums. That means one of several things. Pete could be representing the official government in an official, but covert, capacity. He could be tied into the branch of the Kaliningrad *mafiya* that controls, or hopes to control, the mining and distribution of amber in the Baltic States. He could have stolen the pieces we saw tonight and hopes to bribe me with them in order to get his hands on even more valuable goods."

"Like the Amber Room?"

"Or information about who stole it and how it was smuggled out of Russia and, most important, why."

"Greed," she said succinctly.

"Of course. But greed for *what*? The amber itself? Money? Revenge? Political power? Pete could be after any or all of them. He's neither timid nor stupid."

Honor glanced quickly at Jake. In the pale light washing between clouds, there wasn't anything inviting about his expression. He looked as remote as midnight. Uneasiness flickered through her. This was the Jake she didn't know, the one who could hold a gun with the safety off and every intention of pulling the trigger if he had to.

"Who do you think stole the amber?" she asked.

"Kyle signed for the shipment and drove it out of Kaliningrad. I traced him as far as Russia before Donovan International started slamming doors in my face."

"What does that mean?"

"Just what I said. Donovan International has more pull than I do. They didn't want me asking questions."

"That's ridiculous. We want to find Kyle as much as you do. More. We love him."

"Yeah. That's why your family doesn't want me to find him."

"Look," Honor said through clenched teeth, "Archer told me that the evidence against Kyle was just a bit too pat to believe. As if he had been set up."

"Maybe he wasn't very clever about what he was doing."

"Why can't you believe that he might be innocent?"

"Because that would make me guilty. No thanks, buttercup. I'm not hanging for your brother's sins."

"Couldn't someone else have stolen the damned panel and hidden it in with the legitimate stuff? Why does it have to be you or Kyle?"

Jake muttered something under his breath. He looked in the mirrors for the tenth time in two minutes. Still no one following them. He flicked on the safety and put his gun in the glove compartment.

"Your brother was in lust with a Lithuanian freedom fighter—or terrorist, depending on your politics."

"Lust? Love is a four-letter word, just like the others you use. You can say it. Your tongue won't rot."

"Crap."

"That's another four-letter word," she agreed coolly. "Unlike some men, Kyle is capable of love as well as lust."

"Is that another shot at me?"

"It's a fact. Take it and tuck it."

"Consider it tucked. Now here are a few facts for you. You aren't going to like them any more than I liked being set up to take Kyle's fall."

Honor's hands tightened on the steering wheel.

"I own a company called Emerging Resources," Jake said. "The major part of my business is advising First World corporations on how to work with the Russian Federation, which is teetering between Second World status and the toilet."

She threw him a quick look. He was watching the mirror on the passenger side.

"With intelligence and sweat and luck," he said, "Russia can be kept from sliding into fiscal and social chaos—and dragging a big chunk of the world down with it. Hard currency is one key to any country's survival. In Kaliningrad and Lithuania, I ended up as an unofficial adviser on how the government could get the most hard currency out of their amber. Do you understand the difference between hard and soft currency?"

"A hard currency can be traded for any currency in the world," Honor said tightly. "A soft currency can't. Outside the country that issued it, soft currency can be less valuable than good toilet paper."

"You're a Donovan," he said, smiling thinly. "You understand international business. Without hard currency to buy goods on the world market, not much is possible for Russian Federation countries but charity, poverty, stagnation, and ultimately revolution. Sensible people know it and design national policies accordingly."

"So where does theft and the Amber Room come in?"

"Not under sweet reason, that's for sure."

As Honor turned onto Marine Drive, clouds swiftly ate the light, leaving behind a deeper gloom.

"The Amber Room comes under greed, revenge, and politics," Jake said. "For Russia it's a symbol of Nazi greed, Russian blood, and the agony of World War Two, plus the greatness of a czarist Golden Age that Russians are afraid they'll never know again. Communism gutted the economy and the people's spirit worse than the czars ever did."

Honor remembered the intense conversations she had had with the Donovan when she first suggested that she and Faith do business outside of First World countries. He hadn't been thrilled, despite the fact that the Donovan males were doing just that.

"Dad says pretty much the same thing," she said. It's the one thing he and Archer agree on. But why would the Russian government steal its own Amber Room?"

"Same reason the Italian mafia stole one of Italy's great paintings—*The Nativity* by Caravaggio. Competing interests. Crime and legitimate government may overlap, but they aren't the same. Yet."

"You said something about Lithuanian terrorists. What would they want the Amber

Room for? To swap it for arms?"

"That's one possibility. If they were really smart, they would use it as a lever to pry themselves farther apart from Russia and get their own currency, a real rather than a toothless local government, real autonomy, that sort of thing. Unfortunately, right now Russia can't afford to turn loose any more pieces of its former empire without inviting total collapse."

"What about the woman? What's her interest?"

"Marju?"

"No. The one in the red coat."

"Oh. That's Ellen Lazarus. We used to work for the same outfit."

"The U.S. government?" Honor asked evenly.

"Part of it. Nobody works for all of it, not even the president. As for Ellen, it's simple. She wants the Amber Room."

"Why?"

"She didn't say."

"Guess."

"Politics. International leverage. You stroke mine and I'll stroke yours and we'll all have a fine time for as long as it lasts."

"Jake Mallory's First Principle," Honor said sardonically. "For as long as it lasts."

"Beats fairy dust about love, life, or country ever after, world without end, amen. Nothing lasts forever, honey."

"Even amber?" she challenged.

"Even that. It comes close, though. When you hold a Neolithic figurine in your hand, time peels away until you can almost touch the yearnings of the people who put their own souls into a simple carving..."

The husky resonance of Jake's voice shivered through Honor. He loved ancient amber the way she had always dreamed of being loved by a man.

Yet he had turned down the very thing he loved so deeply.

"Why?" she asked.

"Why what?"

"Why did you refuse Resnikov? Didn't you believe he would follow through with his promises?"

"It didn't matter. I only work for one employer at a time."

"Yourself?"

"Mostly. Lately I've found myself working for a sharp-tongued buttercup."

"Who has found herself the employer of a lethal darlin'," she retorted.

"Sometimes flowers just don't get the job done."

Carefully Honor let out a breath that kept trying to break. She wanted to stay close to Jake so much that it scared her. She was in over her head in every way that mattered. She would survive falling in love with the wrong man.

She wouldn't survive trusting the wrong man in a deadly game of greed and amber.

"If it helps," Jake said, "as your official *ginteras*, I come with the Donovan International seal of approval."

"What?"

"Unlike a certain razor-edged buttercup, Archer figured out real fast that I wouldn't hurt his little sister. He offered to whitewash me if I'd take you away from the line of fire."

"I don't understand."

"No shit," he said roughly.

She bit her lip against the scalding words crowding her tongue. A tirade wouldn't help right now, even though it would feel almost as good as shaking Jake Mallory until his big white teeth rattled.

"Let me get this straight," she said neutrally. "Archer offered to clear your name if you would take me away from here?"

"Yes."

Honor didn't know what to say.

"You don't believe me," Jake said, watching her.

"I don't know what to believe."

"Ah, the lady learns."

"Listen, you smug—"

"Sorry," he said over her words. "I'm a little edgy myself, okay? If I didn't know you were damned intelligent, I would have stuffed you in a kennel cage and mailed you back to the Donovans C.O.D."

"Thanks, I think. You turned down Resnikov and you turned down Archer. Why?"

"I don't trust Resnikov."

"Do you trust Archer?"

"In all but this. When push comes to shove, it's me or Kyle. I know how any Donovan will choose."

"Archer wouldn't go back on his word to you."

"He loves you and he loves Kyle. Only a fool asks a man to choose between two things he loves equally. You can't predict the outcome."

Honor opened her mouth and then closed it without making a sound. She knew that Jake was right. If she had to choose between siblings...she couldn't.

Rain started spitting down. She turned on the headlights and finally found the windshield wiper control. Road dirt smeared across the window until Jake reached over and turned on the washer. The glass cleared into two curved views of a gray universe.

"What do you believe?" Honor asked finally.

"Fuck believing." Jake's voice was cold. "I *know* that I didn't steal the amber, much less a panel of the Amber Room."

She wanted to doubt him.

She wanted to believe him.

She was being asked to choose between two people she loved, Kyle and Jake. Her mind could give her a lifetime of reasons to chose Kyle. Her gut simply rebelled at making either choice.

"If there were another suspect, any other suspect," Honor asked almost desperately, "would you believe Kyle was innocent?"

"Hell, yes! I've been going through it in my mind since I heard about the theft, looking for another explanation. Any explanation. I thought the charming son of a bitch was my friend."

She opened her mouth and thought better

of it. Instead of defending her brother, she listened to her one-night, once-in-a-lifetime lover.

"At first I couldn't believe Kyle had screwed me like that," Jake said. "I even thought he might be in trouble and I could help him. Jesus, was I ever a fool."

The pain and self-contempt in Jake's voice made Honor wince. It was an exact echo of how she had felt after Archer told her who her fishing guide really was.

"I started asking questions," Jake said, "and Donovan International came down on my head like a hundred-year flood. Next thing I knew people were offering to kill me unless I shut up and got out of town. I kept pushing. The Donovan clan didn't like it. They had me thrown out of that half of world."

A seething kind of silence closed over the car. After a few miles, Honor broke it. "What about the woman?"

"Ellen?"

"No. Mariyoo whatever."

Jake looked startled. "Marry you?" Then he understood. "Oh, *Marju*. What about her?"

"If Kyle stole anything—and I'm not saying he did—then isn't there a chance that she knew what was going on?"

"Yes."

"And?"

"She says Kyle used her to get to the Amber Room."

"That's not his style."

Jake didn't reply.

"Damn it, it's true!" Honor said. "Kyle wouldn't do something like that, especially to someone he loved."

"Lusted. Not the same thing."

"No shit," she said bitterly.

Jake felt like pounding on the dashboard. The certainty that Honor was slipping away from him had put a deadly edge on his temper. He told himself all the reasons why she had a right to feel used, took a slow breath, and then another.

He still felt like hammering on the dashboard.

"What makes you so sure Marju didn't use Kyle?" Honor asked.

"No motive."

"How about sixty million bucks?"

"How about the fact that Marju's connection to the panel came from the Forest Brotherhood?" Jake countered.

"So?"

"She's a heavy-duty Lithuanian patriot. The Forest Brotherhood is a Lithuanian patriotic organization. She might steal the Amber Room from one love, the Brotherhood, and give it to another love, Kyle, but she wouldn't steal it from him and the Brotherhood both. No motive. Either way, she already had the damned thing, so why steal it from herself in the first place?"

"What about Snake Eyes?"

"If he had the Amber Room, he wouldn't be hanging around here."

"The same could be said of everyone."

"Except Kyle," Jake said evenly. "He isn't here."

"Neither is Archer. Does that mean he stole it?"

"Makes sense to me. Archer is the one who shut down Russia around my ears."

A few more miles went by in tight silence.

"What if Kyle didn't steal the panel," Honor said finally, "but is being blamed for it?"

"Great. Who stole it?"

"I don't know! Maybe they all did it and ganged up on Kyle!"

"They? As in Russia, Lithuania, the United States, and various international crooks of unknown origin, including me?"

"Easy for you to ridicule, but I don't hear you coming up with anything better."

"I don't have to. I already have a suspect who is a dead match for the facts."

"Your facts need rearranging."

Jake swore wearily. "Any one of a thousand people could have stolen the panel, but that doesn't explain why Kyle and the shipment went missing together, does it?"

"But someone could have just slipped the panel in with the rest of the amber when it was loaded. Kyle didn't have to know anything about it."

"I packed every piece of that shipment myself. There was nothing but raw amber. Nothing."

Honor's eyelids flinched. She didn't say a word.

"I turned the truck over to Kyle," Jake continued relentlessly, "to take to the driver he had hired. Before the truck left Kaliningrad, the driver was murdered and dumped by the side of the road. A man matching Kyle's description was seen driving the truck over the Russian border. The truck hasn't been seen since. Kyle has. Here. Two weeks ago. Not once in the four weeks he has been missing did he call his loving family to let them know he was all right. Now, tell me again how I'm a cold-hearted son of a bitch to think your brother is guilty."

Honor's expression went from stubborn to despairing.

Jake should have felt better that she finally seemed to be believing him. He didn't. It was hard to feel good about anything that made Honor look like she had been hit by a truck.

The silence made the rhythmic clicking of the turn signal seem as loud as a drum roll.

The unmarked police car was still parked in the small turnout near the cottage.

"He's going to rust right into the ground," Honor said in a harsh voice.

"Who?"

"The cop with the radar unit."

"He doesn't give a damn about writing tickets. He's watching your driveway, not traffic."

"Wonderful. What if I flip him off just to let him know I care?"

"He has an eight-hour shift. He can spend

340

it giving you a hard time or he can sit there and read girlie magazines."

Honor kept both hands on the wheel as she turned into the driveway.

"How long will it take you to pack?" Jake asked.

"No time at all. I'm not packing."

With an effort he managed not to say the first red-hot thing that came to his mind.

"What do you have against coming to my cabin?" he asked evenly. "My bed is bigger than the one here. You'll be able to put your whole damned suitcase between us."

Ignoring him, Honor got out of the truck.

Jake opened the glove compartment, grabbed the gun, and caught her before she reached the front door.

"No," he said through his teeth. "Let me check the place out first."

"I locked it."

He gave her a disgusted look. "You've got a good brain, buttercup. Use it."

She looked at his gun. "I find it hard to believe that I'm a—a target or whatever."

"Believe it. You're the key to the Donovan castle. Someone could grab you and open negotiations for the Amber Room."

"I don't have it."

"The Donovans do."

"Like hell!"

"Prove it."

Her mouth opened. Nothing came out.

"Now you're catching on," he said. "You can't prove a negative. Give me the key."

"I thought all you secret agent types carried a lock pick."

"Lock pick? Sure thing. I have one right here." Jake lifted his boot to kick in the door.

"Never mind," she said quickly. "Here."

"Stay outside until I come back for you."

"This is ridiculous."

"Amen. Stay here."

Divided between anger and a nagging fear, Honor waited. Though it wasn't long before Jake returned, it felt like an hour to her.

"Like I said," she muttered, stepping around him to get through the door, "this is— Damn! I forgot."

"I didn't. Watch your step. Paper can be as slippery as ice."

Picking up what she could, Honor threaded her way through the mess the intruder had made. Finally she reached the desk. The answering machine didn't show a message light.

"Sure you wouldn't rather come to my cabin?" Jake asked. "I'm not the world's neatest housekeeper, but I'm better than this."

She didn't bother to respond.

"Hell," he muttered. "I'll check on the boat, then I'll be back to help you put this together."

Before Jake got his foot out the door, the telephone rang. Sourly he thought that whoever was spying on the cottage had a good communication network. He and Honor hadn't been back five minutes and already the fun was beginning.

She grabbed the phone. "Hello?"

"Hello. Who is this?"

"Honor Donovan. Who are you?"

"We have not met, but Kyle has talked much about you. My name is Marju. Kyle is my fiancé. May I come and talk with you?"

18

"Well?" Honor asked impatiently, trying to look past Jake's shoulders. She was eager to see the woman who claimed to be Kyle's fiancée.

"She's alone."

He watched Marju get out of a beat-up rental job and pick her way through the mud and puddles toward the front door.

"Wonder if she and Ellen went to the same school?" Jake asked idly.

"Spy school?" Honor asked, startled.

"Locomotion."

"What do you—oh, that," she said, understanding when she saw Marju walking. Even though the black skirt and sweater weren't particularly stylish, on her they looked like Paris originals. "Whew. I think some women are born walking like that. No practice required."

"You ought to know."

She gave Jake a sidelong look. "I don't move anything like that."

"You do it better."

"Ha. No way do I walk like I have the secret of the universe tucked between my thighs."

He made an odd, strangled sound and then laughed out loud. As he turned toward her, the backs of his fingers brushed down her cheek and across her lips. "You're one of a kind, honey. Whatever happens, I don't regret meeting you."

Honor looked at the laughter and shadows in Jake's eyes and knew he was telling the truth. Before she could think better of it, she found herself whispering a kiss across his fingers. Whatever his motives for answering her ad, he had protected her as much as he had used her; and he had been a hungry, generous lover who made her feel like the most desirable woman since Eve.

"Does this mean I'm forgiven?" he asked huskily.

"It means...I don't know what it means." But she was afraid she did. It meant she was an idiot. She cleared her throat. "It means we need each other until this mess is cleared up, so we might as well bury the hatchet."

"Damned by faint praise again. But I'll take it. It's better than the deep freeze and a razor tongue."

A knock on the door saved Honor from having to answer. She opened the door and started to say something, then she simply stared. Though Marju was not conventionally beautiful, there was something about her that was electrifying. Charisma, sheer animal presence, whatever—the woman radiated on every band of the sexual spectrum.

Honor's stomach sank. She could understand all too well how her brother could have lost his head over this woman.

"Come in," Jake said dryly to Marju. "Don't worry about the silence. Honor will get her tongue back real quick."

"Jay? Is it really you?" Marju asked. Her huge, dark eyes opened wide. The flecks of gold that rimmed each black iris exactly matched her burnished blond hair. A small, pale hand closed around Jake's wrist. "Where is Kyle? Is he well?"

"Yes, yes, I don't know, I don't know." He led Marju in and closed the door. "Honor Donovan, meet Marju. I'd give you her last name but you would hash the pronunciation so badly there's no point. Call her Jones. It worked for Kyle. Marju, the awestruck woman is Kyle's sister."

Honor held out her hand. "Hello, Marju. Susa would kill to paint you."

Marju shook hands briskly despite looking confused by what Honor had said.

"Susa is my mother," Honor explained. "All the kids call her Susa. She paints. Landscapes usually, but she makes exceptions for exceptionally interesting faces."

Marju smiled uncertainly. "Oh. This is good?"

"If you don't mind holding still for her, it's great. Come in and sit down. You'll be my first sister-in-law. As soon as we find Kyle, of course. Coffee? Tea? Something stronger?"

Long, natural lashes swept down over

Marju's eyes. Again, she smiled uncertainly.

Jake sighed and began translating. His Lithuanian was marginal, but his Russian was excellent. So was Marju's.

Honor's Russian was zilch. She waited with increasing impatience.

"Okay," Jake said finally, turning to Honor. "Marju speaks four languages, including English, and understands three more. But school talk and real talk aren't the same. Slang is a problem for her."

"Got it," Honor said. "Er, that is, I understand."

"If it would not trouble you," Marju said, smiling, "a cup of coffee would be welcome."

"I'll get it," Jake said. "You two get acquainted."

"What about you?" Honor asked him.

"Jones and I already know each other."

"Biblically speaking?" Honor muttered before she could stop herself.

He didn't answer.

Marju settled gracefully onto the worn sofa and crossed her elegant legs. Though Honor and Jake had picked up the worst of the mess before Marju arrived, some papers still stuck out from a cushion. Honor snatched up the strays, put them on Kyle's desk, and pulled a dining chair up opposite the sofa.

Despite the fact that Marju was inches taller than Honor, she seemed almost fragile as she sat on the little couch. Her pale hands were laced together until the knuckles showed white. Her delicate feet were crossed at the ankles. Her long, elegant neck was bowed with jet lag or simply a lifetime of talking to shorter people.

"Have you heard from Kyle?" Marju asked anxiously.

"No. Have you?"

"Oh, no." Long lashes blinked rapidly. Tears hovered. "I had hoped," she whispered. "He loves his family so..."

"Certainly no more than he loves the woman he's going to marry?"

Marju smiled wanly. "You are kind, but I have much knowledge of men. They want a woman's sex greatly but they love very little. Women love greatly and pray to be loved just a little in return for their sex."

Honor swallowed and tried not to think of herself and Jake. "Some men are different."

"Of course," Marju said huskily. Tears threatened to spill. "I thought Kyle was such a man, once. He is not, yet I cannot stop my love for him."

A box of tissues appeared between the two women. The flowery pink design looked odd in Jake's big hand.

"Jones can't make it through an evening without crying," he said. "It's the Lithuanian blood. Drama sucked in with Mama's milk and all that."

Marju gave him a watery smile. "Ah, Jay, you still have not forgiven me for choosing Kyle."

"Are you kidding?" Jake said. "I'm down on my knees twice a day thanking my first wife."

"For what?" Honor asked sharply.

"Teaching me that sex wears off about three weeks after the ink on the marriage license is dry. You still like your coffee with a shot of vodka, Jones?"

"Please, yes."

"I'll see if Kyle has any."

Honor tried to hide her reaction. She didn't like vodka under the best of circumstances. In coffee it was unthinkable. But then, Kyle had always been attracted to the exotic. Blonde, dark-eyed, cat-graceful Marju "Jones" was about as exotic as it got.

"Er, how did you and Kyle meet?" Honor asked.

"At a beer hall. What the English call a pub. I was there with my cousin, who works in the amber mines. Kyle was there with Jay. Oh, such laughter they had. It was so artless, so confident, so *American*. I think I fell in love as I stood there."

"You wouldn't be the first," Honor said dryly. "Kyle has been knocking them dead—er, attracting the opposite sex—since he learned how to smile. Rather like you, I suppose."

"Please?"

"Surely you know how you affect men just by walking into a room?"

Marju shrugged. "It does not last."

"Must be fun while it does," Honor said wistfully. "So you looked right past Jake to Kyle?"

"Jake?"

"Jay."

"Ah. He is *tres magnifique,* very much male,

348

but next to Kyle...the comparison is not fair. No man can stand next to my sweet angel Kyle."

Honor blinked. "Sweet? Angel? Kyle? Are we talking about the same man who short-sheeted my bed, stuck a turtle down my T-shirt, and put honey in my braids?"

"It is different for a sister, no?"

"It is different, yes!"

Marju laughed softly. "You are very like Kyle. So open. So kind. So..."

"American?" Jake asked from the kitchen. "As in naive?"

"Yes!" Marju said, clapping her hands. "Naive. It is perfect!"

Honor eyed her enthusiastic sister-in-law-to-be and told herself that the woman's grasp of American English wasn't good enough for her to understand that *naive* wasn't exactly a compliment. Puppies, kittens, and kindergartners were naive. Adults with those romping, innocent qualities were often described as stupid.

"I guess Kyle wasn't expecting you," Jake said, handing Marju a cup of coffee. "No vodka."

Marju gave him a gentle, sad smile and sipped the coffee. "Ah, that has not changed, has it? You make fine coffee, even without the dear bite of vodka."

"Just one of my many charms."

Though Jake was smiling, Honor could tell he didn't particularly care for Marju. Not too surprising. No matter what he said about being grateful not to have caught Marju's eye, it still had to rankle.

"Forgive me for being blunt," Honor said, "but when was the last time you heard from Kyle?"

"Four weeks ago. The night I gave him with my own hands a panel from the Amber Room."

Honor didn't know what to say.

Jake did. "*Shit.* I told Kyle that you were trouble."

"It is I who have trouble," Marju said, weeping soundlessly. "He said he would sell the panel and we would live in Brazil, where we would be warm and safe for the rest of our lives. I believed him! I betrayed my family, my people, my country. All of them. For him." She crossed herself quickly. "May God forgive me, I still love him. I still believe he will telephone me..."

With a disgusted sound, Jake shoved a wad of tissues into Marju's hand. "Here. Wipe your nose."

Honor just closed her eyes and tried to balance Marju's description of Kyle with the brother she had always loved.

It was impossible.

An irrational anger burned through Honor, a primitive hatred for the beautiful stranger who was damning Kyle with every word, every tear. In that instant she understood completely why tyrants killed messengers who brought bad news. Right now Honor hated everything about the divine Miss "Jones."

"Who was Kyle going to sell the panel to?" Jake asked as Marju's tears subsided.

"He did not tell me."

Jake grunted. "How did you get your hands on this supposed piece of the Amber Room in the first place?"

" 'Supposed'? There is no doubt!"

"Bullshit. There's always doubt."

"If you could see, you would not doubt," Marju said.

"How did you see it?" Honor asked before Jake could say anything.

"There is an old patriotic group known as the Forest Brotherhood," she began. "They began in the—"

"Forget the history lesson," Jake said impatiently. "How did they get the Amber Room?"

"History is necessary," Marju countered, her voice cracking with anger. "Only Americans live in a world that is new each day. The rest of us live with the past every moment!"

"Yeah. And then you spend the future rehashing wars your ancestors lost," Jake said.

"You are so American!" Marju said, throwing up her hands in despair.

"Thank you."

Honor cleared her throat. "About the Forest Brotherhood and the Amber Room...?"

For a moment longer Marju glared at Jake. Then she turned back to Honor. "At the end of World War Two, the Germans tried to steal the Amber Room from Russia. Some of

351

the Forest Brotherhood worked loading German ships at Königsberg, what we now call Kaliningrad. The Brotherhood told others, loyal Lithuanians in the Russian navy, which ship to sink. Afterward, they salvaged the Amber Room from the sunken ship and hid it deep beneath the altar of an ancient church, in the catacombs. They waited for Lithuania to become free once more." Her mouth turned down bitterly. "But the Russians conquered."

Honor looked at Jake. He shrugged and didn't say anything. He had heard similar stories about the Amber Room for so many years that it was impossible to say which one was more or less plausible than the others.

"How did the Brotherhood keep a secret for so long?" Honor asked Marju. "Especially one that big."

"Dead men do not gossip," she said simply. "The Russians slaughtered all but one or two of the Brotherhood. Knowledge of the Amber Room came down through the men of my mother's family. A cousin told me."

"Why?" Honor asked.

"He wanted me."

Honor didn't doubt that. "And you ran to Kyle with the good news."

"I did not know Kyle very well at that time."

"Too bad it couldn't have stayed that way," Jake said sardonically. "When did you tell him?"

"Six weeks ago. That is when he talked of love and marriage and Brazil. Poor fool that I am, I b-believed—that he loved m-me!"

Honor ripped a tissue out of the box and stuffed it into the other woman's hand. "Blow."

The brisk sympathy steadied Marju. She blew into the tissue, wiped her nose, and blotted her widely spaced, incredible eyes. Part of Honor took a mean pleasure in the fact that even an exotic like Marju couldn't cry and get away with it entirely. The red nose definitely detracted from the rest of the package.

Marju gave a shuddering sigh, sipped coffee, and collected herself.

"How big is the panel?" Jake asked.

"Perhaps one by two meters," Marju said.

"Heavy?"

"Not in the way of stone. But the wood backing, the frame, made the whole awkward to handle."

"Who helped you?" Jake asked.

"No one! I could trust no one but my very own love. Yet I should not—should not have— t-trusted him." Her breathing fragmented into tears.

Jake handed her another round of tissues and waited impatiently for the storm of weeping to end. He had never understood how Kyle had put up with Marju's tears and tirades. Among Baltic peoples, Lithuanians were famous for their low flashpoint and keen sense of personal drama. For Jake it was a wearing combination.

"Pull yourself together," he said finally. "This isn't helping anyone."

Marju gave Honor a look of mute appeal. Honor sighed, smiled, and patted the other woman's shoulder.

"Don't worry about Jake," Honor said. "American men are uncomfortable around tears, but he'll put a sock in it for now." She gave Jake a hard glance. "Won't you?"

He looked at his watch, then out the window. Even in the more protected areas, whitecaps showed in a solid wall. Haro Strait would be a washboard roller coaster. The "sheltered" water around the rest of the islands wouldn't be much better.

"Have a good cry, Jones," Jake said. "Get it out of your system. It's pretty dirty out on the water right now anyway."

"Too much slang," Honor said.

"You're assuming she's listening to anything except her own sobbing."

Honor put her hands on her hips. "This may come as a rude shock to you, *buttercup*, but when a woman discovers she has been betrayed by the man she loves, she's entitled to a good cry!"

"You didn't. But then, underneath all that feminine fury I guess you knew I didn't really betray you."

"The jury is still out on that one," she shot back. "Don't push it."

"Truce, not an end to the war, is that it?"

"Bingo."

Both of them became aware at the same time that Marju was watching them with a look of concentration, as though she was having trouble following their words.

"Sorry," Honor said. "We didn't mean to leave you out. As you undoubtedly know,

354

Jake can be...difficult."

"But of course," Marju said, bewildered. "He is a man."

Honor laughed.

"Right," Jake said curtly. "So you carried the panel to Kyle in your own little hands. Then what?"

"I used a handcart, not my hands. Together Kyle and I loaded it into the truck. After that, he went to pick up the driver at the pub near the waterfront, you remember it?"

"I remember. Then what?"

"I do not know. Soon Kyle's brother—"

"Which one," Jake interrupted.

"The cold one. Archer? Is that his name?"

"Yeah."

"He was not very understanding," Marju said, blinking against tears. "He did not want to hear that Kyle had used me—used me to—"

"Hell," Jake said under his breath. He waited for the crying to subside before he asked curtly, "Where is the rest of the Amber Room?"

Marju shook her head and spread her small hands as if to show they were empty. "I was never told. My cousin simply brought me the panel, I took it to Kyle, and we put it into the truck as I told you."

"So only your cousin knows where the Amber Room is now?" Jake asked.

"Yes."

"Where is he?"

"I do not know."

The look on Jake's face said he wasn't surprised. "How can you get in touch with him?"

"I? That is not possible."

"Sure it is. He's your cousin. Call an aunt or grandmother or something."

"My whole family is against me! Would you trust the woman who betrayed everything for her lover?" she asked bitterly, tears brimming in her voice and eyes.

Jake grunted. "Then why are you here?"

"I thought if I could t-talk to Kyle, he would—would—" Tears overflowed. Marju's beautiful eyes vanished behind a mound of crumpled tissues.

"Christ," Jake hissed.

He looked at Honor and jerked his head toward the kitchen. After a small hesitation she left Marju and followed him.

"I have to pick up some stuff at the cabin," he said, "but I don't want to leave you here alone."

"I'm not alone."

The sounds of heartbreak from the living room underlined Honor's words.

Jake hissed another word under his breath. "If you don't hear from me in half an hour, call this number," he said, pulling a business card from the pocket of his wool shirt.

" 'Ellen Lazarus, consultant,' " Honor read out loud. She looked at him questioningly. "The lady in the red jacket?"

"Yeah. After me or Archer, she's your best bet."

"For what?"

"Getting through the fairy dust without choking to death. Half an hour, right?"

Honor nodded. "But wh—"

The word ended in a startled sound when Jake brushed a kiss over her lips and followed it with a quick, secret caress from the tip of his tongue.

"Jake!"

"Truce, remember?"

"That's not my idea of a truce!"

"You're right." He bent his head and did a thorough job of kissing her. She didn't respond as he had hoped. On the other hand, she didn't fight him. Reluctantly he lifted his head. "Better, but not nearly up to the previous mark. Good thing we have lots of time to work on the fine print in this truce of ours."

"But I didn't say anything about kissing or—"

"Don't forget," he interrupted, opening the back door. "Half an hour. Beginning now."

The good news was that no one was parked on the highway across from Jake's driveway. The bad news was that the tire tracks in the mud didn't belong to any vehicle he had ever owned. Nor did they look like they belonged to Ellen's snappy little four-wheel-drive rental. These tires were seriously bald. It was a wonder the vehicle had made it up the driveway without sliding off into the forest.

Jake turned the steering wheel sharply and brought the truck to a slithering stop so that it blocked the driveway as thoroughly as a metal cork. The cabin wasn't in sight. Neither was anything else but mud and fir trees stirring in the rain-wet wind.

With one hand Jake stuffed the truck keys into the pocket of his jeans. With the other he popped open the glove compartment, grabbed the gun, and shoved it through a loop on his belt at the small of his back. He had been told that some people found the feel of a gun reassuring. To him, the damn thing just felt cold.

Cursing Kyle, ancient wars, and modern fairy dust, Jake eased out of the truck and into the forest. By the time he had gone fifty feet, water was trickling down his collar from the drippy, cold-fingered caress of fir boughs weighed down by rain and pushed by the wind. Water was also trickling down his chin and over his wrists. He ignored the irritation and concentrated on the forest, the uncertain footing, and the cabin that was beginning to condense from the gloom ahead of him.

There was no sign of a vehicle. For a moment Jake thought hopefully that someone had just gotten lost, realized it, and slid on back to the highway. But something in the scene ahead didn't fit with that cozy idea. Jake wasn't going to move until he figured out what was wrong.

Concealed in the dripping embrace of the forest, he waited while wind moaned high in the treetops, masking all noise except the slap and smash of waves at the base of the nearby cliffs. Suddenly a gust of wind pushed the back door open.

Jake stared at the dark gap. It was possible he had forgotten to lock the door and had left it ajar for the wind to play with....Possible, but not very damned likely.

He drew the gun, took off the safety, and ghosted across the small clearing near the back of the cabin. A moment later he was in the door and making a rapid survey. Nothing showed over the gun barrel but two wood kitchen chairs, an electric stove, a sink, and a table covered with mail he hadn't bothered to open.

Wet footprints still glistened on the floorboards. Whoever was inside hadn't been there long.

Letting out his breath very slowly, Jake listened. Small noises came from the direction of the bedroom. He smiled. The bastard hadn't finished yet.

Ignoring the mud and forest litter stuck to his boots, Jake reached the bedroom in a series of smooth, soundless strides. A quick, thorough look told him there was only one prowler in the room. The man had his back to Jake and was searching through dresser drawers with impatient movements of his hands. Yet for all his hurry, he wasn't making a mess.

A pro. Not good news. But then, Jake hadn't expected any.

The prowler didn't know anything had gone wrong until his right cheek was mashed into the cottage wall and a gun barrel was screwed beneath his chin in such a way that no matter what he did, he couldn't see who was holding him. Nor could he get away from the gun by throwing himself to the side or going limp.

As soon as the prowler realized that he was trapped, he went very still.

"Finished yet?" Jake asked in Russian.

The man sagged in relief and started cursing in the same language, asking what his partner was doing here—they were supposed to rendezvous at the realty sign down the road, remember?

"How's your English?" Jake asked in that language.

The man went stiff.

"Good enough to understand me," Jake said. "What are you looking for?"

Silence.

Jake grabbed a handful of hair and smacked the man's head against the wall again. The gun barrel never moved from its painful niche beneath the Russian's chin. His head was jammed back on his shoulders from the pressure.

"Wrong answer," Jake said calmly.

"Money. Liquor."

Jake rattled the man's teeth again. "I'm losing patience."

"Drugs!" the man gasped.

This time the clock on the dresser rattled when the Russian kissed the wall.

"They aren't paying you enough to be a hero," Jake said, "but so far it's been a really bad day all around for me. If you want to play hardball, you just found your pitcher."

He repeated it in Russian to make sure there was no misunderstanding.

Even then, it took five minutes for Jake to explain the ground rules. By then the prowler had decided he really didn't want to play any more games.

Jake dragged the Russian's head out of the toilet and braced him against the lip of the cold porcelain bowl. Coughing, sputtering, dazed, the man gasped for air.

"Start talking," Jake said. "I've got better things to do than wash your face."

"The box!" the man said in Russian. "I give, not steal!"

Jake buried his left hand in the man's hair, jammed the gun barrel under his chin, and hauled him to his feet. The way he was being held, even if the Russian was still feeling playful, he would have a tough time laying a hand—or a foot—on Jake.

"Where?" Jake asked.

"Where?" The Russian blinked rapidly. "Where what?"

The next time the man got his face out of the toilet, he had no trouble understanding what Jake wanted, no matter which language was used. The Russian led him promptly, if awkwardly, to the basket where Jake kept his dirty laundry. Beneath the shirts, shorts, socks, and a towel was the superbly made leather box Resnikov had offered only a few hours before.

Jake didn't touch the box. He just looked

at it and thought about all the possibilities. No matter what kind of a spin he put on it, the day had just gone from bad to worse.

"You need some more time to learn English," Jake said to his captive. "When you 'give' somebody something like this, it's called setting them up. But don't worry. A few years in jail for breaking and entering should do wonders for your command of American idioms."

Predictably, the man didn't think much of the idea. Jake didn't care. He tied the Russian up with knots that got tighter the more he struggled. Then Jake picked up the phone and called Honor. She answered on the first ring.

"Are you all right?" he asked immediately.

"Fine, but I'm running out of Kleenex."

"Give her a roll of toilet paper."

"You're all heart."

"Finally figured that out, did you? I need an hour, starting now. Then if I'm not back, call—"

"Ellen Lazarus," Honor finished curtly. Then, as though she hadn't meant to, she added quietly, "Are you okay?"

"Yeah. Just taking care of some odds and ends. See you in an hour."

Jake hung up and called the Chowder Keg. As he had hoped, Resnikov was having a leisurely lunch of clams and beer while he waited for his men to come back and report that the box was hidden in Jake's cabin, awaiting discovery anytime Resnikov wanted to start whispering in the U.S. government's ear.

"Pete, it's Jake."

"Mallory?" Resnikov's voice was both surprised and pleased. "I did not expect you to change your mind so quickly. Or is it simply that you are no longer with the lovely Miss Donovan and thus are able to speak more freely?"

"Listen up. This is important."

"Yes?"

"I'm sending back your gift," Jake said distinctly. "If I see it again—or any other amber that can be traced back to stolen Russian museum goods—I will personally burn it to dry my socks. Then I'll come looking for you."

Jake hung up, stuffed the box beneath the prowler's ropes, and dragged him out in the rain to a rendezvous with the realty sign just down the road.

19

After Marju left, Honor started making salmon salad in an effort to do something normal while she tried to reconcile what Marju had said with the brother she had always known. She had barely gotten the bones out of the salmon before there was a knock on the front door.

"Come on in, Jake. The door is open," she called. Then she remembered that it wasn't. She had thrown the dead bolt. Being a target was not only unsettling, it was inconvenient. "Coming!" she called, absently wiping her hands on her jeans as she hurried out of the kitchen.

She stopped short of the door when she saw the strange car parked in the driveway.

"Who is it?" she asked through the closed door.

"Ellen Lazarus and Special Agent Mather. We would like to talk to you."

"Whose special agent?"

"The U.S. government's," said a male voice.

Honor considered letting them stand out in the rain but decided against it. Jake had nominated Ellen as third-string protector, after himself and Archer.

"Wouldn't do to irritate the friendlies," Honor muttered. But it was a tempting thought. Marju's sad revelations had put Honor in a lousy mood. She couldn't help thinking about Kyle and amber...yet she couldn't bring herself to believe that her brother was a thief. She simply couldn't. It felt *wrong*.

Abruptly Honor unbolted the door, opened it, and stepped back. Ellen and Mather moved inside and dripped on the mat Kyle had put next to the threshold for just these soggy Pacific Northwest moments. Beneath their unbuttoned waterproof coats, both agents were wearing business suits. Mather's was a neat navy pinstripe. Ellen's was a rich burgundy with dark blue trim. Neither of them offered to show any identification.

"I suppose it would be cheeky to ask for ID,

since we're on the same side and all," Honor drawled. "So I'll settle for business cards to add to my collection."

Ellen opened a navy purse that was big enough to put a cat in. Mather reached into the breast pocket of his suit coat. Each handed her a card.

Sourly Honor noticed that, like Ellen, Mather was a consultant. "Do you consult on anything in particular?" she asked, sticking the cards in a hip pocket of her jeans.

"We're generalists," Mather said pleasantly. "However, if you require something more specialized, we can call in the people who carry badges."

"Thanks, but I don't think my heart could take the excitement." Honor turned and headed for the kitchen. "Talk to me in here. I'm making lunch. But if you came to cry about something, forget it. I'm fresh out of Kleenex, even in my purse."

As though testing the truth of Honor's words, Ellen glanced at the black backpack that lay half open near the couch. Both agents followed their reluctant hostess into the kitchen. On the unstated theory that one woman always understands another woman better than any man could, Ellen took the lead.

"You don't look like you've been crying," she said.

"Not me. My brother's fiancée." Honor searched the mound of salmon flakes in the bowl for more bones. "You might have heard of her. Marju, lately of Lithuania."

"We've heard of her," Ellen said. "We've being trying to talk to her for several weeks."

"Why?"

For an instant Mather looked impatient, but he didn't do anything about it. Ellen just acted as though she hadn't heard the question.

"Did Marju say where she was staying?" Ellen asked.

"No."

"Don't you think that's odd?"

Honor shrugged. "I just met her. I have no way to judge her behavior."

"What did she want from you?"

"Same thing everyone else does. Kyle."

"If they're engaged, surely they're in touch," Ellen said.

"Not lately, according to her."

"Do you believe her?" Mather asked.

"Why shouldn't I? God knows the tears were real. Besides, if she knows where Kyle is, why was she crying on my shoulder?"

"Perhaps she thought he might have shipped something home," Mather said. "Or to you."

Honor scooped up a stray flake of salmon, popped it into her mouth, and chewed thoughtfully. "It's possible."

"That Kyle shipped something to you?" Ellen asked.

"No, that Marju thought he had."

"Did your brother ship something to you?" Mather asked bluntly.

"Which one? I have four."

"Kyle," Ellen said, her voice crisp.

"He shipped me something. It's on the

desk. Be careful with it. Amber can shatter like glass."

Mather left the room with impressive speed. He reappeared a moment later with a piece of amber in his hand. "This?"

Honor glanced up from stirring the salmon in an idle search for bones. "That's it. Great piece, isn't it? It has clarity for radiance and smoky tendrils of cloud for mystery."

Neither agent looked impressed.

"This is all he sent?" Mather asked Honor.

"No. There were twelve other pieces."

"Raw or worked?" Ellen asked.

"Raw, like that one." Honor pulled mayonnaise out of the refrigerator and reached for a spoon. "Faith works the amber herself, just like the other gemstones."

"What else did Kyle send you?" Mather asked.

"When?"

"In the last month."

"Nothing. Not a card. Not a letter. Not a phone call. Not one damned thing." The spoon rang against the side of the salmon bowl as Honor knocked off the mayonnaise with unnecessary force. "But I don't expect you to take my word for it. So do everyone a favor. Look for whatever you hope Kyle sent me and let me eat my lunch in peace."

"You don't mind if we search the house?" Ellen asked.

"You won't be the first," Honor muttered.

"What?" Mather said.

"What kind of a search are you talking

about?" Honor asked quickly. "The kind where everything bigger than a matchbox is turned inside out?"

"No."

"Bigger than a breadbox?" she asked.

Mather looked at Ellen.

"Yes," Ellen said.

"Bigger than a computer?" Honor persisted.

"What is this, Twenty Questions?" Ellen snapped.

"No," Honor said, "it's me trying to figure out how much of a mess you'll make in your search."

"Two feet by two feet is the smallest size we're interested in."

"Fine," Honor said. "Search the house. Search the garage. Hell, search the barbecue. Search the boat while you're at it. Save the Coast Guard a few steps. On second thought, forget the boat. I'd really like to see Captain Conroy dance on and off the *Tomorrow*'s swim step in this weather."

Surprisingly, Mather smiled. It didn't last long, but it gave Honor hope that he was human underneath the pinstripes and tie.

"Unless you really object," Mather said to her, "I'll search the boat."

"Go ahead. But if you find anything, I get to see it."

Mather turned to leave.

"Wait," Honor said.

He looked back.

"You didn't answer me," she said. "If you

find anything, I get to see it. Otherwise you can go out and get official pieces of paper telling me that I have to let you be on my brother's property. Do we have an understanding?"

He looked at Ellen, who shrugged. "Sure," she said. "Start in the kitchen. I doubt if there's anything in the boat."

Mather began opening kitchen cupboards. He was quick, thorough, and neat.

Ignoring him, Honor started chopping up celery and green onions for the salmon salad. Before she was finished, Mather moved on to the living room.

"How did you meet Jake Mallory?" Ellen asked.

Honor's knife hesitated for a fraction of a second and then sliced on through the last of the green onions. "He answered my ad for a fishing guide."

"Is that what he told you he was? A fishing guide?"

"Pretty much."

"And you believed him?" The amusement in Ellen's voice was just short of outright sarcasm.

The knife whacked through the celery with savage speed. "He can run the boat and we caught a fish," Honor said. "That's good enough for me."

"Miss Donovan..." Ellen began.

"That's me," Honor said, dumping celery and onions into the bowl. She reached for a lemon, sliced it in half, and started squeezing it over the salmon as though something more interesting than a lemon was in her grasp.

"Are you hostile to us because of Jake?" Ellen asked.

"Nope."

"Why, then? If you have nothing to hide..." Ellen smiled and waited expectantly.

From the living room came the sound of desk drawers opening. Honor's breath caught; those were the same noises that had awakened her the night before. She paused in the act of slicing through a second lemon, hardly able to believe it was only last night that she had gone screaming down the path and into Jake's arms.

So much had happened, so quickly, so completely, nothing would ever be the same again. Yet it seemed like Kyle had always been missing, she had always been afraid, she had always known Jake.

You're losing it, Honor told herself. *Get a grip. The smiling blue-eyed lady waiting for your answer isn't a Barbie doll. She's real bright, twice as ambitious, and she wants the panel from the Amber Room.*

Mather moved on to the bedroom. In the kitchen, a steel blade sliced through a third lemon and smacked into the wood cutting board.

"What do you want from me?" Honor asked finally.

"Cooperation."

"You're getting it." Honor began squeezing the remaining lemon halves into the salmon salad mixture.

"Are we?"

"Correct me if I'm wrong, but isn't that your partner going through my closet right now without so much as a piece of official paper in sight?"

"If you want to avoid this kind of intrusion in the future, let Mather be your, um, fishing guide."

"Can he run a SeaSport?"

"If he can't, I'm sure we have someone who can."

"So do I. His name is Jake Mallory."

"You've known him, what—two days?"

"The proof is in the pudding. Or in this case, in the salmon salad."

"He's very good in bed, isn't he?" Ellen asked in the same casual tone of voice.

"The salmon? I wouldn't know. I've never slept with one of them."

Ellen smiled briefly. "You know I meant Jake. Such stamina. Unusual in a man over twenty."

"I'll take your word for it."

"While you're at it, take my word for this. Jake wants the same thing from you that we do."

"Then you're out of luck. Ménage a trois isn't my style. I'm the old-fashioned type—one of any sex at a time."

Honor finished squeezing and started stirring with more force than the salmon needed. Ellen's fingernails beat a brief tattoo on her purse. The sound of dresser drawers opening and closing came from the bedroom.

"Do you really think that all Jake wants from you is your rather ordinary body?" Ellen asked curiously.

"What does that have to do with Mather going through my underwear?" Honor retorted. She prayed that her expression didn't give away what she was thinking: after spectacular pieces of work like Marju and Ellen, Honor knew just how a very small brown hen would feel in a peacock parade.

Ellen tried another approach. "Have you ever heard of the Amber Room?"

"Yes. It's not in my dresser drawers. Guaranteed."

"Either you're quite smart or quite stupid."

"When you figure it out, tell somebody who cares."

"What if I were to tell you that Jake was thrown out of Russia and is suspected of setting up your brother to take the blame for the theft of a panel from the Amber Room?"

Honor yanked out a loaf of bread and began slathering salmon salad over one piece. Part of her was glad that she already knew the unhappy truth about Jay/Jake Mallory. Most of her just wanted to grab the stunning, chatty Ms. Lazarus and drop her off a cliff.

"Miss Donovan? Did you hear me? Jake is at best your competitor and at worst your brother's killer."

"Is that the official U.S. position?" Honor asked.

"It's one of them."

"I don't like that one. Tell me another."

"Kyle stole a panel from the Amber Room."

"Nope. Don't like that one either."

"Take your pick."

"None of the above."

Honor slapped a second piece of bread on top of the first and took a big bite. It tasted like library paste. She had forgotten to add salt or pepper, but she was damned if she would let on how rattled she was by looking for such obvious seasonings now. Grimly she chewed, swallowed, and took another bite.

Mather walked into the kitchen. "I couldn't help overhearing," he began.

"Yeah, right," Honor said. "That popping sound we just heard was your ear coming unstuck from the door."

"Since it's obvious that Miss Donovan already knew the real reason for Jake's interest in her," Mather said, "why don't we tell her some things she might not know?"

Ellen tilted her head and appeared to think it over. "Sweet reason?"

"It works for some people."

"Damned few," Ellen said. Then she shrugged. "Go ahead."

"As a member of a family that is involved in international trade," Mather said, "you are aware of the new world dynamic since the Berlin Wall came down."

Honor nodded and went to the refrigerator to look for a Coke. The sandwich definitely needed help getting down her tight, dry throat. She hoped that the poker face she had learned at the hands of four sister-baiting brothers was firmly in place. She didn't want to reveal any bleeding wounds to the pinstriped shark.

"Countries that once depended on a vast central government for order, economy, and direction were thrown without preparation into a free-market situation," Mather said crisply. "Some nationalisms and religions took the remains of their soviet wealth and went to war. They took a big step backward fiscally. They became, or are fast becoming, Third World economies. Are you following me?"

"Tanks, bombs, and bullets alone aren't the kind of foundation you build a new society on," Honor said, putting the can of soda on the counter with an impatient movement. "Civilian infrastructure is the first lesson of noncommunist economies. Some of the folks over there are still learning it. The longer they wait, the farther back they slide into the swamp of soft currency, poverty, and anarchy."

Mather looked relieved. "Good. You understand. It will save us all a lot of trouble."

Honor doubted it. Instead of saying so, she took a bite out of her sandwich and concentrated on chewing and swallowing.

"You wouldn't know it from reading American newspapers," Mather said, "but there are literally dozens of groups competing for power in the former Soviet Union. We only hear about the most obvious ones or the ones that—"

"We're on a short clock," Ellen interrupted. "The point is simple: the new Russian Federation is a collection of nuclear bombs with their fuses lit. If the wrong people end up with the Amber Room, there's going to be a nasty war. We'll all be downwind of the fallout."

Mather's disappointed expression almost made Honor smile; he looked the way she had felt when Jake wouldn't let her rhapsodize to the Coast Guard about the SeaSport's big engine. Apparently the emerging former E-Bloc economies were Mather's passion.

"Um, yes," Mather said. "Marju Uskhopchik-Mikniskes is a Lithuanian separatist."

"Kyle's Marju?" Honor asked.

"Yes. Ms. Uskhopchik-Mik—"

"Call her Jones," Honor interrupted dryly.

Mather hesitated. "She is, or was, part of a plot to sell the Amber Room for money to use fighting Russia."

"Tanks, bombs, and bullets?" Honor said.

"Exactly," Ellen said. "But Marju's playmates are out of the running now. We think they stole the Amber Room, or at least a panel of it, from the Kaliningrad *mafiya*. You've heard of them?"

"According to Archer, they have all the class of the Colombian cartel and twice the brutality," Honor said. "The bad news is that they have more international connections and a broader 'tax base' than Yeltsin."

"If Archer knows that, why is he holding us at arm's length?" Mather asked impatiently. "He must know they're after Kyle."

Both agents looked at Honor.

"Ask Archer," she said. "He just gives me orders, not explanations."

"No wonder you have a smart mouth," Ellen said. "Older brothers will do it every time."

Smiling slightly, Honor decided that maybe she wouldn't throw Ellen over a big cliff after all. Just a little one. Just enough to muss up her sleek hair.

"You want some salmon salad?" Honor asked.

Ellen smiled and shook her head. "Thanks, but I'm on a diet."

Honor cheered up even more. "That's worse than having an older brother. How about you, Mather?"

"I'm an older brother."

"Why am I not surprised?"

"Oh, he's not too bad," Ellen said, giving Mather the kind of sideways look that was guaranteed to make a man feel one hundred percent healthy. "He's trainable."

"So are gorillas," Honor said. She took another bite of her sandwich, sighed, and reached for the salt.

"Has Jake told you that the Organizatsiya could be involved?" Ellen asked.

"With gorillas?" Honor asked, startled.

Mather looked at the ceiling like he expected to find God there. "No, with the Amber Room."

"Jake mentioned the *mafiya*."

"They aren't the same," Ellen said. "The Organizatsiya is an export. They prey on the Russian emigrants in various countries. The *mafiya* stays home. The Organizatsiya is pretty much independent of the Old World, although they take people who are shit-listed in Russia and give them a safe place to be until the folks back home forget or are paid off. The *mafiya* repays the favor by finding work in Russia for Organizatsiya thugs who are wanted in the United States or other countries."

"Cozy," Honor said. "How is the United States doing on extradition treaties with the Russian Federation?"

"We're working on it," Ellen said. "But the Organizatsiya and the *mafiya* aren't the only players to be reckoned with when it comes to the Amber Room. There are several, legal, factions of the Russian government in the competition. There's the Yeltsin faction, of course. One of his closest advisers is a born-again Russian nationalist. For him the Amber Room is the Holy Grail, a rallying point for the consolidation of Russia."

Honor grabbed the pepper grinder and went to work on what was left of her sandwich. But she was listening carefully, and Ellen knew it.

"This adviser will do whatever he has to, however he can, in order to secure the Amber Room," Ellen said. "And he has the backing of the legal government. The second major faction is run by the communists. They long for the bad old days. Anything that helps Yeltsin hurts them."

"The communists would just as soon the Amber Room stayed lost?"

"For now, yes," Mather said. "Definitely. That could change if—"

"We'll worry about that changing when it does," Ellen interrupted. "For now, we've got enough snakes on our plate."

"Two kinds of legal Russian factions, two kinds of illegal ones," Honor said. "Plus Lithuanian liberationists. Does that about cover it?"

"That only covers the obvious ones," Ellen said. "There are at least five more Lithuania-first groups. None of them agree on anything except burying the local competition and then mopping up on the international scene. All across the former Soviet Union there are similar groups, both legal and not, motivated by nationalism, tribalism, religion, survival, vengeance, and/or simple greed."

Honor grimaced. "You can't tell the players without a scorecard."

"In the new Russian Federation," Ellen retorted, "they can't print scorecards before the players change."

Instead of responding, Honor took a bite of sandwich. None of what she had heard so far sounded like it would make finding Kyle any easier.

"At this time in the Baltic states and Russia," Mather said, "the Amber Room is a very powerful cultural symbol. It means something different to each group, but it means something to *every* group. Anyone who wants to curry favor with or force concessions from the Russian state wants the Amber Room as a bargaining tool."

"And you think my brother stole it."

"No matter who stole it," Ellen said quickly, "Kyle is the one who stuck the hot potato in his truck and took off, leaving a dead Lithuanian driver behind."

"Which means you think Kyle killed that man."

"He didn't die of a heart attack," Mather retorted.

Honor's mouth flattened. She took another small bite of her sandwich. Salt and pepper improved the taste of the salmon salad, but nothing was going to take the dryness of fear out of her mouth. She sipped soda from the can, waited for the fizz to settle in her mouth, and swallowed again.

"Look," she said, "Kyle hasn't called me. He hasn't written me. He hasn't sent me a piece of the Amber Room."

"What about your family?" Ellen asked.

"If they knew where Kyle was, they wouldn't leave me dangling, wondering whether he was alive or dead or hurt or..." Honor's voice faded. She swallowed hard and set the half-eaten sandwich aside.

Ellen's expression said she wasn't as sure about the Donovan clan as Honor was, but she didn't argue the point. "Why did you come here?"

"Archer asked me to."

"Why?"

"He didn't say."

Mather muttered something that sounded like "a real cluster fuck." Beneath all the pinstripes lurked the soul of a pottymouth street cop.

Honor didn't even look his way. She had

heard it all before, in preschool.

"Did you ask Archer?" Ellen said.

"Yes."

"What did he say?"

"It doesn't matter. He didn't tell me."

"So you packed your bags like a good little sister and came running, is that it?" Ellen asked sarcastically.

Honor went back to her original idea: Ellen, a big cliff, and a long drop.

"Yes," Honor said through her teeth. "It may be hard for you to understand, Ms. Consultant, but I love my brothers even though they often drive me nuts. That's the way love works. When you love people, you don't demand long explanations and justifications. You simply do what you can when they need you. It's called loyalty."

"It's called stupidity," Mather said.

"Only if you always come out holding the slimy end of the stick," Honor retorted. "So far, the score is about even in that department, although I will never admit it within hearing of my brothers."

"But—"

"Give it up, Ellen," Jake said from the living room. "It's the Donovan clan and to hell with the rest of the world."

Honor and Mather looked toward the living room. Ellen gave a heartfelt curse before she turned around.

Jake looked like he had rolled around in a mud puddle.

"What happened to you?" Honor asked.

"I like walking in the rain."

"Next time take some soap and do your clothes."

Smiling, Jake walked between the two agents and stopped in front of Honor. His smile didn't reach his eyes. He framed her face in cool hands and kissed her. Honor stiffened, but she didn't draw back. She sensed that he was sending a message to the U.S. government that had nothing to do with sex.

She was right. And she was also wrong. Jake's eyes might have been remote, but he was fully aroused beneath his muddy jeans.

The stark hunger of his body, the tenderness of his kiss, and the watchfulness of his eyes undermined Honor's certainty that all he wanted from her was a means of getting to Kyle. Off balance, almost disoriented, emotionally and physically exhausted by the past few weeks, she held on to Jake's forearms to steady herself.

He kissed her again, less gently, more completely. When he lifted his head, his eyes were as hot and hungry as his body. There were muddy streaks on her face from his hands.

"You were right," Mather said to Ellen.

"Told you, babe," she said. "That slow, eat-you grin of Jake's gets them every time."

Honor flushed. Jake put his thumb over her mouth in a gesture that was both caress and warning.

"Sorry I was late," he said to her, ignoring the agents. "If I'd known you had company, I would have taken a shorter walk."

"How long have you been here?" Honor asked.

Jake looked from her generous mouth to her breasts with their nipples hard against the soft bronze sweater, to her hips leaning toward him...and he smiled slowly, all but licking his lips. "Ellen is wrong. There's nothing ordinary about your body."

Honor knew she shouldn't laugh, shouldn't feel pleased, shouldn't do anything but throw all three people out of her life; and she knew she wouldn't. If she had to trust one of the three, there was no doubt which one it would be.

Until she found Kyle, she was bound to Jake Mallory as surely as if she had spoken vows.

And afterward? Honor asked herself silently.

The answer came immediately and without comfort. She would deal with the afterward mess the same way she was dealing with the Kyle mess. One disaster at a time.

She drew a shaky breath and ran her fingertip over Jake's mustache. "You," she said huskily, "are a very bad dog."

"Does that mean you're going to spank me?"

His hopeful look dragged a broken laugh from Honor's throat.

Despite the laughter, Jake saw the bleakness in her eyes and knew how close to falling off the edge she was. He caught her palm against his mouth, kissed her, and turned to look at the two agents.

"Any more questions?" Jake asked.

"Cooperate with us," Ellen said, "or we'll

take you both out of the game."

"If you thought that would do any good, you'd have done it already," Jake said. "Next threat?"

"Damn you," Ellen snarled. "You think you're God Almighty."

"No, you do. That's why you get pissed off when everyone doesn't kneel on command." He looked at Mather. "You have anything else to add?"

"Just curious. Why won't you work with us?"

"What makes you think we won't?"

"What?" Ellen and Mather demanded as one.

"Think about it. And while you're thinking, check on Petyr Resnikov."

Mather looked at Ellen. She was watching Jake like a barefoot hiker would watch a snake rustling through the nearby grass.

"What about Resnikov?" she asked bluntly.

"If I show you mine, will you show me yours?" Jake asked.

Ellen laughed curtly. "Babe, we don't have anything new to show each other."

"As long as we keep our clothes on, we just might."

Honor flinched and looked at her feet. She knew it shouldn't bother her that Ellen and Jake had been lovers, but it did. Ellen was just too damned sexy for any man not to regret losing her. Even more depressing, there was obviously a very agile brain running Ellen's Playmate-of-the-decade body.

Brutally Honor told herself it didn't matter. She wouldn't have to worry about a lifetime of unhappy comparisons in Jake's mind. She and Jake were, as Ellen would put it, on a short clock.

"Did you know that Pete was going to buy me?" Jake asked.

"Did he try?" Ellen asked.

"What do you think?"

She took her time answering, obviously thinking through the implications and possible outcomes of answering or not answering Jake's question.

"All right," she said. "Resnikov couldn't buy you so he got cute. What happened?"

"Is he yours?" Jake asked again.

"He's ours the same way Russia is our ally in this brave new world."

"Neutrality most of the time, favors some of the time, and trust none of the time," Jake summarized.

"That's it. What happened?"

"When I wouldn't agree to outright purchase, I found one of his men in my cabin planting stolen amber artifacts."

Honor snapped her head around toward Jake so fast that her hair flew out. "What happened? Is that how you got muddy? Are you all right?"

"Were the artifacts from the Amber Room?" Mather demanded.

Jake laced his grubby fingers through Honor's and squeezed gently, silently telling her not to worry.

"Nothing that modern," Jake said. "Stone Age artifacts. Very, very nice bits of work. They defined 'museum quality.' One of them even had an inventory number inked on the back."

Mather pulled a cellular phone out of his pocket and began punching in numbers.

"Where are the pieces now?" Ellen asked.

"I sent them back to Pete with a message."

"Yeah, I'll bet." Bright red nails tapped on navy blue leather. She glanced at Mather, who was speaking softly into the phone, but not so softly that the others couldn't overhear.

"Forget it," Mather said. "We already know that the primary subjects are back together."

Jake bent and said against Honor's ear, "How does it feel to be an official primary subject of the U.S. government?"

Gooseflesh rippled on her arms as the warmth of his breath stirred her hair, yet the knowledge that she was being watched so closely made her stomach lurch.

"Is Resnikov still eating clams?" Jake asked.

There was a long silence while Mather listened.

"Stay with them," he said finally. "Tell the SEAL to stay with the boat. We'll be in touch."

Honor looked at Jake. "The seal? As in bark-bark, give me a fish?"

"As in navy commando," he said softly, and hoped he wouldn't have to meet Ellen's SEAL up close and personal.

Mather flipped the phone closed and stuffed it back in his pocket.

"Well?" Ellen asked him.

Uneasily Mather looked at Jake.

"Don't worry about me," Jake said. "I

already figured out that every time Pete takes a crap one of your men is sitting in the stall next to him. So your guy just told you that two muddy clowns turned up at the Chowder Keg and told Pete what he already knew—no sale. Again. As for the SEAL waiting around for you, he's the squared-away, buffed-up, hell-on-two-feet dude who's getting the best out of that Bayliner every time we go out on the water."

"Did Jake miss anything?" Ellen asked Mather.

"Just what Resnikov said to the men."

"Yeah?"

Mather shrugged. "It was in Russian, but our guy could tell that Resnikov wasn't pinning medals on them and kissing their hairy cheeks."

Ellen resumed tapping her fingernails against her purse.

"Did you eat all the salmon salad?" Jake asked Honor.

"How did you know I made salmon salad?"

He bent down, kissed her, and whispered, "I tasted it."

"It's in the refrigerator," she muttered.

"What kind of bribe would I have to offer to get you to make a sandwich while I shower?"

"Get rid of our guests. I've had it way past up to here."

"Okay." Jake straightened. "Good-bye, Ellen. Take your friend with you. When I have something I want to share, you'll be the first to know."

Ellen's red-lacquered nails went still. She looked at him for a long moment and decided it was the best deal she was going to get right now. She turned to Mather. "C'mon. Let's see where Marju Unpronounceable is staying."

The front door had barely closed behind them when Jake turned to Honor.

"Start packing," he said.

"I don't want to go anywh—"

She stopped talking. No one was listening. The back door had already closed behind Jake. Hands on hips, she watched him trot down the path to the boat. A minute later he reappeared with a nylon duffel in his hand. Clean clothes, no doubt.

Before he reached the door, Honor was in the kitchen making a salmon salad sandwich. No matter how irritated she was, a deal was still a deal.

But if Jake wanted any packing done, he could damn well do it himself.

20

When Jake emerged from the bathroom he was wearing fresh jeans, a clean wool shirt, and boat shoes.

"What happened at your cabin?" Honor asked the instant he walked into the kitchen.

"Just what I told Ellen. Nice necklace you're wearing. Did you design it?"

"Yes. What didn't you tell Ellen?"

He gave up the idea of changing the subject. "The men were from the Seattle branch of the Organizatsiya. That's the—"

"—overseas mutation of the Russian *mafiya*," Honor finished impatiently.

Jake raised his eyebrows.

"Ellen mentioned them," Honor said. "How did you know who the men were working for? Were they carrying membership cards or special guns or something?"

"I asked them."

"And they told you?"

"Yeah."

"Just like that?"

"Are you sure you want to know?" he asked softly.

Honor looked at Jake's eyes. There was a lot more darkness than silver in them.

"Right," she said. "Next topic. Does that mean your good friend Pete is *mafiya?*"

"Not necessarily." Jake finger-combed his wet hair. "Besides, it doesn't matter. Crooks are politicians and politicians are crooks and everyone swaps favors and whores when they think no one is watching."

"Charming worldview you have."

"Thank you. It's the result of a lifetime of study. Are you planning on eating that sandwich or does it have my name on it?"

She handed over the sandwich and a paper towel to serve as a napkin.

"Are you packed?" he asked.

"I was too busy being domestic in the kitchen."

Jake chewed, swallowed, and watched Honor very closely. She had turned away and was rinsing a mayonnaise-covered spoon in the sink.

"Good sandwich," he said. "I'll clean up here while you pack."

"No need."

"Why?"

"I'm not going anywhere that I'll need a change of clothes."

"It's always a good idea to have a change of clothes aboard the boat."

"I'm not aboard the boat." Honor looked out at the blue-white, wind-tossed sound. "Thank God." She looked back at Jake. "Or is the wind supposed to drop?"

"Not today."

She bit her lip. Relief that she wouldn't have to go out on the rough water warred with the chill dread that never stopped gnawing on her: Kyle needed help and she was the only one in a position to give it.

Jake had no trouble following the direction of Honor's thoughts. Her face was almost as expressive as her body had been while he made love to her. He set the sandwich on the counter, dipped an edge of the paper towel in the running water, and turned Honor into his arms.

"What—" she began, startled.

"You have dirt on your cheek. Since it's my fault, it's only fair that I clean you up."

Honor's breath caught at the cool touch of the paper towel as Jake wiped off the smudges his muddy fingers had left on her face when he kissed her earlier. He hesitated, then kissed her again. This time when he lifted his hands her face was clean and flushed.

"I didn't have any mud on my mouth," she said.

"Sure you did."

"I'm not going to pack."

"Okay."

She blinked, caught off balance again. "Just like that? Okay?"

"Just like that. And like this."

He kissed her again, letting the leash on his hunger slip enough to make both of them breathe hard. When he finally let go of her, she looked at him with puzzled, gold-green eyes.

"Jake?"

"Yes?"

"What am I going to do with you?"

"I have a few modest suggestions."

"Modest?" she said skeptically.

"Maybe *modest* is the wrong word. Let's get naked and see if I can find the right word."

She smiled, but it slipped until it was as sad as a smile could be.

Jake saw the change and knew what caused it. She didn't like wanting a man she didn't really trust. Rationally he couldn't blame her for not believing that he wanted her more than he wanted her brother's hide. In her shoes he would have felt the same way. Yet that lack of trust was going to make things even more dangerous. For both of them.

"I should have just stuffed you aboard the

Tomorrow and sailed over the horizon before Archer could call or Ellen could poison the well," Jake said quietly. "Then you would still trust me. But I didn't and you don't and we're stuck with it. *Shit.*"

Honor started to say something, then simply shook her head. He ran his fingertips over her cheek in a gentle caress and released her.

"Did Marju say anything useful?" he asked.

"How do you define *useful?*"

"Helping us find Kyle, the amber, or both."

"No. She wanted to move in with me."

Jake turned back suddenly. "And?"

Honor's mouth turned down. "I gave her all my spare cash and said there wasn't room here for a third person to live. That makes me an unfeeling bitch, but I'm carrying all the chain I can swim with right now. I can't carry her, too."

He let out a hidden breath. He had been wondering how he would get rid of Marju without looking like an insensitive American male.

"Marju is a big girl," Jake said. "She's been through wars you can't even imagine. She'll do fine on her own."

"She seemed awfully upset."

"It's a cultural thing. Lithuanians are kind of the Italians of the Baltic, famous for emoting all over the place. Believe me, you're more upset than Marju is."

"I hope so."

"I know so. How much of that salmon salad did you make?" he asked, turning away again.

"A quart or so. There's enough plain salmon left for an omelet tomorrow and pasta tomorrow night."

Mentally Jake went over the supplies in his truck, her kitchen, and already on board the *Tomorrow*. The food probably would last longer than the gas, even in weather like this.

He looked out at the water beyond Amber Beach's protected shore. Whitecaps leaped on most waves. Streaks of foam had formed. Long, wind-driven swells were humping up in the dark blue water. Small craft warnings would be going out soon, if they weren't already posted.

He had planned to pull a switch and take his own boat to the last place Kyle had entered into his chart plotter, but the *Better Days* wasn't as big as the *Tomorrow*. Even though his boat was seaworthy enough to take on near-gale winds, as long as small craft warnings were out the Coast Guard had the right to decide what small craft should be on the ocean and what should stay in port.

The *Tomorrow* was twenty-seven feet long, technically above the size limit of "small craft." None of the boats following him were that big, except perhaps the elusive Olympic that Conroy had seen. If the rest of the folks kept on following him with their little Tupperware navy, they would be in for a hair-raising ride.

With hidden impatience, Jake reviewed what had to be done before he took to the water again. It would be hours until it was dark enough for him to sneak out, put on his diving gear, and go over the hull of the *Tomorrow* for any little presents left behind by Whidbey Island's navy SEALs. He would rather have spent the time until dark naked with Honor in a bed the size of Texas instead of standing on one foot and then the other. But getting his hands on her sweet body wasn't real likely right now. Or any time soon.

"To hell with sneaking around," he muttered. "It's not like it will come as a big surprise to anyone. They're probably wondering why I haven't done it before now."

"Hello?" Honor said. "Are you talking to me?"

"I'm going diving."

She looked out the window. Something cold and unpleasant slid down her spine at the thought of being out on the water. Even the little beach was feeling the impact of the wind now. Instead of lapping at the rocky shore, the waves were smacking against stone and exploding into foam that was whipped quickly ashore. Spindrift was sticking to tall rocks. Tall, powerful fir trees were swaying like dancers in the wind.

"You're diving in that?" Honor asked.

"No. Below that."

"You're nuts."

"Blame yourself. You vetoed a much better idea."

"What are you talking about? I didn't veto—"

"Sure you did," he interrupted. "Remember? Us, in bed, naked?" He smiled at her expression. "Don't worry, honey. I've got a different kind of skin diving in mind at the moment. But hold the good thought."

"I'd feel better if you smiled with your eyes, too."

"So would I. But life's a bitch and—"

"—then you die," she finished with a catch in her voice. "Jake, don't go diving. It's too dangerous."

Honor knew it was stupid to let him see her worry for him, yet she couldn't do anything about it. Even though her mind and her instincts were locked in uncivil warfare over what to do about Jake Mallory, the thought of him being hurt made her want to throw herself into his arms and hold him close.

And then she realized that he was already holding her, rocking her against his chest.

"It's all right," Jake said. "I'm only going as far as the dock. I won't leave you to face the wolves alone."

She barely kept herself from telling him that she wasn't worried about herself. Giving that away would have been really stupid. She was in more trouble than he was.

He wasn't fighting himself along with everyone else.

Honor went down the path to the boat beside Jake, hugging her wind jacket around her. The temperature was over sixty, but the wind made it seem closer to thirty. Jake didn't seem to notice it. He was wearing a dive suit that fit like skin and a tank of air held on by a harness. Tight black gloves covered his hands. Big flippers and a mask dangled from his right fist. Hoses and a metal gauge lay over his shoulders.

He should have looked awkward, but she kept seeing him as he was beneath the suit—nearly naked and sexy enough to make her forget all the reasons she shouldn't be thinking about what she couldn't help thinking about.

"You must be freezing," she said.

"Not yet. That will come after I've been in the water for a while."

"So don't go in!"

He didn't say anything.

"Why do you have to look at the *Tomorrow*'s hull? Has it sprung a leak?"

"Just checking."

She waited, but he had no more to say on the subject of why he was going for a dive in a gale. It had been the same every time she brought it up in the past hour. Silence or a change of subject.

"Why won't you tell me?" she asked.

"Because you have enough to worry about."

"And this is helping me how?"

Jake sighed. "I figure by now the SEALs have used the *Tomorrow* for a training exercise. I'm just going to make sure they haven't done any damage."

It wasn't the whole truth, but it was as much as he was going to tell her. She was strung tight enough as it was. If she knew he was going to take Kyle's boat out after dark, it wouldn't help her nerves at all.

"You think they sabotaged the *Tomorrow*?" Honor asked, suddenly angry.

"No. I'm just being careful."

"Paranoid."

"That too."

A gust of wind made Honor stagger. Jake steadied her with his free hand.

"Go back to the cottage," he said. "I'll be fine."

" 'I'll be fine,' " she mimicked savagely. "Like hell. You're not supposed to go diving alone."

Jake knew that, but he was doing it anyway. Sometimes it was safer to break the rules than to be the only one playing by them.

He walked out onto the dock. She was right on his heels.

"Go back to the cottage," he said again. "I won't be long."

"Good. I'll be right here the whole time."

"We don't have a second suit. If I get into trouble, what could you do?"

"Dance a jig on the dock."

"Want to be in on the kill, huh?"

She shivered. The thought of him being hurt was bad enough. The thought of him dying made her cold all the way to her soul.

"Sorry to disappoint you, buttercup," he said, "but I *am* going to disappoint you on that one. No victory dance over my dead body."

"That's not funny," she said through her teeth.

"Not for me. But I'm not half as mad at me as you are."

In a seething kind of silence Honor watched

while Jake finished suiting up on the dock. Soon he was turning on the compressed air and checking the flow. Satisfied, he put in the mouthpiece. Moments later he stepped off the deep end of the dock and sank beneath the choppy water.

Honor could barely follow the trail of bubbles for all the wind and froth. Every time she lost all sign of Jake, she thought about what it would be like if he didn't surface at all, ever.

"Get back up here, Jake Mallory," she said to the dark water. "I'm not nearly mad enough at you yet!"

By the time he finally surfaced, Honor had thought about many things, none of them guaranteed to make her feel all warm and squishy. Jake's easy strength as he levered himself from the cold water onto the dock told her that he was doing better than she was. She could barely feel her fingers, and her toes were numb. She wasn't dressed to be out in this kind of wind.

"Did you find it?" she demanded as soon as he removed his mask.

"Find what?"

"The tracking gizmo," she said impatiently. "Did the water freeze your brain?"

"I don't remember mentioning any tracking gizmo." He sat down and began removing the flippers.

Wind whipped hair across Honor's mouth and eyes. Impatiently she pushed it away. "Contrary to my performance in the past day or so, I'm not completely stupid. The SEALs aren't going to blow us up, but they sure might make it easier for Ellen and the boys to track us. So did you find it?"

"Yeah."

"Where is it now?"

"I attached it to the dock."

"Well, that should reassure them that we're not going anywhere."

"That's the idea," he said, standing again. "C'mon. Let's get in out of the wind."

Frowning, Honor followed Jake up the path, certain she was missing something. She was still trying to figure out what as he went into the bedroom to get out of his dive suit. Though the door to the bedroom stayed open, she didn't go in. She didn't trust herself not to offer to help unzip his high-tech skin. Worrying about him under the water had made it nearly impossible to stay mad at him on land.

Jake stepped into the shower and rinsed off the dive suit. He dried it like a second skin, then peeled off the cold water diving hood and went to work on the rest of the suit.

"Don't they have someone watching the house?" Honor called from the living room. "Whoever the guy was that called and told Mather the 'primary subjects' were back together again?"

"Yeah."

"Do you think he can see the dock?"

"Probably."

"Then he'll know you know about the gizmo."

Jake decided he should have left Honor

out in the wind a little longer. Her mind was still too sharp.

"It's possible," he said finally. His voice was muffled because he was peeling off the top half of his wet suit.

"Then what's to stop them from sticking another one on?"

"Nothing."

"Then why did you bother to go gizmo-diving in the first place?"

Jake sighed and told Honor what she really didn't want to hear. "Because they won't come back until well after dark, and by then the *Tomorrow* won't be here."

Silence came, followed by, "Where will it be?"

"Out there," he said, waving in the direction of the islands.

Honor could see the islands through the bedroom window. They rose above the wild water like distant, blue-black whales.

"You're kidding, right?" she asked, afraid that he wasn't.

"Wrong."

He peeled off the bottom half of the dive suit, went to the shower again, and rinsed off his flippers, dive gloves, and tank harness. He could still hear Honor above the sound of the shower, but he pretended he couldn't. He already knew that she didn't think much of going out in rough weather. Normally he didn't either. Not much had been normal lately.

Honor stalked into the bathroom, hands on hips and flags of anger flying in her cheeks.

The sight of him naked but for some kind of diver's jockstrap didn't improve her temper one bit.

"Jacob Mallory, look at that ocean!"

"I've been out in worse."

"I haven't!"

"That's okay. You aren't coming with me. You're going to call Ellen and tell her we had the mother of all fights and you've decided to join her team."

"No," Honor said flatly.

"That means you're coming with me."

"But—"

"There's no other choice," Jake said ruthlessly, brushing past her on the way from bathroom to bedroom. "I'm not leaving you alone with the likes of Snake Eyes on the loose."

Honor followed Jake farther into the bedroom, then wished she hadn't. The bedroom really had a stunning water view. Up until this moment she had loved it. Now she felt like hiding; the sea was angry and violent, as bad as her nightmares of being scared and wet and facedown in a leaky boat that smelled of fish.

"Call Ellen," Jake said softly, touching Honor's suddenly pale cheek. "She'll take care of you."

"No."

"Look at me."

Honor turned away from the water. Despite Jake's gentle voice, his gray eyes were no more peaceful than the sea.

"If I find Kyle," Jake said clearly, "I will do

everything I can to bring him back safely to you. I promise you."

"No," she whispered.

Anger and impatience and something else, something painful, changed Jake's features. "You really don't trust me."

"That's not it."

"The hell it isn't." He turned away and grabbed jeans and underwear from the duffel he had brought. "Well, you're shit out of luck, buttercup. It's Ellen or me." He stripped out of the wet jockstrap and pulled on dry underwear. "No third choice." He yanked on the jeans. "I don't have time right now to arrange for baggage handlers to take you to Tahiti. Ellen's boss is getting impatient. They could pull the plug on me, and then I would be shit out of luck right along with you."

"Jake, that's not—"

He kept on talking. "Once the elephants start to play, dumb pieces of grass like me get trampled in the mud. Kyle has the Donovan family to wash him off and coo over his wounds. I don't have anyone but me. I have to find out the truth about that amber, because nobody else cares. That means you're going to Ellen and I'm going to sea. If that throws a kink in your plans, then that's too damned—"

His tirade stopped abruptly. Two cold, gentle hands were stroking his bare back.

Jake turned around so fast that he almost knocked Honor over. "What do you think you're doing?" he demanded.

"Reasoning with you." She stroked his

chest, tangling her fingers softly in the silk cord that held the amber medallion in place.

"Reasoning?" he asked.

"Uh huh. It's working, too. See how much more reasonable your tone is?" Honor's fingertips traced the intertwined dragons and the male warmth beneath. "Why weren't you wearing this the first time we made love?"

"You didn't know who I was. The medallion would have raised too many questions. I didn't want to answer them."

"Amber man," she said sadly.

He shrugged, but his breath broke when her fingers went from the medallion to his nipples. They turned to tiny stones beneath her curious fingertips.

"Nice try, but you still only have two choices," Jake said through clenched teeth. "Ellen or me."

"I'm thinking."

One of Honor's hands trailed down his chest to his navel and then on to the finger-width of black hair that led down the center of his briefs. He rose to meet her with a speed and force that sent an answering flood of arousal through her.

"What are you thinking?" he asked.

"I was wondering how you would taste."

Jake's breath locked in his throat. "You're supposed to be thinking about your choice—Ellen or the boat. No matter how much I want you or how good you give it to me, you still only have two choices."

"Are you accusing me of trying to seduce you

in order to muddle your mind?" Honor asked.

Slim, caressing fingers slid inside his briefs. Her hands were no longer cold. Or if they were, he didn't notice it.

"Aren't you?" he asked.

"Would it work?"

"No. Yes." His breath hissed as she stroked the pulse beating so hotly beneath smooth skin. "Damn it, I can't think when you do that."

"How about when I do this?"

Her hands moved quickly and his briefs slid down to his knees, then his ankles. The heat of her mouth was every wet dream he had ever had rolled into one. Distantly he told himself that he was stronger, tougher, meaner, all he had to do was grab her by the arms and lift her to her feet and that would end her silly attempt to change his mind by offering sex.

And he would do just that—when he was certain he couldn't take it one more instant. Until then, he would take it like a man, silently, muscles clenched, sweating from head to heels, breathing like a racehorse coming down the home stretch.

"That's it," he said hoarsely.

"But I was just getting the hang of it," she protested, tracing with her tongue the pulse that beat so violently.

Jake kicked aside his briefs, lifted Honor, and wrapped her legs around his waist. "Get the hang of this."

Her pupils dilated with pleasure as he peeled off her pants and sank into her. Her response was a rhythmic contraction and a wave of heat that almost stripped away his control. Hotter than her mouth, deeper, sweeter, she was all around him, he was flying and falling at once, spinning.

"I'm losing it," he said raggedly.

Honor didn't hear him. She was already lost.

21

When Jake came into the kitchen carrying his duffel, Honor was wrapping up salmon sandwiches to take on the boat. Other bags of food stood ready on the counter.

"Did you find enough tie-downs for your Zodiac?" she asked.

"Yeah."

"I can't believe it fit beneath the radar arch."

"That was the easy part. Getting the Zodiac down to the boat in this wind was a lot of fun."

"You should have let me help you."

Jake agreed, but he wasn't about to admit it. "I still think you should call Ellen. You would be safe."

"I would go crazy worrying about Kyle and you."

"You trust me with your body but not your brother, is that it?"

"No. That's not it."

He looked at Honor's stubborn profile. "I don't believe you."

"I can't help that." She stuffed sandwiches into plastic bags and ignored him.

Jake bit back a savage comment. No matter what she said now about trusting him not to hurt Kyle, she hadn't mentioned love in all of the wild, windswept hours they had spent in bed waiting for full darkness to come...and wishing it never would.

"What if I just bundle you up and drop you on Ellen?" he asked roughly.

"I'd tell her where you were."

"You won't know."

"Seal Rock."

His head turned swiftly toward Honor. "When did you learn how to read the chart plotter?"

"Watching you. Seal Rock is the only route Kyle entered that we haven't tried."

"There's no guarantee he's anywhere near there."

"I know."

"Then why are you going?"

"I told you."

"If you trusted me, you would stay on land."

"Typical male logic—wrong." Honor picked up the food bags and met Jake's glance squarely. "You're wasting time."

"What if something happens to you?"

"What if it happens to you?"

His mouth flattened. He went through the arguments in his mind again. He had tried all of them twice, some of them three times.

Honor wasn't buying any of them. He had all but come right out and said he was looking for Kyle's corpse and he didn't need her for that. The heavy hints had seemed to go right over her head.

Then he had seen the fear and grief in her eyes and felt like a murderer.

"Stay here," Jake said gently. "Believe me, it will be easier on you."

"No."

"You're not being reasonable!"

"Takes one to know one."

He dropped the duffel on the table and began cramming in supplies. "If you get seasick and scared, don't come to me for sympathy."

"I figured that out already."

Jake didn't doubt it. With a muttered word he hit the light switch, throwing the kitchen into the same darkness that filled every room but the bedroom. He stood impatiently, waiting for his eyes to adjust to the moonless night.

"What about the bedroom light?" Honor asked after a few moments.

"Leave it on."

"Why?"

"If the spy thinks we're wrestling in the sheets, he won't wonder why the rest of the place stays dark."

"Don't people turn out the lights to make love?"

"Did we?"

"I didn't notice. Did we?"

Despite his irritation, Jake couldn't help smiling as he thought of Honor all flushed and passionate, then sated and sleepy, then her curious mouth arousing him all over again while he watched and wondered how he had gotten so lucky and unlucky at once: Honor was a lover who matched his own hungry sexuality; she was a woman who didn't really trust him.

He had a bad feeling that she was planning on ending their affair after he found Kyle.

"Any darkness that came was due to sunset creeping up on us," Jake said. "I was enjoying every bit of the view. Especially the look on your face when you came that last time."

"Jake!"

"What? Don't tell me you didn't like it."

Honor hated the blush she knew was staining her cheeks right then. It made her feel like a schoolgirl. Jake's slow smile gleaming in reflected light told her that he liked teasing her. He also liked satisfying her.

"You're trying to get my mind off going out on the water, aren't you?" she asked.

"Is that what I'm doing?"

"Yeah."

"Is it working?" he asked.

"Sometimes."

But there was a catch in her voice that told Jake this wasn't one of the times. He put an arm around her and pulled her close, comforting her even though he had sworn he wouldn't.

"Last chance," he said softly. "Stay with Ellen."

"No."

For an instant his lips brushed Honor's

hair. Then he released her and headed out the back door. Together they hurried down the path and into the strong wind. For part of the way, forest screened them from any watchers. For the rest of the path, they would have to depend on darkness and luck.

"The dock will be slippery," Jake warned her in a low voice. "So will the boat."

Honor didn't doubt it. She could almost taste the salt spray in the air. She definitely could feel it in the sting of wind-driven dampness against her skin.

Though the moon hadn't risen yet, there was enough starlight to see that the water was white as much as it was black. Even in the sheltered cove, wind waves more than a foot high broke against pilings and threw water onto the floating walkway. The only good news was that the tide wasn't particularly low—the ramp leading down to the dock wasn't as steep as it would be in a few hours, or as slippery.

Holding the supplies, Honor cautiously crept down the ramp and onto the dock. Before she reached the boat, Jake had unloaded his stuff and was taking hers. He stepped back down into the boat, set the supplies in the cabin, and returned to the dock just as she was lowering herself into the boat.

Jake was right. It was slippery. If she hadn't been wearing deck shoes, she would have been on her hands and knees.

He lifted her aside, opened the engine hatch, and squatted on his heels. He took a deep breath, then another. No smell of gasoline. He would risk it.

But first he removed a small flashlight from his jacket pocket and aimed a pinpoint of light into the compartment. Everything looked the way he had left it—shipshape and ready to go. He stood and lowered the heavy cover into place.

"I'll turn on the blower," Honor said quietly.

"No. Sit in the pilot seat and don't touch anything."

"But—"

"No blower," he said over her protest. "No lights. Nothing."

"But—"

"Do what I say or get off the boat."

The low, flat order told Honor that she wouldn't win this argument. Besides, he was the expert, not her. If he didn't want to use the blower, who was she to argue?

She ducked into the cabin, tossed her backpack into the V berth, and climbed into the pilot seat.

Jake was right behind her. He leaned across the helm seat and started the engine. Even the wind couldn't completely muffle the sound. Very soon someone would figure out that the throaty growl belonged to a boat. Then Ellen would get a call. He doubted that she was sleeping on the Bayliner. It would take her a few minutes to get to her boat. Not much of a head start for him, but it would have to be enough.

Instead of giving the engine time to warm up as usual, Jake went right back onto the dock and started casting off lines. Carrying the stern line in his hand, he leaped aboard and took up the controls.

As soon as his hands wrapped around the wheel, Honor let out a breath she hadn't known she was holding. Very quickly the *Tomorrow* was free of the dock and heading out into choppy, wind-tossed water. Away from the shelter of the headlands at either end of Amber Beach, the waves doubled in size.

Honor reminded herself that it didn't matter, a boat could float on waves of any size. She wished she believed it in her gut as well as her head. It seemed that her instincts and her mind had been in a state of war ever since Jake Mallory walked into her life.

Instantly she told herself that she wasn't being fair to Jake. Kyle was the one who had turned her life upside down. All Jake did was turn the whole mess inside out—and her with it.

But it was too late for regrets. She had made her choices and now she was at the mercy of the wind, the ocean, and a man she trusted more than she should.

In troubled silence Honor watched while Jake bent over the chart plotter, called up the menu, and punched in his choice. A dotted line appeared on the radar screen. He turned the helm until they were on course and nudged the throttle up.

For a time she took the tension and the

pitching waves in silence. Then she started asking questions. "Do you think we got away without anyone noticing?"

"Doubt it. But by the time they can do anything about it, we should be off their scope."

"What about the Coast Guard?"

"Their chopper is at Sand Point, twenty minutes away. We'll be long gone by then."

"Won't they look for us?"

"Clouds, wind, and night are on our side. We'll run without lights in the lee of the islands and hope the Coast Guard doesn't find us."

The SeaSport lurched as it dropped down off a wave. Though Jake wasn't going as fast as usual, he still wasn't exactly crawling. Honor had to brace herself on the bulkhead to stay in the seat.

Switches clicked and the windshield wipers rushed to clear salt water from glass. Not that it mattered. Without a moon or even the bow floodlight turned on, there wasn't much to see.

The cry of wind and the smack of waves on the hull became a kind of silence that ate at Honor's already frayed nerves. The more her eyes became accustomed to the dark, the more she realized how much white water there was.

"What about logs?" she asked finally.

"You see any?"

"No."

"Neither do I."

More noisy silence. The cabin was dark but for the chart plotter's screen and the eerie green glow of the radar screen showing islands and the occasional bright spot of navigation markers.

"What's that way off to the left?" Honor asked.

"A tugboat with a barge in tow."

She looked at the radar screen. "How can you tell?"

"Look out the window. See the lights on the 'Christmas tree'?"

"The what?"

"The tall mast. All tugs have them. The number of lights tells you how long the towrope is. The color of the running lights tells you whether it's coming or going. This one is starboard to, headed out. We'll cross well behind it and whatever it's towing."

Honor turned away from the radar screen and looked out over the water. Sure enough, the boat had a vertical line of lights. "Not my idea of a Christmas tree. Too skinny."

Without answering, Jake adjusted the radar screen to maximum range. Other than a big oil tanker on its way to March Point, there was nothing on the water but wind, waves, and islands. He settled in for a long, bumpy ride.

"Any lights behind us?" he asked after a time.

"Not the last twenty times I looked."

He smiled briefly.

"What does the radar show?" she asked.

"Nothing following us."

"Do you think we got away clean?"

He grunted.

The ride went from lumpy to rough as the *Tomorrow* emerged from the lee of a small island.

"Looks like we got away," Jake said, smiling at Honor. "If anyone but the Coast Guard spots us now, we'll look like vacationers who decided to weigh anchor and find a calmer spot to sleep."

"How long will it take to get to Seal Rock?"

"I don't know. Depends on the wind outside the islands."

Her hands locked on the bulkhead as the boat slid sickeningly down the side of a wave. She was certain the waves were bigger than they had been.

"Jake?" she asked.

"It's all right, honey. If I thought the ride was more dangerous than leaving you behind, I would have tied you up and stuffed you in a closet."

"You wouldn't have." But even as she protested, she knew that he could have done just that. "Why didn't you?" she asked, curious.

"I knew you wouldn't forgive me. But if I'm wrong and anything happens to you, I'll never forgive myself."

"Don't be ridiculous. Everything that happens isn't your fault. I'm a functioning adult, fully capable of making my own decisions and living with the results."

"I'm sure your brothers will see it that way," Jake said ironically.

"That's their problem."

"As long as it's my ass they're after, it's my problem too."

Honor opened her mouth and then closed it again. Jake was right. The Donovan males were very protective of their sisters. Sometimes it was endearing. Most of the time it was a pain in the rear.

"Go into the V berth and try to sleep," Jake said. "It could be a long night."

"Sleep? In this?"

Honor braced herself as the *Tomorrow*'s bow bit into a wave and shot through to a sudden downward swoop on the other side.

"This looks worse than it is," Jake said. "You should see what it's like in the Aleutians when storm winds are blowing and the sea runs forty to eighty feet high. Of course, the boats are a lot bigger, too."

"Eighty feet!"

"And up."

"Why does anyone go out in that?"

"Money." He checked the radar screen closely, watching it through several sweeps. The blip he thought he had seen didn't reappear. "Go ahead, get some sleep."

"I'd rather see the waves and worry than not see them and worry even more."

Besides, it was better than thinking about Kyle and his sexy, forlorn fiancée, the woman who had unintentionally damned him with every word she spoke.

I believed him. I betrayed my family, my people, my country. All of them. For him. May God forgive me, I still love him. I still believe he will telephone me...

Grimly Honor clung to the console and stared out into the churning darkness, trying to think of nothing at all.

Honor awoke the instant Jake started to ease out of the V berth beside her. Not far above her face, the transparent hatch cover showed nothing more than the silver torrent of moonlight that had made the last hour of their journey easier for Jake and more terrifying for her.

She really would rather not have known how wild the sea became before he finally anchored in the lee of an island and let the gale blow on without them.

"Where are you going?" she asked. "It isn't even dawn."

"Just checking the boat. Go back to sleep."

"Oh, sure. 'Go back to sleep,' " she mimicked. "Next time I go to a tennis match, I'll know how the ball feels."

"It wasn't that bad."

"It was worse."

"Next time I'll stuff you in the closet."

"Next time I'll let you."

His smile flashed in the moonlight as he bent down and kissed the corner of her mouth. "I'll hold you to that."

Thirty seconds after Jake left the berth, Honor began to get cold. The sleeping bag they had been using as a blanket was plenty warm as long as he was beside her, radiating heat.

Without him the berth felt like a pie-shaped slice of refrigerator. Even fully dressed in shoes, leggings, jeans, sweater, and sweatshirt, she wasn't really warm.

She inched past the electronics toward the cabin. The tension in her body, the feeling of having to remember to breathe, was so much a part of her now that she almost didn't notice it. The dreams she was having were different. She couldn't get used to them, the raw fear and the feeling that no matter what she did nothing got done, that Kyle was calling her name and his innocence into the darkness and wind, slipping farther and farther away from her with every cry....

The door to the head opened and closed behind Jake. Shivering, she eased past him in the narrow aisle.

"Remember how to use it?" he asked.

"Yes. I particularly remember how cold the seat is."

"Never noticed."

"Try sitting down when you pee."

The door slammed, leaving Jake alone but for the muttering of the radio. He smiled slightly; she really wasn't a morning person. The middle of the night, however...

He turned up the radio, tuned to the marine weather station, and listened while he put coffee water on to boil. He was still listening when Honor emerged from the head, shivering. He handed her a bright orange float coat. It would be too big for her, but it would help to warm her.

"What's the weather like?" she asked, pulling on the coat.

"SSDD, until the high breaks up."

"What does that mean?"

"Same shit different day, until the weather changes."

"Goody," she said sarcastically.

"You bet it is. As long as the wind holds, we won't need to worry about being overrun by the Tupperware navy."

Honor blinked.

Despite the urgency and impatience gnawing at him, Jake smiled at her look of sleepy confusion. "Pleasure craft," he explained. "Made of cheap plastic."

The effort it took for her to smile told him just how edgy she felt. Underneath her forced calm, she was vibrating like a wire too tightly stretched.

And so was he. He had shared the good news about the wind, but not the bad: diving wouldn't be any fun, for either of them.

He changed to the hailing band on the radio and listened. Nothing. He surfed through the other channels several times, listening. Nothing. For all that he could hear on the radio, they had gotten away clean.

He wished he believed it.

They washed down salmon sandwiches with hot coffee. Dawn was barely a hint of gray on the eastern horizon. Jake hit the blower. A few minutes later he started the engine. While it came up to operating temperature, he went to work on the chart plotter again. Nothing new there, either.

"Seal Rock?" Honor asked.

He grunted.

"You don't sound very enthusiastic," she said.

"I'm not. It will be cold, rough, and windy."

"Isn't there a lee side?"

"Only if you're a seal and it's low tide, when the rocks are above water."

"Then why are we going? Kyle won't be there."

"You have a better idea?" he challenged.

She bit her lip and shook her head, not trusting her temper enough to respond. It wasn't Jake's fault she felt like she was breathing nettles.

He sighed and cursed under his breath. He really didn't want to point out that on Seal Rock they were looking for something that didn't have to breathe oxygen—like amber or a dead body.

"Sorry," he said, pulling Honor close. "Right now I'm not any happier about this mess than you are."

"He's not your brother," she said against Jake's flannel shirt.

"But you're his sister."

While Honor tried to make sense of Jake's words, he went out on the bow and pulled up the anchor. Before she had time to get nervous about being adrift, he was back in the helm seat. Anxiously she looked to the east, needing dawn in a way she couldn't explain. If only there was enough light, surely she would be able to see where Kyle was, wouldn't she?

Dawn hadn't arrived yet. The wind had. It caught them as soon as they left the lee of the island. But by the time they hammered through the waves to Seal Rock, it was light enough to see everything.

There was nothing to see except foam.

Even though her head had known it would be this way, disappointment broke over Honor in a long, cold wave.

Kyle, where are you?

"He can't be dead," she said hoarsely. "He's my brother…"

Jake saw a tear slide down her cheek. He had tried to prepare her for the bleak reef. Obviously he hadn't done a very good job.

"You believe he's dead, don't you?" she demanded. "A thief and a murderer and *dead!*"

"It's one explanation for his disappearance," Jake said in a neutral tone.

"He isn't dead," she said, her voice ragged. "What else is around here?"

"Water."

"You know what I mean!"

"This may surprise you," Jake said bitterly, "but I didn't come here just to rub your face in the most probable explanation for Kyle's disappearance. This is the last place Kyle recorded on the chart plotter. Period. No hidden agenda."

"If Kyle can't be here, why bother?"

"Because there's a chance, just a chance, that a panel from the Amber Room is tied to the bottom somewhere around Seal Rock."

"And if you find it, you'll be back in business."

Jake didn't say a word.

For a time Honor tipped back her head and closed her eyes as though to stop tears from falling. It didn't work. "How long will it take you to search for the amber?"

He grimaced. There was nothing in her voice, no color, no life, like a room with no light in it.

"Not too long," he said. "There are only a few places where it would be safe to stash the panel."

She blinked hard and looked out at the ragged rock and white water. "What are you talking about? You could hide the Queen Mary out there."

"If something is down there, it has to be safe from tides, currents, and storms. We get some pretty steep tides around here, so you're looking at least fifteen feet down."

Unwillingly Honor turned and faced Jake. His expression was intent, his eyes like hammered silver as he stared out over the nasty-looking rock.

"Kyle was limited by the amount of air in his tank," Jake continued, "even if he had a spare. I'm betting that he free dove to check out possible hiding places. I doubt that he went much deeper than twenty-five feet, because it gets real dark in these waters and the breath is squeezed right out of you by pressure unless you're used to free diving."

"As far as I know, he always used a tank."

"That's what I figured. According to the charts, there are maybe five places near Seal Rock that meet the requirements of tide, relatively calm water, and depth."

"You've spent a lot of time thinking about this, haven't you?"

Jake ignored the accusation in Honor's voice. "Yes. Ever since I found out that Kyle's dive equipment was missing along with his Zodiac."

"Why didn't you say something to me?"

"You believe he's innocent. That doesn't leave much to talk about, does it?"

"You believe he's guilty. That doesn't leave much to talk about, does it?"

"How about me?" Jake demanded. "Do you think I'm guilty of stealing the amber?"

"No."

His eyes widened in surprise. "Archer does."

She shrugged. "Archer is wrong."

"What makes you so sure?"

"Observation. I watched you with Resnikov's amber. You appreciated all of it, but your real passion was reserved for the Stone Age carvings. The Amber Room isn't Stone Age."

"You don't think I'd do it for sixty million bucks?" Jake asked curiously.

"Money isn't your passion either."

He would have preferred to have Honor's faith in him based on something warmer than observation—something like the unqualified love she gave her brother—but Jake wasn't in a position to be fussy.

"Kyle's passion is ancient jade," she continued, "not ancient amber, and he doesn't need money."

"If you're looking for a motive, don't forget Kyle's other passion," Jake said evenly. "The very modern Marju."

"He left her!"

"Did he? Or did he run out of luck doing something dumb in order to finance his love life?"

The downward curve of Honor's mouth said that she didn't like thinking about her brother's fiancée, a red-hot motive for real stupidity.

"He still didn't need money," Honor insisted.

"How long would Kyle's personal checkbook hold out living high in Brazil? Not the Donovan family money, but his own?"

A ripple went through her body, a signal of the tension that was increasing with every word Jake spoke.

"Don't ask me to believe Kyle is a thief," Honor said harshly. "Please, *don't!*"

Jake reached for her, wanting to hold her and comfort her. She drew back as though he had offered to hit her. His mouth thinned in anger and frustration. She might trust him when she thought about it, and she sure enjoyed sex with him, but she still lumped him with her brother's enemies.

"It will be slack tide soon," Jake said, turning away. "I'll drop anchor and get the dive gear ready."

Instead of answering, Honor grabbed a fishing rod and a heavy lure and went out on the stern. The motion of the boat in choppy water had become so familiar to her that she didn't even notice it. She simply widened her stance, lifted the rod, and sent the lure whipping out over the water with all the force of her fear and anger behind it.

Honor didn't say anything when Jake went over the stern and into the water wearing wet suit, mask, hood, flippers, and snorkel. She didn't seem to notice when he finally returned and put on the air tank. Yet when he went off the swim step and sank below the cold water, she shivered as though she were chilled clear through. After a few more casts she reeled in, put the rod in a holder, and stretched her aching arms.

No matter how carefully Honor looked at the ocean around Seal Rock, she saw no sign of Jake other than the dive buoy he had set out. To make the time pass more quickly, she went inside the cabin and tried to sketch. The pencil felt awkward in her hand. The images in her mind were more horrifying than artful.

With a sound of disgust, she put away her sketching materials and looked around. At home she would have paced away her nervous energy. But there wasn't room for pacing on the boat, and the substitute she had discovered—casting—didn't appeal to her right now.

The radio crackled, making her jump. She heard the Coast Guard "All Stations" broadcast for information about a twenty-seven-foot

SeaSport, name *Tomorrow*, probable destination the San Juan or the Gulf Islands. Hurriedly she stepped up into the helm seat and switched from the hailing channel to the work channel.

No one answered the Coast Guard's query.

After a few minutes of listening, Honor let out a sigh of relief. Her glance fell on the chart plotter. Jake had left it on, displaying the last entry Kyle had made. She stared at the representation of Seal Rock and the dotted lines that seemed to circle around the rock at random. Seven "hits" were recorded.

Honor went back to the menu, called up the first stored route, and looked at it. Nothing had changed since the last ten times she had stared at it, silently demanding that the chart give up its secrets to her. She called up the second route. Nothing new. The third. The fourth. The fifth. The sixth.

"Where are you, Kyle?" she said aloud. "Damn it! Where are you!"

One by one, she retrieved and stared at all the routes Kyle had stored. Like her attempt to sketch, no inspiration came.

"If you weren't trying to hide something, why doesn't your log show that you went to these places?"

Silence and a slowly subsiding wind were her only answers.

Honor pulled Kyle's logbook off the dash and flipped through it as she had many times before. Nothing new leaped out at her.

"Kyle, you're going to have to help me on

this one. I have the key, but it's no good without the lock. *Where did you hide the lock?*"

As soon as Honor said the words, a thread of excitement snaked through her. Almost afraid to believe, to try, and then to suffer disappointment all over again, she shut down the electronics with trembling fingers. Moments later she turned on everything again, as though she had just come on board and was starting up the boat for a day of fishing.

Two separate sets of buttons lit up once more. They were the only access to the normal functions of depth sounder and chart plotter. They were also the only access to whatever unusual functions Kyle had added to the electronics.

"Which set of buttons is the lock?" Honor asked, staring at the machine. "Or is it both, half on one set and half on the other? And which half? Or is it every other, back and forth?"

There was only one way to find out. Starting with the keys that held letters rather than numbers, Honor punched in Kyle's password, which could be rendered in numbers or as a word. Either way, it permitted access to his bank accounts, his computer, his telephone answering machine, everything.

Nothing happened.

She clenched her fist, shut off the electronics and started them again. This time she punched the password into the upper set of buttons. The picture on the chart plotter flickered, then went blank. Honor's groan turned into a sound of surprise as the screen flickered again, then called up a different chart.

Honor was still staring at the screen, trying to make out the location of the route, when she felt the boat shift as it took Jake's weight on the swim step. She slid out of the helm seat and hurried to open the door.

"Jake—" she began.

"No," he interrupted curtly, peeling off the dive harness. "I didn't find anything."

"I did."

22

It took an hour for Honor and Jake to get to Kyle's last, hidden route: Jade Island. Very small, uninhabited, and too far off the common routes to need navigation markers, the island was inaccessible a lot of the time by anything but a Zodiac or a kayak. During high tides there were several narrow channels leading through the rocks, reefs, and rafts of seaweed to the island itself, but there were few people who would risk their boats on the unmarked rocks.

"I can see why Kyle took the Zodiac," Jake said as he completed circling the island. "We're lucky the tide is up. Otherwise you would get a chance to find out how you do in an open boat."

Honor shuddered.

Jake tried the south side of the island first. After he threaded through the obstacles, he discovered a trough of deeper water surrounding much of the island itself. There was no year-round freshwater spring, no beaches except at low tide, and no good fishing or crabbing; in all, there was nothing to recommend Jade Island but isolation and scenery. The scenery, at least, could be duplicated on the more accessible islands.

Jake stood in the stern well, still in his dive suit, handling the *Tomorrow*'s aft controls with the unthinking skill of a man who was thoroughly at home.

A few feet from him Honor looked through binoculars at the uneven, rugged stone wall rising from the sea. She felt a hundred years old and frozen to the marrow of her bones. She didn't even have the relief of tears. The disappointment she felt was so deep that it was impossible to cry. She had been so triumphant when she had finally found the hidden chart and so relieved that she was almost light-headed.

"Let me look," Jake said, taking the binoculars from her. "You're making yourself sick staring through these."

Even though the wind had fallen off steadily and whitecaps were disappearing, there was still a noticeable chop beneath the *Tomorrow*'s white hull. Yet it wasn't seasickness that was making Honor's skin feel clammy. It was the suffocating fear that she had done everything she could and still had failed her brother completely.

There was nothing on the tiny island but rock, fir trees, and more rock.

Jake divided his attention between driving the very slowly moving boat and looking through the glasses. Numbly Honor waited for him to tell her what she already had seen for herself: Kyle wasn't there.

But when Jake lowered the binoculars, all he said was, "Let's try the north side."

Her shrug said more than words. She didn't think the other side of this unforgiving island would have anything to offer but more disappointment.

Slowly the *Tomorrow* cruised the length of the north side, picking through obstacles to the deeper water close to shore. Other than being in the lee of the southeast wind, and having more trees, the north side of the island wasn't much different from the south. There was no place to run a Zodiac up onto a beach because there were no real beaches.

Turning away from the empty island, Honor fought the cold tide of despair that kept threatening to overwhelm her. She had been so certain that Kyle would be there, safe, able to explain everything that had happened....

So certain, and so wrong.

"What does the bottom look like?" Jake asked in a clipped voice.

Honor didn't answer.

He set his jaw. He had been in a lethal mood since he discovered how little Honor trusted him; she had known Kyle's access code but hadn't mentioned it until an hour ago.

The rational part of Jake admitted that he

could hardly blame her. But he wasn't feeling particularly rational at the moment.

"Go inside and check the fish finder," he said
without lowering the binoculars. "I need to
know what the bottom is like. I'll tell you if
I see anything."

Honor went into the cabin and switched the
lower screen from chart to fish finder. She stared
at the gaudy blue-and-red display while the
boat crept closer to the island. The angle of
approach Jake chose was very shallow. Each
time the depth changed more than a few feet,
she read out the number in a voice loud
enough to carry through the open cabin door
to the stern.

"Forty-four, forty-one, thirty-two—going
up fast. Twenty-five. Twenty. Fourteen.
Nine!"

Jake reversed the throttle, killing all but a
tiny bit of forward momentum.

Honor glanced up and gasped. The rugged
cliff looked close enough to touch. "Jake, the
rocks!"

"I see them. We can get closer if we have to.
There's still water to spare under the hull. What
does the radar show?"

"An island right in front of us, what do
you think?"

"Behind us," he snapped.

She forced herself to look at the radar screen
instead of the looming cliff. An island was back
there, too. She tried to remember its name. All
she could think of was her sense of failure, the
aching feeling of having come so very close but

not close enough to make a difference.

"I can see the little island we came past to get here," Honor said. "That uninhabited one on the left, about a mile off. You know which one I mean?"

"Yes."

Jake also knew that a small boat could hide quite handily in the island's dense radar shadow. But there was no point in bringing it up. Honor was unhappy enough without adding more to her worries.

Besides, he couldn't be sure they were being followed. He was just being paranoid about something that probably was no more than an occasional flicker way out at the edge of the radar screen. Getting sucked back into Ellen's world had that effect on him. He didn't like living in a place where everyone had false smiles, multiple motives, and top secret agendas.

He adjusted course to go around a small nose of rock, then ducked back into the cabin and slid into the pilot seat. Honor was staring out the window. The bleak expression on her face told him exactly what she was thinking.

Jake handed over the binoculars. Silently she took them, turned her back, and began examining the shoreline through as much magnification as her stomach could take.

Slowly the *Tomorrow* made its way around a small headland. The opposite side of the headland was a very shallow cove that might have had a rough, rocky beach at low tide, but the tide wasn't low at the moment. A light breeze played over the steep slope dropping down to the shore. Fir trees came all the way to the waterline and trailed their shaggy green arms in the sea.

"Stop!" Honor said suddenly.

Jake didn't have brakes, but he did what he could. He shoved the shifter into neutral, then into reverse for a few seconds, then into neutral again. The boat began drifting. He corrected with the shifter rather than the wheel, holding the *Tomorrow* as nearly stationary as he could in the wind and current.

The shore was less than thirty feet off the port side of the boat. The bottom was at sixteen feet. He watched Honor, the depth sounder, and the shore. Without removing the binoculars she fumbled open the side window and leaned out.

"What is it?" he asked.

"I don't know. Go back to where that bunch of fir trees comes down to the water and get as close as you can."

He looked to her left and saw a dense growth of young trees. Gently he powered backward until the boat was opposite the firs. Abruptly the bottom leaped up to meet the surface.

"That's it," Jake said, reversing. "There's a reef. Any closer and I'll be on the rocks."

With a frustrated noise, Honor leaned farther out the window, banging her elbows in her eagerness to get a better look. The shore was still ten feet away, the fir branches were rippling in the wind, and the boat was constantly adjusting to the restless, choppy water.

"I can't see if it's a—" she began. She made

an odd sound. "It's a dive tank!"

Jake couldn't see anything but the back of her head and the rocky shore they were drifting closer to with every passing second. He looked at the bottom and made up his mind. This would have to do for short-term anchorage. At least they were on the lee side of the island, as long as the wind didn't shift.

He threw the controls into reverse, backed out, then switched to neutral. "I'm going to anchor here."

Honor barely noticed him going to the bow, letting down the anchor, and then backing the boat off to set the hook. The engine noise stopped. She kept staring through the glasses until her eyes ached, praying that she would see her brother.

All she saw was an on-and-off glint of metal where the dive tank lay hidden in the thicket of fir trees.

"Kyle!" Honor called. "Are you here? Are you all right? Kyle! Can you hear me?"

Only the sigh of evergreens and the restless slapping of water against rock answered her.

"Do you know how to shoot a gun?" Jake asked.

Honor backed out of the window so fast that she rapped her head. "The basics, why?"

"How basic?" he asked.

"The end with the hole in it points toward the target. Don't close your eyes when you pull the trigger."

"That's pretty basic." He bent down and opened a compartment beneath the table.

"How good a shot are you?"

"I'd probably do better tying the gun on the end of my fishing line and throwing it like a lure."

The corner of Jake's mouth turned up in a reluctant smile. "I'll bet you would." He straightened, gun in hand, and headed for the stern of the boat. "I'll take this with me."

"What?" She stared at the black weapon and then hurried to follow him out into the stern. "Why do you need one?" she demanded as he shoved the gun into a waterproof dive bag and clipped the bag to the webbing belt around his waist. "Kyle wouldn't shoot you! Why are you carrying a gun?"

Jake looked up. There was no smile on his face. "I'm not planning on shooting your precious brother. I promised you that I wouldn't hurt him. My word might not mean anything to you, but it does to me."

"That isn't what I meant," Honor said, touching Jake's arm. Cool neoprene covered it. "You're in no danger from Kyle, so why take a gun?"

"I'm the nervous type."

"Damn it, Jake, what aren't you telling me?"

He hissed a word under his breath and looked into Honor's angry, anxious eyes. It would be so much easier for both of them if she just trusted him. But she didn't.

"According to Ellen Lazarus," Jake said, "two Russians were sent to take care of Kyle. One killer washed up dead. The other one didn't.

Feel better now that I've told you what I wasn't telling you?"

"No." Honor's hands fastened around Jake's upper arms. She was shocked by the tension and strength in him. "If there's a—a killer waiting for you, don't go ashore!"

When Jake realized that she was worried about him as well as her brother, some of the tension eased from his body.

"You're not thinking very clearly, honey. Somebody has to check out that dive tank." He bent and gave her a swift, hard kiss. "Don't you get worried just because I am. I'm paranoid, remember? That means no more hanging over the rail and yelling for Kyle."

Unhappily she bit her lip, but she didn't protest.

"Stay here until I come back for you," Jake said. "If you hear gunshots, get on the radio to the Coast Guard and stay on until you see them or the SEALs coming over the swim step. Don't try to go ashore. Okay?"

"Can't I help you?"

"Sure. If you see anyone but me or Kyle, hit the boat horn."

"I meant coming ashore with you. I can take the cold water for a few yards."

"You'd be surprised how quick it gets to you. But even if you could take it, I don't want you to leave the boat."

"But—"

"Remember the night the guy trashed Kyle's house?" Jake interrupted.

"Yes."

"Don't sneak up on me," he said simply.

"We'd both regret it. Okay?"

"No, but I'll stay on the boat anyway," Honor said. "Unless you or Kyle is hurt and needs me. Then I'll do what I think is best, up to and including going ashore."

It wasn't quite the answer Jake wanted but it was better than an outright refusal. He went over the stern gunwale onto the swim step. The twenty feet to land wasn't worth the trouble of putting on swim fins to cover. He lowered himself into the water and scissor-kicked until he could stand. When he got to the rocky shore, the reef shoes he wore were better than no protection at all, but they weren't climbing boots.

Cursing, scrambling over slippery stones, he pushed among the prickly, flexible young firs. It didn't take him long to find the dive tank shoved back into the greenery. There was a name etched onto the cylinder: "Kyle Donovan."

Without moving, Jake examined the dense growth of firs beyond the air tank. There was no sign of breakage, no path battered through the stubborn growth, no primitive camp concealed beneath the boughs.

No corpse, either.

Mentally he reviewed the shoreline for places where an inflated Zodiac could be hidden. Zero. As for the island itself, he hadn't noticed many places where a man could hide himself, much less set up a concealed camp.

Jake backed out of the firs and headed uphill, using the shallow crease of a ravine as a trail.

The ravine went all the way to the top of the island, which was about two hundred feet at its highest. He didn't go that far. After a short, sharp scramble he pulled himself up to another row of wind-stunted trees.

And found himself looking right into the barrel of Kyle Donovan's twenty-two pistol.

"If you shoot me," Jake said harshly, "don't shoot the next one up the hill. That would be your sister Honor."

Kyle's eyes narrowed as he tried to see the man outlined against the bright sky. "Jay? What the hell are you doing here?"

"Looking for you."

A sweeping, predatory glance cataloged Kyle's gaunt face, hollow eyes, and trembling hand holding the gun. His dark blond hair was streaked with dust and his green-gold eyes burned with fever. There was a tear in the shoulder of his dive suit that could have come from a fall, a knife, or a bullet.

"What's this about Honor?" Kyle asked hoarsely.

"Honor is with me."

"Get her out of here."

"Why?"

"It's dangerous!"

"You're the only one I see holding a gun. Are you planning on shooting her?"

"Hell, no."

"How about me? You planning on shooting me?"

Kyle gave him a blank, disbelieving look. "Why would I do that? The only one I'm aiming for is the Russian who shot up my Zodiac after I put my elbow in his buddy's throat."

"Was that about a week ago?"

"I guess. The days kind of run together...." Kyle's eyelids lowered wearily. Adrenaline began to fade into the fatigue brought on by hunger and thirst and lack of sleep. "Do you have any water?"

Jake glided closer, waiting for exhaustion to make Kyle careless. "I can get some water, but not with you holding that pistol on me."

Kyle looked at the gun as though surprised to see it was still in his hand.

And then it wasn't. It was in Jake's hand and Jake's arm was barred against Kyle's throat, slamming him down against the rocks. Kyle thrashed once, then stopped struggling.

"It's a good thing I promised Honor not to hurt you," Jake said through his teeth. "I don't like having a gun held on me."

Abruptly he straightened, freeing Kyle, who struggled into a half-sitting position.

"I didn't know it was you," Kyle said, shaking his head.

Jake grunted.

With a sigh Kyle slumped back into the rocky crevice where he had been hiding.

Swiftly Jake finished his inventory of Kyle Donovan. In addition to the bloody gash high on the left shoulder, his dive suit was dirty all over and torn at one knee. The reef walkers he had on his big feet were ragged. His long-limbed, muscular body wasn't up to its usual level of effort; obviously just sitting up taxed his strength. His hands were scraped and bruised, his color was bad, he looked haggard and pretty well used up, but he didn't seem to be in danger of dying right away.

Jake let out a silent breath. He really hadn't wanted to face Honor over Kyle's dead body.

"About that water..." Kyle said in a hoarse voice.

Instead of saying anything, Jake sat on his heels and grabbed the younger man's wrist. The pulse was light, rapid. "Stick out your tongue."

"What?"

"Jesus, you and Honor. Argue about the color of the sky rather than follow a simple order. Stick out your damned tongue."

Kyle smiled. His dry lips cracked and bled. He licked up the moisture hungrily and stuck out his tongue at Jake. "How's it look?"

"Bloody awful, but not dangerously dehydrated. When was the last time you had water?"

"Did it rain last night?"

"Yes."

"Then it was last night. But it wasn't enough."

"Didn't you have any water with you?"

"Some, but I didn't plan on staying for a week."

"What about food?"

"Shipwreck menu," Kyle said huskily. His eyelids closed. "Shellfish and seaweed."

The sympathy Jake felt irritated him almost

as much as having a gun held on him. "Where's the amber?"

"The stuff you signed over to me is at a Kamchatka fishing camp."

"What about the rest of it?"

Kyle's eyes opened. "What?"

"The Amber Room," Jake said savagely. "What about it?"

Suddenly Kyle looked twice as haggard as he had before. "So you *were* part of it. Shit! I couldn't believe you set me up to die!"

"I didn't, but you set me up to take the fall for the stolen amber."

"Like hell," Kyle said, his voice hoarse. "I didn't even know something was wrong until the driver I picked up tried to kill me."

"So you dumped his body and—"

"He was breathing when I left him," Kyle interrupted.

"He wasn't when they found him."

Kyle closed his eyes in a grimace of pain. He looked like a man who was reaching the end of his endurance.

Jake sighed and swore under his breath. What had been a straightforward, if bitterly painful, assignment of blame for the theft of the amber had just gotten real complicated. Even so, Jake was relieved that Kyle had been fooled rather than crooked.

"Don't feel sorry for the bastard you chucked out of the truck," Jake said. "He's the one who jumped you, not the other way around."

Kyle didn't answer.

"When did you find out you had a panel of

the Amber Room?" Jake asked.

Slowly Kyle's eyes opened. They were bleak and measuring, as though he regretted the loss of his gun. His whole body had changed. Despite his exhaustion, he could still gather himself for an attack. "How do you know about that?"

"A former associate told me."

"Russian?"

"American. Some of the folks I worked for before I started my own company."

"Oh. Them. Hell, this is a royal cock-up, isn't it?"

"Yeah. Do you have the amber?"

Kyle nodded.

"Here?" Jake asked.

"Out there." Wearily he waved at the water.

Jake squeezed Kyle's right shoulder reassuringly and stood up. "I'll bring water. And Honor, no doubt. I should break your neck for not telling your family that you're all right, but I promised not to touch you."

"Bring the water and then get her away from here."

"You're not thinking very well. The lady doesn't take orders any better than any other Donovan."

"And you do?"

"Sure. I'm a regular little altar boy."

Kyle gave him a tired smile, winced, and fell back into an uneasy state that was neither consciousness nor sleep, more of a drifting that was broken by adrenaline-filled wakefulness at every unusual sound.

The next thing Kyle knew, Honor was kneeling at his side, trying to get him to sit up.

"Don't pull on that arm," Jake cautioned her. "It's hurt."

"You said he was all right!"

The anger, fear, and love in her voice made Kyle want to smile, but he knew better—his lips were too sore. Like his eyes. Dry and wanting to stay in the dark.

"There's nothing wrong with your brother that antibiotics, a glucose drip, and twenty-four hours' sleep won't cure," Jake said. "You awake, Kyle?"

"Sort of," he said hoarsely. "Water?"

"Right here. I'm going to help you sit up so you won't choke." Jake slid his arm under Kyle's shoulders and lifted him.

Breath hissed through Kyle's teeth.

"What is it?" Honor asked.

"Ribs," Kyle said. "Bastard kicked me."

"The driver?" Honor asked, remembering what Jake had told her as he hustled her into the Zodiac.

"One of the Russians they sent after me," Kyle said.

"The one who washed ashore about a week ago?" Jake asked calmly.

"Let him drink before you grill him," Honor said curtly.

She unscrewed the cap from a two-liter bottle of water and held it awkwardly to Kyle's lips. At first more dribbled down his beard-stubbled chin than went into his mouth. But after a few swallows, he got the hang of it and began drinking greedily.

"Slow down," Jake said, pushing the bottle away. "If you keep gulping like that, you'll get sick all over your loving little sister."

Sighing, Kyle closed his eyes and settled back against Jake's arm, only to flinch when something touched his sore lips.

"Easy," Jake said. "Honor is just putting some goo on so you don't bleed every time you smile."

"What is it?" Kyle asked.

"Chicken manure," she replied. "That way you won't lick it right off."

He laughed, then hissed when his ribs caught him.

"What happened to your arm?" Honor asked.

Kyle looked at her as though wondering how little he could get away with telling her.

"Forget protecting her," Jake said. "She's a lot tougher than you think."

"I got too close to a bullet," Kyle admitted, "but the ribs hurt more now."

Honor made a low sound and bit her lip.

"Hold still," Jake said to Kyle. "I'm going to open up this sleeve for a better look."

He took his dive knife from its sheath and gently sliced fabric away from Kyle's left shoulder. Honor took a steadying breath and leaned closer. Just below the shoulder, his arm and dive suit were crusted with a mixture of grit and blood. A finger's width of skin was gone from the outer arm. Puffy flesh oozed where it wasn't scabbed over.

Very gently Honor touched the unbroken skin around the wound. It was hot. "It's infected," she said unhappily.

"Not dangerously," Jake said.

"How do you know?"

"No red streaks on his arm," he said, looking at Kyle. "How does your stomach feel?"

"Fine," Honor said.

"Not you. Kyle."

"Thirsty."

Jake looked at the sea and saw only what he had seen before—water, rock, islands. Yet he couldn't shake the memory of the elusive blip on the radar and the Olympic that Conroy had talked about and Jake had never seen.

"You can drink all you want once we get you aboard the boat," Jake said. "We're getting out of here."

"The amber," Kyle said. "I have to—"

"Tell me where it is," Jake interrupted impatiently. "I'll come back for it as soon as you and Honor are safe."

Kyle started to speak, then shook his head.

"What is it?" Honor asked.

"Can't risk it," her brother said.

"What do you mean?"

Kyle just shook his head. Underneath a month's growth of bronze beard stubble, his face was set in the same unyielding lines Jake had come to recognize in Honor. Donovans were stubborn to the soles of their feet.

"Kyle?" Honor asked. "What can't you risk?"

"Leaving the amber alone with me," Jake said

savagely. "But that shouldn't surprise you, buttercup. You don't trust me either."

"That's not—hell," Kyle said roughly. It took too much trouble to explain, especially with a dry mouth and a fuzzy mind. "Do you have an air tank along? Mine is about done."

"I have a tank," Jake said.

"GPS unit?"

"Yes."

Kyle sighed and almost smiled. "No wonder you have your own business. Not much gets by you."

"Where is your GPS?" Jake asked.

"It sank with my Zodiac."

Honor's breath came in audibly. "What happened?"

"Bullets," Kyle said, his voice as worn out as he felt. "Jay, I want your word that you'll bring the amber up before you take me off the island."

"No!" Honor said. "You need a doctor more than we need any amber, no matter how fabulous."

Though red and gritty, Kyle's eyes hadn't lost their penetrating clarity. He looked at Jake and waited.

"Your sister is right," Jake said. "You need a doctor."

"I'll keep."

"So will the amber."

"That's just it. I was in a hurry when I sank it. It could tear loose and float away at any moment."

"Let it," Honor said curtly.

"You don't mean that," Kyle protested.

"The hell I don't."

"Explain it to her," Kyle said wearily to Jake. "I'm not up to the job."

As Kyle lifted the water bottle back to his lips, Honor turned on Jake, fixing him with gold-green eyes that were as determined as her brother's.

"There's nothing you can say that would make me value the amber more than I value Kyle's life," she said.

"That's just it," Jake said reluctantly, for he really wanted Honor off the island and safe. Unfortunately, her safety was directly linked to that of the panel from the Amber Room. "Your brother was the last one to see the panel. If you were someone like Snake Eyes, would you believe that Kyle had lost it?"

"But—"

Jake kept talking. "Or would you believe that he had stashed it somewhere until all the fuss died down? And believing that, Snake Eyes will grab whatever lever he thinks will make Kyle feel talkative. A much loved younger sister, for instance."

"That's ridiculous," Honor said.

Jake knew better. He turned back to Kyle. "You have my word. Where did you sink the amber?"

23

Honor was so furious with the two bullheaded men in her life that she stayed on board the *Tomorrow* while Jake took his portable GPS receiver and the Zodiac to the coordinates Kyle gave him—right in the middle of the offshore rocks. Kyle came as far as the island's waterline, but no farther. He sat with his back against a rock, sipped from the two-liter bottle, and watched the dive buoy Jake had set out a hundred feet beyond the shore and about the same distance from the *Tomorrow*.

Plainly Kyle meant exactly what he had said. He wasn't going to leave Jade Island until the amber was safe. Even with the GPS unit, locating the sunken panel wasn't a certainty. Ten yards, give or take, could be a long way in the cold, dark, unpredictable waters of the San Juan Islands.

Frustrated, Honor waited in the stern well of the *Tomorrow*. There was no room for her to pace and no outlet beyond yelling at her brother for being such a macho idiot as to worry about her instead of about himself. Yelling at him wasn't much fun. He just ignored her.

She looked at the rod in the holder to the left of the open cabin door. The gear was rigged and ready to fly. The tip was bowed with the weight of the lure.

"There's always that," she said beneath her breath. "In fact, I could screw up, cast in the wrong direction, and 'accidentally' brain my stubborn brother. Maybe it would knock some sense into him."

But Honor made no move to pick up the rod. Restless, anxious, on edge, feeling hunted and jailed at the same time, she paced as best she could in the confined area of the *Tomorrow*'s stern. She began to regret not being ashore where she could berate her brother without straining her voice.

Abruptly something that looked like a shallow rectangular box popped out of the water barely thirty feet beyond the *Tomorrow*'s hull. Jake surfaced right behind the box.

"Found it!" he yelled.

Smiling despite his cracked lips, Kyle lifted the water bottle in silent salute. Before he could muster enough energy to call out his congratulations, someone else did.

"Excellent, my friend! Now bring it to shore before I am forced to shoot Ms. Donovan."

Honor spun toward the sound of the voice.

Two hundred feet above Kyle, Petyr Resnikov was crouched on the crest of the island's steep slope. He had a sniper's rifle in his hands.

The barrel was pointed at her.

"Do not move, please," Resnikov called in a voice that carried easily down the slope and over the water. "An accidental death at this point would be regrettable, but I have had many regrets since the Berlin Wall fell. I would survive another one. Ms. Donovan would not. Jacob, if your hands go beneath the water, I will shoot your delightful lover. Do we have understanding?"

447

Jake understood all too well. For the moment he was as helpless as Kyle. "I understand."

"Excellent. With understanding there will be no need for death. Ms. Donovan, take one step forward and close the cabin door. Just that. No more."

"Easy does it, Honor," Jake said. "Nothing cute. Pete is worried about you getting on the radio. Make him feel good."

Honor couldn't see if the rifle barrel followed her the one step toward the cabin door, but she was certain it did. She jerked the door out of its stop and slammed it shut.

"Stay in my view, Ms. Donovan," Resnikov said. "If you do not, I will surely kill your lover and your brother. That would be regrettable and so unnecessary."

She flinched and stopped thinking about going overboard or throwing herself flat on the deck, out of Resnikov's sight.

"Jacob. Bring the box to the shore. Remember, I can see your hands very well through the scope, whereas you cannot be certain where my attention is."

Jake already had figured that out. What he hadn't come up with yet was a way to get up that slope and grab the rifle before Resnikov shot everyone in sight.

Slowly Jake put his hands against the edge of the box. He kicked his feet, pushing the box ahead of him in the water.

"At first I was troubled by your presence," Resnikov said to Jake. "You are a formidable foe. On reflection, I decided that to have you here is a bit of good fortune for all of us. You have the experience not to, um, lose your cool and force me to kill. You know that death is not necessary for any of us. Only the Amber Room is necessary. Bring it to me, Jacob."

There was a good possibility that Resnikov was telling the truth, that he wouldn't kill anyone unless pushed to it. But it wasn't a possibility Jake wanted to bet anyone's life on. Especially Honor's.

"Slowly, my friend," Resnikov cautioned as Jake stood in waist-deep water, pushing the shipping box toward shore in front of him. "I must always see your hands. Do not remove your fins when you come ashore."

"Why?" Jake said as he slogged through knee-deep water. "I can barely walk in them and you have a rifle on me in any case."

"Yes. Comforting, is it not? Leave the fins as they are. The dive cylinder, however, you may remove."

"Afraid a bullet would ricochet off the tank?" Jake asked.

"It is possible, yes?"

Cursing, Jake splashed ashore as noisily and awkwardly as possible. It wasn't hard. The big fins were meant for ocean diving, not walking along a rocky shore. While he thrashed around removing his tank and harness, he was careful not to look at Kyle.

Jake was certain Honor's brother would try something. He only prayed that Kyle was thinking well enough to wait until Resnikov came down off the slope to inspect the amber. Until then, they didn't have a snowflake's chance in hell of getting their hands on the Russian without getting killed in the process.

"Kyle, if you are gathering yourself to stand or roll into the trees, do not," Resnikov said crisply. "I would surely shoot your sister. Remember, I would rather shoot no one."

"But you will," Kyle said, his voice savage.

"It is my worst choice. Please do not make it my only one."

Pale, tight, Honor stood rigidly and watched while her brother slowly relaxed. Only she could see the rock that was now clenched in his big fist.

"Just take the damned amber and get out," Kyle snarled.

"I will," Resnikov assured him. "First, however, I will see that I have genuine goods. You will assist me in that, will you not, Jacob?"

"Sure," Jake said acidly. "Always glad to help a friend."

Honor couldn't see the Russian's reaction. His face was hidden behind rifle and sniper scope.

"Open the box, my friend," Resnikov said.

Jake looked at the shipping box. It was nailed shut. Water ran from every seam. The edges were so badly matched that they leaked even after being swollen from submersion in salt water. The inked words on the outside had faded and run, but were still legible: "Fishing Greatness/Camp of Kamchatka." Then there was another stamp: "dried ice, game fish, PERISHABLE."

"Open it, huh?" Jake called to Resnikov. "Easy for you to say. I don't have a pry bar."

"Use the knife you wear. When you are finished, cast the knife into the water."

Without a word Jake pulled his diving knife from its sheath and went to work on the box. Taking it apart was a lot easier than he thought it would be. Like the wood, the nails were made of inferior material. They had already begun to rust.

He ripped off the lid and tossed it out of the way. A thick, opaque plastic bag lay inside the remains of the shipping box. Sitting on his heels, he cautiously slit the bag down one edge with his knife. When he finished, he put the knife back in its sheath.

"No!" Resnikov said. "Throw the knife into the sea."

"There's more wrapping."

Resnikov hesitated for a moment before he said curtly, "Continue. But I do not forget about your knife, Jacob."

"For the man with the rifle, you're sure nervous."

"I have seen you move," the Russian said, "in that pub in Kaliningrad. It was very instructive for me as well as for Kyle Donovan."

"Get real," Jake said. "You're twice as fast as I am."

"I thought so, once. Now I do not wish to put the matter to a contest."

Jake fished around in the plastic until he pulled out a bubble-wrapped rectangle that was perhaps three feet long by four feet wide and less than a foot thick. With great care he slit the clear, broad tape that held the edges of the bubble wrap together.

Golden fire shimmered up through the opening he made.

"Throw the knife into the water!" Resnikov called.

Jake looked up the slope. He couldn't see the other man's eyes, but the rifle looked steady and comfortable in his hands. His pale hair gleamed in the sunlight like another shade of amber. The rifle had no shiny surfaces to attract attention. It wasn't an exhibition piece or a bit of modern military art. It was all business, and the business was killing.

"I think there's more plastic wrapping underneath the bubbles," Jake said.

"Then you will be required to use your teeth. The knife, Jacob. *Now*."

He tossed the knife into the water. It sank out of sight. Slowly he turned back to the box. For once in his life he wasn't eager to see the amber that lay within its protective nest of air bubbles and plastic. Slowly he began peeling away plastic until nothing was left but amber itself.

It was like unwrapping a piece of the sun.

A hundred shades of gold burned beneath his hands. Even as Jake's mind registered the extraordinary skill of the nameless artisans who had created the amber mosaic, a ripple of awe went down his arms. Hair stirred in primal reflex.

Slowly he lifted the mosaic and tilted it first one way and then the other, sending light pouring over its surface. Embedded in the dazzling golden display was an elaborate capital R made of red amber. Above the R was the austere crown of the Romanovs, also in red amber—austere, but far from unassuming. The rich, rare amber announced the presence of one of the great royal families in human history.

Great, and very dead. Power was a sword with no reliable grip and many lethal edges.

"Is it genuine?" Resnikov called.

"Real or fake, it's damned extraordinary," Jake said clearly, turning the panel, absorbing it into himself as though it were truly radiating warmth. "Sunlight and wealth and pride made tangible. A declaration of eternal power that only proves how transient power is. See my name and know how great I am...or was, because I'm dead as coffin nails now and so is my empire."

"Is it genuine?" the Russian demanded.

"Hell, Pete, how would I know?"

"Do not test my patience."

"Right now, I can't test anything. My kit is back in my truck. Come down and have a look for yourself." *Please,* Jake added silently. *Get within my reach for just a second.*

Just one.

"Are you in place?" Resnikov called out.

"What—" began Jake. Then he stopped.

The question hadn't been for him. It was for the woman who was stepping out from cover less than twenty feet away, a machine pistol in her hands.

Suddenly some things that hadn't made sense, did. Unfortunately, it was too late.

"Hello, Jones," Jake said. "I was wondering how Resnikov was going to get down that slope without taking the rifle off us. Now I know. Did you slip a tracking device in Honor's backpack while you were crying on her shoulder?"

Marju smiled. "But of course. She is so like Kyle. So wonderfully naive."

Honor stared at Marju and wanted nothing more than to wrap her fingers around the woman's elegant throat. The realization that she had led Kyle's enemies right to him made her sick.

"Naive, huh?" Jake said. "Well, it beats being what you are."

"What is that?"

"Stupid. Naive can be educated. Stupid goes all the way to the bone."

"I am stupid? Who is holding the weapon? Who is not?"

"Well..." Jake said, straightening.

"Not to stand!" Resnikov called to Jake. "Not to take the hands from panel! Sit on ground, feet in front. Now!"

Though Resnikov's English got worse under pressure, there was no trouble getting his meaning. Jake sat.

Under cover of the panel, he worked his feet free of the awkward flippers. Then he held the panel and waited for Marju to demonstrate her stupidity by getting too close to him. Without seeming to, he watched her intently while she picked her way past Kyle, just beyond the younger man's reach.

"Don't do it, Kyle," Jake said urgently. "Pete still has the rifle trained on Honor."

"I wasn't planning to," Kyle said. "I learned to recognize when she's teasing me. I wouldn't touch the bitch with a stick."

Jake let out a hidden breath. Apparently Kyle had gotten to the bottom line without losing his head. That was one of the things Jake really liked about Kyle; when his crotch wasn't involved, he was smart. Of course, the same thing could be said for other men—like J. Jacob Mallory, for one.

From the corner of his eye, Jake watched Marju's approach. She chose a position midway between himself and Kyle. It meant she had to pretty well turn her back on Honor, but that didn't seem to worry Marju nearly as much as keeping the men quite literally under her gun.

"I am ready, Petyr," she called.

Slowly Resnikov lowered the rifle. He knew his time of greatest danger would be while he came down the hill, when he couldn't keep the rifle trained on everyone in sight.

Jake knew it, too. He wished he could call out to Honor to stay quiet for just a bit longer, just one more minute, just until Resnikov was too busy keeping his balance on the steep slope to worry about anything else. But saying anything would just call attention to Honor.

That was the last thing Jake wanted to do. So he sat quietly while sweat gathered beneath his dive suit and ran coldly down his body.

Rifle in one hand, balancing himself with the other, Resnikov began climbing down the slope. Jake watched with an intensity that was tangible. Normally the Russian was as coordinated as a gymnast, but he had been lying up in the cold rocks long enough for muscles to stiffen. On the third step his foot slipped. Instantly he caught himself and glared at the people below.

No one had moved.

With more care for the loose rocks, Resnikov started down again.

Jake measured the distances and angles and didn't like any of them. Marju might have been stupid to trust Resnikov—or vice versa—but she wasn't giving away much on tactics. Short of rolling down the hill like an avalanche, Resnikov wouldn't get in her way.

The Russian's foot slipped, skidded, slipped again. He took a fast step, then another, but it was too late. His balance was gone. With a curse he windmilled to the ground.

Honor yanked her fishing rod out of the holder and sent the lure flying with every ounce of her strength. Eight ounces of lead and a treble hook thudded into the back of Marju's head. She staggered, crying out in pain and surprise.

Jake came off the ground like an explosion. He knocked Marju senseless with a swift chopping motion of his hand, grabbed her pistol, and spun toward Resnikov.

Kyle was on top of the Russian.

"Get out of the way!" Jake yelled, sighting over the barrel of the machine pistol. "I've got Marju's gun."

There was a turmoil of knees and elbows. Then Kyle rolled aside and pushed himself to his feet. Resnikov made whistling noises but didn't move otherwise.

"Don't worry about him," Kyle said hoarsely. "All he cares about is dragging air."

Jake took in a little air himself, then let it out.

"Kyle!" Honor called. "Are you all right?"

"Tired. Thirsty. Disgusted. Surprised. When did you learn how to cast?"

"Jake taught me."

Kyle looked at the man who was shoving Marju's pistol into his dive belt. "You got her to handle a rod? You must be some kind of, uh, teacher." The tone of his voice said that Kyle had noticed every time Resnikov called Honor Jake's lover.

"Maybe she's a hell of a student," Jake said.

He went to Resnikov and looked at him skeptically. Without warning the side of Jake's hand shot out and connected with the Russian's head. He made a stifled sound and went limp.

"Tie them up with fishing line before they

come to," Jake said, turning toward the boat. "I've got a call to make."

"Ellen?" Honor asked.

"Yeah. Don't worry. I'll drive a hard bargain. By the time I'm done, your brother will be a bloody hero."

"What about Marju and Pete?" Honor asked. "What will happen to them?"

"Who?" Jake said sardonically.

"What is that supposed to mean?"

"I'll let Ellen explain it to you. She's good at making people believe that what happened didn't happen at all."

24

"I still think you should have gone to the hospital," Honor said, frowning down at Kyle. "You leaned on Archer all the way home from the clinic."

Kyle smiled up at her from the comfort of his own bed. "The view is better here and it's going to be a gorgeous sunset," he said, waving to the window. "The nurse is a real nag, though."

"Nurse?" she retorted, pulling the down comforter up to his chin. "I'm the doctor or I don't play, remember? And as doctor, I think you should—"

"Relax," Archer interrupted. He set down a pitcher of juice and a glass on the bedside table. "Like the real doc said, Kyle is fine as long as he keeps guzzling fluids that don't have alcohol or caffeine in them."

"Easy for you to say," Honor said, glaring up—way up—at her oldest brother. "You're not the one in bed."

Archer smiled wearily. "I'd like to be."

He looked it, with his rumpled outdoor clothes, dark beard stubble, and grim lines on either side of his mouth. He had his mother's black hair and his father's eyes, a mixture of gray and blue and green that changed with his clothes or his mood. At the moment Archer's eyes were almost as dark as the circles beneath them.

Honor fought against the sympathy she felt for him. Despite the smudges beneath his eyes, he was disgustingly fit and too quick for a little sister's comfort. His big hands were deft and steady as he poured a glass of juice for Kyle.

"Quit fretting over him," Archer said again, setting the glass on the table and turning toward Honor. "He'll be back to tormenting you in a day. Two, max."

"I can't take it easy! Last night I went to sea in a small boat in a gale, picked my way through horrible little rocks shortly after dawn this morning, watched people holding guns on—"

"It's over," Archer interrupted, giving her a hug that lifted her off her feet. He rocked her from side to side as though she were a little girl again. "Kyle is all right and so are you. Everything's okay."

Honor wanted to keep on snarling at her older

brother, but right then he looked every one of his thirty-four years.

Normally she would have been sympathetic, but she was still simmering from the discovery that Archer, Lawe, and Justin had concealed Kyle's disappearance from her for two weeks—for her own peace of mind, of course. The fact that he had been on her mind constantly during those very weeks didn't impress Archer.

Male logic was a bright red pain.

" 'Take it easy,' " she said scathingly. "'Everything's fine.' Yeah, right. Like you. You look like you've been pulled through a knothole sideways. When was the last time you slept?"

Archer put her down, smiled crookedly, and turned away to talk to Kyle. "I got hold of Justin and Lawe. They'll be here in a few days. The Donovan is flying in tomorrow. Mom dropped her latest project and will be here with paint spatters from hair to heels along with Dad."

"Maybe I'll rethink the hospital," Kyle said, only half joking. "Dad will be pushing stateside desk jobs again and I'm not up to arguing."

Archer handed the glass of juice to Kyle. "Drink up. You'll need all your wit and reflexes in order to dodge the old man."

"Speaking of reflexes, where's Jay?" Kyle asked. "I still can't believe how fast he took care of Marju and Pete."

"Jay's with Ellen Lazarus," Archer said, yawning. "Dirty job, but somebody's got to do it."

Kyle shot a quick glance at Honor. "Jay and Ellen are old history."

"You can quit but you can't get out of the game," Archer said.

"You ought to know," Kyle muttered.

Honor turned to her oldest brother. "You know Ellen?"

Without answering, Archer reached for the thermos of coffee Honor had made for him. Scolding him the whole time, of course, but still taking care of him.

"No, Archer doesn't know Ellen," Kyle said. "But he knows the game."

"Which game?" Honor asked.

Archer shook the thermos. Empty. He looked hopefully at his sister.

"Nope," she said. "I made the first. It's your turn."

"Wait for Jay," Kyle said instantly. "He makes great coffee."

"What do you care?" Archer retorted. "You won't be drinking any for twenty-four hours."

"Just the thought of someone drinking your coffee will be enough to put me in the hospital for sure," Kyle said.

"In that case, I will personally feed you the first cup," Archer promised.

His easy-moving kind of stride reminded Honor of Jake's. She frowned, remembering Archer's description of Jake:...*moves like a fighter.*

Kyle looked at Honor's frown. "It really is ancient history with Jay and Ellen."

"Jake's a big boy," she said, shrugging.

"Ellen's a big girl. What they do is their own business."

"You don't mean that."

"I mean exactly that," Honor said flatly. "I hired Jake to help me find you. Jake signed on with me to clear his name. We both got what we wanted. Now the job is finished and so are we."

"But—"

A knock at the front door of the cottage interrupted Kyle.

"I'll get it," Honor called to Archer.

She hurried from the room before Kyle could say any more about Jake. It really was hard to tell your brother that the man he thought was just right for you didn't happen to want you for anything more than a brief, sizzling affair.

Sex wears off about three weeks after the ink on the marriage license is dry.

Just as Honor's hand touched the door handle, the lessons of the past few days caught up with old habits. "Who is it?" she asked.

"Company," Jake said.

Honor took a moment to smooth all expression from her face as she brushed futilely at toast crumbs on her black sweatshirt and tight, faded jeans. Then she took a steadying breath. She was thirty years old. Certainly she could look a former lover in the eye without flushing and remembering all the stupid things she had said to him about love.

She opened the door. Jake, Ellen, and Resnikov were standing on the small front porch.

"You might have mentioned the other two," Honor said coolly to Jake.

"I said 'company.' "

"Your point?"

"I'm family, not company." He turned to the other two. "Remember our deal. Five minutes apiece and no follow-up without the full might and majesty of the law."

Gently crowding past Honor, Jake walked into the house.

Moving like people with a big job and only a little bit of time to work, Resnikov and Ellen followed. Both of them looked freshly washed and pressed. Ellen was back in her clear red jacket.

"Kyle is too ill to talk," Honor said bluntly.

"No, he isn't," Archer called from the kitchen. "You have five minutes each and no return trips without a subpoena."

"Sounds like a bloody tape recording," Ellen said to Jake. "Did you two set this up in advance?"

"Didn't have to. Archer is like me—he knows the unwritten rules. Pete, you drew the short straw so you go first. And remember, Honor and I saved your ass."

"I didn't hear about that," Ellen said to Jake. "I heard you knocked Petyr *on* his ass."

"I did him a favor. With Marju, Pete was in the position of the male praying mantis courting a female," Jake said ironically.

"Meaning?" Ellen said.

"The females have been known to eat the males during mating, saving the useful portion for last. In order to avoid being a tasty memory, a male brings the female a juicy bug to distract her. Then he hops on and prays he's finished before she is."

Ellen looked speculatively at Resnikov. "So it was getting down to the short strokes with Marju?"

The Russian was puzzled until Jake translated the idiom. Resnikov laughed, shrugged elegantly, and headed for the bedroom without waiting to be shown where it was.

"So it was him," Jake muttered.

"What?" Honor asked.

Jake didn't answer.

Resnikov opened the bedroom door and walked in, leaving the door open behind him.

"The amber panel," he said to Kyle without preamble. "How did you get it to Petropavlosk?"

Kyle reached for the glass of orange juice and drank. Even when he was finished, he didn't say anything.

"We will find out who helped you," Resnikov said.

"Not from me."

"I can make doing business in the Russian Federation quite difficult for Donovan International."

"Shit happens."

"Your family might feel differently."

"His family," Archer said, coming in as far as the doorway, "backs him to the last drop of blood, sweat, and tears."

Jake smiled sourly. No news there. "Next question, Pete. Time's wasting."

"Did you approach Marju about stealing the panel?"

"No."

"That is not what she says."

"Just because she was working for you doesn't mean she can be trusted," Kyle said.

The weariness in his voice could have come from exhaustion, but Honor suspected it didn't. Being used by someone on the way to another goal was enough to give a saint a sour view of humanity.

Kyle wasn't a saint.

"Marju was not working for me in the way that you mean. Our collaboration came later, as a matter of mutual convenience," Resnikov said. "How did she get the amber panel?"

"I don't know," Kyle said.

"I find that difficult to believe."

"Why? Do you trust everyone you screw?"

The Russian looked amused. "That would not be wise."

"Marju didn't trust me. She used me. Big difference."

Honor flinched with silent sympathy for her brother.

"What do you know that might help me?" Resnikov asked Kyle.

"That depends," Jake said before Kyle could answer. "If you're working for the Russian government, we can't tell you much that you don't already know. Marju's cousin, according to her, was her source for the amber."

Resnikove turned quickly toward Jake. "Do you believe that?"

465

"I believe her cousin is a fast-rising *mafiya* star whose buddy tried to kill Kyle and ended up dead himself. If the Kaliningrad *mafiya* had the panel, then the cousin was Marju's connection." Jake looked at his watch. "My turn," he said to Resnikov. "Were you the one who searched this place?"

"Yes."

Honor stiffened.

"Were you on the freighter that nearly ran us down?" Jake continued.

"No." Resnikov looked toward Honor. "I had nothing to do with that misunderstanding. The captain has contempt for little boats. As for Vasi, he received a harsh lecture delivered by me for his part. He has enough English to warn you, but he enjoys—how do you say it?"

"Being an asshole?" Jake asked.

"Yes. It is the reason he left Russia."

"He gets in my face with that seiner again and he'll be looking for a new place to live."

Resnikov nodded. "I said something very similar to him."

"You weren't aboard the seiner either, were you?" Jake said. "You were in Vasi's Olympic, keeping us in sight by keeping the Coast Guard in sight."

The Russian smiled. "You nearly caught me at dawn."

"There were two people aboard. Who was the other one?"

"Marju."

"Her again," Jake said. "A real piece of work, that one."

"She has her uses," Resnikov said. "When you refused my offer, I sent her to enlist her fiancé's sister in our cause."

"Marju and I were never engaged in anything but sex," Kyle said bluntly.

"But Honor did not know that, did she? What would be more natural than a loving sister helping out a grieving fiancée?"

Kyle's expression went from disgust to anger. "It's a good thing it didn't work, Pete. I would have taken you apart for dragging Honor into this mess."

"Why? She was very much a part of the game," Resnikov said matter-of-factly.

"Honor had nothing to do with any of it!" Kyle said.

"She had Jacob Mallory."

"You were the one who told me to get rid of Jake," Honor said suddenly. "That's why your voice seemed familiar."

"I did not succeed in separating the two of you," Resnikov said, shrugging. The look on his face said that it wasn't a defeat he accepted graciously.

"Were you the silent caller, too?" she asked.

Again, Resnikov looked puzzled. Jake spoke a few swift sentences in Russian. Before he was finished, Resnikov was shaking his head.

"My guess is Pavlov," Jake said to Honor. "He likes scaring women."

"Where is Marju?" Honor asked.

Resnikov looked at Ellen. She looked right back at him.

Jake looked at his watch. "One more, Pete."

"The panel," he said instantly to Jake. "Is it genuine?"

"I was going to ask you the same thing."

"You examined it."

"So did you."

"You are better," Resnikov said impatiently.

"I'm not good enough to look at a piece and say yes, no, or maybe. I would have to run some tests. To do that, I would have to have the panel. I don't. Uncle does."

"The amber is genuine," Resnikov said.

"Genuine Baltic, Mexican, Dominican, or all three?" Jake asked evenly.

"Baltic, solely."

"If you know that, you have a better idea where the panel came from than I do."

"But—"

"Time's up. Say good-bye, Pete. Ellen wanted privacy for her questions."

Resnikov hesitated, then gave in. He was in no position to push and he knew it. "There will be other times."

"Not if I can help it," Jake said.

Ellen waited until the front door shut behind Resnikov and his car headed out the driveway.

"How did you get across Russia with the panel?" Ellen asked Kyle.

"Dollars," he said succinctly. "You would be amazed what hard cash buys in the former Soviet Union."

"Who did you buy?"

"Same people you do—whoever is for sale."

Ellen gave Kyle a cool look. "You're not being much help, babe."

"Unless you owe someone more than money," Jake said calmly to Kyle, "tell Uncle the method and keep the names to yourself."

Kyle hesitated.

Archer came into the bedroom and leaned against the door frame. "That's good advice. Don't make any enemies until you have to."

"I used the Russian military in Kaliningrad," Kyle said to Ellen. "They haven't been paid in so long they're selling everything from socks to fighter jets in order to eat. They got me and the shipment to Kamchatka. I gave the truck to someone who was my height and coloring. He drove to Russia and disappeared with the truck to draw people off my trail."

Archer and Jake exchanged swift looks.

"Nice work on short notice," Archer said simply.

Jake nodded.

The look on Kyle's face said that he wished he had been smarter sooner—with Marju, for instance.

For about ten seconds, the sound of Ellen's red nails tapping against her leather purse was the only break in the silence.

"Okay," she said briskly. "You're in Kamchatka. Then what?"

"You saw the shipping carton for the amber," Kyle said, his voice rough. "What do you think?"

"I think you went to that fishing outfit on

the Kamchatka Peninsula and Vlad Kirov got you out of there along with the amber panel."

Kyle nodded.

"So that really was you who came in through SeaTac?" Ellen asked.

"Yes."

"Hell. I owe that guy in Immigration a twenty. I really thought it was the DOA using your passport. How did you kill him?"

Simultaneously Jake and Archer said, *"No."*

They didn't say anything else. They didn't have to. Ellen moved on to her next question without a pause.

"If you were Marju's dupe, why didn't you call your family when you needed help?"

The corners of Kyle's mouth turned down. "I thought I could take care of it myself. I sure as hell didn't want to put their necks on the line."

"Was Jake in on it with Marju?"

Kyle stared at her.

"Oh, come on," Ellen said impatiently. "It wouldn't be the first time in history that a best friend and the best friend's girl get it on in the sack and then dump one corner of the triangle."

"Jay didn't like Marju. He tried to warn me." Kyle shrugged. "I didn't listen. When it came to her, all my brains were below my belt."

Ellen started to ask another question.

Jake beat her to it. "How did you find out about the amber panel?"

"In other words, who betrayed Kyle?" Ellen asked.

"Yeah."

"Marju."

"Wrong answer," Jake told Ellen. "Marju doesn't have the kind of connections to get to you."

"What will you give me if I tell you?" Ellen asked.

"What do you want?" Jake replied.

"Is the panel genuine?"

"Like I told Pete, I haven't done tests."

"All I want is your expert opinion," Ellen said.

"You'll get it. Who betrayed Kyle's escape route and destination to the Russians?"

The agent's black eyebrows rose, revealing the intense blue of her eyes. "You planning a little revenge?"

"Why, is the leak one of yours?"

"No. The leak was Kirov's brother-in-law. He's a screw-up with a gambling habit. He traded the information about the amber panel for his gambling debts with the *mafiya*."

"And word got back to Pete."

Ellen shrugged. "You know Resnikov better than I do, babe."

"I doubt it. From the start you were all over this panel like a cat covering shit," Jake said. "That tells me you already had a line on the Amber Room scam."

"So you think the panel is a fake?" she asked quickly.

"For several years the Russian government has been openly making a replica of the Amber Room, trying to reclaim a lost bit of heritage," Jake said. "Then the government ran out of money for art, along with everything else. The artisans weren't paid. When they began making amber artifacts on their own and selling them the same way—on their own—the *mafiya* moved in. They high-graded or outright stole amber from the Baltic mines and put the artisans to work making copies of old imperial splendor and selling them overseas."

"Was the panel you saw part of the scam?" Ellen asked.

"It could have been. It also could have been real. Before you twist an opinion out of me, call your boss."

Ellen went still. "Why?"

"If the Amber Room has been rediscovered and the communist nostalgia buffs in the military have it, or the Lithuanian separatists have it, Russia is in deep kimchi. If the room is fake and in the hands of people who want power more than money, the legitimate government of Russia still has the problem of proving the fraud or going right back into the kimchi. If the room is an outright *mafiya* hoax, a lot of money changes hands and it's politics as usual. Before you box in your boss with my answer, make sure it's the answer Uncle is ready to live with."

Silence and the tapping of fingernails. Then Ellen gave Jake a genuine smile and headed for the door. "It's a shame you got out of the business. See you around, babe."

The door closed behind her.

Jake let out a long breath.

"Is Pete *mafiya,* government, or freelance?" Kyle asked.

"Good question," Jake said. "He used to be government, but that doesn't mean he won't work whatever side of the street he happens to be on."

Honor began rubbing her temples. Trying to keep track of who was doing what and with which and to whom—maybe—was enough to give her a headache.

"Call Pete a twenty-first-century entrepreneur," Archer suggested blandly. He looked at Jake. "Is Marju being 'debriefed' by Ellen's people?"

"Probably. If Marju can't cut a good enough deal with Uncle, she'll go back to Russia and keep on selling out the Lithuanian freedom fighters. Or maybe she's doubling for them against the Russians. The facts fit either way."

"I'll bet she's doubling," Kyle said bitterly.

"Why?" Jake asked.

"The only real passion she ever showed was for freeing Lithuania from Russia."

"Then why did she team up with Resnikov?" Honor asked.

Kyle's mouth lifted in an acid smile. "No doubt she had a plan for killing Resnikov and taking the panel for her precious Brotherhood. We're lucky she didn't kill us in the bargain."

Honor blew out a hard breath. "What about

Snake Eyes? I suppose he's the Fairy God-mother in drag?"

"Nope," Jake said. "He's *mafiya*. Marju's cousin probably told him about the panel and he got greedy."

"Where is Snake Eyes now?"

"On his way back to Kaliningrad if he's smart," Archer said. "If not, he'll be caught, doubled, and sent back."

"Doubled?" Honor asked.

"Sent back as a spy in exchange for not doing time in the United States."

"That's it!" she announced, closing her eyes. "I have a headache."

Seconds later her eyes flew open. Jake was standing so close to her that she could feel the warmth of his breath. His fingers slid into her hair, rubbing her scalp, tracing all the tight muscles from her neck to the top of her skull.

"Headache, huh?" he asked. "I have just the thing."

"Since when does spectacular sex cure headaches?" she retorted.

Then she remembered that two of her broth-ers were in the room.

Archer snickered.

"Who said anything about sex?" Jake asked, but his eyes told her that he liked the idea. "I was talking about taking the *Better Days* up the Inside Passage to Alaska."

"What is the *Better Days*?" she asked.

"Jake's boat. Another SeaSport," Kyle said.

Jake ignored everyone but Honor. "What do you say to a boat trip that's long enough for me to teach you everything I know?"

"About fishing?" she asked in disbelief. "Why would I do that?"

"I'll let you use my rod," he offered with a slow grin.

Honor's mouth opened. No sound came out.

"It's customary for newlyweds to take a honeymoon," Archer added blandly.

"Butt out, Archer," Jake said. "Remember what I told you earlier."

Honor looked at her oldest brother. "What is Jake talking about?"

"He said if I leaned on you or got between you two, he would take you so far away from the Donovan clan that it would take a day for e-mail to reach you."

Her eyes widened. She looked at Jake almost warily, afraid to hope and unable to do anything else. "We're not married, so there's no point in a honeymoon."

"We will be," Jake said.

"Why?"

"Because you love me."

She closed her eyes and smiled sadly, "Wrong answer, Jake."

"Because I love you."

Her eyes flew open, wide and questioning.

"You have my word," he said simply.

Honor stood on tiptoe and wound her arms tightly around his neck. "In that case, love, let's go fishing."